CW00797196

Anne Whorlton

Family Matters

Enjoy reading!

Anne x

Also by Anne Whorlton

In Lily's Books

Note: The story is set in 2019, which is why there are references to Her (now late) Majesty Queen Elizabeth II.

ISBN: 978-3-00-076526-1

Edited by Shirley Enoch

Cover design and typesetting by Ken Dawson, Creative Covers

For Wolfgang,
with love

xxxxxxxx

CHAPTER 1

MISS LAVENDER THOUGHT she had seen it all, but this was really taking the biscuit!

Walking down the rainy High Street of Bishops Bridge, an elderly couple were pushing an old-fashioned black pram with large, shiny silver wheels, bending forward to – as she had presumed when she had first noticed them a minute ago – speak to the baby inside. They were making funny faces, too, probably in an attempt to make the little one laugh. Devoted grandparents, she had thought and smiled, they don't even mind the weather. But just as she was about to turn away from the door, two distinctively wrinkled, fat dog faces appeared from underneath the hood of the pram. Two pug dogs it seemed, one black, the other one cream, were the lucky inhabitants of the pram, and the recipients of their obliging owners' full attention! They were yapping frantically now while drooling strings of saliva all over the pram.

Miss Lavender shuddered. A dog lover herself, she could not bear to witness such disgrace, and quickly retreated to the safety of the back of her store. On her way, she stopped and thought for a moment. There was a sign that politely asked customers to leave their dogs outside, but it did not say anything about prams – or dogs in prams, come to that. What if they came in?

Just then the door opened, and – thank God – not the pug owners, but Jessie walked in, shaking her head in disbelief.

'Did you see that??'

'And good morning to you, my dear. Did I see what? The pram pugs?'

'Yes! It's absolutely *inconceivable*, isn't it? I mean, really – even pugs can walk, can't they? They do have legs. Who are these people? I have never seen them before. Maybe they are new here? Or on holiday? Gosh, I hope they are not staying at Lily's!—Oh, and good morning, Miss Lavender. I got a bit carried away there, sorry. How are you?'

Miss Lavender raised her eyebrows behind her horn-rimmed spectacles that were sitting almost on the tip of her long, slightly crooked nose, making the old lady look sterner than ever. 'Well – it's been raining all week now, so I suppose I'm a bit low in spirits, missing my daily walks, but otherwise I'm fine. What can I do for you?'

'Oh! I almost forgot. I need some sugar.—No, don't worry, please, I'll get it.' Picking up two packets of sugar from the shelf behind her, Jessie put them on the counter and got out her purse.

'Have you heard from Daisy and Oliver? Are they moving in any time soon?'

Oliver Clifford-Jones was the new vicar who had moved to Bishops Bridge with his wife Daisy shortly after Easter. Due to ongoing renovation works in the Rectory, they had had to set up a temporary home in one of the newly built holiday cottages on Fern Hill Farm where Jessie's friend Lily lived with her eccentric great-aunt

Abigail and an assortment of animals. Unfortunately it was not nearly as quiet and peaceful on the farm as the young couple had anticipated. For one thing, Lily's donkey, William, woke them up every morning, and for another, the cottage came with a winged resident who liked to entertain them with free concertos at night: a friendly barn owl who lived in an ancient oak tree next to the cottages. No wonder Oliver did not know when to write his sermons.

'Oh, no. Not for at least another month, I think. But Oliver is busy enough getting to know his new parish for now, and Daisy loves being on the farm, and helping Abigail with the ponies. Abigail says she already doesn't know how she ever managed without her. She used to take part in horse riding events before she married Oliver, and I believe she did very well, too. Oliver says she has taken it upon herself to break in that high-spirited young stallion of Abigail's.'

'Dancer? Oh, brilliant! Louisa May has been wanting to ride him ever since Abi first started to give her lessons this spring.—Anyway, I must be going. Goodbye, Miss Lavender, have a nice day!'

***

JESSIE'S CAFÉ WAS small, but very popular with locals and holiday makers alike, or walkers who passed through the village and were inevitably drawn in by the delicious smell of Jessie's trademark cinnamon swirls. It was only half past ten when Daisy came in and already the place was buzzing.

'Morning, Daisy! How are you?'

Giving her skirt a customary brush with her hands, Daisy smiled at Joseph, the local vet, who was standing at the counter waiting to be served. 'Good morning, Joseph. I'm fine, thank you.' She always said that, even if it wasn't true. Well, today it was – or at least, it was not completely *untrue*. She had seen worse days.

'I'm glad to hear that.—Oh, and can I have two cinnamon swirls as well, please?' he asked, turning his attention to Jessie, 'It's going to be a long day.'

Jessie, who already looked hot and exhausted, nodded. 'Tell me about it! I have a party of ten coming for afternoon tea today, and I still have scones to bake and sandwiches to prepare. Thank God Lily has offered to help, I wouldn't know what to do without her!— Morning, Daisy! Just a moment, I'll be right with you.'

Daisy loved the way everyone treated her and Oliver as if they had always lived here, when in reality it had only been a couple of weeks since they arrived. She knew that this was partly to do with them living in the cottage on Fern Hill Farm and Lily being about the same age as she was, but still. They had only been there a few days when Lily had knocked on the door of the *Lapwing* and asked them if they would like to join them for an evening at the local pub. Oliver had been busy but insisted she should go, and she had had a great time – that was, after she had recovered from the shock that there seemed to be a cow named Daisy on one of the neighbouring farms. So when Lily had introduced her, this had led to raucous laughter among the friends, and Daisy, thoroughly humiliated, had wanted to turn and run away. But Lily had been quick to calm her, explaining that *the Daisy Cow* was a very special cow and that there was absolutely no shame in having her for a namesake.

'Oh yes, you could say that!' Ben (who Daisy had noticed drank a lot more than any of the others) had nodded vigorously. 'Very special! Ask Susanna, our local artist – she has painted the Daisy Cow so often, she can paint that cow in her sleep! Lucy here just got married, and of course she also got a picture – where did you put that, Lu? Not in the bedroom, I hope?'

Ben had winked at Lucy who had stuck her tongue out at him and laughed as she took the glass of elderflower cordial Greg had brought her. Lucy had been the only one who was not drinking, and it had not taken long for Daisy to figure out why: newly married to Greg, she was pregnant, of course – and looking radiant, too. She was so pretty with her glossy, chestnut curls which she wore, nineteen-fifties style, in a soft curly bob that bounced when she laughed – and, being of a natural happy disposition, Lucy laughed a lot. Daisy knew it was wrong, but she could not help envying her. If only *she* could be as happy! If only *she* could laugh like that, and make others join in. But then, she did not have much reason for laughing, did she?

Yes, you have, she had reminded herself. You have quite a lot to be grateful for: stop pining for the things you cannot have. Or maybe not just yet.

'Right, what would you like?'

'Sorry?' Startled, Daisy looked up to meet Jessie's gaze. 'What did you say?'

Jessie grinned. 'You look just like Louisa May when she is dreaming about ponies!'

'Do I?'

'Yes! I can see two tiny ponies dancing in your

eyes where other people have their pupils! I'm sorry to interrupt your happy dreams, but it's very busy, so can I just take your order?'

Happy dreams, Daisy thought, biting her lip. Hardly! But she quickly collected herself and chose two slices of carrot cake. She was on her way to see old Mr Barnsley who had been down with the flu and did not trust himself to leave the house just yet. Widowed for many years now, Mr Barnsley lived all by himself in a large, rambling old house on Brook Lane, with only his Golden Retriever, Honey, for company. The kind old gentleman was almost blind, which was why Honey was the only dog allowed entrance to Jessie's café.

'I'm so glad you have taken over Louisa May's riding lessons now,' Jessie said as she cut two generous slices of carrot cake. 'Abi is wonderful, to be sure, in her own, eccentric way, but you have a way with young girls that Abi—well. Let's just say she is of a different generation. Don't get me wrong, I love Abi! Everyone does. Anyway, here's your cake. That's five-sixty then, please.'

Daisy smiled warmly. 'Thank you, Jessie. I love working with Louisa May. She is a real credit to you.' Then she took out her purse, paid in cash, and dropped an extra pound into the cute Mrs Potts character teapot that sat on the counter, along with a matching Chip cup and saucer. The cup contained free rhubarb custards for children to take. Funny, Daisy thought, I am sure I saw Joseph dipping his hand into that cup just now.

As if on cue, Joseph gave her a mischievous wink as he took his lunch parcel and coffee from the counter, shamelessly taking another sweet from the little cup, and popping it into his mouth. 'I'll see you at the pub tonight.

You are coming, aren't you, to support our team?'

'Team?'

'Yes. It's quiz night at the *Dog & Partridge*. We thought it might be useful to have a vicar on the team – and an equestrian, too. They do ask the most absurd questions sometimes, like—oh, God, what was that last time? Oh yes: What horse carried her rider through the Olympic Games at Stockholm, half unconscious with pain, in nineteen-bloody-fifty-six?'

'That would be Halla, the only horse ever having won Olympic gold three times in a row, and a total of seven Olympic medals in her life. The name of the rider was Winkler, I think.—They did not really ask *that* question in a pub quiz, did they?'

Joseph's face reddened. 'Erm, no. I think it was on last week's *Who wants to be a millionaire*, but—how on earth do you know all this?? I have never even heard of that horse!'

But Daisy just shrugged. 'I hail from an equestrian family, I suppose it's in my genes. I'll see you tonight then, Joseph, and rely on you to answer any other animal-related questions.'

When Joseph had gone, Jessie shook her head, laughing. 'You are amazing, Daisy! Even if it is in your genes as you say … You used to ride in competitions, too, didn't you? Did you do show jumping, too?'

'Sometimes, yes, but mostly cross-country. I gave up riding professionally when Oliver and I got married. And,' she added a little self-consciously as she took her cake, 'I admit I have only heard of Halla the wonder horse because we have family in Germany. Anyway, thanks for the cake, and I'll see you at the pub tonight then. Bye!'

She had nearly reached the door when this was pushed open by an elderly couple with a large, black pram.

'Sorry, no dogs in here!'

Daisy nearly dropped her cake. Wondering why on earth Jessie was talking about dogs when the couple had a pram and not a lead, Daisy stopped dead when the woman bent forward to peep inside the pram and cooed, 'But our dogs are *very* well-behaved – aren't you, darlings?' Clucking at who, or whatever, was inside the pram if not a baby (presumably two small dogs), she went on, 'And I *promise* they won't—'

'No!' Jessie's voice had taken a noticeably sharper edge. 'Sorry, but no. The café is too small and it's not fair on other customers who would dearly love to bring their four-legged friends. Guide dogs only, I'm afraid.' A little gentler now, Jessie suggested, 'Why don't you take them home and come back without them? Or take some cake back to your house?'

The woman hesitated. 'I don't know … Arthur?'

'No. If we can't bring the dogs, we won't come at all. And we will tell everyone that this is not a friendly café. How dare you be so rude to new customers, I wonder?' And with a tug on his wife's sleeve, the man pulled the pram back and manoeuvred them both through the door. 'We'll go to Helmsley, Harriet. There are plenty of dog-friendly places there.'

The door had only just closed behind them when everybody in the café burst out laughing.

CHAPTER 2

WHEN DAISY APPROACHED Mr Barnsley's house, she found him in the garden watering his roses. Not wanting to make him jump, she cautiously called 'Good morning, Mr Barnsley! It's Daisy. I have come with some cake. Do you have time for a cup of tea?'

'Oh!' The old man turned his face in her direction and smiled. 'Daisy! That is lovely of you to come and see me. My daughter is coming to collect me any moment though, so perhaps we must have that cuppa some other time.'

Daisy returned his smile, even if he could not see it. 'That's alright, I like carrot cake. I'm sure I will find somebody to share it with. Are you going to stay with your daughter for a few days then? She lives in Ripon, doesn't she?'

'Yes. But she is just taking me to the hospital to get my wheezy old chest x-rayed. Doctor says he doesn't like the sound of it, and Jane insists we should get to the bottom of this. A lot of fuss about nothing, I am sure! But there is no arguing with Jane, there isn't. And talking of Jane—' He tilted his head to one side and listened. 'I think I can hear her car now. Is there a light blue Volkswagen Beetle coming up the lane?'

Daisy turned around and waved to Mr Barnsley's daughter who was just pulling up on the side of the road. 'Yes, here she comes. Well, I will leave you to it then, and pray that it's nothing serious. Goodbye!'

A bit at a loss as to what to do with herself (Oliver had gone for what he called a 'business walk' with the church warden, Alan Becket, to discuss the progress the builders were making on the Rectory and the new youth group he was planning to set up), Daisy turned around and walked back to Miss Lavender's shop. Maybe Miss Lavender would have time for a coffee. After all, it was eleven o'clock, the perfect time for a little coffee break, even if she knew the old lady only ever drank tea. Loose tea, preferably Darjeeling, with a squeeze of lemon, and served in one of her pretty willow ware porcelain cups. Daisy had inherited a willow ware tea set from her grandmother and when she had first been to have tea with Miss Lavender (shortly after their arrival), she had been so excited to see that they looked almost alike.

'Morning, Daisy! You alright?'

Daisy looked up to see Lily standing on the porch outside her shop, holding a parcel in her arms. 'Yes,' she called, 'I'm fine!'

'Good. Will you join us for lunch at the farm later? I don't have much time, so it will probably be omelette and salad and Abi's homemade bread, but you are very welcome to join us. And Oliver, of course. Oh, and talking of Oliver,' Lily added, lowering her voice even if there was nobody around, 'I heard the village school mums talking about him this morning, and do you know what they said? He is such a handsome young man, and so charming! It's true, I swear! The girls are all wanting to join the junior bellringers now – they will be terribly disappointed to find that boring old Alan does the bellringing practice, and not Oliver. But he has other plans, hasn't he? For the youth?'

Daisy nodded. She loved to hear other people praising Oliver and was happy for him that things seemed to be going so well. 'Yes, as a matter of fact, he is just talking to Alan about setting up a youth group. Or two, rather. One for the younger ones, and another one for the older ones. He has been in touch with the North York Moors National Park Team, and they say they are always happy to welcome new volunteers, especially young people.'

'Ooh, but that's great! If Oliver puts his mind to it, I'm sure it won't be long before we see Rosedale's teenagers doing river surveys and camping in the wild, watching the stars. Abi says there has been a lot of trouble with bored teenagers in the valley over the last few years. They go up to the old castle and party there at weekends, leaving their rubbish behind, or even act out a drunken Dracula in the old churchyard if the fancy takes them, and post their horrid videos on Instagram or YouTube. That's the older teenagers, of course. I'm not sure Oliver can reach *them* – but it's worth a try. Anyway, I've got to go. I'll see you later at the farm?'

***

'So, WHAT DO you think? Should I try that?'

Miss Lavender (who had been more than ready for a break as she was not feeling particularly well this morning, even if she would never admit as much) stirred her tea, put the dainty little silver spoon carefully back on the saucer, and took a sip before answering Daisy's question. 'What, organising a choir? Well, whyever not, if that's what you want to do. I'm sure you would get quite a few of the girls to come and sing. Jessie's daughter has a lovely voice, and her friend Celine is part of a local Youth Theatre Group who do musicals. The more popular and modern the choice of songs, the better your chances, I suppose, but yes – why not?'

'Well,' Daisy said, picking at her cake, 'I would love to, but – but what if nobody turns up? Or what if the children don't like me? They all love Oliver, I know that, but—'

'Yes, dear, I know, but this is about you now, not Oliver. About what you want to do. Apart from forming a church choir, which is all very well, but – that will not fill your days, will it?'

'Um … no, I suppose it won't, but …'

But Miss Lavender had not finished. She might not even have expected her to answer. 'Now I know you gave up event riding when you got married, but what did you do then? In the three years you lived in Derbyshire, for example?'

Waiting to get pregnant, Daisy was about to blurt out, but stopped herself just in time. Even to her, that sounded silly and very naïve.

She fiddled with her napkin. 'I – I gave violin lessons to some of the children in the parish where Oliver was curate. And later, I worked at a riding school just outside Buxton, too, three or four times a week. I gave riding lessons, and I helped with the training of their event horses, too. I have a degree in horsemanship, you see. From the Royal Horse Association.'

'I see. And – if you don't mind me asking – why don't

you work with horses anymore? Why have you even given up event riding, if you were good at it, and your heart was in it, too?'

Daisy squirmed. She had not known Miss Lavender long enough to be astonished at her direct questions. If she had, she would have known that the old lady never asked personal questions. Never. And she certainly did not answer any, should anyone dare ask them. Daisy had no idea that the person who was the most surprised at her own questions was Miss Lavender herself. As it was, Daisy was perfectly oblivious to her host's remarkably uncharacteristic behaviour, so all she could think of now was how to explain that over the last five years, she had tried everything to get pregnant.

Because, more than anything, she wanted to be a mother.

'I … well. Because – if I had followed my career, it would have taken me away from Oliver, and that was not how we – I – thought marriage should be. Leading separate lives before we had even … you know, started a family. You see, before I met Oliver, my father used to take me to all these competitions, or if he was not available, my brother would come with me. We grew up with Thoroughbreds, you see, so for all of us siblings, it was only ever horses …' A smile brightened her face, making her sad blue eyes shine for a moment. 'I met Oliver at a race. He was there with a friend who was keen on horse racing, though I believe he only went for the fun of it. During a break, we were both queuing for an ice-cream, and he managed to drop his into my – well, it landed on my blouse.' The 99 Flake had plunged right into her cleavage when they had bumped into each other, but Miss Lavender did not have to know these intimate details, even if Daisy had laughed at the time. She had been in a buoyant mood that day, having just won a series of events with her precious horse, Destiny.

'That's nice. Now, about the horses – why don't you ask Abi if she can help you? Maybe you can at least take on a few more pupils. I'm sure Abi wouldn't mind. She always says her ponies don't get enough exercise these days.'

Daisy sighed. 'Yes, I suppose I could …' But the truth was, she was not thinking about horses now. She was thinking about the thing that troubled her the most, even more than leaving her career, and her beloved horse behind. Only last week, when they were talking on the telephone, her mother had suggested she make an appointment for her with a private consultant in London. To talk about the conception problem. But she could not bring herself to talk to anyone about it, least of all a stranger. These days, she did not even talk to Oliver about it. Only last week, she had secretly done another pregnancy test while Oliver thought she was cleaning the bathroom. Dropping on her knees as she waited for the result, she had whispered, 'Please let me be pregnant, God. Please. And – and if I am not, please – help me to cope. Amen.' Then she had looked at the little window of the test stick and burst into tears – one line, not two. Another crushing *no*.

'I'm afraid I have taken up too much of your time, Miss Lavender. I am sure you want to get back to your shop. I'll see myself out.' With that, Daisy put her empty cup down with a slightly trembling hand and rose to her feet.

Miss Lavender frowned at her young visitor over the rim of her glasses, not at all sure what to make of it. But then she reminded herself that that was what happened if you broke your own rules – no prying. No personal questions you would not feel comfortable answering yourself. 'Well, if you're sure—'

'I am. Now I remember, I think I promised Oliver I would plant the flowers we bought at the garden centre on Saturday. He will be home for lunch, so I had better get back and make a start. Goodbye, Miss Lavender. Thank you for the tea.'

When Daisy had gone, Miss Lavender flipped her shop sign back to *open*, and looked at her delicate Tiffany wristwatch with the sparkling diamonds set around the oval dial – her mother's watch. The hands were at a quarter past eleven. She could close the shop now and take an early lunch break. A little walk might do her good, and stop her mind from brooding, too. But then she saw the Colbecks approaching, waving to her as they were crossing the bridge, and she dismissed the idea of a walk. Though she put on a smile to welcome her customers, she could not deny the fact that Daisy's visit had rather unsettled her. Something in what the vicar's wife had said had stirred a memory in her, though she could not put her finger on what it was now. And even if Daisy had not found the courage to tell her what was really troubling her, Miss Lavender knew that it was usually the unspoken things that mattered the most, just like the invisible wounds were the hardest to heal.

As she of all people should know.

CHAPTER 3

OLIVER FOUND HIS wife sitting on one of the metal benches in the churchyard. Her head bent low, her lips were moving in fervent prayer, and his heart went out to her. She had been crying, too; he could tell from the swollen eyes that were looking back at him when he called her name. Her beautiful, clear blue eyes, like the summer sky, now clouded over with sorrow and pain.

'Hello, my darling – how long have you been sitting here?'

He went to sit beside her and took her hand. 'I thought you were going to come back to the farm for lunch. Lily was getting worried, so I came to find you. It's half past one.'

'Oh! I'm sorry. I didn't mean to worry you, or Lily. I must have forgotten all about the time.' Resting her head against his shoulder, she sighed. 'It's so quiet and peaceful up here – I am glad we came to Bishops Bridge. I love this churchyard.'

Oliver followed her gaze across the low wall that surrounded the old churchyard. 'I know you love being up here – that is why I always know where to find you.' He smiled, and they sat there for a few minutes saying nothing, just taking in the scenery.

Before people had settled in Bishops Bridge in the mid-fifteenth century, they had lived here, on top of the hill, and worshipped in the old church of St Mary's. Though the church itself lay in ruins, the churchyard was still in use today, and there were services traditionally conducted here on Boxing Day and Easter Monday. Oliver had already decided that that was not nearly often enough and that from now on, there would be regular open-air services during the summer months – weather permitting, of course.

He had found a book about the history of Bishops Bridge in the library at the Rectory (Reverend Thompson having left most of the books connected with either the church, or the village), and learned that local historians thought it likely that when the Black Death had come to the hamlet of Broughton in 1428, it had killed most of the inhabitants and driven the surviving two dozen or so down the hill. The village of Bishops Bridge was named after the stone bridge that was later built across the stream, and the Bishop who had come from York to bless the new settlement upon its foundation in 1430.

Daisy on the other hand, who was not much of a reader, had only half-heartedly listened to an enthusiastic Lily when she had taken her on a discovery tour of Bishops Bridge. For someone who had only moved here a little over a year ago, Lily knew the most extraordinary things about the area. Daisy had asked her why people had not simply gone back to worship in the old church. Lily had said they had at first, but could not be bothered to keep it up in the long run when no one lived there anymore. So in 1786 they had had a new church built down in the village, where it stood in the centre of the green, and near the stream.

'I don't know if it's true,' Lily had mused, closing the church's heavy oak door behind them as they had stepped out into the sunlight again, 'but they might also have been afraid because they believed the place to be cursed. Fact is, people did not go back to live on that hill until much later, in the early seventeenth century, when farmers began to settle there and work the land. It's mostly sheep farms, and some cattle. And the Mavericks' grand estate of course, Birchwood Park. Whatever is going to happen to that place, now they are both dead …'

Daisy did not care why the people had never gone back; she just loved the idea of there being two churches, even if one of them was a ruin. And she did not care about the Mavericks either, since she had never met them. She just loved sitting here, alone, or with Oliver, and dream. It really was the most romantic of places and a source of inspiration for poets, writers, and painters. She had done some sketching here, too, though she never had the patience to finish any of her pictures. She preferred the violin to the paint brush. Most of all though, she preferred riding.

While she found her thoughts turning to her horse again, Oliver was studying her face. There was far too much on his beautiful wife's mind these days, far too little of which she would share with him. It had not always been like this. They used to be so close when they were first married. In many ways, they still were, but Oliver was no fool – he knew she took her temperature every day, he knew she did a pregnancy test once a month, sometimes more often than that. He had noticed her drinking only decaf these days and only allowing herself the occasional glass of wine. She carefully tried to avoid leaving pieces of evidence lying about the place, hoping he would not notice. But he did notice. He had seen the empty test kit packages in the bin outside, and he doubted they were Lily's. He had found the thermometer, too, along with a miniature notebook, in her bedside table drawer when she had asked him to find her earrings one day, no doubt in a rare moment of distraction. They had been in the process of getting ready for a night out, and she had probably not given a thought about the contents of her drawer. It would not normally be a problem, anyway – they used not to keep things from each other. It made him all the sadder to see that she seemed to feel the need to do so now.

He wished she would talk to him, but she had become like a closed book on that subject – the Baby Issue, as he secretly called it –, pretending she was fine when it was obvious she wasn't. He wasn't either, but that was a different matter. As a man, he kept himself busy (and it turned out there were hundreds of things to keep him busy in his new parish!), and tried his best to remain positive, hopeful, and cheerful. There did not seem to be another way.

Oliver did not realise he was also being scrutinised by his wife. Daisy, who was sitting quite still, looked for all the world as if she was watching the sheep in the field, but every now and then she would cast a quick glance at her husband, recognizing that worried frown on his face as he stared ahead towards the ruined nave of the old church. Roofless and without any of the original walls remaining apart from a few arches where the stained-glass windows used to be, St Mary's had been left exposed to the elements for centuries. Blackbirds were hopping up and down the paved area where once the feet of worshippers had trodden, picking between the ancient stone slabs in search of food. It was the most peaceful and the saddest picture at the same time – what would the church have looked like five or even six hundred years ago? What would it have felt like to come here to worship (apart from cold, Daisy thought, shivering as the clouds were covering the sun just now) as a peasant with no shoes on your feet, never mind a penny to spare for the alms' box, or a warm meal to look forward to after the service?

We should be so grateful, she thought. We have everything we need, and more. Why can't I be more grateful? Why can't I be happy and content with what I have?

Her gaze resting on her husband's face, Daisy gave an inaudible sigh. Lily was right, he *was* a very handsome man – it was, in fact, the first thing she had noticed about him. At six foot two, he was quite tall, and she had not been able to ignore the muscles underneath his shirt the day they had met at the race. Even then, she had loved the way he had raked his hands through his thick, dark brown hair and had to admit it was not so much about the hair (which she thought was too long and rather untidy at the time) but his strong, tanned hands. But what had ultimately made her fall in love with him had been his eyes, and the way they crinkled at the edges when he smiled. Only a few days before, her sister Eleanor had asked her what the author of the book she was reading meant when she described eyes to be "the colour of the sea after a storm". The moment Daisy looked into Oliver's eyes, which were grey with a hint of green, she knew. She did not tell Eleanor, of course. She would not have heard the last of it. Her older sister was a terrible tease, always had been.

It pained Daisy to see him so troubled now, especially as she knew she was the cause of his worries, but there seemed nothing she could do about it today. Some days were fine, most were okay, and some – like today – just unbearably hard.

Oliver turned his eyes on her and smiled. 'Will you come home with me then? Lily has put our dinner in the oven. But she had to get back to her shop, so she gave me a lift into the village. I thought we could walk back together. What do you think?'

'Yes, that would be lovely. I have got my bike, but I can push it along as we walk. And Oliver?'

'Yes?'

'It's *lunch*. You just said *dinner*. Dinner is what we have in the evening. I can see country life has rubbed off on you already, at least where language is concerned!'

Now Oliver laughed out loud. 'Oh, Daisy! I love you so much! Come on then, home for lunch – we can have tea later. Oops, that's dinner then, of course.' Taking her hands, he pulled her to her feet, gently pushing back a stray curl of her blonde hair as he bent down to claim a kiss. 'And I know you love me, too, dinner, lunch, or tea.'

'Of course I do,' she smiled, 'which is why you are going to take me out tonight. It's quiz night at the *Dog & Partridge*, and this time I'm not going without you! You can have a pint of Guinness.'

'Or we could go early and have our dinner there – I hear the shepherd's pie is excellent. And we could share a sticky toffee pudding.'

Daisy's eyes widened. '*Share*? Sticky toffee pudding? I don't think so!'

***

WHILE DAISY WAS getting ready to go out, Oliver sat on the patio behind the cottage talking to Alan Becket, who had called with some good news: It looked like they were going to move into the Rectory before the summer was over – 'with any luck, in July or early August,' Alan said. 'That is, if they can fit your kitchen before then. Have you chosen the tiles yet?'

'My wife has, yes. And she has mentioned something about bringing home some paint charts, too, and choose the colours for the walls herself … we will pay for any extras. I just want her to be happy at the Rectory, you know, and feel quite at home.'

Alan assured him that he understood (he didn't really, of course, but that was because he did not know about their troubles – how could he?) and that he did not see any problem in them choosing their own colours.

When he had rung off, Oliver sat there for a few minutes, pondering on his own words as he gazed across the fields. *I want her to be happy there, and feel quite at home.*

He knew that Daisy was in no hurry to leave the farm. She would happily stay in this little cottage for ever. If they were not meant to have children, what on earth were they to do with all those rooms? There were six bedrooms altogether, and a studio flat above the stone built double garage. Maybe he should have insisted they move somewhere else. A lot of vicars did not live in the actual vicarage these days but preferred smaller, more modern accommodation that suited their needs better. But since they had come as far as they had, it seemed a little late now to change their minds.

'Daisy? That was Alan with some good news about the Rectory. He says we can do the rest of the downstairs painting ourselves while they get the first floor ready next week. Didn't you say you would not mind doing a bit of DIY with me?'

Not having heard her husband coming in, Daisy dropped her pearl necklace as she jumped in surprise. 'Oh!'

'Sorry I made you jump. Here, let me do that for you.' He stood behind her to put the necklace, a treasured keepsake from her much beloved late grandmother, around her slender neck, kissing her soft, creamy skin as he fastened the clasp. 'Mmm, you smell good. Penhaligon's?'

Daisy nodded. Her sister Kate had given her *The Favourite* for her last birthday – personally, she thought it was rather too heavy. She preferred the zesty scent of *Quercus*, but sadly, the bottle was empty – and she could not very well wear Creed, her wedding scent, for an evening at the local pub. She knew she already had a reputation for being posh; the last thing she needed was for the other girls to notice her expensive taste in perfumes.

'So what do you say?'

'To what?'

'To the good news – about the Rectory. And the DIY.'

'Oh.' Pulling up the straps of her silk camisole, Daisy got up to slip on the pale pink cotton shirt she had laid out on the bed along with a long, white skirt. 'Yes, that sounds good. When can we start?'

He smiled. 'Tomorrow, if you like. Or as soon as you

have chosen the colour and bought the paint. Just please don't ask me to come along – you know how hopeless I am when it comes to colours. You can go with Jessie, or Lily.'

'Well, I'd still like to go with you. You are my husband, and we are going to live in the house, aren't we? Even if it's just the two of us.'

The words had slipped out before she could stop herself and she turned away from him, ashamed. Why couldn't she just relax for one single evening? Why did every little thing have to evoke that kind of thinking in her? He had only been talking about choosing colours, for goodness' sake, not nursery wallpaper!

'I'm sorry!' She buried her face in her hands and began to cry.

'Oh, darling.' Oliver took her in his arms and held her close. 'My poor darling! I think going out tonight will do you good, hm? Bit of distraction … and sticky toffee pudding.'

She laughed under her tears then, but he could see she was still upset when she pulled back a minute later to finish getting dressed. As he watched her slip her pearl bracelet over her slim wrist, he wondered if coming here had been such a good idea after all. He had hoped that they would find country life more relaxing, and that Daisy, being a country girl at heart, might be happier here. But it seemed that nothing, not even a farm full of ponies, could help her come to terms with the fact that she was not able to get pregnant. Maybe it was time to sit down and discuss alternatives. Daisy was so fragile these days; she could not go on for much longer, and the longer they waited, and the more often they got their hopes up for nothing, the harder it got. For both of them.

CHAPTER 4

'SORRY I'M LATE! It was one of those days ...'

Jessie flopped onto the bench next to Lily and rolled her eyes. 'As if those pugs weren't enough to put up with – or their owners, for that matter – they have to be friends with *the Johnsons* of all people! They sat in their garden all afternoon, with their yapping pugs dashing about the place, and poor Ossie chasing after them barking his head off. I don't know if he was trying to herd them or something. Honestly, that dog needs a job! I don't know what the people at the rescue centre were thinking when they let them choose a border collie. I always assumed that adopting a rescue dog was a long and complicated procedure, with application forms to fill in, and home visits and so on, before anyone could officially adopt a dog, let alone a collie! These people should not have a dog at all, but that's a different matter. Needless to say, the afternoon tea party retreated inside after a while, while the outside tables remained empty despite all that glorious sunshine. I'm sure those pug owners did that on purpose. Sweet revenge and all that.'

Ben, who had just finished his first pint, put an arm around her shoulder. 'Aw, come on, Jess, don't be so hard on your neighbours. They are just lonely old people with nothing else to do. Why don't you let me buy you a drink? Glass of wine with a splash of lemonade?'

Firmly removing his arm from her shoulder, Jessie made a point of moving a few inches away. Then she cleared her throat and said, 'Yes, a glass of wine would be most welcome. Anyone else joining me? Oh, and talking of joining, Nate is coming, too. I hope you don't mind, but I asked him to come along, since Louisa May is spending the night at Celine's, and we have the evening to ourselves for once.'

'Why would we mind – on the contrary, we should feel honoured that you'd want to spend your precious evening off with us. You so rarely get to spend some time on your own, the two of you.—Hey, Nate! We're here!'

Lucy waved enthusiastically when a tall, handsome man walked in, scanning the room. With his collar length dark hair, lanky frame, and horn-rimmed glasses, Nate Sullivan was the epitome of the cute geek type. Dressed in a white, open-necked shirt and blue jeans, a leather jacket over his arm, he stood there looking a little lost. But then he spotted first Lucy, then Jessie, and his whole face lit up.

'Hello!' He kissed Jessie's cheek and sat down on her right. 'Sorry to keep you waiting. They haven't started yet, have they?'

'What, in that noise? No.' Getting to his feet, Ben asked in a tone of forced joviality, 'Anyone else up for another drink? Nate?'

'I'm fine with water for the time being, thank you.' Reaching for the jug on the table, Nate helped himself to a glass of water. Just as well he wasn't looking, or he would have noticed Ben sneering at him. In Ben's opinion, a man who did not drink was not a man at all – but then he would never accept the man who had come to steal his girl, regardless of his drinking habits. It did not matter either that Jessie had never actually been his girl in the first place. It had only ever been one-sided, and Ben knew that. But still—

'Ben?'

At the sound of Jessie's voice, Ben turned around. She might have no taste when it came to men, but God, she was pretty!

'What?'

Don't, she mouthed, shooting him a warning glance. Her cornflower blue eyes were sparkling, but if she was hoping that that would put him off, she couldn't have been more wrong. On the contrary, it made him want to walk over to her, grab her, and kiss her. Full on the mouth, and in front of everyone. Especially Nate Sullivan.

For a moment Ben seriously contemplated doing it, but then he thought better of it. Instead, he scoffed, as if to defy her, and strode purposefully to the bar where Mike was already getting his next pint ready.

'Forget it, mate,' Mike said, pulling the tap, 'you can't win her back. Not now she's back with her daughter's father. You cannot beat family, and you know it. Just be happy for her, eh? Let it go.'

Ben mumbled something under his breath, held his credit card against the machine, and took his pint without so much as a comment. He knew he stood no chance against Nate, and ought to forget about Jessie, but it still irked him to see them together. He knew he was being unfair, that he should be happy for her – for the three of them – but found that he couldn't. All his life he had been waiting for a woman like Jessie, and now he had lost her before she had even been his … Shaking his head angrily, he drained half his glass on his way back to the table. That didn't make sense, not even to him. A man could not lose what he had never possessed.

'You forgot our wine,' Lily said, shaking her head at him as he sat down opposite her. 'You really are becoming more scatterbrained than Joseph these days!'

'Oi!' Joseph nudged her. 'Careful there! I'll go get your wine. Anyone else? Daisy? Oliver?'

Just then Patrick Alderson, the village blacksmith, leaped onto the stage, grabbed the microphone and called out a cheerful 'Good evening, everybody!' With his good looks, laid-back attitude and irresistible schoolboy charm, Patrick was easily the most popular bachelor in the village, and he knew just how to make the girls swoon.

'Are you ready for a really tough quiz? Brains sharpened, pencils alert? Great, let's go! Here is the first question, and it's about ...'

'Music,' Greg said and pushed notepad and pencil towards Ben. 'He *always* starts with a music question.'

' … music! What was the name of Paul McCartney's band that split up in 1981?'

'Oh God, that's so easy!' Finishing his pint, Ben put the glass down with a thud and scribbled *The Wings* on their answer sheet. Wiping his mouth with the back of his hand, he fixed his eyes on Nate as he gave a loud belch.

'Wait till he gets going,' Lily remarked drily. 'You might want to go easy on the alcohol, Ben, we still need your brains.'

But Ben was not listening. He was watching Nate whispering something in Jessie's ear which made her blush and giggle, wishing he could punch the man's face.

'In which country do we find the Spanish Riding School, where the famous Lipizzaner horses perform to classical music?'

'Well, not in Spain, or they wouldn't be asking,' Greg frowned, and Lucy was about to write *Vienna* when Lily shook her head and whispered 'Austria'.

'Oh yes, of course – Vienna is the city, isn't it? Not the country. Silly me.'

Daisy, who knew the answer, but had not been quick enough, smiled fondly at Lucy. She was by far the prettiest of them all, and yet she was such a lovely, unpretentious girl. And she had to be clever too, running her uncle's hardware shop in Kirkbymoorside and repairing her dad's tractor at weekends. What would they do without her, when she had her baby? But before she could start getting all maudlin again, Oliver nudged her just in time for her to hear the next question.

'What does a luthier do?'

Nate frowned. 'A what?'

Daisy took the pen and wrote 'someone who builds and repairs string instruments', feeling the tension ease off as she closed her eyes and heard her grandmother play *Greensleeves* on her violin. She had bequeathed the beautiful instrument to Daisy, claiming that she would be the only one who would truly appreciate it.

'Your brothers and sisters, they have nothing but horses in their heads. You are the only one who has inherited the musical streak from your mother's side of the family, so you should have this violin. I know you will not only treasure it, but play it, too. And that is how it should be. An instrument, and especially a violin, must be played, and played with love, or it will die.'

With her beloved grandmother now gone, Daisy treasured the beautiful instrument more than ever. And although Oliver knew how much it meant to her, she would not tell him that she sometimes took the violin up to the ruined church on Broughton Hill, and played it there, among the ancient headstones of the old churchyard. Then the sweet melody would carry over the moors, echoing from the hillsides, and for once, Daisy would feel at peace with the world, and with herself.

***

'Is ANYONE STAYING for another drink?'

Their team having come third (out of six teams that was not altogether bad, Lily said), most of them were getting ready to go now, but Ben was clearly looking for a drinking companion. Or someone to pour his heart out to, Daisy thought, feeling a bit sorry for him. She knew Ben was in love with Jessie and that he stood no chance against Nate. Trying to get her husband's attention, she winked at him, at the same time nodding subtly towards Ben. If anyone could get that man to talk, it would be Oliver. Greg and Lucy had already left, and poor Joseph, having been up since the early hours, looked ready to drop.

Thankfully, Oliver took the hint. 'I might, actually – if you don't mind going home with Lily and Joseph, Daisy?'

'No, I don't. I'm shattered. And I know I shouldn't have had wine, it always makes me so terribly tired. I'm sure I'll have a nice old headache tomorrow morning, and it will serve me right, too.'

Ben rolled his eyes – whether at Daisy's claiming to get a headache from one small glass of Pinot Grigio, or at the prospect of having to spend the rest of the evening with the vicar, she could not tell – then thought better of it and slapped Oliver's back. 'Right then, good man, let's get ourselves some pints before they close the bar. It's another hour, so we can still get enough beer to see us home nice and drunk.'

'It's *safe and sound*, Ben, not nice and drunk!' Lily shook her head. 'And Oliver, if he gets nasty, you need have no qualms about leaving him. The landlord knows him well, he can always put him up in the pigsty if he can't trust him to walk the distance to his mum's house. His parents live on the lane to Rosedale Abbey,' she explained, looking at Oliver. 'That big white house on the right; you might have noticed it on your walks. And very nice people they are, too, the Cartwrights. Well respected in the village,' she could not resist adding.

Ben scowled at her, but Lily just gave him her sweetest smile and said, 'Come on, Daisy, let's get you home. I dare say you look done in.'

'Oliver and I are thinking of getting a dog,' Daisy said as she climbed into the back of the car, 'I grew up with Retrievers, and Oliver has always said we should have a dog as soon as we are settled. I know he would love a lassie dog, like Lucy's Hamish. Or perhaps we might adopt one. Didn't Jessie say there was a rescue centre near Thirsk?'

'Do you mean will they have any more dogs like the infamous Ossie?'

Joseph slipped behind the wheel and started the engine. 'Oh come on, Lily, give that dog a break! It's not his fault his owners can't look after him probably.—Oi!'

Pressing the button for the electronic handbrake, he leant over the wheel and squinted into the dusk. 'What the hell was that?'

'What was what?'

But Joseph had already got out and was running up the lane towards the bridge, leaving Daisy and Lily to exchange confused glances.

'Did you see anything?' Lily pressed her nose to the window. It was not quite dark yet, but the sky was overcast, and the shadows already long and dark. She wound down the window and stuck her head out, but whatever it was that Joseph had seen, it must have run away.

'No, I'm afraid I didn't.'

'Hm.' Lily pulled her head back in and shook it as she closed the window. 'Well, whatever it was, I hope he'll be back soon. I'm tired!'

While they waited, Daisy began to twist and turn her wedding band around her finger. It had become too wide recently. She would have to take it to the jewellers to have it made tighter if she did not want to risk losing it.

'You know, I have been thinking about …' Daisy faltered, not sure how to go on. Or if to go on at all. The truth was, even before Miss Lavender had mentioned it this morning, she had been thinking about asking Abi for help. She knew she would probably let her use the farm – and the ponies, of course – to give riding lessons to the local children, or even set up a business of sorts, if they were to stay here. The trouble was, she was not entirely sure that that was what she wanted. What if she fell pregnant? What if she didn't? She sighed. What if, what if, what if …

'Thinking about what?'

'Oh,' Daisy mumbled, shaking her head, 'never mind.'

Lily probably knew she *did* mind, but thought it better not to ask. If Daisy did not want to talk about it, then she would be the last person to force her now. Having come here raw with grief after the devastating loss of her boyfriend just over a year ago, Lily knew what it meant to have people trying to get you to talk when all you wanted was to be alone with your grief. And whatever it was that Daisy was grieving for, or missing in her life, it would take a lot of time, patience, and kindness for her to get over it. Thank God she had such a wonderful husband in Oliver. Lily hoped Daisy knew just how lucky she was.

'I missed it! Bugger!'

Joseph was leaning against the side of the car, panting and shaking his head. 'Sorry, ladies,' he gasped, still out of breath. 'But at least we can go home now. Funny though – I could have sworn … oh, anyway. Let's get you ladies home.'

'What did you miss? What was it?'

'I thought it was a dog, but maybe it was just a large cat or something,' Joseph said as he drove across the narrow bridge and turned left onto Brook Lane. 'It was definitely four-legged and very fast – too fast for me to catch at any rate! I really need to get fit this summer. And I must stop using the accident as an excuse for not getting on with it!'

Daisy, who had been about to close her eyes, as she was feeling quite drowsy, leaned forward in her seat. 'What accident?'

'I had a rather scary encounter with a herd of cows last autumn. Trampled me down, they did. Eight weeks in hospital, four in rehab, and another four at home being mollycoddled by my mother.' He rolled his eyes. 'No kidding! I was so glad to get back to work, although I was only allowed to handle hamsters and guinea pigs for a while. Moving to Fern Hill Farm was the best idea I had this spring. And not only because of Abi's baking!'

'Oh,' Daisy said. 'You must have had a guardian angel then. Cows can be quite dangerous, can't they, when they feel threatened?'

'Oh, aye, they can, especially when they have calves. They get fiercely protective then.'

'Yes, I can imagine they would. I am glad you survived that attack and are quite well again. Oh sorry,' she said, unable to suppress a huge yawn, 'I am so tired! Do you mind if I close my eyes for a bit?'

'Not at all,' Lily said. 'We will wake you when we get home. Though the bumps in the road are likely to keep you awake, anyway.'

Daisy nodded, already dozing off. Hopefully, she would be asleep by the time Oliver got back from the pub. He could tell her about Ben tomorrow. Although knowing him, he would probably not tell her anything. And as it was none of her business what Ben might or might not have told her vicar husband in confidence, it was just as well. What they should really talk about, of course, was what she was supposed to do with herself, now that they were stuck in the middle of nowhere. Especially if she did not get pregnant.

CHAPTER 5

A FEW DAYS later, when Oliver had gone to meet the electrician at the Rectory, Daisy took her morning tea to sit on the patio behind the cottage and watched the ponies. Abi had put her three stallions in this field, and it was a joy to watch them, playfully challenging each other as they ran from one field into the next. Well, Dancer and Willoughby were playing, while twenty-year-old Ronnie was quietly grazing in a sunny corner at the far end, looking up every now and then as if to make sure the youngsters were sticking to the rules. As far as Daisy could tell, they were, mostly. Dancer, whom she had been asked to break in, still found it difficult to submit at times, and to know when he had better back off. But for now, they seemed to be doing alright.

Her phone rang, and she turned to pick it up from the table.

'Hello?'

'Daisy? It's Abi. I'm sorry to bother you so early, but I've just had a call from Jonathan Hunter who says there were people trespassing the Mavericks' land and feeding Angela's horses God knows what. Angela Maverick died earlier this year, you see, and her husband—well, never mind. I can tell you about that later. Anyway, Jonathan is a neighbour, and he was working in the field bordering on the Mavericks' estate when he saw those ramblers feeding them sweets and trying to climb on their backs. Ignorant townies. Jonathan chased them away and checked the horses. He says they seem to be okay, but he had to get back to his work, of course, so he asked me if we could come and get them? That is, he asked me, but I thought you could help me perhaps? If you like?'

'I'll be over in a minute.'

As soon as Daisy entered the farmhouse kitchen, she was hit by the irresistible smell of freshly baked bread. There was a cafetiere on the table, which was set for three, Daisy noted. But there was no sign of either Lily or Joseph. Maybe they would be back for ten o'clocks. That seemed to be a Yorkshire tradition. One of the many traditions around here, she thought and smiled.

'The Mavericks' land? Isn't that the rather grand estate up on the hill, at the end of the lane? Lily told me the owners had passed away recently.'

Abi nodded as she poured them a cup of coffee each, despite Daisy's protest that she had just had breakfast. 'Yes, that's the one. Birchwood Park. Angela Maverick died earlier this year, as I said, and her husband … he took his life a few weeks later.' She shook her head sadly. 'Poor Charles. Couldn't live without his beloved Angela. And now there is only Ellen, their daughter, but she lives in London, studying for a degree in opera singing. She has been struggling to keep on top of things, poor lass. I don't think she will keep the place – it is far too large, and the death duties will probably eat away most of her inheritance, sad as it is. I am sure it must have been hard for her to go back to London, but she was determined to keep her promise, bless her. Keep on singing, that's what her mum used to say. They say it was the last thing she ever said to Ellen. Keep on singing ... she has always sung, that lass. Ever since she came, and from what I have learned, all her life. She is adopted, you know,' Abi explained while she poured more coffee. 'The Mavericks could not have children, and it had always been a burden, especially for Angela, who often felt lonely when her husband was away on business. Charles worked a lot – he was something big in the textile industry, had his own business which he sold last year when his wife was diagnosed with terminal cancer. He wanted to be at home, and care for her, right to the end. Which he did – sadly though, that end came rather sooner than expected. She passed away in February, and then *he* took his own life a few weeks later, leaving poor Ellen to fend for herself again.'

Seeing the horrified expression on Daisy's face, she nodded. 'I know. It's awful. The funeral was the saddest I have ever attended in my life. It was heartbreaking. Now I'm sure Reverend Thompson tried his best, but— oh, Daisy! Those horrible people! You would have been appalled.'

'Hold on! Is that the girl Oliver told me about when we first came here? The one who was shunned at her father's funeral because—well, because what? Because he had committed suicide? Because she was only adopted? Because she never was one of them??'

Abi, who was buttering a thick cut slice of bread, paused for a moment, holding the knife in mid-air. 'Yes. To all of those questions. I know it's awful, and highly unfair, but I'm afraid not everybody here is friendly. Most of us are. But – well, not everyone.'

Daisy was speechless. When Abi put the slice of bread before her, complete with a generous spread of strawberry jam, she began eating it mechanically, all protests forgotten. She could not believe what she had just heard. Talk of the cruelty of humans! There seemed to be no limit to it. Not even here in peaceful Rosedale. Or maybe it wasn't so peaceful after all?

'It's just a handful of people, really. Most of whom do not even live here. Charles's brother and sister-in-law, for instance, who had always assumed that they would inherit. But they left everything to Ellen. The estate, the cars, the horses, the flat in London, and the family home in Argyll – which is more like a small castle, really – and the money of course. Every single penny. And then there are some here who would turn their nose up at Ellen being adopted, just like you said. She had been in foster care for most of her life, the poor girl, and came here when she was nine. She was bullied at school because of that – and her constant singing perhaps, which did make her a bit of an oddity, but I suppose that was her way of coping with difficult situations. Then she was sent to Ampleforth College, where she finally began to thrive and blossom. She came home every weekend but seldom ventured further than the church, where she would sit and sing, or pray. They were very religious, the Mavericks. All of them, even that brother of his and his stuck-up wife. I don't know if they might be Catholics – do Catholics still believe suicide to be an unforgivable sin these days? Do you know? But you are not Catholic, are you?'

'No. But even if I were, I would not condemn people who commit suicide. Or any sin, for that matter. It is not our place to do so, is it? We are forgiven because Jesus died for us. For all of us. No exceptions.'

'Hm. If you say so. Still, that is what they did – it's just one family, and their neighbours, but that was enough. One of them claimed to be Angela's best friend. And she was, I think – most of the time. But she never concealed her feelings when it came to the adoption of Ellen. Marion Higgins came to Birchwood Park the day Ellen arrived and told Angela exactly what she thought, and how they would live to regret it.' Abi shook her head disapprovingly. 'They didn't, though. Ellen turned out to be a tonic for them both, and has been such a credit to them! Some people say Angela and Charles saved Ellen, but others say it was the other way round: that Ellen had come to save *them* from their loneliness. They were a very happy family,' she added wistfully.

There were tears in Abi's eyes, though whether they were angry or sad tears, Daisy could not tell. Possibly both. Her heart went out to her, and to Ellen, although she did not know her. She had seen the grave though and read the inscription on the marble headstone.

In loving memory of my dear parents, Angela and Charles Maverick. Sadly missed, forever cherished.

Daisy sighed. 'Poor Ellen. She certainly does not deserve that. No one does. Who did you say those people were? Those who shunned her at her father's funeral?'

'Marion Higgins. She is worse than her husband, really, but then *he* never says much to anything or anyone. One of their daughters was Angela Maverick's godchild – I suspect they expected their Jocelyn to inherit something, too. But she only got a brooch to remember her godmother by, and that was that. She can sell it, it's probably worth a fortune. How Angela could have been friends with that woman, I will never know. They knew each other all their lives. Went to school together and so on. Oh well. – More coffee?'

Daisy shook her head. 'Shouldn't we get going? To get the horses, I mean?'

'Oh yes, we will go in a minute. But I made breakfast for Lily and Joseph, and they never turned up, did they? No point in pouring good coffee down the drain. It's from Nate's roastery.'

'Okay … so, what about the others who also shunned Ellen, or said nasty things? You said they were neighbours. Of the Higgins, or of the Mavericks?'

Abi's lips formed a thin line. 'They are neighbours of the Mavericks. Although they live a bit off the track, keep themselves to themselves. They are very strange, the Matlocks. Always have been. They only eat fruit, and drink warm water. Very odd. They have a pony they left to graze with Angela's horses. A very naughty Shetland Pony they claim to have rescued from a circus. They have not been looking after it, though, not even when Angela had passed away. It did not matter at first when Charles was still around, and I believe there were two girls from Helmsley who used to come a couple times a week to ride, but they stopped coming after Charles's death. So then the Hunters offered to look after the horses, as they are the nearest neighbours, apart from the Matlocks, of course. But they have so much to do with their farm and Jonathan's elderly parents and … oh, never mind. I told Jonathan I would phone Ellen, and ask her if it is okay for us to bring them here. I'm sure she'll say yes, but I do want to ask.' She got up to get the telephone. 'They are Thoroughbreds, by the way, so I thought I would ask you to look after them. Would you like that?'

Daisy stared at her open-mouthed. Thoroughbreds? Left to themselves on a deserted estate? How could Abi even ask?

'Of course I'll help! I'd be delighted!' She jumped up, her eyes bright with excitement. 'Come on, let's go! I can drive the truck if you like. I presume they have one?'

Abi smiled. 'They do, yes, and I'm glad because mine is quite old, and not in good shape. Let me just make that phone call, and then we are ready to go. They are wonderful horses. You will love them.'

I already do, Daisy thought as she sprinted across the yard to the cottage. She whistled softly as she changed into an old pair of jeans and her favourite fleece sweater with *Hammond Hall Stud* emblazoned on it. For the first time since they arrived here, she felt she had a purpose. And not just a purpose – she was on a mission.

***

'BUT WHAT ABOUT the pony? We cannot leave him here all by himself, even if he does not belong to the Mavericks.'

They had just led the two mares – one chestnut, one bay – into the Mavericks' horse truck. A very large, luxurious, and almost new truck, as Daisy could not help but notice. Nor could she help noticing the Land Rover standing in the spacious garage, along with a dark green Jaguar E-type that looked as if it might be a genuine classic and worth a small fortune. All the while a rather shaggy looking brown Shetland Pony had been watching them, and now it was standing at the fence, gazing across at them with huge, sad eyes. Or what they could see from those eyes, as they were mostly hidden underneath a filthy mat of long, brown hair.

Abi sighed. 'You're right. We can't just leave him. But we can't just take him either, or they will accuse us of stealing him. Not that they ever cared for him in the first place. I think he has been lodging with the Mavericks since the day he came. He is not old, I think,' she said, running a hand along the pony's neck. 'Nine or ten perhaps. He would make some little girl a lovely riding pony, or pet.' When she withdrew her hand, it was black and greasy. 'Uugh, but he is in dire need of a shower! Poor little sausage. – Do you want to stay here, while I walk over to the Matlocks' place and ask them what they want us to do about their pony? I don't think I'll be long.'

'In that case, I am quite happy to wait here.' Daisy rubbed the velvet nose of one of the mares, who in turn let out a soft snort of contentment. 'You can go and have tea with the Matlocks. Oh no,' she said, putting a hand over her mouth, 'they don't drink tea, do they?'

Abi shot her a look. 'If I didn't know you better, young lady, I'd say that was cheeky! Now then, let's get this over with. But I'm sure they will be more than happy for us to keep him.'

Daisy smiled. 'If that's the case, I am sure William will be pleased to have a companion. He is just about the same size, too.'

'Ha! That's what *you* think. William will stick with his Lady Greys and this one,' Abi said, tickling the pony's chin, 'will team up with Myrtle as soon as he sets foot on the farm. Or hoof. I would wager my second-best hat, if Myrtle had not eaten that the day before Lucy's wedding.'

'Good luck!' Daisy called after her, but Abi was

already gone, heading down an overgrown footpath. Turning back to the pony, Daisy said, 'You are a nice pony, aren't you? You just need a bit of brushing up, and you'll be fit to sit down for afternoon tea with us. Only in the orchard, of course.'

The pony said nothing. Instead, he pushed his nose inside her pocket and ate all of the sugar lumps. Still munching, he then pushed open the gate, trotted towards the horse truck, and climbed in, squeezing in between the two Thoroughbreds. For him, the matter was settled.

***

'THAT WAS QUICK! You cannot have been gone for more than ten minutes. What did they say? They did not want any money, did they?'

Abi climbed into her car and stuck her head out of the window. 'No. He wasn't in – he always goes foraging on Thursday mornings, apparently – and she told me exactly where to stick it. The pony, I mean. And otherwise. Horrible people! So rude. I mean, if they want to live on berries and mushrooms, then that's their decision, but they can at least be polite.' She looked at Daisy. 'I must say I'm feeling a bit bad about this. I should have offered to take the horses in the first place. Would have saved poor Ellen a lot of trouble, and the Hunters, too. Maddie Hunter is a lovely lass, and ever so helpful, but she has a lot on her hands as it is. Anyway. We've got the horses, and the pony, and we are going to take them all back to Fern Hill Farm where they can stay as long as they want. I don't mind.'

I'm sure you don't, thought Daisy, hiding a smile. 'So

you are going to keep him then?'

'Frankly, I don't see what else we can do. He seems to have made up his mind, anyway. And I have a feeling he will let us know what else he has set his stubborn mind on.' With a sigh and a shake of her head, Abi started the engine. 'One of these days I'll just register Fern Hill Farm as a charity for rescue ponies. I might as well, at the rate I am going.' Waving a hand through the window, she called, 'I'll see you at the farm!'

***

BY THE TIME they had settled the horses and finished cleaning the pony – Daisy thought she had never been so dirty in her life, but the pony looked a lot better, and had collapsed onto his bed of straw as if he had no intention of getting up again any time soon – it was almost five. Oliver was back and curious to hear the whole story over a cup of tea. He and Daisy were having tea, anyway, while Abi had poured herself a neat whisky.

'And I deserve it, too, after all that trouble. I'm sure I will sleep like a log tonight! Thank you for your help, Daisy. I could not have done this without you.'

Daisy smiled. 'It was a pleasure, and an honour. Two Thoroughbreds, and such beauties, too! Does Ellen not ride?'

'I don't know, to be honest. I don't think I ever saw her on horseback, but she might just not have ridden outside the estate, which is quite large enough of course. When I asked her what to do about the horses this morning, she just said I should get them and keep them safe until she knew what she was going to do with them. For now, they are safe, and that is all that matters. I stopped at the Hunters' farm on the way and told them we've got the pony, too,' she said, taking a biscuit, 'so I can call Ellen later and tell her not to worry. She has enough on her plate as it is, poor lassie.'

Oliver nodded. 'I wonder if there is anything we can do to help? Except looking after her mother's horses, I mean. She will still be grieving, even when she comes back, and perhaps not be able to cope with everything at once. It is rather a lot for her.'

'Too much, if you ask me.' Daisy poured herself another cup of tea. 'Especially after what happened at the funeral. She did not deserve that. No one does.'

'No,' Abi said quietly, as she looked out of the window, 'she most certainly didn't. She is such a lovely girl. Misses her parents terribly – you would never guess she was adopted. They were very close.'

'So you said, yes.' Daisy avoided Oliver's eye, hoping he would not seriously think about adoption now. Some days she did wonder what went on in her husband's mind. But then they had not talked about it for months. Maybe it was time they did.

'Maybe I should invite her to stay with us for a while when she comes back after her exams,' Abi contemplated, pushing a piece of shortbread around on her plate. 'I have a feeling she might not like to be up there all on her own.'

'I wouldn't, if I were her,' Daisy said with feeling. 'I'm sure she will appreciate your offer, Abi, even if she says no. It's very kind of you.'

'Nonsense. It's what anyone would do around here. Except the Higgins and the Matlocks perhaps.'

Oliver grinned. 'Yes, except those. Oops! Sorry, I

shouldn't say that as a vicar.'

But Abi just shrugged and finished her whisky. 'Oh, don't worry, I'm not going to tell anyone. And for what it's worth, Oliver, you are not only a vicar, are you? You are also human. You have feelings, opinions, and attitudes, same as anyone else. Anyway, I am going to check on—oh, hello, Lily. I didn't hear you come in. Aren't you working?'

Lily pointed to the clock on the wall. 'It's six o'clock?—Ooh, tea, lovely!' Flopping down on a chair, she shook the tea pot to find it was empty. 'Ah, just my luck. Hi, Daisy. What's this I hear about you having adopted Angela Maverick's horses?'

Abi, who had taken the tea pot, nearly dropped it. 'You can't have heard about *that* already!' But Lily laughed. 'News travel fast in this village, as well you know! I met Madeleine Hunter outside my shop. And then I saw that posh horse truck rumbling past, which is kind of hard to overlook.' She bit into a shortbread. 'And you have rescued the pony, too? The one the Matlocks claim to have saved and then dumped on the Mavericks?'

'Well, we didn't have much of a choice,' Abi remarked drily. 'He simply opened the gate and walked straight up the ramp into the horse box, as Daisy tells me. He did not stop to ask.'

'Open the gate? How?'

'Well, I don't know, do I? We were busy leading Angela's mares into the horsebox, and I am certain I closed the gate after them. Or maybe I didn't?' Abi cast a glance at Daisy, who nodded solemnly. 'You did. I saw you closing it.'

Lily laughed until the tears were rolling down her cheeks and got up to cuddle Theo, Abi's ancient wirehaired dachshund. He was snoozing in his bed by the Aga, as was his habit at this time of day – or any time of the day, really. 'Your mummy has a talent for picking up four-legged troublemakers, hasn't she? First the goat, and now a circus pony!'

Daisy though, who had been itching to show Oliver the horses, tugged at his shirtsleeve. 'Will you come to the stables with me? Please? I can't wait for you to meet Ruby and Starlight. They are such beauties!'

Oliver looked longingly at the shortbread – but, knowing he stood no chance against his wife when it came to horses, he gave a sigh and pushed back his chair. 'Alright then, let's go. Thanks for the tea, Abi – and the shortbread!' And helping himself to another piece, he followed his wife outside.

'He really adores her, doesn't he?' Lily observed when they had gone. 'I think they are a lovely couple. Though why she always looks so sad, I would like to know. Do you have an idea?'

Abi picked up the plates and cups and took them over to the sink. 'I do, yes. But I have a feeling she doesn't want to talk about it, so I don't want to speculate. I may be wrong, for all I know. Is Joseph coming tonight? I haven't seen him at all today. Though I did set the table for three this morning. And ended up on my own – well, with Daisy. Not complaining, of course. She is a delightful young woman.'

'Oh, gosh, I'm sorry. We had dinner in Helmsley last night and then stayed at his house, as he was on early morning duty in the small animal practice. He is going to come here later, though I'm sure he'll be worn out, so we can have our usual glass of sherry in front of the fire. As we do.' She shared a smile with her great-aunt but froze when she heard a loud shriek from the yard, followed by raucous laughter.

'What the—'

'I don't believe this! I just don't believe this!—Abi!!!'

Abi sighed. 'Oh dear, what now? Goat – or pony?'

'Or both?' Lily suggested, deadpan. Throwing a dish towel at her niece, Abi went out to see what the trouble was.

CHAPTER 6

'I THINK WE deserve this tonight,' Oliver said, putting two glasses of wine on the coffee table. 'Or you do, anyway. You have done a fantastic job today, Daisy! I'm so proud of you.'

'Are you?' Daisy tried not to think about the effect the alcohol might have on her chances of conceiving. She was too tired to argue though, and anyway, it had not helped before, had it? Her not drinking, and cutting down on caffeine and red meat, even though she loved her steak. Not to mention giving up her career … of all the things, that had been the hardest. Whether it had been worth the sacrifice, she was not sure now. Probably not.

She and Destiny had been a brilliant team and won countless competitions all over the UK – mostly cross-country, but also the occasional triathlon, which involved show jumping and dressage as well. But that was before she had married Oliver and given up event riding. It had been a terrible wrench, and no one – except perhaps her father who had heard her crying as she had packed her riding equipment away and kissed Destiny goodbye the day before her wedding – knew it had all but broken her heart.

'I am. You are wonderful with horses. And I know

they cannot replace Destiny, my darling, but they are—'

'*No horse* can ever replace Destiny.' She had not meant to speak harshly, but just hearing the name of her beloved horse brought tears to her eyes. Why did he have to bring this up now? Didn't he know how much it hurt her when he referred to her old life as if it was a closed chapter? And why did it even have to be closed? Why did it have to be over, just because they were here now, and she was … well. Not a mother.

'Of course not.' He reached for her hand, but she withdrew it. She didn't know why she felt she had to punish him. It was unreasonable. She knew he meant well. He always did.

'But it's a start,' Oliver said, refusing to give up yet. 'There is no one better suited for the job in hand than you, and Abi knows that. I'm sure Ellen will be very grateful to you for looking after her mother's beloved horses. And,' he added, raising his glass, and winking at her, 'who knows where this might be leading?'

Into another dead end of course, Daisy thought, but chinked her glass against his. They were not her horses, and they might well be gone by the end of the summer. What then?

Stop it, she chided herself. Just stop it! You are being unfair as well as ungrateful, and it is not like you to be so mean. He never asked you to give up riding. It was your choice, remember? Your choice.

'I'm sorry,' she whispered, suddenly close to tears. 'I don't know what's wrong with me. You are right, it has been a wonderful day. There is a lot to be grateful for. Let's – let's just leave it at that, okay?'

He looked at her for a long time before he finally

nodded. 'Of course. I didn't mean to upset you, darling. I'm sorry. Please forgive me.'

'It's okay.' She sipped her wine. 'Mm, this is a very good wine. Is it the one my father gave us?'

'No. It's Marks and Spencer. I bought it on the way home, along with the stir-fry. Talking of stir-fry, I am absolutely starving. Do you mind if I start cooking?'

'Not at all. I'll help you.'

'You know,' Daisy said later, when they were sitting on the sofa, eating their dessert (he had remembered to buy her favourite chocolate eclairs, too), 'I am really quite pleased with myself today, if you don't mind me saying so. Even if I could have done without that pony and his tricks! I don't think I have ever seen a horse quite so full of mischief as this one.'

When she had found him in the corner of the field behind the barn, covered in stinking black mud, she could have murdered him – well, almost. Because after all her hard work, he had gone and enjoyed a good old roll, looking worse than when they had first encountered him at Birchwood Park. A lot worse. And he had not seemed in the least perturbed.

'There stands a pony without conscience,' Abi had remarked drily, and they had all nodded in solemn agreement as they stared at the mud-caked pony. What else was there to say? Though how he could even have escaped from his stall, or got into the field when the gate was closed, was beyond them.

'Maybe he jumped?' Lily suggested.

'Maybe he did – you never know with circus performers like him!'

To which Lily had replied they should call him Jolly Jumper then. And as no one could deny the fact that he *was* a jolly little fellow, for all that he was so naughty, and could not have got into the field unless he had literally jumped the fence, they all agreed it was a very good name.

'Aw, but he is funny, isn't he?' Oliver grinned, putting his empty plate down and stretching out his long legs. 'I can't remember the last time I laughed so hard. I think he is charming – in his own way.'

Daisy pulled a face. 'Very funny, yes. You did not have to clean him! But you're right, he did make us laugh, didn't he? I'm not sure Ellen will want to keep *him*. Oh, I wish there was something we could do to help her, Oliver. She must be so wretched, the poor girl.'

Talking about Ellen seemed safer than talking about herself, or her feelings. And really, when you looked at it, her situation was infinitely better than young Ellen's, wasn't it? Nobody had died, let alone committed suicide, and left her to pick up the pieces. At least she had a purpose now, a job to do. Thank God for these wonderful horses that had ended up on Fern Hill Farm – even if they did not compare to Destiny, they were perfectly lovely, and they had come at just the right time. They were, in fact, the answer to her prayer.

'Well, you are helping her now, aren't you? By looking after her mum's horses. I'm sure she'll appreciate that. Also,' Oliver said, placing his hand over his wife's, 'I hope these horses will help *you*, darling. They are magnificent creatures, and they will need exercise, too – good job you brought your riding equipment to Yorkshire when you heard we were going to stay on a stud farm for a while.'

'Yes, good job I did …' She picked at her eclair, lost

in thoughts. Then she looked at Oliver, a mixture of mischief and fierce determination showing in her eyes. 'But I will not waste my time on that Jolly Jumper fellow! He can stay as muddy as he likes, for all I care. It's not as if anyone is going to enter him for the Great Yorkshire Show.'

Oliver raised his eyebrows. 'No? I am sure he would come first in the class – let me think … naughtiest pony?'

'Yes, well, if there was a class like that, he would easily win it!' she laughed, picking up her glass. 'Maybe there is a local show that would allow him to take part. I'm sure Lily would be delighted to enter him. As for me, I am quite content to ride Angela Maverick's wonderful horses. Who do you think I should try first, Ruby or Starlight?'

***

It was early morning, and it was still dark when she crept down the passage of the old house and slipped out of the back door and down the stone steps into the garden. From here, she ran across the lawn and, pushing through the cast iron gate, on to the stables where her horse was waiting for her. Only Destiny did not know she was hers, of course, as they had only brought the beautiful chestnut mare home the day before.

Her very own horse.

She was terribly excited about the prospect of their first proper ride. Having lain awake all night, she could not wait until sunrise, never mind until after breakfast when her father had said they would go on a ride around the estate together.

Daisy pushed the sliding door open and slipped into the dimly lit stable. It was cosy and warm in here, and smelt of horses and straw and leather. The tack room was situated at the front, with an oval shaped silver nameplate for each horse's bridle and saddle, hung on opposite walls of the room. Only Destiny didn't have a nameplate yet. Daisy smiled as she walked past the open door. She would get the saddle later. For now, she just wanted to see her.

'Good morning, my beautiful,' she said, speaking in the same tone she would use for her young nieces and nephews. 'Did you sleep well?'

The beautiful mare turned around and watched her with large, liquid eyes that betrayed only mild curiosity. Daisy stepped closer, stretching out her hand for the horse to sniff. 'You don't know me yet, do you? I am your new mistress. You don't need to be afraid,' she said, curving her hand over the horse's nose and stroking it lightly. 'I only want to say good morning. There now,' she whispered, slowly working her way down the mare's gracefully arched neck. 'There now, my beautiful …'

Opening the stable door, she slipped a head collar over Destiny's noble head and led her down the passage. When she had fastened the lead rope to one of the iron rings in the wall outside the tack room, she went to get Destiny's brand new bridle and saddle, all the while humming softly.

Destiny stood quite still, but Daisy could sense her inquisitive eyes on her, following her every move. She could feel the horse was just as excited as she was. She would have to be careful, or Destiny would break into a wild run the moment she was in the saddle, or even before. Concentration was paramount. And patience. If she could not teach Destiny to be patient and wait, she would leave the horse in charge, and that would not do. She would need her freedom, of course, but she was not allowed to be in charge while carrying a rider. But Daisy had not grown up with racehorses for *nothing, and sat in the saddle from an early age; she knew what she was doing. Only when she had fastened the saddle, and checked the bridle once more, she took the head collar off and led Destiny outside into the early morning sunshine.*

'Look, Destiny. This is your new home. Do you want to go and explore? Yes?'

The horse snorted softly and thumped a hoof on the ground, and Daisy laughed. 'You do, yes? Come on then, I'll show you. Easy now! No rush. We have all the time in the world …'

She was just going to put her foot in the stirrup when she woke up.

She was in the cottage on Fern Hill Farm, and Destiny was in Suffolk, and not here. Turning aside so Oliver would not wake up, Daisy pulled out a tissue from the box on the bedside table and wept quietly.

CHAPTER 7

St Peter's was always cold, even on a summer day, and Miss Lavender pulled her shawl around her shoulders as she entered the church. She came here every morning to pray, and on this particular morning she had come with a purpose to pray for Daisy Clifford-Jones. Ever since Daisy and her husband had moved to Bishops Bridge, Miss Lavender had been convinced that something was troubling the beautiful young woman with the deep blue eyes. Even though she was always friendly, always gracious and kind, there was a deep sadness in those eyes that touched Miss Lavender's heart. Even when she smiled, she looked sad.

And that, the old lady thought as she sat down in her usual place (third pew on the right, without exception), is sad. And definitely not right. While Miss Lavender knew that some people thought the vicar's wife aloof, she suspected there was more to Daisy Clifford-Jones than met the eye. A lot more. With her seemingly cool demeanour, her refined way of speaking, and her timeless, elegant style (Daisy was the only woman Miss Lavender knew who preferred skirts to trousers, even when riding her bicycle!), even Miss Lavender had to admit the vicar's young wife looked a little out of place in this remote part of the North York Moors. For what it was worth, she did not even look like a vicar's wife. Although what a vicar's wife was supposed to look like, she did not know.

And yet, she sensed that something was missing in Daisy's life. Of course she missed the horses, and her riding career. But she had a feeling that that was not all. There was something else ... but what? That was what she had come to pray about today. As Miss Lavender was not in the habit of asking people about their feelings (just as she would not talk about hers), never mind getting involved in other people's lives, she would do what she always did in such cases: She would ask God.

***

WHEN SHE LEFT the church half an hour later, Miss Lavender felt better for it, though still not sure about what to do. Should she invite Daisy for tea, and try and get her to talk? Would she tell her what really troubled her then, instead of going on about choirs and other matters of interest strictly to do with her husband's church? She sighed. Probably not. Glancing at the clock in the church tower, and realizing with a frown that it was later than she had thought, Miss Lavender decided to give her morning walk a miss. It was just beginning to rain, anyway, and the last thing she needed was a bad cold. At her age, this could well mean having to close the shop for a whole week.

'Good morning, Miss Lavender!'

Madeleine Hunter was standing by the steps to Miss Lavender's porch, waving. 'I know it's not nine yet, but we have run out of porridge oats, and I was wondering if you would be so kind and sell me some? Please?'

Miss Lavender sighed. She had not even had breakfast yet. But then neither had Madeleine perhaps, and she was pregnant. 'Of course. Come on in, Madeleine.'

'Did you know Miss Abigail has taken Angela Maverick's horses to Fern Hill Farm? I am so glad, and relieved! I tried my best, but it was just getting a little too much with the farm, and Freya needing constant attention, and the little one in here,' she placed a hand over her rounded belly, laughing softly. 'I am always rushed off my feet! And they are such precious horses. The vicar's wife is looking after them, Daisy. I saw her riding Starlight across the Wilkinson's field the other day. Or was it Ruby? Anyway, she looked very much at home in the saddle. Elegant, too. Abi says she used to do event riding before she got married.'

Miss Lavender was in the process of unlocking the door when she stopped for a moment. Was *that* the missing piece? The event riding? No. She shook her head. She knew she had been a professional rider. Daisy had told her so herself, hadn't she?

'Yes,' she said, turning the key, 'she told me about that.'

'Well, she must have been good. Shame she gave that up, wouldn't you agree? – Do you have coarse oats, too? Jonathan likes those better. Oh, and a jar of black treacle, please.'

Shame she gave that up …

Miss Lavender frowned as she thought about this. But then she shook her head, determined not to let herself agree or disagree on anything, never mind discussing Daisy's private affairs with a customer. Deciding to ignore Madeleine's remark, she got the two items and placed them on the counter, hoping she would get to have her breakfast after all.

'She always looks a bit sad, doesn't she? Daisy, I mean. But when she is riding, she looks happy. I suppose it's because she is in her element then. Even Jonathan noticed when she went past our farm the other day. And he is not exactly the most sensitive type, never mind romantic! He's a good husband of course, don't get me wrong.'

'Don't you worry, my dear, I won't. And unless you need anything else, that's five-sixty, please.' Much as she liked Madeleine, that woman could talk for England, and the old lady's patience was wearing a bit thin.

'Oh! Yes! Sorry. I'm babbling, I know. Jonathan always tells me not to—here you are, Miss Lavender. Five-sixty. Oh, and can I have a bag of barley sugars? I always like to have a few in my bag in case … you know.'

Miss Lavender didn't know, but went to measure one hundred grams of the sweets into a paper bag. 'That's six-eighty then, please.'

'Of course. Here you are.' Madeleine put some extra coins on the counter and took her shopping. 'And thank you for serving me, Miss Lavender. That's very kind of you. Goodbye.'

The old lady smiled. It was hard to resist Madeleine's charm. 'Of course. Give my regards to your husband, and enjoy your breakfast. Goodbye.'

As soon as Madeleine had left the shop, Miss Lavender locked the door and went upstairs to her flat to put the kettle on. She did not need much, but two slices of buttered toast with her tea, and a little bit of peace and quiet was all it took to get her ready for another day. For some reason though, she did not seem to be able to get into her routine today. She regretted not having been able to do her walk, and Madeleine's words about Daisy had got her thinking about the vicar's wife again. She didn't know why, but she could not shake off the feeling that she must have seen Daisy before. But where? She hardly ever left her safe haven here in Rosedale, and Daisy had said she had never been to Yorkshire. So where could they possibly have met? It didn't make sense.

A professional … used to do event riding … must have been good … shame she gave that up.

The words kept tumbling about in her head, getting mixed with the vision of a girl with deep blue eyes looking back at her inquisitively, until the old lady could not bear it any longer. Pushing back her chair, she cried, 'Oh, for heaven's sake, what is it? What, Lord?'

***

DAISY PUT ON her riding hat and fastened it, clipping the chin strap carefully in place. Then she gathered the soft leather reins in one hand, took the stirrup in the other, and closed her eyes briefly before swinging herself onto Starlight's back. Slipping her right foot into the other stirrup, Daisy patted the mare's neck. 'Don't you worry, my lovely, I've done this before. We'll be fine, you and me.'

As she pushed Starlight into a light trot, her body moved instantly with the horse's, and Daisy felt more joy than she had felt in months. Years, possibly. I should never have given up riding, she thought as she bent down under the low branches of an ash tree. I should have stood my ground …

But she did not want to be bitter about this. Not on such a beautiful day when she was riding down the lane towards the village, anticipating a long, leisurely ride through the fields and the woods. Starlight was amazing. Spirited and lively, and yet at the same time willing to submit. Destiny had always wanted to run, faster and faster, and jump any hurdle that came their way. Her brother Simon used to call her a show-off. 'She knows she's brilliant and she wants everyone to know. She will take you anywhere, that one. Soaring the heights. You'll be on the front page of every horse magazine in the country before long, mark my words.'

All of Daisy's siblings were passionate about horses and riding – Eleanor, Daisy's eldest sister, took part in international horse jumping events, and Simon was a champion jockey who earned a fortune at the racecourses around the British Isles and beyond. Kate, the youngest, had specialised in dressage and rode her Warmblood mare, Willow, from victory to victory. George, the eldest, had taken over the management of Hammond Hall Stud a few years ago, when their father had had a heart scare. He ran the place together with his wife, Helen, who was just as mad about horses as the rest of them. Albert was the only one who had only ever ridden for the sheer pleasure of it. He, too, had left his horse behind when he got married. But while Albert's stallion, Firefly, was used for breeding and had fathered many a promising foal, Destiny had become her nieces' pet horse.

On entering the village, Daisy waved to a group of school mums who were standing on the other side of the bridge, chatting, and laughing. They must have just dropped off their children at the village school. Daisy sighed. This should be me. I should be one of them by now. Kissing my little girl, or boy, goodbye, and going home to do the things I could not do while the children were around, demanding my attention. Like riding my horse …

She had always wanted to be a stay-at-home-mum, like her own mother had been. Of course, she had helped her father to run the estate, but first and foremost, she had been a mother. Though she had given up her career, Daisy had hoped they would be able to keep a couple of ponies for their children, and she would teach them to ride. At least, that had been the plan. Or the dream.

Or nothing, as it turned out.

'This way, my lovely,' Daisy said, gently steering Starlight in the right direction. She did not want to go all the way round the valley, as it was a hot day, and there was no shade on the other side. 'Yes, that's right, we are going into the woods, and then perhaps on to Rosedale Abbey. It's too hot to go all the way up to the kilns, like I did with Ruby yesterday. Sorry, my beauty. No adventures for you today.' She laughed softly, then gave a little sigh. Though she would not describe herself as the most adventurous type, she could not help feeling that life was somehow slipping through her fingers like grains of sand, without anything ever happening. The truth was, she was not only unhappy, she was also bored.

She could keep herself busy with church and choirs and looking after Ellen's horses of course. She could even take more pupils and teach them to ride. She enjoyed working with Louisa May, and she had to admit she quite liked Abi's sturdy Welsh Ponies. They were good-natured and easy to handle, except Dancer perhaps, but he was only young and had never been properly trained. All it took was for her to ask Abi …

So why didn't she? Because the truth was, deep in her heart she was still waiting. Except that she was getting more and more disillusioned with every passing month. This miracle they had both been praying and hoping for so fervently, took such a long time in coming, she had almost given up hope it would ever come at all.

What if it never happened? What if she simply was not meant to be a mother?

'Then,' she whispered, 'I will have to find another purpose, or I will simply die of boredom.'

Perhaps it was time to find out what that purpose was, she thought as she patted Starlight's neck and let her walk up the hill, and deeper into the woods. Even though they were in the shade of the trees, it was still very warm, and she did not want to exhaust the horse. But she wanted to get to the top, and look down onto the shimmering lake one could only see from up there. Lily called it the Lake of Shining Waters, quoting from one of the many books she seemed to know by heart. A true bookworm, Lily was constantly quoting from some book or other, whether people knew what she was talking about or not. Daisy did not read much, except books on horses, or stories in which horses were the main characters (classics like *Black Beauty* and *War Horse*, which she always cried her way through because they reminded her of Destiny). And advice books on how to get pregnant. Not that she would tell anyone about those, or be careless enough to leave them lying about the cottage. She kept them well hidden at the back of the wardrobe, together with her journal and a whole box full of pregnancy tests. She had ordered them online, too ashamed to ask for a test kit in a pharmacy, or put it into her basket at *Boots*.

And that, too, will have to stop, she thought. I need to focus on other things. I need to leave the past behind, and move on. Whatever God's plan might be for me on this earth, I am sure it cannot be that of me being stuck in a waiting room.

***

A SMART BLACK and burgundy coloured carriage came into sight when Daisy passed through the village on her way back to the farm. She recognised the two Lady Greys, Clover and Delilah, from a distance and put up a hand in greeting just as Abi called, 'Hello, Daisy! Lovely day for it, isn't it?'

But her words got somewhat lost in the excited squeals and laughter rising from the back seat of the carriage where, to Daisy's surprise, the two Marston children were sitting, holding hands with each other as they took in the excitement of Bishops Bridge's High Street. At twenty-eight and twenty-four, they were not children but adults, but, having both been born with cerebral palsy, Edmund and Victoria still lived at home with their parents. Henry and Eliza Marston had made it their lifelong commitment to care for them, insisting that they alone knew what was best for their children. They did not want them to live in a care home and only see them at weekends. Everybody in the village admired them for their courage and determination, and everybody was fond of Edmund and Victoria. Susanna Harper came once a week to paint with them, and Abi often invited them to come over and pet the ponies. And since Daisy had come to the farm, they visited even more often, having taken a liking to "the beautiful lady", as Abi insisted Mrs Marston had said. Daisy had blushed at the compliment and since then she had been trying to think of a way to help these two. After all, they were God's children, too, and deserved every bit as much happiness – and fun – as any other.

'Hello, Victoria, hello, Edmund,' she called as she came to a halt next to the carriage, smiling at the two. 'Are you having fun?'

Victoria did not speak and just smiled shyly back at her, but Edmund shouted, 'Yes!' He was grinning from ear to ear, and Daisy felt a rush of warmth filling her heart. Such simple joys, she thought. The little things that make us happy, put a smile on our faces.

'Oh, that's good. And have you been to your mum and dad's farm, too? Did they see you riding in the carriage?'

'They–they–t–took a p–picture,' Edmund said with some difficulty but was pleased when Daisy raised her eyebrows and said, clearly impressed, 'They took pictures, too? Oh good! You must show me the pictures when your Dad next brings you to the farm. Can I ride home with you? Do you think Starlight can keep up with the two Lady Greys?'

This sent Edmund into a fit of laughter, and for the next minute any kind of conversation was impossible because of his incredibly joyful, but rather loud and ongoing laughter. Some people stopped to see what was going on and waved and called 'Hello!' when they recognised Victoria and Edmund (or "the village's favourite inhabitants", as Lily fondly described them). Miss Lavender came out and brought a bag of pick and mix (though you could not pick the sweets yourself in her shop, as she insisted she was "not a supermarket") for them to share and stopped for a little chat with Abi. Then she turned to Daisy and said, 'It's good to see you, Daisy. That's a lovely mare you've got there. Is this Starlight or Ruby?'

'Starlight,' Daisy replied, patting the horse's neck. 'You can tell by the white star on her forehead. And she has two white stockings, too. Ruby is a golden chestnut with no white at all. She's beautiful, isn't she?'

Miss Lavender smiled. 'She is. And you look very happy, Daisy. That's good.'

Shortly after that, they rode home together, dropping Victoria and Edmund off at Brook Farm, and by the time they arrived at Fern Hill Farm, Daisy felt happier than she had felt in a long time. Edmund and Victoria would come over next week, and she would introduce them to Jolly Jumper. Maybe the little fellow would be just the pony for these two. If nothing else, he would make them laugh.

CHAPTER 8

JESSIE WAS BROWSING the Barbour website for knitted jumpers, thinking she might treat herself to something nice. Nate had asked her and Louisa May to join him for a boating holiday in Norfolk later in the summer, which would help them reconnect, and come to the right decision in due time. Because whichever way you looked at it, if they were to have a future together, they could not live fifty miles apart, and have their respective businesses to run as well. More than anything, she wanted Louisa May to have a father, and for them all to be a proper family at long last.

She stopped as the cursor hovered over the *Add to basket* button. Okay, she thought, that is what *I* want. But what about Louisa May? What would she think about us getting married, and perhaps having more children? What if she didn't like the idea, no matter how cool she thought Nate was with his own coffee roastery and driving a Jaguar?

Bringing up Louisa May on her own had been her choice after all. Okay, so she had only found out that she was pregnant when Nate had already left for Africa after A-Levels, but she could have got in touch, had she really wanted to. The fact that her then eighteen-year-old self maybe just didn't have the courage was not enough of an excuse to keep the existence of his daughter a secret for so many years, and she knew that. There would have been plenty of opportunity to find him and tell him that he had a daughter, but she had let them all pass. And over the years, it had just become harder and harder and … well, then came Lily. She had given her a book called *The Fine Art of Coffee Making*, written by Nate Sullivan, on her birthday last year. Fate? Or destiny?

Either way, she was glad Lily had not only bought her that book, but bullied her into signing up to that Barista Masterclass at Nate's coffee shop in Durham. She knew that had she found him happily married with kids – and she had to admit she was surprised to find that he wasn't, given that he was handsome as well as charming and immensely successful – she would have left Durham with her certificate, and that would have been it. Or maybe she would not even have stayed for the course. At any rate, she would never have told him about Louisa May. But he wasn't married, and there weren't any other children. And here they were, making plans for the future, as if the last fifteen years had never happened …

Only they had, hadn't they? Or how was she ever to forget what had brought them together in the first place? They had only ever been friends at school, until that fateful night when she had come running to him, grief-stricken and desperate to be held in his arms, comforted, and loved …

Just then her gaze fell on the date on the screen of her laptop, and she froze. The fifth of June. Fifteen years today – and she had not even thought of Michelle until now! Did that make her a bad sister? Possibly. Although her mother had not even phoned her yet, which was unusual. But then it was only just six. Maybe Mum was still in the churchyard, putting flowers on Michelle's grave. Freesias and tuberose with their strong, sweet scent, grown in a special spot in her garden. And every year on the twelfth of June, she would make up a posy with lavender and lady's mantle, and a single pink rose in the middle, and take it to the churchyard. She always went alone. Her father went, too, but sometimes he chose the day after, or the day when the funeral had been.

Her sister's funeral.

Jessie felt hot tears forming at the back of her eyes, filling them faster than she could find a tissue to wipe them away with. It was no use. There were too many, and they were coming too fast. It didn't matter. She wanted to be sad, and cry for the sister she had loved so much.

'Michelle,' she whispered, 'Michelle …'

Even now she could see herself standing at the top of the stairs, trying to take in the horribly surreal scene below. The two policemen taking their hats off. Speaking in low voices that were not low enough. With a beating heart, her throat as dry and rough as sandpaper, and clammy hands that were holding so tight to the railings that her knuckles turned white, Jessie had heard every word. Every single, inconceivable word …

We are so sorry … there has been an accident … your daughter …

And then she had heard herself screaming. 'No! No! Nooo!'

Strangely enough, no one else had heard her. No one had looked up to see her standing there, shaking her head in wild despair. She had screamed inside her head.

… killed instantly … no comfort, I know, but – she never felt any pain …

Then, while her father had put an arm around her mother's waist and gently steered her to the sofa, Jessie, unnoticed by her parents, had rushed to the bathroom to be violently sick.

Even though it was so long ago, she still remembered every single detail of that terrible night. Michelle had been knocked over by a car while skating along the winding country lanes in Lincolnshire, where they had grown up. Having left the house in a fury after an argument with their mum (probably about some trifling matter or other; it had not taken much to wind Michelle up, as she had always been the more highly-strung of the two sisters), Michelle had never come home. To this day, her mother had not been able to forgive herself for letting Michelle go. Even today, she would not get behind the wheel, and if Jessie had not decided to move to Yorkshire when Louisa May turned four, the poor girl would never have been allowed a bike, never mind skates. If her mother knew Louisa May loved nothing better than to race up and down the High Street with her inline skates, holding on to the back rack of her friend's bike, she would have a heart attack.

Just as well she doesn't then, Jessie thought and blew her nose. Then she got up to throw the tissue in the bin – and crashed into Louisa May. Standing in the door to her mother's bedroom, a can of coke in her hand, she looked more embarrassed than concerned, as any fourteen-year-old would who had just caught her mother crying.

'Hey, mum – you alright?'

Coming over to the desk, she glanced at the screen

and said, 'Ooh, that is a nice sweater! That pale yellow one. Are you going to buy it?'

'I might, yes … although it is rather a lot of money for a cotton sweater. Do you think it would suit me?'

'Definitely. And of course it's expensive, it's Barbour. But you never go shopping, and treat yourself. Go on then, buy it. You'll look great!' And after a long thirsty swig of her coke, she added cheekily, 'Nate will *love* you in it.'

Despite her cheeks being still wet with tears, Jessie could not help but laugh. 'Alright then, if you say so.'

'I do. Yellow really suits you. Makes you look young. Although,' she added, tilting her head as she scrutinised her mother, 'you don't really look like thirty-three. Josy's mum is only thirty but looks much older. But then she smokes and drinks and only eats junk food. I mean, *only*. Like, all the time.'

'Thirty? Then she must have been …'

'… sixteen when she had Josy, yes. And seventeen when she had Ginger. And eighteen when she had Amber and Billy. And they all have different fathers, too. Except the twins, obviously. But Josy says they never see any of them, so it doesn't matter. Her mum has a new boyfriend, and Josy hates him. He drinks and smokes and sits in the flat all day, playing computer games with his cap on and expecting Josy and her sisters to bring him beer and cigarettes. Mum?' Tugging at Jessie's sleeve, she said, 'I'm glad you found Nate. He's not exactly cool, but that's alright. Josy's mum's boyfriend is a biker and plays in a band, which might make you think he's pretty cool, but … he's not *nice*. Nate is a snob, but that's alright. I'd rather have a snob for a father than a drunk and drug addict.'

Jessie laughed. 'Well, I'm glad we are agreed on that! When does he play in a band or go biking then? If he sits around in the flat all day?'

'At weekends, mostly. And he crashed his bike some weeks ago, so he can't ride that anymore. Came home in a foul mood, Josy said, and smashed her computer screen just out of spite. But she says it's alright, as soon as the baby is born, he will move out. They always do, apparently.' Louisa May bit her lip. 'Mum? Nate won't leave us again, will he?'

Suddenly she looked so anxious, so vulnerable and young, Jessie's heart went out to her, and she hugged her daughter tight. 'No, sweetie, he won't leave us. He loves you far too much, and he is so glad to have you in his life. Us. And I'm sorry to hear that about Josy. Does she have anyone she can talk to? Apart from you, I mean?'

'She's okay, I think.' Louisa May shrugged. 'As soon as she's done with school, she'll find herself a job and move out, she says. Can't blame her, can you?'

'Of course not. But that's another two years … maybe she would speak to Oliver? Or to Daisy, if she would rather talk to a woman?'

'She has talked to the school counsellor, I think. But they say as long as there is no evidence of violence or neglect, they can't do anything. And he doesn't beat them, so …' She shrugged again. 'Anyway, she wouldn't talk to a vicar. And I like Daisy but … she is a bit stuck up, isn't she? The way she talks – God, you'd think she was royalty! She's worse than Miss Lavender, and *she's* posh! Are you sure they are not related?'

Jessie laughed. 'Quite sure!'

Already on her way out, Louisa May turned around

and asked casually, 'Can I go and meet the others in the village after tea? I'll do the dishes, too. What are we having, anyway?'

'I thought we could have bangers and mash, if you like?'

'Yeah, fine. Do you want me to peel the potatoes?'

'That would be nice, yes. Then I can place my order. Unless you want to add something to the basket? I could save it until the weekend, if you like?'

'Nah, you're alright. You order posh Barbour, and I'll browse the charity shops in York with Josy on Saturday. Can I go? To York? And to the village tonight?'

Jessie sighed. 'Okay. I can take you to Kirkbymoorside on Saturday morning, and then you can take the bus from there. And you can go into the village tonight – as long as you promise not to get yourself into trouble, and be home before dark.'

Her daughter rolled her eyes. 'Mum! There is nothing anyone can get up to in *Bishops Bridge*, and it doesn't get dark before ten in June!'

'Yes, but I still want you to be back *before* ten. At nine, actually. You are fourteen, Louisa May, not sixteen.'

Her daughter pouted. 'It's not like we are going to a club or anything. We are just going to sit on the grass and *talk*.'

'And I don't mind you sitting on the grass and talking. As long as you get home at nine.' Deciding she would place her order later, Jessie shut the computer down and turned around. 'Remember, there are no street lights along the lane, and—'

'Yes, mum. I know. And I haven't forgotten what happened to poor Auntie Michelle either. The auntie I never knew. You and Nana both make sure I never forget.'

Jessie stared at her daughter, too stunned to speak. *You and Nana both make sure I never forget.*

Forcing herself to take a couple of deep breaths, she got up very slowly and walked past her daughter and down the stairs. Only when she had reached the bottom of the stairs, she turned back and said icily, 'Well then – I suppose you will not walk out on me after an argument either, will you?'

***

'I MUST SAY that looks great – for someone who has never painted a wall in her life, you have done a fabulous job! That green is really nice. It will go very well with the cream kitchen units.'

'Yes, that's what I thought.' Stepping down from the ladder, Daisy looked critically at the kitchen wall before turning to Oliver. 'You don't think it's too dark?'

'No, it's great. What is the colour called again?'

'Thyme. And the lighter green over here is sage.' Daisy pointed to the opposite wall with the window overlooking the gravelled yard. The sink would be fitted underneath the window, so she could look outside while doing the dishes, just like in the *Lapwing*. Not that there would be much going on in the yard here, other than a few birds hopping about, or maybe the odd rabbit. On Fern Hill Farm, there was always something going on, always someone to chat with, or just wave to as they passed through the yard … in other words, life on the farm was never boring. What on earth was she going to fill her days with here?

'Daisy?'

She shook herself. 'Yes?'

'You were miles away! Dreaming about your new kitchen?'

Daisy shrugged. 'Maybe … I'm sorry, you were saying?'

'I said I didn't realise you had chosen two different shades of green – clever idea. And the tiles were … beige and brown, weren't they? Like in our cottage?'

'They're actually the same.'

'Oh.'

Now Daisy laughed, in spite of herself. 'Oh, Oliver! You really didn't notice, did you?'

He shook his head. 'No. But it makes sense – I know how much you love the cottage. It feels like home to you, doesn't it? Especially now that Ellen's horses have arrived.'

'Yes. I—' She stopped herself just in time. *I wish we could stay right there, in that cosy little cottage.* But she had a feeling he already knew that. He did know her very well. And what was more, he understood her better than anyone.

'I know,' he said, looking at her with so much love she felt she did not deserve. 'I know you wish we could stay in the cottage, rather than move into this big old house. I'm sorry, darling. But you will still be able to go to the farm every day, look after Ellen's horses, ride them … and we will do our best to make ourselves quite at home here. Tell you what, why don't we go back to the cottage when we're finished, grab a few things, and have a candlelight picnic here? We can walk back in the dark, or just stay here and sleep on the floor. In which case I would get the toothbrushes, too.'

But before Daisy could decide whether it was a very romantic or a crazy idea – the bathrooms had been fitted but they still did not have a kitchen, never mind furniture – there was a knock on the door.

Oliver frowned. 'Oh no … who can that be now? People know we haven't even moved in yet. I hope it's not some ruffian looking for a place to sleep.'

'Ruffians?' Daisy raised her eyebrows. 'This is Bishops Bridge, Oliver, not York, or wherever you would find those. Go on then and see who it is. I'll clean the brushes.'

A minute later she could hear a deep, booming voice in the corridor. 'Evening, Reverend. Sorry to disturb you but there are some youngsters that have been sitting in the church car park all evening, drinking beer and smoking and playing loud music. Thought you might like to know. I believe it's the same gang that normally meets up at the old castle at weekends. I told them to clear off, but they got quite cheeky with me, so I thought I'd get you to come – you're quite good with them youngsters, aren't you? From what I've heard.'

Daisy shut her eyes. Of course he would go. He had to, she knew that. Being popular in the village and forming youth groups was one thing but telling them off when they did wrong was quite another. She sighed. She just hoped he wouldn't be too long, or their romantic evening would be ruined before it had begun.

'Thank you, Mr—'

'Cartwright. Alexander.'

'I'm Oliver. And if you give me a minute to explain things to my wife …'

Daisy sighed. 'It's fine,' she called, coming to introduce herself to Mr Cartwright, 'I heard you. Go on

then, and tell them they can have their parties elsewhere.
– Good evening, Mr Cartwright. I'm Daisy.'

'So pleased to meet you. Call me Alexander. I believe
you have met our son? Ben?'

'Oh! Yes, I have. Right,' she said, brushing Oliver's
arm and trying to sound brave, 'you go then, and I'll clean
up.'

***

'WE WERE JUST *talking*, mum, really! I told the boys to
turn the music down the minute we saw Oliver coming,
and they did. Anyway, I don't know what the fuss is about.
It's not that I drank anything other than coke, and you
know I don't smoke. I wouldn't with my asthma, would
I? I'm not stupid.'

Louisa May was sitting on the sofa with a mug of
hot chocolate, staring defiantly at her mother. She was
wearing red lipstick and mascara – and a mini skirt Jessie
could have sworn she had never seen on her daughter
before. She certainly hadn't worn it when she had left the
house shortly after tea.

Jessie sighed. 'Of course you are not stupid. It is
because you are not that I am concerned. You said you
were going to meet your friends in the village to sit and
chat and—'

'Which is what we did …'

'Which is what you did, yes. And those so-called
friends smoked and played loud music and drank beer …
did they smoke grass, too?'

'Ye–es … some of them. Not me though. Can I go
to bed now? We are all to come and clean up at the castle

tomorrow morning. Oliver is going to meet us at seven, to make sure we all show up.'

'At the *castle*?' Jessie nearly dropped her mug. 'Why, I thought you were sitting in the church car park?'

'Well … um … we were, but – we'd been up to the castle first. They always meet there on Friday nights – the others, I mean. Not me, I've never been before! Or not at night, anyway. So, um …'

Jessie paled. 'But you – you are not telling me you climbed those walls, are you? I know they do that, and then drop their beer bottles and think it's great fun. Philip Colbeck told me about that. He has chased them away many times, but they keep coming back …' She gave her daughter a stern look. 'So you admit you've been up there? Do you have any idea how dangerous that is? And in the dark, too! You could have broken your necks, and then what?!'

'I only climbed the *stairs*. I didn't sit on the wall, and I didn't throw any bottles down either. I told them not to, actually, but they wouldn't listen. And I only stayed because I was worried for Josy. She did it to impress Mark – he's in Year 10 and smokes dope. And he has a new girlfriend every week. I don't like him – he'll be like her mum's boyfriends in ten years' time, and I told her as much, but she's mad about him, she won't listen. She asked me to come along, mum. I had to promise. You would have done the same! Wouldn't you?'

She looked at her mother pleadingly, and Jessie's heart softened. 'Of course I would,' she sighed. 'You're a good friend, and you have done right. But I still don't like you hanging around with those older boys. Promise you will not go there again? Or not with them, anyway, and at night?'

Lousia May nodded. 'Promise. Sorry I got you worried, mum.'

Kissing her daughter's hair, inhaling the scent of sweet honey shampoo, Jessie said, 'It's okay. I'm glad you're home safe and sound. Now off to bed with you, or you won't be fit for that Maths test tomorrow.'

'Oh God!' Louisa May groaned, grabbing a cushion and covering her face with it. 'I'd quite forgotten about that! Thanks for reminding me, mum. I won't sleep a wink now.'

But for once, Jessie was unsympathetic. 'Good. I'll wake you at six then, with a cup of tea. Remember, you have to be at the church gate at seven, and catch the bus at ten past eight.'

Reluctantly peeling herself off the sofa, Louisa May rolled her eyes. 'I know! And Oliver will be waiting at the lychgate handing out bin bags, no doubt. I had no idea he could be so stern, when he's normally so cool and laid-back. That look he gave us could have made a flower wither and die on the spot. *I don't want to see any of you around here again unless it's for the service, or youth group, or choir. Or bell ringing practice.*'

Jessie was still chuckling to herself when her daughter had crept up the stairs, muttering about the unfairness of it all.

CHAPTER 9

OLIVER WAS FAST asleep when Daisy crept out of bed at dawn the next morning. Taking her clothes and shoes with her, she went into the bathroom to get dressed, and resisted the temptation of a cup of tea. If she boiled the kettle now, she would wake Oliver, and that would not do. She peered out of the window to check the weather and decided she would be alright in a light sweater, and did not bother to take a coat. Then she slipped out of the cottage (they had not spent the night at the Rectory after all, and Daisy had not even pretended to be disappointed), carefully closing the door behind her.

The rain that had fallen during the night had stopped, and the air smelled clean and fresh. Daisy crossed the yard, passed through the gate and walked down the lane towards the village. She had contemplated taking her bike, but it was in the barn, and she could not risk provoking William into an early morning bray. Lily would have her guts for garters.

It was colder than she had expected, and she walked on briskly, her hands deep in her pockets, until she reached the village. There she paused at the bridge to watch the sun rise behind the church spire. It was a beautiful sight, with the sun bursting through the clouds, as if it could not wait to warm the earth and cheer the weary souls after last night's torrential downpour. The rain and the wind had kept her awake halfway through the night, and even when it had finally ceased, Daisy had lain awake, unable to sleep as she listened to her husband's even breathing. She wished she had his ability to sleep anywhere at any time. When they had visited his brother in New Zealand a few years ago, he had slept all the way to Singapore, where they had to change planes. Maybe she would be more tired once she had got back into the habit of daily rides. She sighed as she pushed herself away from the bridge to continue her way up the hill. Maybe. Maybe not.

She walked past the church, set back on the village green to her right, and smiled when she saw a fat, brown duck waddling down to the beck, followed by a flock of ducklings. Next to the church was the new church hall, which had been built only recently, with a sheltered garden where afternoon teas were served every first Saturday of the month from May through September. At the moment, the church hall also doubled as village hall because that was undergoing renovation work.

'It seems the Rectory is not the only building site here,' Lily had commented when Daisy had seen her coming out of the church hall carrying her yoga mat last Wednesday. She had tried to persuade Daisy to join the class, but Daisy was not the yoga type. She preferred to ride, or walk. Most of all, she preferred to be alone.

When she had passed the Rectory, sheltered from view by an impressive yew hedge and several ancient looking oak trees, the lane narrowed as it bent left, winding its way up towards Broughton Hill. Soon, the castle came into view, and Daisy thought of the group of youngsters

Oliver had ordered to come here "first thing in the morning" to clean up last night's mess. Daisy had been shocked to learn that Louisa May had been one of the party last night. Poor Jessie! She would not be impressed. And on a Wednesday night, too!

'The gate used to be padlocked, Alexander tells me, but they had neither qualms nor trouble breaking the lock. Also, I think it's a shame if people can't visit the castle anymore, and enjoy the view over the valley. I'm sure it's not your regular visitor who has cut through that iron grid to get to the top. But the drunker they are, the cheekier they get – and the more daring. And as they drink a lot … they dare a lot,' Oliver had explained when he had come back last night. 'I hope we can think of some way to stop this ….'

Daisy had not said much on the subject, as she had privately thought that Oliver took his duties rather a bit too seriously at times. Surely patrolling the ruined castle walls at night was not part of a vicar's job, was it?

This morning, though, she found the historic site peaceful and quiet, just as it should be. Leaning with her back against the wall of the gatehouse, Daisy sighed. Oblivious of the thick clouds gathering in the west, she closed her eyes. Up here, she felt more at peace than anywhere else. There was a strange kind of magic about the place, and though she could not explain it, she felt irresistibly drawn here, almost as if by some invisible thread. Was that how the four Pevensie children had felt in the *Narnia* books, when Aslan had called them, she wondered. Who was calling *her* here? And why?

The sudden, sharp cry of a bird of prey circling the air above the fields made Daisy jump. She looked up to see what sort of bird it was, but it was too high up and before she knew it, it was gone. Oliver would have known, or checked on his birdwatching app. The only moorland birds she could easily identify were the curlew (thanks to their distinctive call), and the grouse. Oliver always laughed at the sound the ground nesting grouse made. He said they sounded rather dumb – which they probably were, but Daisy thought they were lovely all the same, and very much part of the landscape here. She knew that driven grouse shooting was still a very popular sport, especially here on the North York Moors, but she hated the idea of the poor birds being shot for the sheer fun of it. Or what people called fun.

Daisy let her gaze wander across the fields that stretched out before her like a patchwork quilt, separated by low drystone walls or hedges, and flecked with sheep. Lambs were skipping and jumping about like live balls of cotton wool, kicking their stiff little legs in the air, and she stood and watched them for half an hour or so, blissfully unaware of the time passing by, and the dark clouds gathering behind her. A smile spread over Daisy's face as she spotted a rabbit family, emerging from their burrow one by one. There was mum – or dad? – and six wee little bunnies. As soon as they had been given the all-clear, they charged off in different directions, and Daisy could not help but laugh at the sight of their cute fluffy white tails bobbing up and down. Finally, she turned away from the gatehouse and crossed the lane to enter the churchyard.

On opening the metal gate, Daisy thought she saw a movement behind one of the withered old headstones, but when she went to investigate, whatever it was – a rabbit, most likely, or a mouse – had gone.

'Funny,' she said to herself, frowning slightly as she walked over to her favourite bench at the far end of the churchyard, 'I could have sworn—'

Startled by a sudden rustling noise behind her, followed by something that sounded like a sneeze, Daisy turned around sharply – but again, there was nothing. There was only the sound of the wind that was much stronger now – and felt distinctively colder, too – than when she had first set off from the farm. She had no idea what time it was as she had forgotten to slip on her watch. Just as she had forgotten to take her mobile, or her key, for that matter. Thinking she would easily be back in time for breakfast, she had not even left a note for her husband.

The first drops of rain began to fall just as Daisy was about to sit down and pray. 'Somehow,' she murmured, 'I get the feeling you don't *want* me to pray, God. Or not now, anyway. But you're right, I should go home before Oliver calls the police. You know what he is like, always worrying about his silly little wife.'

The dog was sitting by the gate, looking up at her with soulful brown eyes, as if he had been waiting for her. It was a cocker spaniel, black with a patch of white on the chest, but he wasn't wearing a collar. He looked very wet, very thin, and very frightened.

'Oh, you poor little thing! What are you doing out here, all on your own?'

Bending down to stroke him, Daisy almost expected him to duck away, even run, but he didn't. Instead, he whined softly and began to lick her hands, as if to say, Now where have *you* been?

Laughing, Daisy dropped a spontaneous kiss on his wet head and said, 'It was you, wasn't it? You were hiding behind that headstone when I came in. Well then, I suppose I'd better take you home. Where do you live, hm?'

She checked his neck carefully, hoping to find a collar yet, but all she could feel was wet fur that was tangled and matted in places, and skin and bones underneath. He was shivering with cold, and possibly with fear. Daisy's heart melted as she picked him up and cradled him in her arms. The little dog turned his face up to her and gave her nose a couple of quick, grateful licks, making her laugh.

'Oh, you are a dear little fellow! Let's go and ask the farmer next door. I think it's the Hunters' farm, I forgot the name – not that it matters, hey? The only thing that matters is that we'll get you nice and warm, and fed before long. And then I'll take you home with me and ask Joseph to check whether you have got a chip. Don't worry, he's very kind. He won't hurt you.'

Biting her lip, she looked up at the sky, and prayed they would not be caught in a thunderstorm before they had a chance to get back to Fern Hill Farm. She was terribly scared of thunderstorms. But she could not let her fears get the better of her now. She had to bring the dog home, one way or another. Wrapping the trembling little creature in her sweater, she held him close to her chest as she ran up the lane as fast as she could.

✳✳✳

'OH, THAT POOR little thing! No, he's not ours. And you needn't bother trying the Wilkinsons and the Talbots either, as they have got collies, not spaniels. Better take him home and get him warmed up and fed. Jonathan can give you a lift later. He should be in for his breakfast any minute, if you would like to wait? I dare say you look like you could do with a nice cuppa, and a slice of my plum bread.'

Madeleine Hunter was about her age, with what looked like a ton of thick black hair curled into a loose bun at the nape of her neck, and warm, brown eyes. When she bent down to place a cushion on the bench for Daisy to sit on, Daisy noticed the tell-tale bump underneath her floral cotton dress and closed her eyes briefly. Not another one! Really, did they all have to be pregnant around here? Was this some sort of virus? Or were there fertility fairies dancing on the moors in moonlit nights? Did only the locals see them, and get their wish granted?

'You're the vicar's wife, aren't you? The one who looks after Angela Maverick's horses now on Fern Hill Farm? Abi told me.'

Daisy could not seem to take her eyes off the bump. She knew she was staring but she just couldn't help it. Why was life so unfair?

Trying to swallow her bitterness – and nearly choking on it, like a pill that would not go down, no matter how much water you poured down your throat – she said, 'Yes, I'm Daisy Clifford-Jones. Daisy to my friends. And I am very happy to look after the horses. They are quite wonderful.'

'Oh, yes. They are marvellous. I wish I could ride them – I used to ride, you know, before I got pregnant. But with this bump I could not even see the horse's neck in front of me now!' She laughed as she handed Daisy a mug of steaming hot tea. 'Do you have any children yet?'

Daisy took the mug, careful not to spill its hot content over the dog. His eyes were closed, and his soft, regular breathing told her he was asleep. Good for you, she thought, and you don't have to answer any uncomfortable questions either. She began to stroke his soft, damp coat while her eyes stared straight ahead, past Madeleine, past the door, and past the pair of small red wellingtons that stood next to a very large black and a medium sized green pair in the hall. A happy family. Mother, father, daughter.

She swallowed. 'No,' she answered at last and began to sip her tea mechanically. It was strong and milky and very sweet. She never took sugar in her tea but was too polite to say anything. It was very kind of Madeleine to ask her in and offer her tea in the first place. She was sure she had other things to do. Weren't farmers' wives always busy?

Much to her relief, Madeleine just nodded and did not pursue the matter any further. Instead, she cut two enormous slices of fruitcake, buttered them generously, and put them on two plates. Handing one to Daisy, she sat down next to her and smiled down at the dog. 'Such a cute little fellow. And you found him in the churchyard?'

'Yes.'

'What were you doing there at this time of day, if you don't mind me asking?'

'Um ... I often come up here in the mornings. I love the romance of the old churchyard. And the stillness. I just sit there and … talk to God.'

Madeleine looked at her, confusion written on her face. 'Talk to God? You mean – you pray?'

'Yes.' Well, what else could she say? That's what prayer was, wasn't it – talking to God.

'Hm, yes.' Madeleine nodded. 'That makes sense. Nice quiet place, too. Very peaceful.'

They drank their tea in silence until they heard the sound of the front door being pushed open and a man's booming voice calling out a cheerful 'Morning! I hope you've got that coffee ready, Maddie, I'm absolutely soaked, as well as—oh! Hello?'

Madeleine's husband, a bear of a man with broad shoulders, ruddy cheeks and laughing green eyes, removed his tweed cap when he saw Daisy sitting on the bench by the Aga. 'I didn't know we had a visitor. Mrs Clifford-Jones, isn't it? I'm Jonathan,' he said, extending a strong, tanned hand.

Daisy took the hand and shook it gingerly. 'Yes. Good morning, Mr Hunter – Jonathan. Please call me Daisy. Your wife was so kind as to give us shelter and tea – look what I found in the churchyard,' she said, indicating the sleeping dog in her lap. He did not so much as lift his head.

'Oh! Was he abandoned, do you think?' The farmer knelt down, placing his large hand on the little dog's head and giving it a very gentle little rub. Whining softly, the dog looked up, gave the hand a tentative lick, and put his head down again. 'Well, he's not from around here. I'd know if he were. What are you going to do with him?'

Daisy shrugged. 'I don't know. First of all, I'm going to take him home, try and feed him, and keep him warm. And then I'll ask the vet to have a look at him, and check if he is chipped. As it happens, my husband and I are still staying at Fern Hill Farm, so we see Joseph Hancock almost every day. How do you know I am Oliver's wife, by the way?'

While Madeleine busied herself with retrieving her husband's breakfast from the oven and pouring him a

large mug of coffee, the farmer sat down on a chair. 'I
didn't. I just took a guess. People say you are a very fine
young lady, and you looked very fine to me, so I figured
it had to be you,' he winked and took a sip of his coffee.

'Oh!' Daisy laughed, blushing self-consciously. 'I see.
I didn't know that that was what people say about me.'
What else might they be saying about her? That she was
aloof? Too grand for this place? That she didn't fit in?

'It is. They also say you are very kind, and charming.
And good with horses, eh, Maddie?' Winking again, he
took the plate from his wife and began to tuck into his
full English, leaving the women to do the talking.

***

IT WAS GONE eight by the time Daisy climbed into
Jonathan Hunter's battered Volvo, clutching the dog to
her chest. She could not wait to introduce him to Oliver.
And of course she hoped they would be able to keep him,
as she was already hopelessly in love.

'So, have you settled in yet? Or are you still at Abigail's
farm?'

'We are, yes,' Daisy fastened her seatbelt and found it
was covered in chocolate. Never mind, she thought. We
have a washing machine. 'But the builders are making
really good progress. We are hoping to move into the
Rectory by the end of the July.'

'Oh, good. It's awfully big though, isn't it? How many
bedrooms are there? Five? Six?'

'Six, yes, and the studio above the garage. It's
ridiculous, I know, but—oh, there is my husband!' she
cried when he saw Oliver coming out of the church.

ANNE WHORLTON

'Would you mind pulling over, please? He does not even know where I have been, I'm afraid I might have got him quite worried …'

Jonathan stopped the car and got out to open the door for Daisy, knowing she wouldn't want to let go of the dog. 'There you go. Now then, take good care of the little one. I hope you can keep him.—Morning, Oliver!' he called. 'I'm bringing your wife. And you are both invited to come to our Midsommer Fest – I'm sure my wife has told yours all about it by now. It's good fun though. Make sure you don't miss it!'

'We won't. Morning, Jonathan.' Oliver came to shake Jonathan's hand, then turned to his wife. 'There you are! I've been looking for you.'

'I know,' she said, waving goodbye to Jonathan, who was in a hurry to get on. 'And I'm sorry. Were you very worried?'

He tilted his head, pondering on her question for a moment. 'A bit, yes. Although I suspected you might have walked up to the churchyard, knowing how you love to be there. I was just heading—oh!' he cried when he saw a wet black nose peeping out from the folds of Daisy's sweater. 'What's that?'

'That,' said his wife, 'is the dog I found in the churchyard this morning.'

97

CHAPTER 10

'THE WHAT?'

'The dog I found in the churchyard this morning,' Daisy explained matter-of-factly. Tugging at her sweater, she revealed the dog that had fallen asleep during the short ride in Jonathan's car. 'Here he is. Isn't he adorable?'

Opening his eyes, the dog looked up at Oliver, and Oliver looked down at him. It was hard to say who was the more surprised. As they stared at each other, one with soft grey, the other with liquid brown eyes, Daisy thought it was like a scene in a movie. She hardly dared to breathe as she watched the pair of them. Then the dog gave a huge yawn, breaking the spell.

Laughing, Oliver held out his arms. 'He is indeed! Very adorable. Come here, little fellow … Where did you say you found him? In the churchyard?'

Daisy nodded as she placed the dog in his arms. 'That's right.'

'I suppose there is no point in me asking how he got there, is there?' Mesmerised, Oliver gazed at the furry little bundle in his arms.

'No,' Daisy laughed, 'there isn't. He was sitting at the gate in the pouring rain looking for all the world as if he had been waiting for me.'

'He did, eh?' Oliver said, tickling the dog's chin. 'Hm … so what are we going to do with you, my lad? Do you want to come home with us? Yes?'

'Of course he does! He looks like he has not eaten for days,' Daisy said, stroking the dog. 'Poor little thing! – You don't think it was wrong of me to take him, do you?' she asked, looking anxiously at her husband. 'But I could not just leave him there, could I? He looked so cold, and frightened. I took him to the Hunters' farm, thinking they might recognise him. But they didn't. They said they had never seen him before, and they did not know anyone who owned a spaniel around here. I thought we would ask Joseph to take a look at him. He will know what to do.'

Oliver nodded. 'That's a good idea. And no, of course you didn't do wrong, darling. You did exactly the right thing. Come on,' he said, leading her towards the car park, 'let's get you home. I dare say this little fellow could do with a hot bath and a good breakfast, and so could you. Perhaps not together though. The bath, I mean.'

***

DAISY WARMED SOME milk in a pan, diluted it with water, and added a beaten egg for good measure, humming softly as she moved around the kitchen. Having poured the mixture into a plastic bowl, she set it down before the dog, stroking his head encouragingly. 'Go on then, eat. You must be hungry.'

After he had sniffed the bowl and looked back at Daisy, as if to ask for permission, the dog began to lap up the mixture until the bowl was empty. Then he licked around the edges, making sure he had not missed a single drop, and lay down with a heavy sigh.

Daisy laughed. 'That was good, yes? I'm glad you enjoyed that. Once the doctor has checked you over, he can tell me when and what to feed you next. We don't want to upset your poor little tummy, do we?'

As if on cue, there was a knock on the door, and Joseph put his head in. 'Hello? Anyone at home?' Stepping inside, he immediately dropped down to the dog and cuddled him. 'Hello, little fellow! Aren't you lucky that our Daisy here found you? – What did you give him, Daisy?'

'Warm milk and water and a beaten egg. He was a bit hesitant at first, but then he lapped it all up in seconds. Thanks for coming so quickly.' She had texted him from the car, telling him they had found a stray dog and were bringing him home.

Joseph nodded, his hands moving expertly across the spaniel's emaciated body, feeling for hidden injuries or swellings. 'He must have been hungry, poor little chap! And you fed him exactly the right thing. His stomach would not have coped with anything solid right now, or too much of anything really. He probably hasn't eaten for some days. Hmm …' He looked up at Daisy, his brow furrowed. 'And you found him in the churchyard? All by himself?'

'She did, yes. Strange as it is. Good morning, Joseph. Good of you to come.' Oliver came in through the patio door, slipping his mobile in his pocket. 'Coffee?' he asked, raising an eyebrow at Joseph.

'Oh, yes, please. Milk, two sugars.'

Daisy sat on the rug and fondled the dog's fluffy ears. 'He was waiting for me at the gate, you know,' she explained, blushing a little as she spoke. 'I know, it's probably silly of me to think so, but I cannot shake off the feeling I have seen him before – and maybe he felt the same about me?—Oh, I don't know what I am saying. You must excuse me, I suppose I am a little tired.'

Joseph chuckled. 'That's alright. I have a girlfriend with more imagination than is good for her at times, I can deal with stories like that. I hear them all the time. Right,' he said, feeling the dog's neck and shoulders, 'let's see if we can find any … no. Just as I thought. No collar, no tag. And my guess is I won't find a microchip on him either. Damned puppy dealers!'

'Puppy dealers?' Daisy's eyes widened in horror. 'Do you think he might have escaped from one of those horrible puppy farms one reads about in the papers?'

'He might have, or perhaps he has run away from his new owners because he was scared. If he was indeed born on a puppy farm, he will not have been socialised, so anything new would frighten him. Likely the owners were inexperienced and didn't know how to handle a young dog in the first place, never mind a lively young spaniel like this one, so … you know.'

'Know what? Do you mean they just took him there on purpose and *left* him?' Daisy cried indignantly.

Oliver put a hand on his wife's shoulder. 'Hey! Don't work yourself up, darling. We don't know anything about how the little one got there, or about his owners, and whether they were ignorant or even downright cruel. For all we know they might be sitting at home crying their eyes out for him. The main thing is, you found him, and he is safe now. Isn't he, Joseph?'

Joseph nodded. 'He is, yes. But he has been around

here for a while longer, I think, so the theory with the owners crying their eyes out seems unlikely. Do you remember that evening at the *Dog & Partridge*, Daisy? When I thought I had seen an animal darting across the car park and disappearing into the trees? That might well have been him.'

Daisy's mouth fell open. 'But – but that's over two weeks ago! Three, I think! He can't have been wandering about this place without anybody noticing him!'

'Well now, I didn't say nobody *noticed* him – but noticing, recognizing, or even catching him is three different things. Come to think of it, I did hear something at the *Red Grouse* last week, when I stopped there for a quick lunch … Dan said something about having been feeding a stray dog some leftovers for some time – they did call the police, he said, but no dog had been reported missing, and then he just disappeared. They never saw him again. So our little stray might have come from somewhere around Castleton and made his way south across the moors, stopping at farms and pubs in search for food. You'll be amazed at how long dogs can go with no, or very little, food.'

Oliver shook his head. 'But how can he have survived without food that long if he is barely more than a pup? How would he know where to find food, or how to cross a road for example, without being knocked down by a car?'

'He may *look* very young, and I admit he is rather a bit on the small side, but he is not a puppy anymore. Or at least not a very young one. I dare say he could be about a year old. My guess is he must have been on the road for a while because clearly, he knows his way around. Don't you, little beggar?' he teased, ruffling the dog's ears.

Producing a scanner, he then began to search for a microchip. Daisy watched anxiously while he ran the device expertly across the dog's chest and shoulders. 'Nope,' he said, 'no chip either. Damn.'

Daisy gave a small sigh of relief and felt Oliver's hand gently moving up and down her back, reassuring her. 'What happens now? Will you take him to the police, or the rescue centre? And will they return him to the people who bought him, even if they were not good to him?'

'Don't worry, Daisy, I'm not taking him anywhere for now. I'll take a few pictures of him, and leave him with you for the time being. Then I'll stop at the police station and give them the details. They will contact you and probably ask you to write a report. And as for ignorant buyers, we don't know if they even exist, so don't panic. He may well be yours to keep yet if that is what you want.'

Daisy looked at Oliver, and he nodded. 'Of course we'd love to keep him. He's a grand little dog, isn't he, Daisy?'

But Daisy was not listening. She was holding the dog in her arms, cradling him, and humming a soft tune while making secret promises to take care of him for the rest of his life.

'Ah, she's in love!' Joseph grinned and slapped Oliver's back. 'You will have to jostle for your fair lady's attention from now on. That dog is a serious heartbreaker! Don't let Lily see him, or we can both set up home in the barn.'

'With the donkey?'

Joseph rolled his eyes. 'Oh, right! I had quite forgotten about *him*! No, not in the barn then. Anyway,' he chuckled, waving goodbye to the vicar and his mesmerised wife, 'I'll see you later.'

***

Daisy had just settled the little dog at the foot of their bed ('but only for the first couple of nights – if he is to stay with us, he'll sleep in his own bed!' Oliver had protested) when Oliver's phone beeped.

'Oh no. Don't tell me you have to go out again.'

'I hope not … no, it's alright. It's just my dad. He wants to know when we are coming to see him. Says it's been a year – it has, hasn't it? My, my …'

Daisy groaned inwardly. She hated going to Kent. Not only was her father-in-law, a retired vicar himself, the grumpiest old man she had ever come across, but also he constantly complained about them not coming often enough. When they were visiting, it was never for long enough either, no matter how patiently Oliver tried to point out that he had a job to go back to. Daisy knew this was partly to do with Oliver's older brother living in New Zealand, but also because Oliver had always been the favourite. While this might touch her, on the one hand, it also made her wary of the old man, on the other. She was not sure if he expected Oliver to look after him when he got to the point that he could not manage on his own any longer. Probably. Thankfully, Rupert Clifford-Jones was remarkably fit for his age and went walking with his friends almost every weekend – not pleasant little rambles, mind you, but proper challenges, like climbing Ben Nevis or the Three Peaks in the Yorkshire Dales. He was a keen skier, too, and went to Switzerland with his friends every year in February. Alpine skiing, of course.

Well, she thought, as she tried to get the dog to lie down again, at least that means we won't have to worry about him announcing he was going to move to Yorkshire and live in the Rectory with us any time soon.

Oliver sat on the edge of the bed, tapping into his phone. 'I should probably go and see him. I take it you wouldn't want to come with me?'

She shook her head, clutching the dog to her chest as if he were a lifebuoy. 'I can't leave him, can I? Apart from the fact that your dad does not like dogs, if I remember correctly.'

'Yes, you're right … anyway, we don't need to discuss this tonight, Dad. I'll call you tomorrow.' He pressed *send* and put the phone on the bedside table, then picked it up again. 'Or maybe I'd better turn it off for the night – oh, why did we ever give him a smartphone and install WhatsApp for him? Stupid idea. Was it mine, or Michael's?'

Now Daisy laughed. 'Oh, Oliver! You are hopeless. Turn it off, and then let's get some sleep before the little one here wakes us up again. I am not sure he is housetrained yet, and you have a wedding tomorrow.'

After a while, she could hear her husband snoring peacefully, while she could not find any sleep. Even the dog lay quite still, and she had to feel him every now and then to make sure he was real, and not just a dream. There was a full moon outside in the now completely dark sky, and Daisy lay for a long time watching the wisps of clouds as they silently floated past the pale silver moon, as if brushing it in their passing.

'Thank you, God,' she whispered, and closed her eyes. 'Thank you.'

CHAPTER 11

'OH, WILL THAT barking never stop!'

Jessie threw her tea towel into the laundry basket by the kitchen door. She had just dried what felt like a hundred cups and plates and saucers because the dishwasher in the café had broken down ('Of course it would do that on a Saturday!') and her nerves were beginning to feel like a threadbare rug, they had worn so thin. Thank God Nate was there to help her today, and keep her calm. She would have closed two hours ago if it hadn't been for him. Ossie had been let out into the garden at ten o'clock on the dot, as usual, and never stopped barking for more than the two minutes it took him to water the plants, and catch his breath. He must have lungs like a whale. She had read that in Louisa May's biology book – blue whales, for example, exchanged between eighty to ninety per cent of oxygen in their lungs each time they breathed, roughly eight times more than humans. And they did not waste their breath barking!

'Can dogs go hoarse?' Nate wiggled his left eyebrow. He was cleaning the coffee machine, and did not seem in the least perturbed by Ossie's frantic barking. That's probably because he doesn't hear it every bloody day, Jessie thought miserably, throwing her hands up in despair.

'What do *I* know? Not this one, apparently!'

A couple who had wanted to sit outside came back in and looked around, hoping to find an empty table, but they were all occupied, thanks to Ossie. Or thanks to the Johnsons, rather. Jessie kept reminding herself it was not the dog's fault. But ever since they put up a new fence – a hideous thing that was at least six feet high and so dense the dog could not see through it, which probably made him even more desperate for attention – the barking had got worse. A lot worse.

'Excuse me, Miss, is there perhaps anything you can do about the—'

'No. I'm sorry, but no. I did try talking to them, but they don't listen. They only put up that blooming fence to rile me, and to keep their dog from getting friendly with my customers. Some used to feed and pet him, you see, through the old fence. It was just a couple of wobbly poles and mesh then, which the dog could stick his nose through,' Jessie explained. 'But not now. So I'm afraid you'll have to endure the barking, or come back another time.'

'Well, that's a shame,' the woman said. 'But can we perhaps have two cappuccinos and two slices of your chocolate cake to take away?'

'Of course. And the cappuccino is on the house.' It's not your fault we have such ignorant neighbours, she wanted to add but thought better of it. She felt she had already said too much.

When they had gone, Nate put an arm around Jessie and said, 'I'll go and talk to them. They don't know me, they might listen. Or I could pretend I'm from the local council, investigating in a case of statutory nuisance?'

She sighed. 'You can try. But don't blame me if they call you names, or throw things at you.'

'They'd better not, or I'll report them to the police for assault.' And with another wiggle of his eyebrow he was gone.

Three minutes later, he was back. 'They didn't open the door. Or perhaps they have gone out?'

'Well, they certainly did not take their dog then. But thanks for trying.'

'Always happy to help. Tell you what, why don't we go out for a meal tonight, the three of us? Would that make up for the troubles of the day?'

'Yes, but only if you promise you'll get your plumber to look at the dishwasher first thing on Monday morning. Have you called him yet?'

'I have, and he'll pop in on Monday afternoon. He'll bring a new dishwasher, too, just in case this one is beyond repair.'

Jessie sighed. 'Well, I hope it isn't, but thank you. It's probably best to be prepared. In the meantime, I'll have to ask Louisa May to help us tomorrow. We can make it up to her by taking her for a pizza and a movie tonight. She is not particularly keen on fancy restaurants, anyway. I know I wasn't at her age.'

'Pizza and movie it is then. We can save the fancy restaurant for another time, when it's just the two of us,' he winked. 'Go on then, serve your customers, I'll finish the washing up.'

***

JESSIE WAS JUST going to flip the sign to *closed* when the

door was opened, and a ridiculously tall, thin model of a blonde came in, turning her head to the man behind her as she laughed. 'Oh, Ben, you are so funny! Really, I haven't had such fun in—hello? You're not closing, are you? Ben said …'

Ben had the decency to flush. 'Yes, well, I told Cindy you made the best cappuccino far and wide. Can we have one, please? Regular for me, and with soy milk for Cindy. We aren't staying long, don't worry. I know you're closing at five.'

Do you, Jessie thought, and wished Nate hadn't gone home yet. He said he had some e-mails to attend to before they went out tonight, and she had assured him she'd be alright for the last hour. Maybe she had been a little hasty.

'Okay,' she said and walked back to her counter, muttering under her breath. He was friendly alright, but she could not shake off the feeling that he had come here for a reason, and not because his new girlfriend – if that was who she was – fancied a cappuccino.

When she brought the drinks to their table by the front window, Ben – still all smiles and friendliness – dropped the bombshell. 'By the way – Cindy here is looking for a place to rent in the village. Would you mind if I showed her around Corner Cottage? Since you were going to move out soon, anyway?'

***

'HE DID WHAT??'

Lily stared at her friend, not sure if she had heard right. She knew Ben was jealous, but embarrassing Jessie in front of her customers? He wouldn't stoop that low, would he? Unless …

'He wasn't drunk, was he?' she asked, rather hopeful.

'No. He was quite friendly, actually. And dead serious. Cindy is his new sales assistant, whatever that means in his books.'

'Well, he sleeps with her, obviously.'

Jessie shrugged. 'I don't care if he does. Anyway, she is his new sales assistant, and she lives in Newcastle, so obviously …'

'Obviously, she would be looking for a place in Thirsk where Ben has his office, or move in with him. Jessie, he just wants to make things difficult for you because he is jealous! I admit it's a low shot but—fact is, he can't evict you just like that. I'm sure he knows that. Talk it over with Nate, and then invite Ben over for a cup of coffee. On his own. I'm sure you can work it out.'

Jessie nodded. 'Okay. But the thing is … well – we *were* actually thinking about moving to Durham. We can't go on like this, Lily, you know that! With Nate's business in Durham, and my little café here …'

'You are not going to leave Bishops Bridge, are you?'

'Well … I have to admit we've been discussing the options, and … well, going to Durham is one of them. I don't want to give up the café, or not yet, anyway, but we need to be reasonable. Nate has his business there, and if we send Louisa—'

'Send me where?'

They both turned around to see the girl herself standing in the door, staring at her mother in disbelief. 'You're not telling me you've been making plans behind my back, are you? Or when were you going to tell me? On the day? Go on, Louisa May, pack up your things, we are moving to Durham? Just like that?'

'No! Of course not. But – oh, why don't you sit down? We can talk about it right now. And no, we haven't made any decisions behind your back. We were just discussing Ampleforth – you did want to go there, didn't you? Nate said he would—'

'I don't care a fucking *shit* what Nate said! You have been talking about me behind my back! That is – that is … despicable! There, I learned a new word in Drama Class. Do you even know the meaning of it? Despicable! That's you. And Nate. Oh go on then, move to Durham and be happy! I am going to stay right here – on the farm!'

And she stomped off, across the bridge, to pick up her bike. Yanking it off the grass, she pushed it for a few metres before she got on and pedalled up Brook Lane at alarming speed. A minute later she was gone.

'Well,' said Lily, practical as ever. 'At least we know where she is going. Don't worry, Jess. She'll come round. And in the meantime, she has Abi, or Daisy, and the horses. They will soon put her right.'

***

IT WAS SURPRISINGLY cold for June, and Daisy was glad she had put on an extra sweater before she had set off for an early evening walk with the little dog. They had not named him yet, as they were not sure they would be able to keep him. Joseph had said to give it a week, then he would issue a pet passport, and he would be officially theirs. For now, they just called him Little One. Daisy had borrowed a collar and lead from Abi but was already looking forward to a trip to the pet shop where they would buy everything brand new for their dog. She could already picture the black spaniel in a red tartan collar and matching lead. He would wear a name tag, too, with their phone number on it, so he could never get lost again.

'You are going to be ours, Little One,' she said as she bent down to ruffle the spaniel's ears. 'And we are going to be very happy. I am so glad you found us. You did find me, didn't you?' The dog did not answer but sat down and scratched his ear with his paw, and Daisy laughed. 'You don't understand me, do you? Never mind. Come on, this way.'

Suddenly, there was a sobbing noise coming from the other side of the beechwood hedge, along with the sound of running feet.

'Lily? Is that you?'

There was no answer, so Daisy picked up the dog and walked back to the gate, turned sharp left, and entered the field where the crying had come from. Only she could not see anybody. Whoever had just run through that field must have been very fast – and very keen to be alone. Unless she had imagined the crying and the running, of course. By the looks of it, she just might have.

'Hello?'

Walking briskly down the field to the gate at the far end, she leaned over the gate and called out, 'Is that you, Lily? Are you alright?'

It was then that she saw Ronnie, Abi's Welsh Cob, on the other side of the field, and a young girl leaning into him, crying desperately. It wasn't Lily though. It was—

'Louisa May!'

She hurried over to the pair, careful not to stumble, or drop the dog. Ronnie might be a gentle giant, but he was still a giant, and a very heavy one at that. She did not want to risk the dog getting under his hooves.

When she reached Jessie's daughter, she placed a tentative hand on her shoulder. 'Don't worry, it's only me. You can tell me to leave you alone, but if you would like to come back to the cottage with me, I'll make you a cup of tea. Or a mug of Horlicks. I've got chocolate, too. Cadbury Little Bars – I always have one of those when I'm upset. Very soothing.'

'It's so unfair!!' Louisa May cried without looking up. 'And mean!'

'I know. I know, sweetheart.' She didn't know what was troubling the girl, but she did know about life being unfair. Or finding it unfair, rather. After all, it was a matter of perspective, wasn't it?

Louisa May turned around, her tear-stained face betraying the state of her misery. 'They want to dump me at Ampleforth and move to Durham. They never even *asked* me!'

Before Daisy knew what was happening, Louisa flung herself into her arms, nearly crushing the dog in the process. 'Oh!' she cried, pulling back in surprise. 'What's that? Is it—oh, my God, it's a dog! How cute is that?!' She stroked the dog's soft fur, laughing underneath her tears. 'Is it yours?'

'I don't know. I like to think he is. We – that is, I found him in the churchyard yesterday morning,' Daisy explained when she saw the confused look on the young girl's face. 'Unless somebody else claims him, he is ours to keep.'

'Aw, he's so *cute*! I hope you can keep him!'

Daisy nodded. 'Yes, we hope so, too. Do you want to hold him while we walk to the cottage? It's starting to rain, and I was going to walk back, anyway.'

Louisa May nodded. Taking the little bundle of fur from Daisy, she held him to her face and giggled when he began to lick it. 'Oh, he's *so* cute! I want one, too! Where did you say you found him?'

***

AT CORNER COTTAGE, Jessie put the phone down and turned to Nate who was rummaging through her fridge in search of something he could cook for dinner. 'She's staying with Daisy and Oliver. Still upset, but Daisy seems to have calmed her down enough to persuade her to call me and let me know where she is. Well, I knew she was heading for the farm, but …' Her voice trailed off. She knew she should be glad that Louisa May was safe, but she could not help thinking about the inevitable argument they were going to have tomorrow. And knowing her daughter, she might well wait until Nate was back in Durham.

'Oh, but that's good then, isn't it? Now we have an evening to ourselves, which I hope we will still be able to enjoy, despite the fact that we should probably spend it trying to figure out what to do.'

Jessie turned around. 'Yes, we should. And I might as well tell you, Nate, I am not going to give up my café. It's the only café Bishops Bridge has, and I really don't want to let people down. Plus, I have more customers than ever now, thanks to Lily's bookshop next door, and our joined garden space. Well, if it weren't for that dog, but …'

'Hey, hey! Not so fast! What about me? And I don't mean my business, since that does not seem to compare to yours, anyway, even though it's ten times as big and more profitable, too. Plus, I have staff to think of – but that's only by the by. What about us? What sort of family life are we supposed to lead if you want to stay here for the sake of that café? Lovely as it is, and thriving, too, but – you cannot stay here, and I there, and … tell me, how is that going to work?'

Jessie bit her lip, trying to ignore the way he had just belittled her business, never mind hurt her feelings. More profitable, my foot. Of course it was more profitable, but that was not the point here, was it? Miss Lavender always said, *not everything is about profit*. But then she was old and wise, and Jessie was sure she had more money under her mattress than she let on. At her age, she could get away with that attitude, while Jessie couldn't. Not if she wanted to persuade Nate to stay here. And she did. Between them, Louisa May and Ben had made her realise that quite clearly today.

'I don't know, to be honest. It's tricky … But I will not move anywhere if Louisa May is not happy to come with us. Also, I don't want her to feel she is being *dumped* at Ampleforth, as she puts it, just because we want to be on our own. I don't know what you think, but to me, that does not feel right.'

'What *I* think? Does that even matter?'

'Of course it does!' she cried indignantly. Why was he being so mean? It was not like him at all. Where the ever relaxed, easy-going Nate who even managed to remain cheerful over a broken dishwasher and a constantly barking dog?

'Well,' he said, 'I suppose the only thing we can do is to leave things as they are, since you are not prepared to discuss alternatives. – What about this school then? Don't they have a deadline? Or have we missed that already, anyway?'

'I don't know. I'm sure we can find out.' She sighed wearily. Didn't he see how tired she was? How a broken dishwasher, a constantly barking dog, Ben wanting to turn her out of her home, and a daughter who had run away because she felt betrayed by her mother was simply too much? Couldn't he see that?

'But why can't we live in Durham?' he persisted, unable to leave it be. 'Then we could rent a cottage here, and you could keep your café for weekends. If Louisa May goes to Ampleforth, she can come here at weekends, and we can all stay at the cottage. And if Ben wasn't threatening to kick you out, you – that is, we – could stay right here, at Corner Cottage. I'm sure we can talk to him, Jessie. He seems a reasonable chap.'

'I'm afraid you'll find him not so reasonable when it comes to me staying at Corner Cottage. He is jealous, Nate! Can't you see that?'

'Oh, I can. I am not blind, you know. I saw his dirty looks in the pub, and I knew it wasn't about me not drinking. It was about me stealing his girl. I know I asked you before, but you never were an item, were you?'

'No! Of course not. I would have told you, wouldn't I?'

'Like you told me about my daughter?'

She stared at him. 'What?'

'Well, you didn't tell me about Louisa May, did you? It took you thirteen years. And if it had not been for Lily—'

'I thought you would never hold that against me. You

promised you wouldn't!'

He ignored the tears in her eyes, or perhaps he was so angry, he did not see them. 'Well, I can't keep that promise if you are being so unreasonable! I am prepared to pay Louisa's school fees, rent a cottage here, and make you my partner in business. And I am doing all of this gladly, because I love you – and Louisa – and I want us to have a future together. But we need to make compromises, Jessie, both of us, if we—'

But Jessie was not listening. She had left the room and shut the door behind her.

***

'JESSIE?'

Nate was standing outside her bedroom door, a bottle of wine in his hand. 'I was going to open this bottle of wine, and I thought you might want to come downstairs? I have found a quiche in the fridge and put it in the oven. I hope that's alright. There is salad, too. Are you coming?'

There was no answer.

'Oh, come on, Jessie. Please! We can talk about it? Or just leave it for now and watch a nice film, I don't mind. I thought you wanted to watch *Captain Corelli's Mandolin* with me. We can do that?'

Still, there was not a sound from the other side. Nate was getting frustrated. Having been on his own for so long, he didn't know how to handle a situation like this. More to the point, he did not know how to handle an upset woman. A woman he had upset to the point of crying. He could hear her sniffling on the other side of the door, and bit his lip. Had she been crying all this time?

While he was sitting on the sofa sulking?

'Please?'

Suddenly he had an idea. Putting down the wine bottle, he cleared his throat and began to sing. And because he could not think of anything better, it had to be *O Sole Mio*. He only knew the one line, so he had to hum the rest and repeat O Sole Mio over and over again, hoping she would put him out of his misery soon.

'Oh, for goodness' sake!'

The door was flung open, and she stood before him, tear-stained face and all, and he grabbed her waist and kissed her before she could say any more.

'But I am *not* going to give up my café!' was the last thing Jessie said before she fell asleep in his arms, twenty minutes after they had started the film.

'Nor do you have to,' he promised, kissing her hair. 'We'll find a way. But not tonight. Come on then. It's been a long day.' And he picked her up and carried her upstairs.

CHAPTER 12

OLIVER WAS JOGGING along the old railway track on Rosedale East Side, panting and secretly cursing himself for not having brought anything to drink. It was hot, and he was out of practice. He had not run in weeks – not since they had moved here, in fact – and was regretting his choice of track. But he had needed to get out and clear his head, and running had seemed the best option. Daisy had had one of her dreams again, and he had spent half the night comforting her. If he had hoped the dog might help her, it seemed he had been hoping in vain.

'It was so real, Oliver! It was really awful!'

'I can imagine,' he had said. And he could. After all, she was not the only one who was suffering because she could not have children. Even if in her dream it had been horses. Horses left to die on a desert island where no grass would grow. The message could not be clearer than that, could it?

'They were painfully thin, Oliver. Just like in the seven years of famine described in the Old Testament, you know. The hunger years. There were foals, too, trying to drink from their mothers. But the mothers would push them away, and leave them to die on the burnt ground. The poor mares barely had enough strength to walk …

oh, Oliver, what does this mean? Do you think it has anything to do with … with …' She could not bring herself to say the word, but he knew what she meant. Of course he knew. Infertility. The dream was just a mask. Just like their happy life was just a mask.

'Bother,' he muttered now, stopping to rub the back of his thighs. Having come as far as he had, he could either turn back now, or go on and do the complete circuit. It would not make a jot of a difference.

Just then something caught his eye in one of the impressive brick arches that lined this part of the track. These arches, as he had read on the information boards put up by the National Park team, were the remains of what had once been the entrances to three huge calcinating kilns. When ironstone had been found here in the 1860s, Rosedale had quickly turned into a beehive of industrial industry. Today, all that was left were the arches, the lone chimney a bit further down the track, and the track itself which had once been the railway line built for the purpose of transporting the purified iron ore to Teesside and County Durham.

'Uh-oh! Is this what I think it is?'

Walking over to one of the arches, Oliver stepped sideways across the wooden fence that had been put up to keep people from climbing around inside the kilns. There was also a warning sign about falling masonry, but apparently, neither of these had stopped someone from stashing an impressive amount of alcohol and cigarettes behind the brick wall of one of the kilns. There was a wooden box, too, that was too heavy to contain only cigarettes. Frowning, Oliver lifted the box and set it on a large, flat rock.

'Hey, Oliver! What are you doing there? You are not telling me you have found the ghost's treasure, are you?'

He spun around to see Lily standing on the track, a heavily panting black and white Springer Spaniel by her side. Inigo was Joseph's dog and, usually, he would accompany the vet on his rounds, but Lily often took him for walks when Joseph was on duty in the small animal practice in Pickering. Being her own boss, she could always close her shop for an hour or two, especially when it was not busy.

'No, I'm afraid no treasure. But I seem to have come across someone's secret stash of alcohol and cigarettes.'

'Oh?' Curious, Lily stepped across the fence, bidding Inigo to lie down in the shade. 'And *stay*! The last thing we need is an injured dog, especially when Daddy is not here to patch you up. – Let me see what you've found … oh wow!' she exclaimed when Oliver showed her. 'That is a lot! They can party all summer. Whisky, too … uh-oh. Do you think it's those teenagers who normally meet at the castle? They always go there at weekends, don't they, and leave their litter behind. Joseph went to give them a piece of his mind some weeks ago, when he was passing late one night, but they just sneered and laughed at him. The only one who has been successful so far in making them clear off is Mr Colbeck. But then he was a policeman, wasn't he, so I guess that gives him the kind of authority you would need to chase them away. – What's in that box?'

'I was just going to open it. You haven't got a penknife with you by any chance? Or better still a putty knife?'

Lily's father was a builder, so at least she knew what a putty knife was. 'Alas, I left the house without my toolbox today, as I didn't know it might come in handy,' she deadpanned.

Oliver laughed. 'Never mind, I'll manage ...' Taking a flat, smooth stone from the heap of masonry, he deftly slid it between the lid and the corpus of the box and moved it up and down a couple of times until the lid opened with a crack. 'I'd say that's done the trick—oi! Do you know what's in here?'

Lily shook her head. 'No, but you're going to tell me – or show me?' She stepped closer, leaving Inigo to explore the grass around the fence with his nose. When she saw what was inside the box, she gasped.

'Fireworks??'

'Hmm ... looks to me like they are planning to play ghost up here one of these nights. Well,' he held up a packet of Cook's matches, 'whatever they are up to, they are in for a surprise when they come back here.'

'Because we are going to take this dangerous toy box away, right?'

'Yep. That, and the whisky, so at least they know somebody found out on them.' Oliver shook his head. 'I mean, if they really wanted to keep it a secret, they might have gone to a little more trouble hiding the stuff. I could see the bottles peeping out from behind that arch when I was standing on the track. I have a feeling they might not be of the brightest sort ... Anyway!' Closing the lid on the box, he turned to Lily and said, 'I'll walk down with you, if you don't mind. I'm not going to run down into the village carrying a box of fireworks and a bottle of whisky. I'll never hear the last of it!'

Lily sniggered. 'Yes, I suppose you're right there. Come on, let me take the whisky bottle. Then they'll think it's a present for Abi.'

Oliver laughed. 'Great idea! Birthday present sorted … no, no, just kidding. Daisy has got something for her, I think. – What do we do about the fireworks? I could put up a notice in the window by the church car park: Fireworks found by the kilns, anyone who is missing them, come in for tea. Sermon included.'

Shaking her head, Lily took the whisky bottle and plopped it into her rucksack. 'Tell me, Oliver, how does Daisy put up with you? Honestly, you are worse than Joseph!'

But Oliver shrugged and gave her a lopsided smile. 'She loves me, that's how.'

***

'Happy birthday, Abi!' Kissing Abi's cheeks, Jessie presented her with a beautiful bouquet and a packet of Nate's signature coffee. 'This is from all of us, and I have a cake, too – shall I leave it in the car, just in case that goat is loose?'

Abi laughed. 'That might be better, yes. In the meantime, see that you get some sausages, before the boys eat them all. Or the dogs.'

Daisy, who was just pouring dressing over a salad she had made, raised an eyebrow at Jessie's daughter, beckoning her to come over. 'Sorry for kidnapping you like this,' she said, once they were out of earshot. 'How did it go? Did you tell them you did not want to go to Durham?'

Louisa May picked up the dog and let him lick her face. 'No. I didn't have to – turns out Mum doesn't want to go either.'

'Oh?'

'Yeah. She says she can't have the café open only on Saturdays and Sundays, it's not worth the trouble of driving down here. And where would she stay? So for now it looks like nothing's going to change, except that they agreed to let me go to Ampleforth in September.'

'Oh. Well, that is good then, isn't it?' Daisy was not sure whether this was good for Jessie and Nate – or for all of them as a family, come to think of it – but felt she was in no position to comment, let alone judge. Not everyone wanted to get married these days, did they? If Nate and Jessie were happy with this arrangement … and providing Ben would let Jessie stay in Corner Cottage …

Louisa May shrugged. Taking the can of coke she had brought, she tapped the lid with her fingernail (Daisy noticed she had put on bright blue nail polish to match the blue streak in her blond hair) and pulled the ring to open it. The *pshht* sound of the fizz escaping from the can made the dog wiggle in her arms, and she put him down. 'As good as it can get, I suppose. Two of my best friends went last year, you see, so it will be good to be together again. I know Mum couldn't afford to send me, or she would have, so—yeah, it's good.'

Daisy nodded. 'I hope you will be happy there, Louisa May. And of course, you can still have your riding lessons at weekends, if you like. Will you come home for the weekends?'

'I think so. Depends on what the others do, I suppose. I don't want to be the baby who always runs back home to Mummy and Daddy at weekends. Well, not to Daddy, in my case. But,' she shrugged, 'you know.'

'I understand. I didn't come home at weekends either,

even if my school was about as close from where we lived as yours.'

'Where did you go?'

'Framlingham College.'

'That sounds very posh.'

Daisy laughed. 'Yes, I suppose it is. But at the end of the day, it is not about how posh or how grand the school is, it is about whether you are happy there or not. And I hope you will be happy at Ampleforth, Louisa May. I am sure that is all your parents want for you – they want you to be happy.'

Louisa May finished her drink and wiped her mouth with the sleeve of her sweater. 'I'll be fine. And I don't know about you, but I'm starving. Can we go back now?'

'Of course. I'm sorry I kept you.'

'Don't be daft. You weren't holding me hostage, were you? Anyway, let's grab some sausages before they feed them to the dogs. Also, Mum has made a cake for Abi. With a goat on it!'

'You are joking?'

Louisa May grinned. ''Fraid so, yes. But I would have loved to see her face!'

***

LATER, THEY WERE sitting around a campfire roasting marshmallows, and for the first time since their arrival Daisy felt completely at home. She still wished they wouldn't have to move to the Rectory, but at least it was close to the village, which meant she could see Miss Lavender more often, which was a bonus. And she could still cycle to the farm as often as she liked.

'I think we should offer to help Madeleine with the catering for her Midsommer Fest,' Lily suggested. 'What do you think?'

'I think that's a great idea,' Daisy said, eager to be able to help Madeleine who had been so kind to her. 'Though I must say I'm not very accomplished in the kitchen – I can make a simple salad, like the one I made tonight. Or a crumble. That's the only dessert I make.'

'Ooh, yummy. Everyone loves a crumble! Wait, I'll get my notebook and write a list. Or you could help with the decorations? Cutting strips of coloured cotton to put in the wish tree?'

Daisy stared at her blankly. 'What sort of tree?'

'The wish tree or wishing tree. Haven't you heard of that tradition? You take a strip of cotton and make a wish while you tie it to the branch of the tree. And then you wait for it to come true or … not.' Everyone laughed, except Daisy who tried to catch Oliver's eye. But he was laughing, too, and not looking at her.

'Not any old tree will do though,' Susanna put in. She and her husband David lived next door to Abi at Rose Cottage. They had brought their baby daughter, Sarah Elaine, and she was rocking her gently in her arms now. With her incredibly long red hair that reached all the way down her back, Susanna reminded Daisy of the Lady of Shalott, as depicted in Waterhouse's famous painting. 'Hawthorns are traditionally used, and the Hunters have the most amazing specimen up there. That tree must have been there for centuries. I don't know if that improves your chances of getting your wish granted, but that's not what it's about, or not at Maddie's Midsommer Fest, anyway. It's just a bit of fun for adults and kids alike. Isn't it, Lily?'

Lily was just coming back with her notebook and obligatory black pen. 'Well, don't ask *me*, I wasn't even here yet last year in June, was I? This is my first Midsommer Fest, too, and I'm really looking forward to it.—Right, so Daisy is making a crumble, and I am making cheese scones and a big bowl of salad. Jessie?'

And while they were busy discussing, laughing, and writing things down, the sun set over the valley, casting long shadows down the hillside.

I shouldn't get so worked up over this, Daisy thought. It's just a silly old tradition. There are lots of those here. Like the devil who was said to be guarding a treasure he had buried in the hillside. What nonsense!

'During thunderstorms, when lightning hits the rocks behind the old iron kilns that you can see from the farm, people believe it's him getting angry!' Abi had explained when they had first moved into the Lapwing in early May. 'At what or who, I do not know, but people believe that he sends the sparks flying off those rocks to warn people off. They say it's *him* growling at us and not boring old thunder that we hear on such nights. It's nonsense, of course, but you'll find that there is a lot of good old superstition around here. And you'd better be careful with what you say from the pulpit on Sundays, young man,' she had said to Oliver, playfully wagging her finger at him. 'Folks around here like their traditions, and they will go to some lengths to defend their local legends. Ghosts included.'

Daisy had felt cold shivers running down her spine, but Oliver had laughed good-naturedly and said he would bear it in mind.

***

THE SUNSET OVER the hills on the other side of the dale was spectacular that night. Lily, Joseph, Oliver, and Daisy were standing at the farm gate, watching in silence as the sun, an enormous red ball, slowly dipped, dipped, dipped behind the shadowy silhouette of the kilns, and was gone. Suddenly the valley lay in total darkness, and the only thing the friends could make out at all were the blurred shapes of the sheep in the field opposite. There were no lights along the potholed lane that led from the village to the remote farms, and the silence that seemed to have ascended on the dale the moment the sun had gone made the atmosphere even more intense.

For a long time, none of them said anything, then Lily let out a long sigh and whispered, 'Isn't this the most *magical* place on earth? Can't you just see how fairies might be playing by the side of the beck now, bowing to each other and fluttering their dainty little wings as they invite their little fairy friends to join in a midnight reel on the water? Can you see the soft ripples in the moonlight, when their tiny feet touch the water's surface here and there?'

Joseph shook his head laughing, and Oliver arched an eyebrow in what could perhaps be described as mild disapproval, but Daisy stiffened in his arms. She did not feel comfortable when there was talk of fairies, or deep waters, knowing this would often bring back memories she would rather forget. Oliver, blissfully unaware of what was going on in his wife's head, assumed she was cold, and said, 'Come on, let's get back to the cottage. You never know what our four-legged little friend might be up to tonight, so we'd better grab some sleep while we can.'

***

'LOOK, THERE SHE *is, playing with her fairies again – hullo, Daisy, how are the fairies today? Oh!' Her cousin Felicity put a hand over her mouth in mock self-reproach. 'I'm ever so sorry, I must have scared them away! I hope they did not drown.' She and Eleanor laughed, and Daisy felt hot tears stinging in her eyes. Why was it that every time her cousins visited they would team up with her older siblings and make fun of her? She normally got on so well with Eleanor, although she was six years older than herself, and she liked her cousins, too – not when they teased her though.*

Normally, Daisy would have been careful not to tempt them by venturing to the pond on her own. But, feeling irresistibly drawn to the water's edge, she had foolishly believed she could slip away unseen while they were all fighting over who got the largest piece of brownie. Of course they had seen her – and come running after her, too, laughing and teasing. She should have known better.

Turning to her cousins, Daisy shouted, 'Yes, you have drowned them all! You can come to the funeral, if you like, and bring some cake, too!' Then she tossed her blond curls over her shoulder, and turned her back to her cousins, hoping they would leave her alone. But that only made them laugh, and soon Daisy found herself joining in. She could never be angry with Felicity and Eleanor for long.

Dorothy, Felicity's sixteen-year-old sister, was carrying little Kate on her hips, and called out, 'Will you be alright looking after this cheeky little butterfly for a few minutes? We were just going to go and get some marmalade sandwiches and lemonade, and then we can have a picnic underneath the willow tree. The boys had all the brownies. What do you think?'

Daisy thought it was a splendid idea and held out her arms to her little sister. 'Come here, Katie! You can sit with me, and I will tell you all about the poor fairies who drowned. Dorothy, Felicity and Eleanor don't believe in fairies, you see, because they are nearly grown up and when you are grown up, you lose your imagination.'

Kate looked up at her with her large, violet eyes. Then she stuck her thumb in her little rosebud mouth and began sucking it, her eyes still fixed on Daisy. 'You think that's an awful shame?' asked Daisy. 'Yes, so do I. Life is so much better if you have imagination.'

She could still hear her cousins and sister laughing as they walked away towards the house while she settled little Kate in the grass beside her and began to tell her about the fairies that lived hidden among the tiny leaves of the water forget-me-nots that grew in the shallow part of the pond. Kate listened intently, all the while watching out for fairies, and when she saw a dragonfly hovering above the surface of the water, its delicate wings shimmering greenish blue in the midday sunlight, she jumped up in excitement.

'Fairy, fairy! Look, Daisy, look!'

It all happened so quickly that Daisy could scarcely remember afterwards, when she tried to explain to her parents between chattering of teeth and hiccups and violent sobbing. One moment Kate was running towards the water, chubby hands waving in the air, laughing – and the next there was a loud splash, followed by a scream.

'Kate!'

Seeing her sister's hand sticking out from where she

knew the water was at its deepest, Daisy did not hesitate for one second but plunged right in after her, without even remembering to take off her shoes first.

The water was cold, dark, and terrifyingly deep, and soon Daisy was fighting for her own life as much as for her sister's. The weight of her shoes and her wet dress was constantly dragging her down, and when her foot got caught in the tangled, sticky mass of the waterlilies' stems, it took her too long to break free. By the time she reached the spot where Kate's hand had been, it was gone.

'Help! Help, help, HELP!'

Daisy sat up with a jolt. Her heart was beating against her ribcage, and her nightdress was soaked in sweat. But when she cast an anxious look at Oliver, she found he had not stirred at all. Neither had the dog, who was sleeping peacefully in the crook of his arm.

'Oh, thank God,' she whispered, reaching for the water glass on her bedside table. 'Thank God …'

Though no one had ever reproached Daisy for being so careless and irresponsible, Daisy had never been able to forget how her sister had nearly drowned that day. All because she had been dreaming and not watching her, like she should have.

Her mother had cried with relief when she had seen Daisy coming out of the pond with a pale but otherwise unscathed Kate in her arms and dropped to the ground, sobbing, and choking. And putting her arms around her two youngest girls, she had held them tight, crying 'thank God, thank God!'

The relief, however, had been short-lived. Although Kate had seemed to recover quickly, she began to complain about nausea, tummy-aches, and tiredness in the evening. At first, her parents had thought it was only the aftermath of the near-drowning experience and had let her lie on the sofa with a blanket and read stories to her until she fell asleep. But then Kate had woken in the middle of the night, shivering and shaking, and with a high temperature. An ambulance had been called and she had been rushed into hospital, a desperately guilt-ridden mother at her side. Kate was diagnosed with a rare complication that had to do with retaining water in her lungs which had in turn caused a dangerous infection. For two days and nights they had feared for her life, until finally the crisis was over, and Kate was safe at last. She had made a full recovery and today, she did not remember the accident at all, as her family had thought it best never to tell her.

But Daisy remembered every single desperate moment. Had Kate died, she would never have forgiven herself, no matter how often her parents assured her that she was not to blame.

Needless to say, she had never wanted to believe in fairies again.

CHAPTER 13

'So this is the dog? The one you found in the churchyard?'

Daisy stood on the porch outside Miss Lavender's shop, holding the dog in her arms. Joseph had just given them the all-clear the other day, saying he would issue a pet passport as soon as they had decided upon a name. Which they hadn't yet. But he had been with them for a week now, and she was excited to go into Thirsk later this afternoon, to buy beautiful things for their beautiful dog. Oliver had dropped her off in the village on his way to Rosedale Abbey, where he had a wedding to conduct, and would come back for them later. She had said she would walk up to the castle and old church in the meantime, hoping to find inspiration for a name there. After all, what place could be more inspiring than the one in which she had found him?

Word had spread quickly though, and here she was, introducing her dog to every Tom, Dick, and Harry in Bishops Bridge. Or, in this case, old Mr Barnsley, who had just come out of Jessie's café, his Golden Retriever, Honey, close by his side. In the background, they could hear the infamous Ossie barking.

'Yes,' she answered patiently, thinking it was not Mr Barnsley's fault that she had been asked the same question about twenty times before.

'This is amazing!' the old man remarked. Tickling the little dog behind the ears, he chuckled. 'What a handsome little fellow! What's his name?'

'He doesn't have a name yet. We have only just been told we would be able to keep him. For now, we just call him Little One.—Good morning, Miss Lavender! How are you today? Have you met our dog yet? I found him in the churchyard last week, all on his own.'

But Miss Lavender was not listening. She stood rooted to the spot, staring at the dog as if it was a ghost.

'Miss Lavender? Are you quite alright? You look a little pale. Would you like to sit down?'

As Miss Lavender was beginning to sway a little, Daisy quickly passed the dog to Mr Barnsley and took her by the elbow, steering her towards the old wicker rocking chair in the corner of the porch. The chair had seen better days, its faded blue colour peeling from the woven seat and back, but it looked solid enough to accommodate its frail owner. The last thing Daisy needed was for Miss Lavender to faint and fall down the steps.

Once safely seated, Miss Lavender began to rock softly in her chair. Back and forth, back and forth. For a long time, she did not speak, but never took her eyes off the dog, who was giving Mr Barnsley the full face treatment now, making the old man chuckle with delight. Then all of a sudden she asked, in a low, husky voice that did not sound at all like her, 'Where did you say you found him?'

'In the old churchyard. He was sitting by the gate, waiting for me. Well – he *looked* like he was waiting for me. Or anyone to take him home. And since no dog has been reported missing, Joseph said we could keep him.

He doesn't have a name yet. We have only just had the good news. About keeping him, I mean.'

Miss Lavender nodded. Still rocking, her watery blue eyes still resting on the dog.

Daisy thought the old lady's behaviour very odd, the way she stared at the dog. Did he evoke some memories in her perhaps? Was that why she was staring so intently at him?

Mr Barnsley seemed to think the same, even if he could not see much. He was very perceptive though, and even Honey was beginning to whine softly, and looking at Miss Lavender, as if she, too, sensed that something was not right. 'Do you want me to fetch Lily?' Mr Barnsley whispered. 'Perhaps she had better call the doctor? If Miss Lavender is unwell?'

'I heard that, Mr Barnsley. And I am quite well, thank you very much. It is not every day that one finds their lost dog again after fifty years – and in the churchyard, too, of all places! I buried him there myself, you see, in 1972. Behind the churchyard, that is. Under the red beech tree near the fence. At least, I thought I did …' A soft smile was playing at her lips, making her look younger. And more vulnerable, Daisy thought, and swallowed.

'But now he has come back to me. Haven't you, Drifter?'

Daisy was glad she was not holding the dog now, or she might have dropped him.

***

'FOR A MOMENT we thought she had lost her marbles. I went to get her a glass of water, and when I came back,

Mr Barnsley had placed our Little One in her lap, and she was stroking him. She looked quite content, and not in the least bit … confused. She did not speak but just smiled and stroked, and then Mr Barnsley sat down with her, and I thought it was the loveliest picture I had ever seen. So peaceful! The two old people and the two dogs sitting on the porch. If I wasn't so fond of our Little One myself, I think I might have left him with her.'

Oliver shook his head. He was driving, and Daisy sat next to him, holding the dog. 'Oh, my! So what's the secret? Did you learn anything about—what did she call him? Drifter?'

'Yes. But she didn't want to talk about him. So, I can only guess she must have had a dog like that when she first came to Bishops Bridge. She said she buried him on Broughton Hill in 1972. That is almost fifty years ago though … How old do you think Miss Lavender is? Seventy? Seventy-five?'

'Something like that. I would put her closer to eighty perhaps.'

'Eighty?? She wouldn't still be running a shop at eighty, would she?'

Oliver shrugged. 'I don't know. If that is all she has … and she is fit for her age, you must give her that. Walks her five miles every day, keeps her mind occupied … so why not?'

'I'm not sure I can believe that! But be that as it may, she did not tell us anything more, and unless she does, we will not find out. In the meantime,' she said, speaking to the dog, 'we will buy you a beautiful collar and lead and a nice, soft doggy bed to sleep in, and a pretty set of bowls for your food and drink, and a rug to lie on, and a brush and – oh, and food, of course, and dog biscuits …'

Oliver laughed. 'Oh, Daisy! You are wonderful! But don't forget we need to buy furniture, too. Unless you want to sit in the dog bed with the Little One.' He winked at her. 'Shall we call him Drifter then? It's a nice name, isn't it? I like it.'

'I don't know … Drifter?' The dog lifted his head. 'Look! He knows it's him. And he was somewhat adrift when I found him, wasn't he?'

'He was, yes. But perhaps you had better ask Miss Lavender what she thinks before you bring him to the church to be baptised.'

'Oliver!' she cried, batting his arm playfully. 'Don't let your father hear that!' Her fearsome father-in-law had been a vicar, too, until his retirement five years ago. Unlike his son though, who was described as modern and laid-back, he had a rather more old-fashioned view on things like baptisms and dogs in churches.

'Ah, but he knows what I'm like,' Oliver said, 'and he has mellowed quite a bit over the years. Retirement does him good.'

Daisy nodded. 'I know. And I shouldn't be so hard on him. Forgive me.'

He smiled. 'Nothing to forgive. I know what a stubborn old mule he is. But then perhaps that has kept him going for so long. Who knows, eh?'

'Yes,' she whispered, absent-mindedly kissing the dog's head, 'who knows.'

For a while Daisy just looked out of the window, watching the beautiful landscape of the North York Moors slip by. But then she turned to Oliver and put a hand on his thigh. 'I love you.' There was a quiet urgency to her voice, and he took her hand and kissed it. 'And I love you. Always have, always will.'

∗∗∗

Miss Lavender stood on a chair in her bedroom, trying to peer into the depths of her enormous oak wardrobe. She was looking for something. Something she had not set eyes on in a very long time, and which she had suddenly remembered last night when she had been unable to sleep. It was the Dog Business that had unsettled her, she was sure of that. If he had not turned up in the churchyard – and on her porch – like some ghost from the past, she might never have thought about the box again …

Although she knew it could not be anywhere else – she had searched the attic, too, just to make sure she had not moved it there at some point – it was neither at the bottom of the wardrobe, hidden behind piles of shoe boxes (most of them containing shoes she had not worn in years, if at all, and should have given to charity long ago), nor was it on the top shelf, where she thought she remembered putting it. She was beginning to get a bit anxious now, doubting her memory. Had she thrown it away at some point? Surely she would remember if she had, wouldn't she?

'It can't have disappeared,' she muttered and decided to give the large bottom drawer one more try. Getting to her knees, Miss Lavender pulled at the two brass knobs. But no matter how hard she pulled, the heavy drawer would not open even by an inch. It remained tightly stuck, as if refusing to reveal its content – all the more reason for the old lady to believe that she was indeed looking in the right place.

'If I can ever get that wretched thing to open!' She sat back and wiped the sweat from her brow. 'I can always ask Oliver tomorrow, I suppose …' She shook her head. No. She did not want anyone else to see it. It was her secret, her past. Her ghosts to deal with.

Again, she gripped the knobs with both hands and pulled as hard as she could … *crack!*

But it was not the drawer that had cracked but Miss Lavender's back. The pain shot through her body like fire, and she cried out loud. 'Ouch!'

For a while, she just sat there whimpering both in pain and in frustration. Then she sat up, straightened her back until it gave another, this time satisfying, crack. 'I will *not* be beat!' Determinedly pushing a wisp of hair from her face, she bent to tackle the stubborn old drawer once more.

It took a few more attempts (and cost her excruciating pain!), but at last, the drawer began to move a little. When she had prised it open by a few more inches, she was able to look inside – and there, right at the back, was something black, and solid: the box.

'Thank God! I thought I'd have to give up after all. Now then, Lavinia Lavender – you have come this far, you are not going to chicken out now. What must be done, must be done!'

Taking a deep breath, she pulled out the box, sat it on her bed, and wiped off the thin layer of dust. On opening the lid, a musty smell hit her nose, and she had to turn away for a moment, preparing herself for what she knew to be inside. Her eyelids fluttered, and she swallowed a few times, but then curiosity got the better of her. With trembling hands, she lifted out the diary and a bundle of letters, bound together with a fraying piece of red ribbon. She would not read them now, but put them aside for later.

Later, as she used to say in those dark weeks following the accident, when I can bear it.

She closed her eyes for the briefest of moments, then she took the silver jewellery box with the engraved L on it. L for Lavinia. She carefully traced the ornate letter with a gnarled finger, memories of the day on which she had been given the box coming back to her with such clarity she could almost picture her sixteen year old self in her parents' parlour.

'For me?' she had asked, looking up from the box to her parents.

'Of course it is for you,' her father had replied and smiled indulgently at her, like he used to in those days. What happy, carefree days they were! 'We only have the one darling daughter, haven't we? It's your birthday present. Go on, open it.'

She opened it now, and although she knew the original contents – the silver locket with her parents' picture inside on one side, and one of her horse, Duchess, on the other – had long gone, sold when she had desperately needed the money, she was not prepared for the emotional shock she got at the sight of what was still in it. What she had put there all those years ago, for safekeeping.

For *remembering*.

She took out the first of three photographs, that of her beloved horse (naturally, after what had happened, she had not wanted to keep the photograph of her parents, although later she sometimes wished she had), and her eyes misted over as she remembered Duchess. There were two more pictures, one of a young man with reddish hair and a kind, round face, and another of a black cocker spaniel with a white breast: Drifter. Miss Lavender smiled as she held the faded picture up against the light, scrutinizing it. He really looked most uncannily like the dog Daisy had found in the churchyard. Maybe she would show Daisy the picture after church tomorrow. And if Daisy was who she thought she was … or might be …

She shook her head. No. She would not allow herself to dwell on Daisy now, or what she thought she had heard Lily say to Jessie in the café a few days ago. There would be a time for that, and that time was not tonight, nor tomorrow. She would know when she was ready.

Squaring her shoulders, and resisting the temptation to lose herself in the photograph – and her melancholy memories – of the young man, Miss Lavender reached into the box once more, knowing that the last two objects would be the hardest to look at.

Nestled on the dark red velvet cushion that lined the box lay the ring he had given her. And curled into it, a lock of soft, black hair.

CHAPTER 14

'YOU'RE LEAVING ALREADY? But it's only half past eight!'

Daisy looked up from her coffee cup as Oliver emerged from the bedroom, dressed in his usual Sunday service attire of smart jeans and charcoal crewneck sweater with his clerical collar underneath. Holding his Bible and hymn book in his right hand and his car keys in his left, he bent to kiss Daisy's cheek.

'I know and I'm sorry, my darling, especially when you got so little sleep last night.' He looked pointedly at the dog. 'Yes, my friend, it's you I'm talking about! You can't keep this up, you know, playing all night. We need our sleep. Is that understood?'

The dog gazed up at him with his liquid brown eyes, as if he would never so much as draw breath again without asking his permission. Then he thumped his tail on the floor and turned his attention back to his mistress. After all, she had toast, and his master had not.

Oliver shook his head, but his eyes were smiling. 'Anyway, I'd better go. Are you sure you're not coming? But you don't want to leave him, right?'

'No. Maybe I'll take him for a walk later or ... you know what,' she said, absent-mindedly dropping a piece of toast. 'I'll come with you. I can walk him while you are in church, and then we can meet at Jessie's … oh. No dogs. I forgot.'

Oliver grinned. 'Oh yes, it's one thing being full of schadenfreude when the pugs aren't allowed in, but quite a different matter when you have your own dog, isn't it? Oh, Daisy, how I do love you! Go on then, pour me another coffee. I'll wait until you are ready, and then we can go together. Even if we can't sit in Jessie's café, we might pick up some cake and knock on Miss Lavender's door. But we'll see her in church, anyway. At least, I will.'

***

DAISY STOOD OUTSIDE Miss Lavender's house and looked up at the windows. There was a light in one of them, which struck her as odd, seeing as it was a bright summer morning. Maybe she had forgotten to switch it off before she left for church. Or even the night before.

'Come on, darling, let's sit by the stream and wait for Daddy to come. I have brought some treats, so we can practise *sit* and *stay*. And play fetch afterwards,' she promised, producing a ball. 'Would you like that?'

The dog gave a bark and wagged his tail, making a group of walkers chuckle as they passed. Daisy waved to them, then turned her attention back on the house. What room would that be, she wondered? The kitchen? She had never been upstairs in Miss Lavender's private flat. Whenever they had had tea, it had always been in her little parlour on the ground floor, or in the small, walled garden behind the house. Daisy had never met anyone who was so fiercely private – and yet, as Lily had pointed out over shepherd's pie and wine in the farmhouse kitchen last night, Miss Lavender had never let anyone come as close as Daisy, and within such a short space of time, too.

'It's like she has adopted you! Honestly, it's amazing! You must have stirred something in her – a long-forgotten memory or something.'

Daisy had looked at her, slightly bemused. Lily was a hopeless romantic; she always saw something that other people did not see. 'A long-forgotten memory? Of what?'

'Well, I don't know, do I? If I did, I would tell you.— Oh, but wait!' she had cried, suddenly excited. 'The dog! She thought it was hers, didn't she, when she first saw him? What did she call him?'

'Drifter.'

'Yes … and you found him in the churchyard. Miss Lavender often goes there, you know, and … I don't know what she does there, really. Pray? Think? Or perhaps remember someone, or something? A bit like you. What do *you* do when you go up there? Except finding dogs?'

'Um … I pray. Usually.'

'There you go! You are very much alike, you know. Are you sure you aren't related? Or have met in another life perhaps? You never know, do you?'

Well, she did know, and the answer was: no. There had never been another life, so logically, they could not have met before.

She often goes there … to the churchyard … and sits and thinks. Or remembers. Or prays.

Daisy shook herself. She had come here to teach the little dog some manners, and play with him, not muse over something Lily had said. Lily simply had too much imagination, that was it.

***

OLIVER WENT TO ring the bell, but there was no answer. He had come to the stream wearing a frown on his face, and called, 'She wasn't in church. That is unusual! Do you think she might have gone out? Maybe caught a bus to York to attend service at the Minster, like you said she sometimes did?'

Daisy had shaken her head. 'No, she would go for Evensong then. Sunday eucharist service starts at half past nine in the Minster – when would she have to leave then, at seven? No, it must be something else that has kept her … maybe she is ill? Lily said she closed the shop early yesterday. Do you know, I think we'd better check on her. I'd never forgive myself if we found her lying on the floor unconscious, and be too late to—'

'Now don't fret, darling,' Oliver had calmed her, 'we will find her, okay? I'm sure she is fine. Maybe she is just tired.'

Standing outside Miss Lavender's shop now, they found the door locked, and nobody answering. 'Now, how do we get in? Have you any idea where she might keep a spare key for the back door? Or maybe Jessie has one, seeing as she is her neighbour in business?'

Daisy slapped her forehead. 'Of course! Now why didn't I think of that! I'll be right back!'

Five minutes later she was back with the key, but hesitated as she held it in her hands, shaking her head. 'I'm not sure I can do this, Oliver … she is such an intensely private person, isn't she? It feels … wrong somehow.'

'I know, but not checking if she is okay feels more wrong – give it to me then. I'll do it.'

She gave him the key and he put it into the lock and turned it. 'Okay,' he said, pushing the door open, 'here we go … Miss Lavender? Are you in? Hello?'

Daisy cringed at his casual *Hello*. With Miss Lavender, it was always *Good morning*, *Good afternoon*, or *Good evening*. *How do you do* was also perfectly acceptable at any time of day, whereas *Hello* was most definitely not. Well, Daisy thought to herself, if she is at home – and, please God, neither ill nor hurt – she will let him know, and no mistake.

But there was no answer, and so there was nothing else for it, they had to go in. Following her husband across the threshold, Daisy put the dog down and said, 'Where is Miss Lavender, Drifter? Can you find her?'

Oliver laughed. 'Daisy! We said we would not call him Drifter without checking with Miss Lavender first. And he doesn't know who she is, anyway. He doesn't even know he's—'

But the dog was gone.

'See? He knows his name! And he knows we are looking for someone, too – or maybe instinct tells him that we do. He might even remember Miss Lavender's scent, and has picked it up. Working cockers are clever dogs.'

'Alright,' Oliver said, still laughing, and took Daisy's hand, 'let's go find the little rascal. But don't be disappointed if we find him in the shop with his nose in the biscuit barrel.'

They did not find him in the shop (and the door that divided the shop from Miss Lavender's private rooms was locked, anyway) but upstairs in Miss Lavender's living room, sitting in front of the sofa where the old lady lay quite still.

'Miss Lavender!'

Daisy rushed forward, dropping to her knees as she took the old lady's hand. It was ice-cold but there was a steady pulse, thank God, and now she could see Miss Lavender was breathing, and quite regularly, too. She was just fast asleep.

Relieved, Daisy was going to turn round to Oliver when she noticed the ugly purple bruise to Miss Lavender's head. She must have had a fall after all. One of her eyes looked swollen, too. 'Oh, Miss Lavender! Oh, poor you …'

Bending over her, Daisy gently touched her forehead. The skin felt cold and clammy, and Daisy looked about the room, hoping to spot a blanket somewhere. There was one draped across the armchair, a large, brown, scratchy old mohair thing that reminded her of the one her Granny used to have on her lap. 'This will have to do,' she murmured, pulling the blanket over Miss Lavender's body. 'I am sorry for it being so scratchy, but it will keep you nice and warm. Oliver is just calling the ambulance … I hope you don't mind. But I think you might have concussion.' And to Oliver, she said, 'Do you want to go and find the bathroom, and get a damp cloth we can put on that bruise?'

Oliver nodded as he put back his phone. 'The ambulance will be here in about ten minutes. You stay with her while I get the cloth. I don't think it will help much now. She will have had that fall some hours ago, by the looks of it. But never mind, I'll get something.'

Gently laying a hand on the old lady's bony shoulder, Daisy whispered, 'Miss Lavender? It's Daisy. You had a fall. The ambulance is on its way to take you to the hospital.'

Suddenly the old lady's eyes snapped open. 'Hospital? Why would I want to go to hospital? And what are *you* doing here, anyway? Shouldn't you be—oh. No, of course not. I am sorry, I must have confused you with someone.' She squinted. 'Who *are* you?'

Daisy gave her a reassuring smile. 'It's Daisy, Miss Lavender. We were worried about you because you did not come to church this morning. So we thought we had better check on you. Look, I have brought the dog, too – the one I found in the churchyard, remember?'

Miss Lavender thought about it for a moment. Then she nodded. 'Yes, I remember. Drifter, isn't it?'

'Yes. Well, he is not—oh, never mind,' she said, deciding now was not the time to discuss minor points like the difference between a dog that had died of old age half a century ago and one who was barely more than a puppy. 'But it was him who found you. He dashed up the stairs as if …' She stopped. *As if he was at home here. Or as if he had been here before.*

The old lady harrumphed. 'Hm. He did, eh? And how did you get in, if I may ask?'

At this, Daisy squirmed. 'We … erm … Jessie gave us the spare key. We just wanted to make sure you were alright, Miss Lavender, or we would never have dreamed of intruding. Please forgive me. Us.'

'Nothing to forgive. You're a good girl, Daisy. I'm glad you came.' And looking down at the dog, she smiled. 'So you called him Drifter then?'

'Well …'

'The ambulance has just arrived.' Oliver turned away

from the window and made for the stairs. 'I'll go and open the door if you don't mind, Miss Lavender.'

'And what if I do? They will take me to hospital, anyway, whether I like it or whether I don't. It's what they do to old people these days. They think we are incapable of looking after ourselves, so they just do as they see fit. – You will come with me though, Daisy, won't you?'

Daisy smiled. 'Of course I will.'

***

DESPITE HER PROTESTS ('I am perfectly fine, young man, there is absolutely nothing wrong with me. It's just a bruise!'), Miss Lavender was taken to York Hospital. Oliver and Daisy followed in their own car, Drifter sitting in the footwell of the passenger seat. Looking up adoringly at Daisy, he seemed to enjoy the car ride immensely.

Once they had found a space in the overcrowded car park, Daisy hurried inside and was relieved to find they had not taken Miss Lavender to a ward yet. 'I know I'm not family,' she explained to the receptionist, 'but Miss Lavender does not have anyone else, so …'

'She is not the only old lady with no one left in the world but her dog, or cat. Some do not even have a pet to keep them company. Sad, really, but what can you do?'

Daisy was thinking about this while she waited for the doctor to take a closer look at Miss Lavender's injuries. She hoped they would not keep her in hospital for too long, knowing how much the shop meant to her elderly friend, never mind her independence and privacy she always went to such great lengths to protect. For the first time since she had known Miss Lavender, Daisy began to wonder if perhaps she was hiding something. Or running away from something – her past maybe? Painful memories that haunted her? Like that dog? What *did* she think about when she went to sit in the old churchyard, as Lily had said?

She often goes there … to the churchyard … and sits and thinks. Or remembers. Or prays.

Daisy took a sip of the tea she had bought from the vending machine and frowned. It was strange though, wasn't it? They were so much alike, she and Miss Lavender, despite their difference in age, and the fact that they were not related, or had never met before. They couldn't have, could they? And the dog story, that was rather eerie, too, wasn't it? Even for someone who did not have the faintest superstitious notions, like herself.

'Mrs Clifford-Jones?'

She looked up to see a young doctor standing in the door, clipboard in hand and a rather tired but sympathetic smile on his face. Daisy wondered how long he had been on duty already. Too long probably, she thought. With hospitals being permanently understaffed, she supposed they did not have much choice, especially not junior doctors seeking permanent employment.

'Yes?'

'I am happy to inform you there is nothing much wrong with your friend except that she has rather severe concussion, and a broken wrist – but she will have to stay here for a few days, I'm afraid. We would like to run a few more tests as her heartrate is not … not quite what it should be. Also, her blood pressure is alarmingly low. She will probably need some help once she gets home. This is actually something we would like to discuss with you before we discharge her. In the meantime, we would appreciate it very much if you could persuade her to … um … make her see she will indeed have to stay here for a few days to make sure she gets all the rest she needs. She would be back behind the counter of her shop tomorrow if we let her. I hope you'll agree with me that that is absolutely out of the question.'

Hiding a smile, Daisy nodded earnestly instead. 'Of course. I will do my very best. Can I see her now?'

***

' … AND THEN I will need my glasses, which I have left on the bedside table, if I remember correctly … or perhaps they are on the bureau in the living room. Or on the kitchen table? Golly, I don't remember a thing! This is very vexing. Anyway, I am sure you will find them. And then I'll need my second best cardigan, the navy one with the pretty pearl buttons. It should be in my wardrobe, for I am sure I have not worn it since last Sunday, and I can clearly remember wearing it for church then. Oh, and speaking of wardrobe,' Miss Lavender said, dropping her voice.

Daisy held her breath, sensing the old lady was going to tell her something of significance.

She was right.

CHAPTER 15

'Va, pensiero, sull'ali dorate –

Fly, thought, on your golden wings, go, rest on the slopes, on the hills …'

Shaking her head angrily, Ellen stared at the lyrics in front of her. It did not work. No matter what her tutor said, for her, English simply did not work here. It was all very well *translating* the text, but *singing* it was quite a different matter. It sounded bland, unemotional. Distant. And so foreign, even though it was her native language! No. She just could not bring herself to sing it, the words would not come. Granted, there were some really good recordings from renowned choirs who had actually sung it in English, and it sounded nice enough – but to her, it was not *Nabucco*. It just wasn't the same.

Pursing her lips, she tapped her pencil impatiently against the music stand. Maybe she should have listened to Katharina, who insisted that the German was the best translation of Verdi's famous slave choir from what might well be his most famous opera, *Nabucco*. Would she have time to change her mind?

Teure Heimat, wann seh ich dich wieder?

Better, but still not quite right. And she could not remember the next line. She could look it up of course, but she needed to hear it, to get the pronunciation right. Her eyes never leaving the notes before her, and still humming softly, she grabbed her phone.

'Katharina? Have you got a minute? Great. Can you come over? I'm on the small stage. Yes, getting ready – or trying to, anyway. Thanks!'

***

'OVE OLEZZANO TEPIDE e molli l'aure dolci del suolo natal!'

'Hm … *where sweet breezes, warm and gentle, perfume the air of our native soil*! Well. It does remind me of Yorkshire, and the Moors, but that's about it. It just doesn't match the Italian. What do you think?'

'I think,' Katharina said, taking a deliciously smelling parcel from out of her bulging shoulder bag, 'it's time you had a break. Let's sit outside for a bit, it's such a lovely day. The fresh air will do you good, and the sun, no?'

Ellen sighed. 'Oh, alright then. But you do know that eating before singing is not good for your vocal cords?'

'Ach, *papperlapapp*! A few pasties won't hurt. *You* can always sing, even in your sleep.'

'Papa-what?'

But Katharina was already marching down the corridor, swinging her bag while singing at the top of her voice. 'Flieg, Gedanke, getragen von Sehnsucht! Lass dich nieder—'

'Flieg, Gedanke? I thought it was *Teure Heimat*! It's confusing!'

Katharina laughed. Holding the door, she let her friend pass through and followed her outside, then led the way towards the formal gardens at the front of the College. 'That comes later on, in the chorus. We can practise while we eat. Or afterwards. You'll pick it up in no time at all, memorising every single word. You are a natural when it comes to languages. Unlike me, for I still struggle in lectures. Thank God it's almost over. I can't wait to get back to Wien, and speak German every day.'

Ellen nodded, dreading the day when she would have to part with her friends at the Royal College of Music. When she would be on her own again.

She had met Katharina at the RCM Opera Studio six years ago, when they had both been new to the college, and they had formed an instant friendship. Both extremely ambitious as well as highly gifted, they had worked hard towards their Master of Performance qualification over the last two years, with Ellen hoping to obtain an Artist Diploma in Opera, which would enable her to become a professional opera singer – something she had dreamed of all her life. Katharina, on the other hand, having grown up in a family of professional classical musicians in Vienna, had contemplated auditioning for the Art Dip programme as well, but she said she was a homebird and did not want to stay in London for another two years. Also, she had received an offer to join the Vienna State Opera for a year, and was excited to go.

Ellen herself had three offers to choose from, including a two-year contract in Verona, but time was running out and she had yet to sort out her parents' inheritance. Maybe it would actually be the safest option to stay on for another two years, plus, she really wanted that diploma. The RCM having become something of a second home to her over the years, she was reluctant to leave – especially as there was in fact no home for her to go back to now. Just a large, empty house on the moors where every room, every piece of furniture, every lingering whiff of her mother's perfume – yes, even the dust in her father's study would remind her of her parents.

Naturally, she envied Katharina for the chance to go home, and catch up with her family before embarking on her career in opera singing. How she would love to go with her instead, if only for the summer!

'When are you going back?'

'I have booked a flight for the twelfth of July. You know you can still come with me? My parents would be delighted to have you. You can stay as long as you like.'

Ellen hesitated for the briefest of moments before she shook her head. 'I'd love to, but really, I can't. I've got so much to do – all the things I couldn't get sorted after Dad's—well. You know.'

Resuming her humming, Ellen walked on. *As long as I keep on walking, and singing, I will be okay.* Just keep on singing, Mama had always said. She had loved nothing better than to hear her daughter sing, and Ellen, sensing that it was what her mum would have wanted, had sung her through her final minutes, tears streaming down her face.

Her dad, a keen walker as well as a true Yorkshireman, had firmly believed that a walk on the moors would always ground you. *Keep on walking, lass,* he had said. *Keep on walking.*

She swallowed. *Dear Papa! Why did he have to go? Didn't he know she still needed him? Hadn't he thought of her at all? His darling girl? Why had he taken that gun from the closet and walked into the wood the day after* she had gone back to London? Why? He had promised he would be alright. He had promised he would take her to Vienna, and Salzburg, in the autumn. And to Verona. It was ironic, really, that she had been offered a job there. She would have to decline, of course. She would not leave England, not now. During her sickness, her mum had listened to them planning that trip, and encouraged them to go, even if she should not recover. And her father had promised her on her deathbed that he would look after their girl, hadn't he? That he would take care of her, make sure she would never have to feel alone and frightened again.

He had not kept any of those promises.

Sometimes she was angry. But mostly, she was just desperately sad. And overwhelmed by what lay ahead. If only she had someone who could help her! There was the solicitor, of course, kind old Mr Hamilton, who had promised to help her sort out the house and everything, but he wasn't a friend. He would not make tea for her when she woke up in the middle of the night crying for her mum. Which she still did frequently. And for her dad, too. Less frequently. Because she was angry. He had *chosen* to end his life, while her mum had fought so bravely right to the end. Why couldn't he have been as brave?

Not that that was reason to call him a coward, like some people did. What did they know of his pain? Nothing. They didn't even know what to say to her, did they? Apart from the usual 'Sorry for your loss, darling.' Why did they call her *darling* when they didn't mean it? And why were some people so cruel as to walk past her in the churchyard, and say nothing? Nothing! Maybe *Sorry for your loss, darling* wasn't so bad after all.

To be fair, a lot of them had offered their help, too. Miss Lavender, Miss Abigail and Lily, to name but a few. And the vicar, though he had been on the verge of retiring, and moving away. He had given her his new telephone number, asked her to keep in touch. And probably knowing that she wouldn't.

'Is this a good spot? We can watch the swans, yes?'

Without waiting for her answer, Katharina flopped down on the grass by the lake and got out two sticky buns covered in icing sugar. Ellen, surprised to find that they had walked as far as Hyde Park, took one (knowing it would hurt Katharina's feelings if she didn't) and devoured it within seconds. She had not realised until now how hungry she was. Licking her fingers, she said, 'Thank you. That was actually really good, and just what I needed.'

Without a word, Katharina handed her the second bun. She ate that, too, though more slowly. Then suddenly, halfway through the bun, she burst into tears.

'What will I do without you? What will I do up there, all on my own?'

Katharina put an arm around her shoulder and waited until the sobbing had ceased a little, then she began to sing. All the way through in German, and then in Italian, where Ellen joined in, just as her friend had known she would.

'O mia patra, si bella e perduta!'

Oh, my homeland, so beautiful and lost …

'But it is not lost, Ellen. Even if you don't think you are going to live there, you do not have to give it up. I'm sure you will find a way to keep Birchwood Park. Your homeland. And you know what? My flight is not until mid-July. Why don't we go up together the weekend after next? After the final concert. What do you think?'

'I think,' Ellen said and leaned against Katharina, 'you are a wonderful friend and I'm going to miss you terribly. And yes, please, let's go to Yorkshire together.'

CHAPTER 16

LILY HAD OFFERED to help Daisy pack a few things for Miss Lavender and take her to York, as Oliver had an appointment which he was unable to cancel. He would need the car, too, but had promised to pick her up later, so Lily would not have to stay in York and wait. Thankfully, Abi had volunteered to look after the little dog.

'I don't mind doing a bit of shopping on a quiet Monday morning in York,' Lily said as she pushed open the door to Miss Lavender's flat. 'And I don't open my shop until two on Mondays, so don't worry about that. Right, what's on her list?'

Unlike Daisy, Lily was not in the least bit shy about entering Miss Lavender's private rooms and opening cupboards and drawers. Daisy was glad she did not have to do this alone, even though she had been asked specifically "to bring the box". Whatever that box contained, it had to be very special.

The telephone rang as they were passing through the living room, and they were surprised to hear an answering machine kicking in. 'Fancy Miss Lavender having an answering machine! Will wonders never cease,' Lily remarked, sending Daisy, being as nervous as she was, into a fit of the giggles.

But they both stopped in their tracks when they heard a girl's voice saying, 'Good afternoon, Miss Lavender, it's Ellen. I just wanted to let you know that I'm coming up to Yorkshire with my German … sorry, *Austrian* friend next weekend. I hope you will be able to make time for a cup of tea. Katharina would dearly love to meet you, and also, there is something I would like to ask you. So … yes, I hope you are well, and I am very much looking forward to seeing you on Friday – probably late afternoon, depending on traffic. Goodbye.'

Lily raised her eyebrows. 'I didn't know they were friends. But then Miss Lavender never talks about private things, does she? Always keeps herself to herself. And by God, Ellen can do with a few good friends, no matter how old and eccentric! You know her story, don't you?'

Daisy nodded, and Lily, not one to waste time, began flinging things into an overnight bag she had brought with her. Daisy opened her mouth to say that perhaps they had better be a bit more careful, but Lily was busy packing and chatting.

'Did I tell you how I first came to meet Ellen? It was last year in October, when Joseph had had his accident – with the cows, you know. She was singing in the church when I walked past one day. And wow, *what* a voice! Quite exquisite. She sang the *Once In Royal David's City* solo in the Christmas Service, too. I've never heard anything like it. I'm sure she will be a great success on the opera stages of the world! Anyway, I thought she could not be older than seventeen or eighteen then; I was surprised to hear she was actually twenty-three, so not that much younger than myself! Well, I will be twenty-nine in September. Time flies, eh? How old are you, Daisy, if you don't mind me asking?'

'I don't, no. And I'm twenty-eight, too. My birthday is in November.—But Lily, shouldn't we stick to the list? Look, it says here … oh!'

Her eyes had caught sight of the box. It was sitting on the bed, with the lid open. Next to it lay an open journal, a scarf, a bundle of letters held together by frayed red ribbon, and a pretty little silver jewellery box.

'Oh. That looks old. And quite special. Did she ask you to bring that?'

Daisy nodded, slowly walking over to the bed. The things smelled old and musty, sending funny little shivers of excitement down her spine. Somehow she had the feeling that whatever was written in those letters and that journal would be of great significance. And what might be in the jewellery box? A ring from a deceased husband perhaps, or an old beau? Or a family signet ring that would reveal Miss Lavender's mysterious past? Even Daisy knew that Miss Lavender could not possibly have grown up here, in rural Yorkshire, not with that posh accent, and her ladylike demeanour. She was definitely from the south, or from London. And most definitely upper-class. Very upper-class. And yet she seemed happy enough running her little convenience store in sleepy little Bishops Bridge …

Daisy shook her head. It was a mystery.

'Wow. Okay. I don't know about you, but I am just dying to know what is in that box – and what is written in that journal! Never mind those letters … love letters, no doubt.' Lily shook her chestnut curls. 'This is so romantic! I wonder if she is going to let you read any of that … now don't look so surprised, Daisy Clifford-Jones, you know very well how fond dear old Lady Lavender is of you! If she is ever going to tell anyone about her past, that will be you. I am absolutely sure of it.'

Dear old Lady Lavender. Daisy's lips twitched. That was a lovely, and very fitting nickname. Lady Lavender … suddenly an image came to her mind, a very fleeting one. That very name in writing … where had she seen that? She could not for the life of her remember. Had it been written in some book? Her father's stud book perhaps? It could have been a horse, couldn't it? A racehorse could well have been registered with that name … No. She shook her head. It must have been somewhere else. Or I am mixing things up, which is more likely.

'What are you shaking your head for now? Come on, get your basket, and pop the stuff in. Carefully, of course. – Will you have time for lunch afterwards? We could grab a sandwich and sit by the river or go all posh and join the queue at Bettys.'

'If you are sure you can spare the time, then yes, that would be lovely. You have a shop to open; I only have a young dog to look after. And no, we will not leave without Miss Lavender's second-best cardigan, or the pleated teal skirt she wanted! You have only put underwear in that bag, and socks. What do you expect the poor lady to wear when I take her to the hospital café tomorrow?'

'Taking her to the café tomorrow, are you? Oh well, I suppose I'd better let you finish here then. You will be more careful, and stick to the list, too. I'll make sure all the windows are closed, in case it rains later. Which I hope it doesn't, because we want to go for an evening walk tonight, but you never know on the Moors!'

Daisy could not agree more. She was still amazed

at how fast the weather could change up here. But she, too, hoped it would stay dry tonight, as she was looking forward to their own evening stroll down the fields with Drifter. They had slipped into this routine so easily; it was already hard to imagine what life had been like without the little dog in it. She smiled fondly as she pictured the spaniel dashing down the field ahead of them, ears flapping, and barking happily. Then she zipped up the bag and sighed. If nothing else, a walk would stop her from brooding over things she could not change, and mysteries that were not hers to solve.

***

'I AM GLAD you found that jewellery box, too – I should have mentioned it, but it had slipped my memory … like so many things these days. Why, if it had not been for Drifter, I might never have remembered anything at all!'

Miss Lavender was sitting upright in her hospital bed, turning the little silver box in her hands. Slowly and softly, but with a visible tremor, her gnarled old fingers moved across the lid, almost as if caressing it. She did not open it though. She knew what was inside that box. For her, there was no hurry. Daisy, on the other hand, could not wait to find out. She knew better than to press the old lady though. Instead, she asked her if she remembered anything about the fall she had taken, or even when it had happened. She dreaded to think that poor Miss Lavender had been lying on the sofa for a whole night, or even longer.

Thankfully, she reassured Daisy that she hadn't. 'No, no. I was in the kitchen, making myself a cup of tea, and then I suddenly felt dizzy … I did not sleep much, I think, and I'm not sure I had any dinner last night.'

'You didn't sleep? And you did not have your dinner? Whyever not, dear Miss Lavender?'

'Now, now, my dear – don't fret. It won't do. If you pour us a nice cup of—oh. No Darjeeling. And no proper china cups either. Shame. I keep forgetting I'm in hospital.' She sighed wearily. 'How much longer did that wretched doctor say they would keep me here? Not all week, surely?'

Daisy smiled. 'We'll see. Now, why don't you tell me what you want me to do about the diary, or the letters – would you like me to leave you alone for a while, so you can read them? I can go to the cafeteria and come back in half an hour, if you like?'

'You haven't answered my question, girl. That won't do.'

'Don't scold your lovely young friend here, Mrs Lavender. She is not a doctor, and she will not decide when you can go home.'

They turned around to see the young doctor who had first seen Miss Lavender when she was admitted yesterday standing in the door, clipboard in hand, his face a rather endearing mixture of amusement and real concern.

'I have the results of your ECG here, and I'm afraid we will need to discuss them first before you make up your mind to go home and open your shop. I will take your pulse and temperature now, and then—'

'For one thing,' Miss Lavender cut in rather indignantly, 'it is *Miss* Lavender, not Mrs, as I am not married. And for another, I am an adult, not a child, and certainly no imbecile. You can talk to me all you like, but

I *will* go home just as soon as this headache has passed, and I can walk again without feeling wobbly. You cannot stop me.'

The doctor sighed. 'I hope I won't have to, Miss Lavender, to be honest. But I would much rather you listened to me, and see for yourself that you cannot simply go home and carry on as before. May I?' He indicated the chair next to her bed and sat down, looking at Miss Lavender's medical records. 'You are seventy-seven years old, Miss Lavender, and live on your own, in a flat above your shop in … Bishops Bridge. Is that right?'

Daisy put a hand to her mouth to stifle a gasp. Seventy-seven! Goodness, she thought. Oliver had been right to suggest she was closer to eighty. She should have retired *years ago*!

'Yes.'

'And you have no family nearby? Children, grandchildren … no?'

'Nobody. Except this young lady here. Who may or may not be family. We were about to find out when you walked in.'

'What??'

But Miss Lavender put a hand on Daisy's arm and shook her head, mouthing, *not now.* Though why she had said as much as she had, Daisy wanted to know. How were they supposed to get rid of the doctor now? He had to be nearly as intrigued as she was, judging by the look on his face. Only nearly, of course. Because it was not his family, but hers. It was not about him, it was about her – and Miss Lavender. The windmills of her restless mind had suddenly switched into overdrive, turning and turning.

... who may or not be family. We were about to find out ...

But how? She was no Lavender, her parents weren't, her grandparents hadn't been Lavenders ... she frowned. It did not make sense. How could they possibly be related?

'Are you alright, Miss? Would you like a glass of water?'

No, she wanted to scream. I just want to be alone with ... whoever Miss Lavender is. I want to know what she means by saying *we may or may not be* family. But she just shook her head. She really did not want to make things any more difficult for the poor doctor. Daisy thought he looked even more tired than yesterday. She hoped that not all his patients were as obstinate as Miss Lavender.

It was in that moment that Miss Lavender chose to tell the doctor, in her usual stern tone, 'I think Mrs Clifford-Jones and I would appreciate some privacy now. You can come back later and tell me what I can and cannot do. In an hour, perhaps?'

Clicking his pen a couple of times, the doctor finally put it away and got up with a weary sigh. A very weary sigh. 'Alright then. One hour.—Miss?' He motioned for Daisy to follow him outside.

When they were standing in the corridor outside Miss Lavender's room, he said, rather urgently, 'Please make sure you are still here when I come back. I might need an ally.'

Daisy smiled. 'Understood. And you have my word, I will not let her stay in her flat on her own, or open the shop for at least another two weeks. My husband and I will look after her, whether she is family or not. She is in our church. My husband is the vicar. Will that do?'

The doctor's face broke into a relieved smile. 'Very nicely, yes. Thank you, Miss.' Then he walked down the corridor, and Daisy hurried back into Miss Lavender's room. Thank God she was the only occupant for the time being. Briefly wondering if she had private health insurance, Daisy shrugged and thought that it mattered very little as long as they had their privacy, and their one hour, and that would have to do.

Meanwhile, Miss Lavender had produced the diary and was holding it out to Daisy. 'Now then. I am not sure I want to tell you the whole story – it is rather a long story, and quite a sad one, too –, but I thought perhaps you might want to read this. Because whatever questions you and I might have – and I can see you have a lot of questions, they are written all over your face – I believe you will find the answers in there. The letters I would like to keep to myself. They are not all Hugh's, anyway, and thus of no interest to you.'

Daisy hesitated.

'Go on then,' Miss Lavender urged gently, pressing the journal into Daisy's hand. 'Read, lass. I am taking a little nap. You can always ask me questions later, should you have any.'

And as Miss Lavender leaned back and closed her eyes, Daisy began to read.

CHAPTER 17

I could hear their raised voices even before I entered the house. Exchanging a meaningful glance with Summers, our long-suffering housekeeper, I tossed my riding gloves and crop onto the bench in the hall, removed my hat and shook out my curls with a sigh. After I had taken a deep breath, I walked towards the closed door of the drawing room, and knocked. There was no answer, but the shouting stopped, dropping down to an angry whispering. I was just about to open the door when it was practically flung into my face, and Mother stormed out. She was crying and holding a hand to her mouth, but otherwise ignored me as she ran past me and up the stairs. I could only shake my head. I knew she would lock herself into her room and cry for hours, then sleep until morning.

Tonight, I am sure, it will be only Father and me at the dinner table. It is on days like these that I wish I had a brother or sister. Someone to share this burden with – the crumbling, and now fast failing marriage of my parents. Alas, there is only me.

I know my parents argue – I can hear them almost every day. And even though they think I don't know why, of course I do: it's because Father cannot keep his hands off other women. He even flirts with the wives of their dinner guests, I swear he does! Quite openly, too. And I am not at all sure everybody ends up in their own beds afterwards. At the rate he is going, I must have dozens of half-brothers and -sisters out there! And no, I don't think this is funny. Not at all.

Mother knows, of course. She probably always knew, right from the start. Though why she has chosen to turn a blind eye on his numerous dalliances over the years, I'll never understand.

Otherwise, I am my parents' only child, and – my father's words! – the "apple of their eye". That would not be so bad, if I didn't know that they are hoping for me to get married rather sooner than later, preferably to a wealthy man, so he can bring more money into the family. Ha! As if we don't have enough of that. If there is one thing we have in abundance, it's money. It can't buy you happiness though, can it? Of which we have daily proof here. I think Mother is depressed. I also think she drinks too much, and I can almost understand her. Almost. I still wish she wouldn't.

My Grandmama Veronica, who is a wonderfully eccentric lady and lives all by herself in a villa in the South of France, also suffers from depression (for some reason this is a well-known fact), but she doesn't drink. She is an artist and paints the most beautiful watercolours. Sadly, we do not see Grandmama often, as she does not get on with Father, and hates England, claiming it always rains here (it probably comes from her having grown up in India, though I forget why). Mother sometimes goes by herself. She took me last year, and we had the most fantastic time, collecting shells on the beach, eating exotic foods like escargots and cuisses de grenouilles, and admiring the sunset from the terrace.

If I ever run away, I'll make for France. I'm sure Grandmama will have me. Maybe Mother should come, too?

Just then I heard the door of Mother's bedroom slam shut, and suddenly everything was very quiet. Thinking I would rather not see Father now, I made for my own bedroom, whistling to Drifter to follow me. We could have a bath together, Drifter and me, if only to annoy Mother. She says dogs do not belong in bathrooms. If she knew he sleeps in my bed every night, she would have a fit.

Same day, after dinner:

Of course it was only Father and me. The atmosphere was frosty, to say the least. I refused to do small talk, and I was in no mood to listen to the lame excuses he was trying to make for Mother either. Headache, my foot! If she didn't a) cry so much and b) drink so much, she wouldn't have headaches. She should go riding, like me, or walk Father's dogs. They are all fat and lazy Labradors. Not nearly as cute as my darling Drifter.

When I went upstairs (I did not stay for coffee), I suddenly had an idea, and I could have slapped myself for not having thought of it sooner. Hugh! I'll go and live with Hugh, not with Grandmama! For as much as I love her, I do not see myself actually living in France, thousands of miles away from everything I hold so dear – namely my dog, my horse, and Hugh.

I met him at the Great Yorkshire Show last summer, where he presented his father's cows. I watched his prize bull, Tristan, win, and smiled at him (Hugh, not the bull) when he walked past me. He stopped, and we got chatting, and then I recklessly accepted his invitation for an ice-cream! (By the way, I had never tasted such delicious ice-cream! Hugh said it was locally made, and he could cycle to the farm that made the ice-cream, making me want to live there, too –but not only for the ice-cream!)

I knew at that moment that we were destined to be together. I can't explain why, I just knew. Not only is Hugh handsome and strong and can lead an eight hundred pound bull around the ring with one hand, but he is also generous and ever so kind. He is also terribly shy, as I was about to find out, because whatever I suggested we do afterwards, he just smiled and said, 'as you wish'. He is at least six foot five, and his arms are covered in freckles and scratches ("been in them gooseberries for me mum"). He has strawberry-blond hair and eyes the colour of green glass. Oh, how I love to gaze up into those eyes!

We met again the next day, and went for a walk – it was so romantic! Unfortunately, we bumped into Mother on the way back, and do you know what she did? She took me by the elbow – and rather roughly, too! – and hissed, just as soon as we were out of earshot (whose ears, I wonder! Hugh's? Or the lady's who sold us the coffee I would not get to drink now),"What do you think you are doing? Parading around the show ground with a farm boy! What will people think?"

To which I retorted, "That I am a very lucky girl to have caught the eye of such a handsome young man?"

Mother's hand came down hard and fast, and left a burning red mark on my left cheek. The shame! It is still with me today (a whole year later!) and will always be for as long as I live. Going to France with Mother? I don't think so. I'd much rather go to Yorkshire and stay with Hugh. He will marry me, and we will have a family of our own, raising our children with love and kindness, and not with money and pretence.

August 28th, 1962

Mother and Father summoned me to the library after dinner. If I am summoned to the library, I always know it's something serious. Like when Father told me that they would not have any more children, and that I was the sole heiress of Hammond Hall, and did I know what that meant?

Daisy put the diary down. Her hands were shaking. The sole heiress of Hammond Hall???

I must have got that wrong, she thought, and looked at the page again. But there it was, clearly written in ink, and leaving her in no doubt at all:

I was the sole heiress of Hammond Hall, and did I know what that meant?

Whether the young Lavinia had known, Daisy could not tell, but *she* most certainly had had no idea this was coming when she had begun to read the diary!

I was ten years old then and not the rebel that I am now, so I looked up at him and said, very solemnly, "A great honour, and a great responsibility."

It was the right answer, and to this day I remember the relief that flooded through me when he smiled and said, "Good girl," and kissed the top of my head. "Now run along." I smiled, too, and ran along. What a silly little goose I was! Little did I know what was to come ...

Daisy shook her head as the words blurred in front of her eyes. Little did I know indeed ...

'Impossible!' she whispered, still staring at the yellowed pages of the journal in her lap. Her mouth felt dry, and she reached for the water bottle she always kept in her handbag. When she had taken a few sips, she turned to Miss Lavender, desperate for answers. Answers the diary might or might not give her. At any rate, she needed to hear it from her. Reading wouldn't do, she knew it wouldn't.

'Miss Lavender? How come you—' But Miss Lavender's even breathing told her the old lady must have fallen asleep. There was nothing else for it – if she wanted those answers, she would have to read on. So she did.

They are going to get divorced. Mother says she cannot stay another week, and is already busy packing trunks to go to France and live with Grandmama. She did not ask if I wanted to come. I don't. I want to go to Yorkshire, and live with Hugh, don't I? And if I had not had those two glasses of wine, I would leave right now! But I don't like driving in the dark, and I need the night to think about what I'm going to pack. It won't be much. I cannot possibly turn up on the Crawfords' doorstep with half the amount of luggage Mother is going to carry to France with her, even if Grandmama is expecting her. For all I know I might not even be welcome, although Hugh only wrote in his last letter that I was.

"You will always find a refuge here, and a home, if needs be."

That was what he promised me, and I shall have to hold him to that. There is no time to write, and ask him to prepare his parents. If Mother cannot stay for another week, I am sure I cannot stay for another day!

Father has a mistress – there is nothing new in that, but this time it is different. This time she is my age, and pregnant. He says he loves her. It's ridiculous of course, but there you go. Grown-ups are so strange, they are not grown-up at all. Or Father isn't, anyway. He must have lost his mind to want to divorce Mother, kick her out, and allow a girl who is barely eighteen to be mistress of Hammond Hall, taking Mother's place! Nobody can ever take her place. For all her faults, she is a wonderful lady, a perfect hostess, and the dearest mother I could have wished for. Sadly, she has become so wrapped up in her depression, that she seems to have lost sight of me altogether. They both have. That is why I'm leaving.

I left the library and went up to my room, and then I sat there for a long time, thinking. I will leave first thing in the morning, just before sunrise. The question is, how will I get to the station? It's raining, and it's two and a half miles to Newmarket. Should I take the Morgan and leave it there? Or better still, drive it up to Yorkshire? That would serve Father right. He loves this car! It's his favourite. He has quite a collection. I might take the little MG ... I could always sell it, should I need the money. I'm not even sure how much money there is in my account. I'll have to find myself a job if I don't want to sponge off Hugh's family for ever. (And I most certainly don't!)

Drifter is looking up at me with his innocent caramel eyes. He doesn't have a clue what's going on! Well, I don't have much of a clue either. But I know I am not going to stay here, and I bend down to Drifter and take his sweet little doggy face in my hands and say,

"We'll get away from here, Drifter. You and me. Tomorrow. I'll wake you quite early, and then we'll be on our way. What do you think, would you like to live on a farm in Yorkshire?"

Daisy put the diary down, stunned. How could this be possible? Lavinia Lavender, the sole heiress of Hammond Hall! Had she really run away? Had she never inherited after all? Though she was dying to know, Daisy knew she would have to wait because her elderly friend – or cousin, or great-aunt, or whoever she was – was still asleep.

'I'd better go,' she whispered, reluctantly getting to her feet. There were so many questions to ask, so many answers yet to be found …

'I'll be back tomorrow though, I promise. First thing.'

She was just wondering what to do about the diary and the jewellery box, when the door was pushed open. A nurse came bustling in, bearing a plastic tray. 'Lunchtime!' she chirped.

Daisy felt Miss Lavender's hand grasping hers. 'Take the jewellery box with you, Daisy girl, and the diary. For safekeeping,' she whispered. 'You can read on, if you like, I don't mind. And yes, please come back tomorrow, if you can.'

'I will,' Daisy whispered back, although why they even bothered to whisper, she did not know. It was not as if the nurse had any intention of letting Miss Lavender get away without her lunch.

'There you go, Mrs Lavender!' An encouraging smile on her red and tired looking face, the nurse placed a plastic tray on the bedside table. 'It's poached salmon today, mashed potatoes, and spring greens.'

Miss Lavender groaned. And then she and Daisy said, in unison, 'It's *Miss* Lavender.'

***

ALL THE WAY back home, Daisy stared out of the window, wondering how on earth that had happened. How had she ended up not only reading Miss Lavender's diaries and learning about her connection with Hammond Hall, but actually being related to her!

'Just one question, please, before I go,' she had said, slipping both the diary and the jewellery box into her handbag. 'And then I'll leave you alone, I promise. Did you – did you know all along? I mean, ever since I came to Bishops Bridge?'

Miss Lavender had pursed her lips. 'I didn't, no. But I heard Lily mention something about the "posh stud farm" you had grown up on in Suffolk at Jessie's café, shortly after you and Abigail had rescued Ellen Maverick's horses. I had come in to get my quiche for dinner that day. You know how I love Jessie's quiches …' She had lifted the lid from her plate, only to put it back again with a weary sigh. 'Anyway, when Lily said Suffolk, I pricked my ears. But then more customers came in, and they did not continue their conversation. It's been on my mind ever since, and I was meaning to ask you … but it was not until you found the dog that everything suddenly seemed to fall into place. And now here we are! A mystery solved.'

She had beamed at her then, as if she had just found the biggest of all Easter eggs in the garden, but Daisy had just stared at her open-mouthed, unable to take in what she had just heard. It was too much, simply too much!

And now here we are …

Well, Daisy thought. That was one way of putting it. Here we are indeed …

The question was, *who* are we? Who was Miss Lavender to her – an aunt? A cousin once, twice, thrice removed perhaps? A great-aunt of sorts?

There hadn't been time to find out about that, as Oliver had texted her to say he was waiting at the entrance and had not found a space in the car park, so would she mind coming down at once?

So Daisy had kissed Miss Lavender goodbye, hardly able to hold back the tears. 'I'll come back tomorrow, and then we will talk about it. And hopefully figure out how we are related. But oh, I am so glad I found you!'

'Now, now,' the old lady had tutted, 'don't cry. There is nothing to cry about – not now. There was a time …' She had shaken her head. 'It doesn't matter now. It's years and years ago. Almost forgotten.'

Almost, but not quite, Daisy felt sure, as she hugged Drifter to her chest and kissed his head.

'Do you want me to stop at Sutton Bank?' Oliver's voice cut through her thoughts. 'There is a signpost to the visitor centre. We could have a coffee and enjoy England's finest view, as described by James Herriot? I am told they do decent cakes, too.'

But Daisy shook her head. She could not wait to get home and go on reading. Find out what had happened next …

Had the young Lavinia really gone to Yorkshire to marry that farm boy? But she had said she was not married. Did that mean she never had been married in the first place? What had gone wrong?

CHAPTER 18

THE BRIDGE CAFÉ was not open on Mondays, but Jessie and Lily were sitting on the steps of the veranda talking about Miss Lavender's accident, and how odd Daisy's text had read that she had sent to Lily from the hospital.

'You don't have to wait for me, Oliver is going to pick me up. I'll see you later on the farm.' Lily put her phone on the floor next to her and shook her head. 'Not a word about how Miss Lavender is, or when she is going to be released, or what was in that box—'

'Well, she might not know *that* herself, if it is something to do with Miss Lavender's past – and the way you describe that musty old box, it looks very much like it is. For all that she has taken so quickly to our Daisy, it doesn't mean she will share her innermost secrets with her, does it? Especially when she has kept them for so long.'

Lily shook her head. 'No, I suppose she wouldn't … oh, look, there are the Colbecks! They have probably tried in vain to do their usual Monday morning shopping, and been wondering what on earth has happened to Miss Lavender … hello, Mrs Colbeck! Hello, Mr Colbeck!' she called, and the couple waved back as they came over now, a little girl dancing at Mrs Colbeck's hand.

'Hello, Lily, hello, Jessie. This is our youngest

granddaughter, Jubilee. She's staying with us for a few days while her mum is in hospital. Nothing serious! Just getting rid of some varicose veins,' Mrs Colbeck explained in a low voice when she saw the concern on their faces. 'But tell me, what's happened to Miss Lavender? Is she ill?'

Jessie pulled a bag of salted caramel toffees out of her bag and offered the sweets to Jubilee, but the little girl shook her head, and went to hide behind her granny's legs.

'She had a fall yesterday morning,' Jessie explained. 'Oliver and Daisy found her and took her to the hospital in York. Daisy has been to see her today, but she did not have any news, except that she has suffered concussion and broken her wrist – or elbow or something. Right hand though, I believe. So, it looks like the shop is going to remain closed for a while.'

'Oh well,' Mr Colbeck said, 'the main thing is it's nothing too serious. A broken wrist can be fixed, and she'll get over the concussion in no time, and do her maths like she used to. I have never seen anyone doing their sums so quickly in their head, and always getting it right, too!'

They all laughed fondly as they envisioned the old lady standing behind her counter, her lips moving quickly as she added up the various prices in her head. Jessie nodded. 'Yes, that's probably true.—Oh, there's the school bus coming! Now I know someone who will have no problem eating all of the sweets in this bag, and without even bothering to share, either.'

A minute later, Louisa May stepped off the bus and came running towards them, an exercise book in her hand. 'Mum, mum, guess what – I got an A for my English essay! Excellent work, Mr Bradshaw said. – Oh, hello, Mr Colbeck! Celine says you are a hero!'

Everyone looked at Mr Colbeck in surprise, including his granddaughter, who was peeping out from behind her granny's back. 'Why are you a hero, grandad? What have you done?'

'Nothing, sweetheart. I just took an old lady home, that's all. She had got lost in the dark, and I took her home.'

Louisa May rolled her eyes as she pulled out a can of pop out of her rucksack. 'Yes, but she was wearing her *nightie*, Mum, and had been wandering around the village for an hour or so. Celine's Nana from Orchard Farm – the one who believes she sees fairies dancing on the water on full moon nights?'

Jessie frowned. 'Orchard Farm? But that's in Thorgill! That's … a good mile from here! How did she even get here, and at night, too?'

Mrs Colbeck shrugged. 'Well, she walked, of course, even if she may not have been a hundred per cent awake. Philip says he was passing the farm at around eleven on Saturday night, on his way home from York. He had his annual meeting with his former colleagues from the Police Force in York, you know. The wives are invited, too, but most of us never go. It's men talking crime … anyway, so Philip was passing the farm, and came into the village, and there she was, wandering about in her nightie.'

Jessie shook her head, confused. 'Celine's parents always keep an eye on her, especially when there is a full moon. They know she is prone to go out then and look for the fairies … how did she escape in the first place?

They are such a caring family, always looking out for each other. I really don't understand.'

'Well,' Mr Colbeck said, eager to close the subject, 'I found her, and that's the main thing, isn't it? She did not come to any harm, and the Barrys were more than relieved when I brought her home. Turned out Mr Barry was watching the football, and his wife had fallen asleep. They had only just noticed that Nana had disappeared, and were searching the garden when I came.'

'That woman! Honestly!' Lousia May opened her can and took a thirsty swig. 'She is so unbelievably sweet, but boy, she is mad! Literally *away with the fairies*. Anyway,' she said, turning her sweetest teenage girl smile on Mr Colbeck, 'Celine says you're a hero, Mr Colbeck, for finding her and bringing her home. – How did you persuade her to get into the car with you, by the way?'

Now Mr Colbeck looked sheepish. 'Oh, you know … I didn't stop to ask her. I just took her by the arm and sat her in the passenger seat and closed the door, then locked it. Policeman's habit, I suppose. No harm done, eh?'

His wife tutted but looked at him adoringly. 'You are incorrigible, Philip! You will never stop helping people and rescuing them if you can. I'm just glad you're retired now, and we live in peaceful little Bishops Bridge where nothing ever happens. We should be quite safe here.' Tugging at his shirtsleeve, she said, 'Come on then, my hero, let's go home. I am planning Toad in the Hole for tea, and Jubilee has promised to find the eggs for the batter. Let's hope the hens have been good.'

'Aren't they always good?' little Jubilee asked as they all strolled across the bridge hand in hand, waving goodbye to Lily, Jessie, and Louisa May.

'Well,' Jessie said and rose to her feet, 'there goes the village hero. And now let me have a look at that essay, Louisa May. I am so proud of you! How about we have a pizza tonight and watch a film on Netflix, just the two of us?'

***

IN THEIR COSY little holiday cottage at Fern Hill Farm, Daisy and Oliver were sitting on what Oliver referred to as 'the dreaded sofa' because of its reclining seats tempting him to fall asleep every time he sat on this particular piece of furniture. They were enjoying a late coffee and Oliver's favourite treats, Thornton's caramel shortbread squares. He insisted Daisy kept the box well hidden, or he would eat them all at once.

'Oliver?'

'Yes?'

'Can I ask you something?'

'Anything. Unless it's do you want another caramel square, because you know I do – and you know I shouldn't!'

She smiled. 'You can eat them all if you like. I don't mind. My question was … um … do I look at all like Miss Lavender?'

He put his chocolate down and turned to her, his brow furrowed. 'Like Miss Lavender? Why?'

'Because I have been wondering … that is, I have found out … you see, I have every reason to believe we are related. I mean – we *are* related, we must be, it's just that I still can't get my head around it …' Lifting up her face, she looked at her husband and said, with a helpless little shrug, 'I still don't understand *how*, you know? She could be a great-aunt, or a distant cousin or something ...'

Now she had his full attention. 'What makes you think that? Has she confided in you and told you something about her past? If so, you would be the first, from what I gather. She never talks about herself, and certainly not about her mysterious past. Everyone in Bishops Bridge knows and respects that.'

'Oh? Then how do you know her past is mysterious?'

'Well,' he said, carefully placing his hands on his thighs. 'If nobody knows anything about it, it's a mystery, right? And nobody does, so there you are. The only thing some people – a very few old people, like your Mr Barnsley, that is – know is that she came here in the early nineteen seventies and bought the shop, and the house. She was not born and bred here. Not in Rosedale, not in Yorkshire. I think we are all agreed that her accent is definitely upper class, and not from around here. So, in answer to your question, yes, I can easily imagine that she is the missing link in your puzzle.'

Now it was Daisy's turn to frown. 'Why would there be a missing link in my puzzle? What puzzle, anyway?'

'Oh, I don't know. Something is missing ... in your family history. I think I heard your brother Simon say something like that once. How he never understood how your grandfather ever came to be master of Hammond Hall when he had not even grown up there, or anywhere near. When he wasn't even ... and then I think he said a name, but I didn't hear him because somebody else was laughing loudly. I think it was at our wedding reception. I had completely forgotten about that. Funny, eh? But whatever that name was, I think if it had been *Lavender*, I would remember that.'

Daisy nodded, dumbstruck. Funny. That was one way of putting it. Why had nobody ever told her? Why hadn't she ever asked? – Because she was a spoilt, privileged, ignorant girl, that's why. Because she had taken growing up at Hammond Hall for granted. They all had, hadn't they? Never knowing how much it must have cost somebody else, many years before they were even born … a young Lavinia, namely. The rightful heiress of Hammond Hall.

'Are you going to tell me then? About your mysterious link to Miss Lavender?'

'Sorry?'

Oliver smiled. 'You were miles away just now! You were going to tell me about how you were related with Miss Lavender – or were you not?'

'Um … I think I'll wait until tomorrow. She has entrusted me with her old diary, and I would like to read it first, if you don't mind.'

His eyes widened. This was getting better and better. 'Her old diary??'

'Yes,' Daisy said rather matter-of-factly. 'The one she kept when she was twenty. That was in 1962. But so far, all I know is that she grew up at Hammond Hall, and ran away to marry a farmer in Yorkshire. Only I think she never did. Marry him, I mean. I suppose I'll find out more when I read this.' She took the diary out of her handbag and showed it to Oliver.

'Wow,' he said and shook his head, amazed. 'Wow. Of course you want to read this, if she asked you to. What a great proof of her trust though! She must be very fond of you, whether you are family or not. Seems like you are though, hmm, if she grew up at Hammond Hall?'

She smiled. 'Yes.'

He kissed her cheek and rose to his feet. 'Well, I'll leave you to it then. Do you want another coffee?'

'Yes, please. And Oliver?'

'Yes?'

'I love you.'

***

Miss Lavender was dreaming she was back at Hammond Hall, crouching down beside her dog.

Would you like to live on a farm in Yorkshire?

It had sounded like the most wonderful adventure! She had been so sure that everything would work out alright, if only she could get to Yorkshire. If only she could get to Hugh. And it *would* have worked out, she was sure even today. If only the accident had not occurred, tearing her dreams apart and smashing all her hopes …

When she had first arrived at Low Farm near the picturesque Yorkshire village of Thornton-le-Dale on that rainy day in late August, she had almost believed she had come home. Soaked to the skin after a twenty-minute walk through the pouring rain (there was a bus stop in the village, but the farm was a good mile up the road), with only her carpet bag and her little dog, she had stood on the doorstep, waiting for someone to hear her tentative knock. The moment the door was opened, and she saw Hugh's mum, all rosy-cheeked and laughing blue eyes, she knew everything was going to be alright. She was going to be alright.

'Oh, you poor lass! Come in! And you, little chap,' she

had said to the dog. 'You are very welcome, both of you. We were just going to have our tea, if you want to wash your hands, you can join us if you like. – Hugh! There is a young lady come to see you. She has brought her dog with her, and a suitcase.'

Martha Crawford had been everything her mother could not be: generous, kind, and blissfully ignorant of the so-called 'rules of society', which only applied to the upper class, anyway, and not to simple folks like Hugh and his parents. She had a great sense of humour, too, and talked non-stop. At first it had been hard to understand the dialect, but after a while Lavinia had got used to it. Although Mrs Crawford had insisted she let her parents know where she was, she had not tried to persuade her to go home. Instead, she had told her nosy neighbours that Lavinia was "a distant cousin of Hugh's who had been sent to live with them because of her fragile constitution", claiming the fresh Yorkshire air would do her good.

And it had. After only a few short weeks, Lavinia had settled in so well, and made herself useful by helping Mrs Crawford with milking, butter and cheese making, and any household chores she had never had to bother about while living at Hammond Hall. Here, she did not mind the work in the least. Soon, she and Mrs Crawford (or Martha, as she was to call her) had formed a strong bond between them, a bond that gave Hugh every hope that his mother might approve of his intention to marry Lavinia. But then her life had been turned upside down once more, in the cruellest imaginable way …

'You'd better go home, lass. I'm sure your father and mother will forgive you the moment they see you, and they will come to love the little bairn, too, once they get over the

shock. The sooner you go, the easier it will be. You have a whole life before you! You don't want to live with me and my sister in a tiny cottage in Burton-upon-Trent and be miserable. You are young, and you will be happy again, in time. God bless you, lass.'

But what about your grandson, Lavinia had wanted to cry, or granddaughter? Don't you want to see him, or her, grow up?

She had been too stunned to ask though, too stunned to say anything at all. Instead, she had thrown herself into the older woman's arms, buried her face in her ample bosom, and cried …

A single tear was finding its way down her cheek now, as she woke up in the still darkness of the hospital room. Feeling the wet sensation on her skin, Miss Lavender put up a hand and laid it against her cheek, as if to make sure she was not imagining things. She wasn't. The tears were real; they felt hot and wet on her skin as they ran down her cheeks, and there were more to come. Lots more. The floodgates had been opened, and there was no holding back now: For the first time in over fifty-five years, Miss Lavender was crying.

CHAPTER 19

Daisy read all night, rereading a few of the entries to make sure she had got it right. She had told Oliver to go to sleep hours ago, for he had several appointments the next day, while she was only going to go into York to see Miss Lavender.

'I can leave Drifter with Lily, and do the shopping on the way back,' she had said, looking up from the diary in her lap. 'We need quite a few things, and I want to get Miss Lavender some nice juice she can drink while she is in hospital. I know she likes Appletizer, so I'll get her a few bottles. Is there anything you want in particular? Except a new packet of those caramel shortbread squares?'

'Don't tempt me! But yes, please. And if you go via Helmsley, you can get us a few pies for tea. I know Abi and Lily love Hunter's pies, too, so maybe get a few more?'

'Yes, I can do that. It's the perfect excuse to stop for an ice-cream, too. Now then, I want to get on with this – kiss goodnight?'

Oliver laughed. '*Now then*! You, my dear Daisy, are turning into a proper Yorkshire Lass, see if you don't! Kiss goodnight indeed. Come on, Drifter, Mummy wants to read Auntie Lavinia's diary.'

After a while, Drifter came pitter-pattering back into

the living room though, hoping to be allowed on the sofa. And so here they were now, the dog curled up in her lap, and she holding Miss Lavender's diary against the light, open at the page where she had stopped reading that afternoon. The date was the 13th of November 1962.

She stared at the first sentence, written in large, bold letters, almost like a headline. It certainly was some news, and of the sort she had not expected. Or not from Miss Lavender, in any case. But there it was, in the same lady's own handwriting:

I AM PREGNANT!

Silly, silly me. What a mess! I am not blaming Hugh, though. Why should I? I knew what I was doing. It was me who seduced him, not the other way round. I wanted him so much the night we came back from the dance at the village hall ... he asked me at least a hundred times if I was sure, and every time he asked, I laughed and said yes. A hundred times yes ... and I'm not sorry either. Not one bit! Hugh says he will marry me, and that's that. We told his parents, of course, and Martha said I would have to tell Father and Mother. I didn't want to at first, but Martha insisted they had a right to know. Well, I'm not sure about that, but I wrote Mother a letter, anyway, and told her she was going to be a grandmother. She is in France now, so I felt it safe to give her my address, knowing she would not speak to Father. I also know they do not really care where I am, even if Martha thinks otherwise. She probably can't imagine what it is like to disown your only child – I am sure they would never do that to Hugh! They may have been shocked to hear our news, but they did not chase us away. They did not even chase me away, and they would have had every right to do so. Anyway, I wrote to Mother – duty done! – and I am still waiting for her reply. I have a feeling I won't get any. I will not bother writing to Father now, or even humiliate myself by calling Hammond Hall. I have had enough. If I never see the place again, then so be it.

Darling Hugh went straight to York to buy me a ring. It's a very simple ring but still, it must have cost him a fortune. Maybe his mother slipped him some money, I don't know. She does love him so very much. She says she only wants to see him happy – why can't my own mother be like that? Hugh Senior does not say much, but then he is not a man of many words.

We are to get married the day before Christmas. I have always dreamed of a winter wedding! If it snows we can put the ponies in front of the sleigh and ride to church in it. Oh, I am so happy! And I will work very hard to make up for this. I promised them I would. We will convert the barn into a snug little home, and be quite happy there. Just Hugh, me, Baby, and Drifter. And all the other children to come, of course. I want five, and Hugh says he does not mind. One day he will take over the farm, and then perhaps his parents will move into the new house, which is now the barn. They are such lovely, kind, and generous people! I am so glad I came here, even if I did not mean to get pregnant and hurry things along like this. But we were always going to stay together, and get married eventually, Hugh says, so that's alright. He is happy. I am happy. I have a feeling his mum is happier than she lets on, and his father will come round. And my parents can get lost for all I care. They will never know their grandchild now, but that is not my fault, is it? Nor is it my loss but theirs.

I have a job in the village shop now, which is fun. I only work in the mornings, three hours every day Monday to Friday, with most Saturdays off. If Mother knew I worked in a shop, she would have a fit! Good thing she doesn't then.

I must go, there is work to do. There always is here, thank God! I can milk a cow, and make butter, and Martha says my parkin is just as good as hers now (Hugh secretly thinks it is better, but he wouldn't tell her so as not to hurt her feelings. They really are the nicest family I have ever known, and I feel privileged to be a part of it when we are married!). Anyway, got to run now, cows won't wait!

Daisy put down the journal and gazed across the moonlit field. She had a feeling Lavinia's story would not come with a happy ending, for all that she had seemed so excited when she had written about her pregnancy, and the life she thought she was going to have on the farm near Thornton-le-Dale. She would not have come to Bishops Bridge, would she, if things had worked out the way she had hoped they would?

Helping herself to another caramel square, Daisy picked up the journal again and read on.

Saturday 25th November

We had a little party tonight to announce our engagement. It was just a few neighbours who came, and Hugh's best friend from school, who is also the vicar. He is going to marry us. His wife, Dora, didn't come, because she had to stay with their children. They have two girls, aged three and five. Oh, I hope I am going to have a girl! On second thoughts, I don't really care. We are going to have more children when we are married and settled in our own home. Hugh has already made a start on that barn conversion with his dad and grandpa. I know his grandpa is secretly making a cradle for us, I heard his grandma telling Martha about it in the kitchen when they were making mint pasties this morning. Now I know they are happy for us, too, I do not mind my own parents' lack of interest so much. At least, I'm telling myself I don't.

'Of course you did,' Daisy whispered, wiping her cheek with the back of her hand, 'of course you did …'

Sunday, 4 December

God, how time flies! Is it really December already? There is still so much to do, and it's only three weeks until the wedding now. We had a practice walk down the aisle today after service. Carl is a kind man, and for all that he is a vicar, he is surprisingly modern in his views. He knows I am expecting but he says as long as we get married it's alright. His wife Dora is the prettiest woman I have ever seen, and their little girls are absolutely adorable! I think Dora and I are going to be good friends. She asked me to come round for tea soon and said I could spend the night before the wedding at the vicarage, so Hugh would not see me before church. She will help me get into my dress, and do my hair, too. I said I would love to and that she was so kind, and she just laughed and said, nonsense, girls must stick together! Eloise and Florence are to be our flower girls. And as I have no other friends here yet, Dora will be my one and only bridesmaid! God, I'm getting giddy with excitement!!!

I wish Hugh's dad would give me away, but he says he can't, so I suppose we will have to walk together, Hugh and me, just like we are going to walk through life together from that day on.

I wrote to Mother once more, but again, no reply. I did not expect her to, but it still hurts. After all, it was Father who wrecked our family, and not me. Well, maybe getting pregnant was not the cleverest idea but still – oh well. Perhaps she will soften a little once we are married, and our baby is born. I will send her a card then, and a picture of her grandchild.

My friend Joan (who always keeps me up to date in terms of what my father is up to – not that I care that much, but I know she means well) wrote to me saying Father is not marrying the little minx after all because she has been having an affair with another man – who might well be the father of the child she pretends to be carrying, but Joan says she isn't even sure she is pregnant after all. She only said so because she wanted to trick Father into marrying her, and now that she has found herself an even richer man, who does not need to file for divorce first, she has had second thoughts. About Father, and about her pregnancy. If I were not so angry, I would laugh. Joan's father works on our estate, so I can trust she is telling me the truth and not just passing on idle gossip. I have had enough of gossip for the rest of my life! And Joan is not the gossiping kind, anyway (that would be her mother, who runs the post office!).

It doesn't matter, anyway. The only thing that matters is that I have found my home with the man I love, and we are getting married in three weeks! We are going to live on this farm with his Mum and Dad and Gran, and everything is going to be fine. What more can I ever ask for?

Daisy shook her head. What more indeed? This was like reading a film script – the setting was coming vividly to life before her, and she could just picture an excited young Lavinia getting ready for her wedding …

Only that wedding day had never come, had it?

Monday 20th December

It's been raining non-stop for two weeks now, the farmyard has turned into the Lake District, and the fields are so muddy even the faithful John Deere got stuck yesterday. Today it is cold though, freezing even, which does not make it better. I can't believe we should have such ghastly weather for our wedding! The men are out mending fences all day, I wonder when Hugh will ever find the time to buy himself a decent suit – never mind getting married! Martha says not to worry, it will all come out right. But I feel restless, and anxious all the same. Is it just the pregnancy? Wedding nerves? Both of it? I have a feeling of foreboding I cannot explain. Something's going to happen, I just know it, and it makes my stomach clench with anticipation.

Last night I dreamed Father had come to the farm to take me home. He dragged me by the hair all the way down to Suffolk – I swear my head hurt when I woke up this morning! I felt it all over, I did, and was relieved to find there was not a single hair missing. But I was drenched in sweat, and I rushed down the corridor to Hugh's room – well, of course he had got up already, as it was seven o'clock, so I dressed and got ready for work. Wednesday is to be my last day at the shop before Christmas. I'll go back then and try to put in as many hours as I can until baby arrives (in June – oh how glad I am we are to have a summer baby! Everything is easier in the summer, and we will have moved into our own little home by then. And as much as I love Hugh's parents, and Martha's wonderful farmhouse kitchen, I must say I can't wait!).

Hugh has just popped his head in and says he is going into town with his Dad on Wednesday, to buy a new tie and shirt, and perhaps a new pair of shoes. His old suit will have to do, there is no money for a new one. I don't mind. He will look handsome in whatever he wears!

Oh, but I didn't tell you about my dress! Dora and I went to York and bought the most beautiful dress! Dora says I cannot wear white now that I have spent a night with Hugh (oops! She blushed when she said that, and then we both had a fit of the giggles!), it would not be proper, and I can't have a veil either, but I don't mind. It's a pale blue silk gown with a high waist, so I will be very comfortable, and my belly won't show too much either. I can't wait for the little one to start kicking and moving around so I feel him, or her! But the doctor says it's too early yet, and to give it another month or so.

I will be a good mother. I will be a good wife. I will do my very best to make them all happy, most of all Hugh, and to prove myself worthy. If I never see my parents again, or my home, or my horse, then so be it. But this is my one chance at happiness, and I will not let it pass. And as soon as we are married, my life can begin at last.

Daisy turned the page, but found it was blank. As was the next one. And the one after that. Frowning, she turned and turned page after page, right to the end. But there were no more entries – they stopped right there, on 20th December 1962.

***

MISS LAVENDER WAS sitting in a chair by the window when Daisy came in. She was wearing her own clothes today, and was tapping her foot impatiently against the leg of the table.

'Oh, thank God you are here. Please, can we go outside? I can't stand this smell!'

Daisy stopped in her tracks. Miss Lavender had not even bothered to say *good afternoon*. That had to be a first!

'I'm not sure you should go outside … hadn't we better ask the nurse?'

But Miss Lavender shook her head. 'Absolutely not. I am determined to sit outside in the sun, and no one is going to stop me.'

Daisy sighed. 'I don't want you to get into trouble, Miss Lavender, which would only result in you having to stay longer. Let me check with a nurse first, please.'

'Hm. Alright then, you tell them.'

'*Ask*, not tell. Wait here.'

Five minutes later, they were back in Miss Lavender's room, but they had opened the window and Daisy had pushed the table underneath it, so they could at least get some fresh air. She had also brought a tin of Abi's homemade shortbread. The nurse had brought tea, and left them to it, on the condition that Miss Lavender would go "straight back to bed" after tea.

'So,' Miss Lavender began, 'you have read the diary?'

'I have, yes. But – it ended quite suddenly. On the day before the wedding. There,' Daisy took a deep breath before she lifted her eyes to meet Miss Lavender's. 'There never was a wedding though, was there?'

Slowly, Miss Lavender shook her head.

Daisy bit her lip, waiting for her to speak, and explain what had happened. She did not have to wait long.

'He died, you know. On that day. His father, too. There was an accident … the tractor had got stuck in the frozen mud, and when they tried to get it out, it turned over and …' Her voice broke, and Daisy handed her a tissue, too shocked to say anything. And what could she have said? I'm sorry? Somehow, that did not seem enough, not even after so many years.

Miss Lavender took the tissue, dried her eyes, and went on hurriedly, clearly wanting to get it over with. 'So they both died, and his mother went to live with her sister in Staffordshire, and I stayed with Dora and her husband until the baby was born.'

Tears shimmering in her own eyes, Daisy held her breath as she waited for Miss Lavender to go on. She didn't though. She just sat there, holding the little silver jewellery box, stroking gently over the intricate *L* on the lid with her gnarled fingers, her eyes closed.

L for Lavinia. Lady Lavinia even. Why had she changed her name? I must not forget to ask her, Daisy thought. But first, I want to know what is in that box.

Slowly, and with trembling fingers, Lavinia finally lifted the lid. She did not open her eyes to look at its contents though. Perhaps it was too painful. Instead, she held out the box to Daisy. Her hands were shaking so much, she nearly dropped the box, but Daisy caught it just in time.

She swallowed before she allowed herself to look inside. Nestled on a frayed burgundy velvet cushion, lay a simple, but beautiful gold ring.

And curled inside the ring, a lock of soft, black hair.

***

'Poor little Timothy only lived for a few days. He was too weak, they said. He just … didn't thrive.'

Oliver and Daisy were sitting on the patio behind their cottage, enjoying the last of the evening sunshine. She had told him everything, from beginning to end, and felt a lot better for it. Oliver was just as shocked as she was when he heard about young Lavinia's fate. He was not surprised, however, to learn that she really was related to the old lady, and that Lavinia's name was not Lavender but Featherstone. Or had been Featherstone, at any rate. She must have changed it at some point. And he was beginning to understand why.

'I knew it! I knew there had to be a connection. And you asked me yesterday, didn't you, whether you were at all alike? You *are*, actually,' he said, holding her at a little distance now as he looked at her. 'You have the same eyes. The cheekbones, too. Have you never noticed?'

Daisy shook her head. 'No, I didn't. Funny, isn't it? Now you mention it, I suppose you're right. Hers are a little bit faded, but … yes. Just as blue as mine.' And she leaned into him and sighed. 'I only hope I will never have to walk through such desperately dark valleys on my own. Poor Lavinia.'

'You will never have to walk alone,' he said, kissing her hair. 'Because you have me. And God. What a tragedy though,' he mused, 'to lose her fiancé, and then her baby, too. Nothing to remind her of him … nothing left of her old life at all. She never went back, did she?'

'No.' Daisy shook her head, biting her lip. Reaching for her wine glass, she twirled it in her hand as she spoke. 'She didn't. And you don't even know the rest of it … what happened next, I mean.'

'Oh dear. More bad news? Darker valleys, even?'

Daisy nodded, still twirling her glass. 'Only a few months later, when Lavinia had left the vicarage and her friends in Thornton-le-Dale, and gone to Thirsk, she received another terrible blow. A telegram arrived from France, telling her that her mother had died in a car crash. Can you imagine the horror? To lose the man you love, your baby, *and* your mother, within a few short months?'

Oliver shook his head, stunned.

'She never had the chance to see her mother again. She never had the chance to tell her she was sorry, or that she loved her. Neither had her mother. One moment was all it took … The accident happened on one of those famously steep, narrow, winding roads in the South of France. They said she might have been drunk, but … oh, what difference does it make?' Daisy put down her wine glass rather abruptly and turned to look at her husband, tears spilling down her cheeks. 'How can God have let that happen? Tell me?'

CHAPTER 20

WHEN ELLEN AND Katharina arrived early on Friday afternoon, hungry and tired after their long journey, they found Miss Lavender's shop closed. A notice had been put in the window which read, 'Closed due to illness – sorry for any inconvenience'.

'That is strange,' Ellen said when she returned to the car. 'But then I was wondering what had happened to her, as she never returned my phone call. Come on, let's ask Jessie. She will have put the notice in the window, and she will know what is wrong with Miss Lavender.' Pushing up the sleeve of her shirt, she glanced at her watch and said, 'Half past four – we might still get coffee and cake. Come on!'

Katharina, still drowsy with sleep (she had been asleep for most of the time, and Ellen had to sing nonstop just to stop herself from falling asleep behind the wheel), clambered out of the car and stretched luxuriously.

'Did you say cake?'

Ellen rolled her eyes and dragged her friend up the steps. 'Yes, cake, and you will love it, too! Jessie makes scrumptious cakes, and her cinnamon swirls are so delicious, you will want to eat them every day. Though I don't suppose there will be any left by now. Anyway, Miss

Lavender seems to have been taken ill, in case you did not hear me just now, and I hope Jessie will be able to tell me what's wrong with her. She always knows everything that's going on here. Here we are – hello, Jessie!'

Jessie looked up from cleaning her counter. 'Ellen! Oh, that is a lovely surprise! Have you come for the Midsommer Fest?'

Ellen shook her head. 'No, we just wanted to spend a couple of quiet days at Birchwood Park, and see Mum's horses. I hear they are in expert hands at Fern Hill Farm?'

'Oh, yes. She's a star, is Daisy. Brilliant with the horses. If you want to meet her, I'm sure you will find her at the farm. Unless she is out riding, or walking her new dog. She found him abandoned in the old churchyard of all places!—Oh,' Jessie remembered, 'or she might be visiting Miss Lavender of course. She had a fall on Sunday and was taken to hospital. From what I hear, I don't think it's anything serious, but they will keep her in for a couple of days. Daisy visits her nearly every day. For some reason they are very close …'

'If she goes to see her every day, I suppose they must be. I'm glad to hear she looks out for Miss Lavender – normally, she is the one who always looks out for others, isn't she? My mum told me how she had given Susanna Harper a job when really she didn't need an assistant, just to help her settle back in and earn some money. Her dad had just died, I think, and she came back to stay with her mum. You probably weren't here then; it must be fifteen years ago or so. And she helped Lily set up her bookshop, too, didn't she? She always does things like that. Not to mention the kindness she has shown to me after – after …' Her voice trailed away, and she stiffened visibly at the sight of a woman coming in from the outdoor seating area. It was Mrs Higgins.

But Mrs Higgins pretended not to see her. She just sailed past them with her head held high and left the shop without even bothering to say goodbye to Jessie – never mind acknowledging Ellen.

Katharina, noticing the sudden paleness that had come across Ellen's face, looked from Ellen to Jessie and frowned. 'What was that?'

'Do you mean *who* was that? That was Mrs Higgins, the most spiteful woman in Bishops Bridge. A horrible person, and an incurable gossip, I'm afraid. She behaved really badly at – at Ellen's dad's funeral. – I'm so sorry, Ellen. Do you need a glass of water?'

Ellen nodded, and Jessie turned to fetch a glass from the shelf and filled it with cold water. Katharina looked aghast. 'That's who she is, eh? Mrs Higgins. I have heard that name – and the story, too. It took me days to dry those tears, didn't it, Ellen?'

'Yes, but it's over now. She's gone. And I would really like to talk about something else if you don't mind.' Ellen drained her glass, but Jessie and Katharina saw how her hands were shaking and exchanged concerned glances.

'Right you are.' Jessie took the empty glass from her and gave her an encouraging smile. 'Now then, why don't you sit down, and I'll bring you two cappuccinos and – what was your favourite cake again, Ellen?'

'I would say your cinnamon swirls, but I don't suppose you have any left at this time of day?'

'I'm afraid not, no. Carrot cake? Sticky toffee flapjack?'

Katharina's face lit up. 'Both, please. And if you have chocolate cake, I'll have a slice of that, too.'

'I'll bring you a cake selection in a moment. All needs to go, anyway, as I will not be open tomorrow. Too much to do for the Midsommer Fest.'

'Midsommer Fest? What is that?' asked Katharina when they were seated, thinking it would be best to distract her friend. She could see Ellen was shaking. No doubt she would rather walk up the hill and sing her heart out now, as was her habitual self-soothing skill.

Ellen shrugged. 'I haven't been in years, not since I was a kid, so I can't really tell you much, except that it's traditionally held at the Hunters' farm around the twenty-first of June. But I'm sure Jessie will be able to tell you more, as she has Swedish ancestors.'

'I have, and yes, I can tell you a little bit more. It used to be a pagan festival, marking the beginning of summer, with lots of rituals such as tying wishes around a magical tree and other things. Many Scandinavian countries name Midsummer's Day after St. John the Baptist now, but essentially it is still the same thing,' Jessie explained as she put their cappuccinos in front of them. 'Anyway, it's great fun. And now I'm going to get your cake.'

While they were enjoying their cake and coffee, Lily walked in. 'Oh! Hello, Ellen! I had an idea you might be coming today. I was just helping Daisy to put a few things together to take to the hospital for Miss Lavender when you called last Sunday, so I heard you on the answering machine. – Don't worry, it's nothing serious! She had a fall and will have to stay in hospital for another few days. Daisy has just gone to visit her, I think. She goes almost every day. Anyway, it's good to see you.' She came over to hug Ellen, then turned to Katharina. 'I'm Lily Henderson. I have the bookshop next door. Well – I'm just closing for the day. But do come over and have a little browse while you are here.' And calling over her shoulder, she asked, 'Have you got a coffee for me, Jessie, and a bun, to get me through the dreaded cash balance?'

***

When Daisy returned from the hospital that evening ('The traffic was absolutely horrendous! I do not know what possessed me to go on a Friday afternoon in the first place!'), she poured herself a glass of cold water and dropped onto the sofa. 'I am shattered! Thank God the Hunters' party is tomorrow – wild horses would not have been able to drag me there tonight.'

Oliver sat down beside her, and put an arm around her shoulder. 'I can easily believe that. So, what's the story? Were you able to solve that family mystery of yours?'

'Nearly. Though you will have to help me with that, Lavinia and I could not figure it out between the two of us ... will you make me a cup of tea, please? And then I'll tell you all about it.'

So when they were settled on the sofa with their mugs of tea and a plate of Abi's shortbread, she told him how Lavinia had gone to live in Thirsk, where she had found herself a job at a newsagent's. She was not happy there though as the proprietor of the shop kept harassing her (whether he had actually raped her at some point or not Lavinia would not tell, but Daisy suspected he might have), so she had gone to work in Amos Woodcourt's delicatessen instead. When kind Mr Woodcourt retired some years later, he even offered the shop to her. But Lavinia had had enough of Thirsk. Using her inheritance –

her father might have disowned her, but her grandmother had left a villa in France to her, which she sold –, she went to open her own little shop in Bishops Bridge.

'I asked her why Bishops Bridge of all places, and she told me she had discovered the village when walking in Rosedale with Drifter and fallen in love with the peaceful Moors. She had her own car by then and loved nothing better than exploring the North York Moors, often walking all day, and in all kinds of weather. "And so we came here, Drifter and me, in nineteen seventy-one, to begin a new life," she said. It was then, by the way, that she changed her name to Lavender. She really wanted to leave everything behind. Forget, even. Though I suppose you cannot ever forget your parents, or your home …'

Oliver nodded. 'No, I suppose not. What was her name then? Not Miller, obviously.'

'She would have been Lady Featherstone. Her father was Sir Winston Featherstone, Baronet. Which is the title my father so reluctantly inherited.'

'I see. So if she had not run away, she would be Lady Featherstone now.'

'Yes. But she did run away, and left all that behind. Name, title, estate. And when she moved to Bishops Bridge, she became Miss Lavender, and all that remained of her old life was Drifter. The faithful little dog died about a year after she had moved here, at the old age of seventeen. She never had another dog. I asked her, you know, and she said she could never have loved another dog as she had loved Drifter. Also, I suppose he was the last link to her past. A past she desperately wanted to forget … and who can blame her? I certainly can't.'

Oliver shook his head. 'Poor Miss Lavender! And she

never re—I mean, she never married?'

'No. And she did not inherit the estate, or any of the money that was left after her father's gambling years. It all went to his nephew in Dorset.'

'Your grandfather?'

Daisy nodded. 'Yes. Edward Miller. He was the only son of old Sir Winston's widowed sister Emmeline. She had lost her husband in the Great War and never remarried. And since his two older brothers had also fallen in that same war, Emmeline was the only family he had left. Except Lavinia of course, but to her stubborn old father, she might as well have been dead, I'm afraid. Anyway, so Grandfather inherited, and moved north with his mother – Emmeline lived to be almost a hundred! – and his son. Who, of course, is none other than my father.'

'Aaah! That explains why there would be no Lavenders in your family. I see. Are you a cousin of Lavinia's then?'

'I thought you might be able to tell me. You know I am hopeless at that sort of thing.'

Oliver took a notepad from underneath the coffee table and began scribbling down names and dates. Then he tapped the pencil against the edge of the table a few times, leaned back and said, 'First cousin twice removed. You would call her great-auntie, I suppose, for simplicity's sake.'

Daisy nodded. 'Yes … that's the kind of relationship we figured out … funny, isn't it? Of all the places God could have sent you to, it had to be Bishops Bridge. If we hadn't come here, we would never have found Lavinia. – Oh, but I can't wait to tell Dad!' Turning to her husband, she smiled and said, 'You were right, you know? About that missing piece in my family jigsaw puzzle.'

'Yes,' he said and took her hand, 'it seems I was.'

They sat in silence for a while, and Daisy, her head resting against Oliver's shoulder, thought about what else she and Lavinia had discussed this afternoon. How she had suddenly started to cry, and – gently encouraged by Lavinia – found herself pouring her heart out about the Baby Issue, and her nagging doubts. And how Lavinia had taken her hand, looked her straight in the eye, and said, very earnestly, 'Daisy. I am very tired, so I will not say much on the matter now. Just this: Listen to your heart. I am sure you will know what to do if you just take a moment to listen to your heart. And talk it over with your husband. He will understand. He loves you, and he only wants what is best for you, I am sure.'

She had bit her lip, not sure where this was leading. 'And what do you think that would be?'

The old lady had sighed. 'Horses, Daisy. Horses. What else?'

What else indeed, Daisy had thought on her way home. And as she fought her way through the traffic, an idea formed in her head. An idea that had been lurking at the back of her mind for a while now, ever since the day the Marston children first came to the farm. When she had seen the joy shining in their eyes at the sight of the horses. When she had heard Edmund laugh about Jolly Jumper, the pony that was driving everybody else insane. Maybe he, like Ossie the ever-barking dog, just needed a job?

'I'll sleep over it. And then I'll do some research. And talk to Oliver. Promise,' she had said aloud, though this time, she was alone in the car. She often found herself talking to nobody in particular when she was driving these days. Or maybe it was just her way of praying? After all, the only one who was always with her was God, wasn't he?

'It's getting late,' Oliver remarked, slowly letting go of her hand as he rose to his feet. 'Maybe we should make a start on dinner. Pasta pesto okay? Since you admit to have forgotten all about the shopping?'

Daisy, lost in thoughts, looked up, a little confused. 'Oh. Yes, good idea. And then I think I will go for a little walk up the hill. On my own, if you don't mind. I need to think.'

'Sure. It's a beautiful night and won't be dark for another couple of hours. How about I meet you at the Rectory later, and bring Drifter? We could stay the night, if you like, now they have installed the bathrooms.'

She smiled. 'That would be lovely, yes. But don't forget to take some milk, as I don't want to go without my tea tomorrow morning.'

'I was rather thinking of a bottle of wine, but yes, I can also bring milk,' he winked, and she slapped him playfully. 'Get away with you!'

'I will, but only as far as the kitchen. You stay right here and relax. You deserve some rest after the day you have had.'

***

'So if Miss Lavender has to stay at the hospital over the weekend, what do you want to do? Do you want to visit her?'

Katharina followed Ellen into the house, carrying her suitcase as well as her old and battered, but much loved leather briefcase containing her notes. She had inherited that briefcase from her great-grandfather, who had played the tuba in the Viennese Symphonic Orchestra. 'And do you think we should go to the party tomorrow? The Midsommer Fest?'

'Oh dear, no. There will be hundreds of people! Every single house on Bishops Bridge High Street will be deserted tomorrow night because everybody will be up here, dancing around that silly old tree. They won't even notice me not being there. As for visiting Miss Lavender, I thought perhaps I could go on Sunday morning, when everyone will be nursing their headaches. Except you, of course. But you can come to York with me, and then we can have tea at Bettys afterwards. What do you think?'

'Yes, that's fine. I have never been to York, I would love to go.'

Ellen placed her suitcase at the foot of the stairs and went through to the kitchen. 'Sorry about the party – if you insist, we will go of course. But I'd much rather walk to the castle and sing there tonight. It's a full moon. Perfect! What do you think?'

Katharina shrugged. 'That's tonight, not tomorrow. We can go, if you like. But first, I need to eat. Shall we pop the pizza in the oven? And is there any chance of a glass of wine?'

'You are impossible! You have just got through a very generous selection of Jessie's cakes!' Ellen laughed, in spite of herself. If only Katharina did not have to go back to Austria so soon. They could go on sharing her parents' apartment in Kensington and come here at the weekends, if they were not otherwise engaged. The flat would feel very lonely after the summer. But she was not sure she wanted to spend the rest of the summer here either. After all, what did she have to come back here for? Or, not to put too fine a finger on it, what did she have to live for, except her music?

'So what? That was over an hour ago! I cannot sing on an empty stomach. It is not healthy. And then we can walk down to the castle for a bit of exercise, and sing. It's not far, is it?

Taking a bottle of Sauvignon out of the fridge, Ellen poured them two generous glasses and handed one to her friend.'Here you go,' she said, raising her glass. 'To friendship and music.'

'To friendship and music.'

An hour later, the two girls walked down the hill to the castle. The sun was just beginning to set and cast a warm glow over the ancient walls of the old church to their left, making Katharina stop and marvel at the romantic sight of the ruins.

'You know this would be the perfect setting for an opera? Look at the light, the shadows! It is *so* romantic! Just imagine … oh! What's that?'

CHAPTER 21

THEY BOTH STOOD completely still as they listened to the sad tune that was coming from within the castle walls. It was exquisite, and utterly beautiful.

'A violin,' remarked Katharina, spellbound. 'Somebody is playing their violin up there.'

Ellen gave her a playful shove, rolling her eyes. 'Well, yes, I can hear that. But who on earth would be playing their violin in a castle ruin at night?'

Katharina shrugged. 'Perhaps the same kind of person as would walk down there to sing, no?'

They giggled, then fell silent again, hardly daring to breathe when the piece (Schubert, Ellen thought, and very well played. To perfection.) drew to a close. But just as soon as the last note had faded, the violinist began to play yet another tune. 'Ave Maria,' Ellen whispered, already beginning to sing as she walked slowly towards the castle gate. Picking up the tune, Katharina joined her, and so they entered the gatehouse through the broken portcullis until they reached the open space behind.

Standing on what had to be the remains of the vaulted undercroft, the violinist was playing with closed eyes against a velvet sky. She was a tall, slim woman in her mid- to late twenties, with softly curled blond hair and smooth, flawless skin. Whether she noticed the singers who had joined her at all, Ellen and Katharina could not tell. She was in a world of her own. Just like they both were when they were singing.

When the *Ave Maria* came to an end, Ellen called out, 'I hope you don't mind us joining you like that? It was impossible to resist, I'm afraid.'

The woman shook her head. 'Not at all. If you don't mind me playing not nearly as well as you sing?'

Ellen and Katharina exchanged glances. 'She does not seem to have a lot of confidence,' Ellen whispered, and Katharina nodded. But confidence or no confidence, she had taken up her violin again and began to play an aria by Bach, *Bist du bei mir*. That was Katharina's song. Ellen watched as her friend stood singing a few steps further down from where their unknown violinist was playing. She thought she had never heard, or seen anything more beautiful. Tears were running down her face, and she did not even bother to wipe them away.

'Thank you,' she whispered when the woman took down her violin and turned to look at them at last. Her eyes were of the most dazzling blue Ellen had ever seen. 'This was so beautiful. We actually came here to sing, but you playing the violin made it even more precious, especially in this setting, and on such a magical night as this. I'm Ellen, by the way, and this,' she motioned for Katharina to come a little closer, as she was standing in the shadows, 'is my friend Katharina from Austria.'

The woman smiled kindly. 'Nice to meet you at last, Ellen. And you, Katharina. Your singing was absolutely wonderful! I am Daisy Clifford-Jones. I have had the honour of looking after your mother's wonderful horses these past two weeks.'

Now it dawned on Ellen – of course, who else could it be? From what she had heard about the vicar's wife so far, it had to be her: beautiful, gifted, kind-hearted, and very shy. There was a look of sadness in those amazing blue eyes though, making Ellen want to reach out to her.

'Ah! I see. I have heard about you. So pleased to meet you at last. Your violin playing is quite exquisite – where did you learn?'

Daisy blushed. 'My grandmother taught me when I was little. Later, I had lessons, and then I played in the school orchestra when I was a teenager,' she added, laughing a little nervously. Ellen thought she was commendably modest for someone who played so well. 'I never pursued a musical career though – I didn't even go to university at all. I'm a horse woman at heart, I'm afraid.' Again, this nervous little laugh that made Ellen wonder what Daisy was apologizing for – surely there was nothing wrong with being "a horse woman", as she called herself? And it wasn't exactly as if her violin playing was rubbish. On the contrary, it was really, really good.

'I hear you are a student at the Royal College of Music in London?'

Ellen nodded. 'Yes, we are both training to become opera singers. Katharina is going back to Austria to join the Vienna State Opera, but I am staying on for my Artist Diploma.'

'Oh! I see. That would be another year then, or two?'

'Two. I could perhaps do it in one year, but … no. Two is fine. Less pressure.'

Katharina nudged her. 'By a fraction or two, yes. You will put yourself under quite enough pressure, just like you have done over the last six years with those high-flying ambitions of yours. I always thought *I* was ambitious,' she explained, turning to Daisy. 'But this one here is in a league of her own. The proverbial Angel of Music.'

'Oh, give over!' Ellen was clearly embarrassed by her friend's high praise, but Daisy could tell she was even more so because she knew her friend's words to be true. She did sound like an angel when she sang – but then so did Katharina.

'Shall we do another song before it gets too dark? I need to get back home, as my husband will worry where I have gone. I told him I would go for a walk, but I suppose I got a little carried away ... as I sometimes do when I play.' This time, her laughter was soft, almost alluring, and Ellen smiled. She liked Daisy and hoped they could become friends, even if she did not intend to stay long in Rosedale.

'Have you seen your mum's horses yet?'

'No, we only just arrived this afternoon. I was meaning to call Abi but somehow forgot about it ...' Mainly because of that stupid Higgins woman. The encounter had upset her more than she cared to admit. She would rather hide on her parents' estate from now on, and avoid mixing with people. At Birchwood Park, she felt safe.

'Why don't you come to the farm tomorrow morning? They have ten o'clocks—um, well, at ten. Abi bakes the most amazing cakes and breads, and everyone is welcome at any time. But I'm sure you know that.'

Ellen smiled fondly. Dear Miss Abigail! She, too, was of the rough-shell-but-soft-heart kind who would go out of her way to help others. 'Yes, I know, and I would love to come. Ten o'clocks sound perfect. You don't mind going to the farm tomorrow morning, Katharina, do you?'

Katharina shook her head. 'Nope. As long as I get to sleep in, I don't mind anything at all. I am so tired! But yes, another song. Shall we do *You raise me up*? Like Celtic Woman in that YouTube video? Even if we are not wearing silk evening gowns and stage make up, I think we might sound just as good.'

Lifting up her violin, Daisy began to play the intro, and then Katharina sang the first verse, her voice soft and alluring, while Ellen waited in the background, gently swaying in accord with the gentle, melancholy tune. Then she stepped forward to sing the chorus, and the second verse. They finished the song together, with Daisy joining in at the very end.

***

OLIVER WAS JUST coming up the lane with Drifter when he heard the music. Having set off to find his wife, worried that she might stay out too late and become frightened in the dark, he realised he need not have worried at all. She was just lost in her music, and by the sound of it, she had been joined by someone who was (or were) just as absorbed in their singing as Daisy was in her playing. It was lovely.

He knew Daisy had come up here to be alone, trying to make sense of it all. And it was a lot to take in. An *incredible* lot. How Miss Lavender had managed to carry such a terrible burden over such a long time was beyond anything he could understand. And now she had confided in Daisy – because Daisy, as it had turned out, was family.

He hoped very much that his wife would never think of herself as unimportant or insignificant any more. He knew she meant a lot to her parents and siblings, and they meant a lot to her. But to Miss Lavender, she must mean the world.

He was just whistling to Drifter to follow him up the muddy track to the gatehouse when he heard laughing and talking, and soon three young women emerged from the castle. One of them was carrying a violin case, waving to him. It was in moments like these that he could not believe that this beautiful, talented woman was his wife, and his heart soared when she turned her brilliant smile on him.

'Hello! Have you been standing there long?'

She came over to kiss his cheek, before turning to introduce the others. 'This is Ellen Maverick from Birchwood Park, and this is her friend Katharina. She is from Vienna, but they are both students at the Royal College of Music in London. Opera, in case you were wondering.'

Oliver smiled. 'I wasn't, no. Hello, Ellen. Nice to meet you, Katharina. I'm Oliver.'

Having shaken hands, Ellen bent down to cuddle Drifter. 'Oh, what a perfect little darling! Jessie told me you were found abandoned in the churchyard. Or did you come there on purpose to find Daisy?' The dog tilted his head as if contemplating her question. Laughing, she fondled his thick, fluffy ears. 'Ah, you won't tell me, what a shame. Then I suppose that will remain a mystery, hey?'

Oliver laughed. 'Yes, I suppose it will. But I like the idea of him having waited for Daisy to find him. Shall we walk you back to Birchwood Park?'

'No, no, you're alright. It is not quite dark yet, and there is two of us. We will be quite safe, won't we, Katharina?'

Katharina nodded as she, too, bent down to stroke Drifter. 'Oh yes. It's not far.'

'Well, if you are sure,' Oliver said, taking his wife's hand. 'Good night then, see you soon.'

'Good night!'

When the two girls had disappeared around the bend, he turned to Daisy and said, 'That was an amazing performance, darling. Wow! Actually, I think the castle would be a perfect venue for private little concerts or plays, wouldn't it? I can see them acting out *The Taming of the Shrew* up there, or *King Lear*. Anyway,' he squeezed her hand gently, 'I hope you are feeling a little better now.'

'Oh yes. A lot better. And it was lovely to have them sing with me. They are extremely gifted though! Oh my. It was the most *extraordinary* experience.'

'I'm sure it was. But you Daisy, you are gifted, too,' Oliver remarked, 'In so many ways! The violin, the horses … I'm sure you could put that to good use even here, and perhaps it would help you to—'

But Daisy grabbed his shirtsleeve, making him stop. She did not want to talk. She just wanted to seize the moment, and be happy. 'Oh, Oliver! Look at the stars – isn't it magical?' Then she suddenly spread out her arms laughing, and he smiled. She looked radiant tonight. And happy. Was it the music, he wondered, or was there something else? Something she might not dare tell him yet, in case it was a false alarm? He would not ask, of course. He knew better than that by now.

'It is, yes. Absolutely. Come on now, darling, let's

go home. You're getting cold. Why didn't you bring a sweater?'

'Oh, I don't know. I forgot … yes, let's go—to the Rectory. Have you brought the milk?'

He winked. 'The milk, the toothbrushes, and the wine. We can have a glass on the patio while it's still light, or we can dance in the moonlight … Remember how we used to do that on our honeymoon? On the boat?'

Daisy smiled, remembering their honeymoon on her godfather's yacht in the Mediterranean. It had been his wedding gift to them. And a very special one, too. 'I do, yes. And yes to all the other romantic things. Wine, dancing in the moonlight … let's make this night count, Oliver. For some reason, I feel like we should.'

He put a hand to her cheek, feeling the softness of her skin. 'Let's make it count then. This night, and every other, too.'

As they walked on, Daisy thought of poor Lavinia who had never had a chance to dance in the moonlight with her husband. Whose son had not lived. Whose life had not worked out at all the way she had wanted. Whose dreams had all come to nothing. Who am I, thought Daisy, to complain when I have so much? I am so lucky. So very, very lucky.

And yet, the further they walked down the hill, the nearer they got to the village, the more anxious she began to feel. By the time Oliver opened the gate to the garden of the Rectory, the sense of peace that had been with Daisy while she was playing her violin in the castle grounds, had left her altogether. Instead, it had been replaced with a growing sense of dread. Her hands felt clammy, and her mouth dry.

'Oliver?'

He was already getting the wine out and did not turn around to her. 'Yes, darling?'

'I—' She shook her head. 'Nothing. Let's go outside.'

Tucking the bottle under his right arm and taking two glasses from the hooks underneath the kitchen shelf, he offered her his other arm and said, 'Come on then, darling. Time to unwind.'

***

WHILE DAISY AND Oliver were dancing cheek to cheek in the moonlight, Katharina and Ellen were standing on the balcony of Ellen's bedroom looking out across the moors, thinking they had never felt such peace before.

'How can you ever think of leaving this place? If this was mine, I would never give it up.'

Ellen sighed. 'I wish I didn't have to. And maybe I won't … maybe I'll just sell the property in Scotland, and keep Birchwood Park … for a little while longer at least. I need the apartment in Kensington, there's no way I could afford living in London otherwise. And it's convenient. But this …' She sighed. 'This is home.'

Katharina nodded. Arm in arm, their foreheads touching, they stood in silence for a long time, until Katharina yawned and announced it was time to go to bed.

But while her friend was asleep the moment her head hit the pillow, Ellen lay awake for hours, staring at the ceiling of her old bedroom, willing the memories to stay with her. Don't go away, she whispered, don't leave me. Keep me company tonight, and stay with me when I go back to London. I don't want to forget, she thought, swallowing back tears. I don't want to forget ever. Her head turned towards the framed photograph of her mother on the bedside table, softly lit by the moonlight.

'Mum,' she whispered, almost choking on her words. 'Mama …'

The first tears spilled down her cheeks, dropping silently onto the pillow. How often had she cried herself to sleep that first summer she had come here, afraid she would not be allowed to stay, afraid the children at school would not want to be her friends, afraid everybody would think her odd, and that she would be sent back to one of the horrible foster homes she had lived at before she came to Birchwood Park. But Angela and Charles Maverick had not sent her back. The children had not wanted to be friends with her, but that was okay: she had been happy enough to be at school and learn, and come back to the place she soon called home. Here, she had always felt safe, loved, and cherished.

'Everybody needs a safe and happy place,' her dad had said to her one day last summer, when they had come back from a long walk across the Moors, 'a place to call home.'

Last summer … when her life was still alright. When they did not know yet what was to come. When she had believed she would always be able to call this her home – her safe and happy place. Now, it was only a large, empty house, filled with expensive furniture, paintings, and all sorts of ornaments her parents had collected over the years. And the memories that still lingered here would soon fade away. Even now it felt cold, and all wrong.

A desperate sob threatened to escape from the depth

of her chest, and she had to put a hand to her mouth to muffle the sound. 'Mama!'

Turning her head, she buried her face in the pillow and cried and cried until she fell asleep, exhausted.

CHAPTER 22

JESSIE WAS HUMMING softly as she prepared her quiches and salads for the Midsommer Fest at home while Nate was holding the fort at the café. He had insisted he would rather come and help than see her losing customers by keeping the café closed on a Saturday.

'Honestly, darling, you cannot run a business like that. I'll come down and do the morning shift, and then we will do the afternoon together. You can close at three, I suppose. Then there is still plenty of time for any sort of preparation – and maybe even an hour on the sun lounger before the party starts. I hereby volunteer to apply the sunscreen onto your back – and wherever else you want it …'

This had made her laugh, and the anger she had felt at being patronised had evaporated. She knew he was right, too – she could not really afford to keep the café closed. So she had got up extra early, made three cakes, flapjacks, and a couple of trays of scones, and put them in the back of Nate's car before kissing him goodbye.

'No lunch menu today, just coffee, teas, and cakes. When you're sold out, you close and come home. I'll come and join you as soon as I can.'

'Good. Oh, by the way – Ben was on the answering

machine, saying you did not answer his messages … I couldn't help hearing as he called while you were in the shower. Do you want me to speak to him tonight? He will be there, won't he? At the party?'

'Course he will. Free drinks, and plenty of pretty girls – he couldn't resist, could he? He'll be sleeping at his parents', so he just has to walk down the hill.'

Nate had nodded. 'Right. I'll make sure I'll talk to him before he is drunk then.'

***

'HAVE YOU GOT the latest Hazel Gaynor book? It's about Grace Kelly and the Monaco wedding in 1956. My mum loves Grace Kelly, so I want to give it to her for her birthday. It was supposed to be published in June, I think … could you have a look?'

Lily nodded, already tapping at the screen of her tablet. There it was, Hazel Gaynor, *Meet me in Monaco*. 'Oh,' she said. 'Publishing date is set for the twenty-third of July, so that's another month. When is your mum's birthday?'

Sally Jones, who ran the *Dog & Partridge* together with her brother Ivan, sighed. 'Bother. It's next week. On the twenty-fifth. Do you have another idea? I was so set on getting her this book. She really loves Grace … by the way, don't you think that the vicar's wife looks remarkably like Grace Kelly?'

Lily paused. Yes. Yes, that was it – that was whom Daisy had instantly reminded her of, the moment she had first seen her! The sapphire blue eyes, her blond hair expertly styled in that classic wave – why, even the clothes she wore! Classic and elegant in style, Daisy was dressed like no other woman in Rosedale. Lily could just picture her on that grand estate in Suffolk she had grown up at, leading a pair of perfectly groomed Thoroughbreds down a long, gravelled lane. Of course there would be no weeds in that gravel. And of course she wouldn't wear jeans but …

'She does, doesn't she?'

'What?'

'Look like Grace Kelly. Daisy Clifford-Jones?' Sally prompted, 'the vicar's wife?'

'Oh. Yes, I suppose you're right … the eyes, the hair … yes. And do you know what, I think I have the perfect gift for your mum. Here,' Lily said, taking a large, heavy book from the shelf that was labelled *Biographies*. 'Grace Kelly: *Hollywood Dream Girl*. It is said to be one of the best biographies written on Grace Kelly. It's a bit pricey, I know, but it's a beautiful book as well as a classic. And it's for your mum.'

Sally shook her head, laughing. 'You are a good bookseller, Lily Henderson! Yes, I'll buy it. Are you all going to the Midsommer Fest tonight?'

'Of course. I wouldn't miss it for anything, as I have never been before. Sorry we won't be at the *Dog & Partridge* tonight then. You'll have to make do with the tourists. Shall I gift wrap the book for you?'

'Oh yes, please do! I am so hopeless at these things. And if we don't get any customers thanks to Maddie's party, we'll close early and come up the hill for a pint.'

***

DAISY KNEW SHE was riding too fast. She knew she was not paying attention either. But all she could think of was how Oliver had deceived her. Gone behind her back, that's what he had done when he had made an appointment with the GP and talked about their Baby Issue. The GP had suggested he took a sperm sample. A sperm sample! How embarrassing was that? She could not even bring herself to say it. Yes, she was a prude, and no, she did not like talking about such intimate matters. But did that give him the right to go ahead and make appointments without even asking her? What if she did not want to find out what, if anything, was wrong? It was their marriage, wasn't it, and their Baby Issue – not only his.

'What's this then?' she had asked when they had come back to the cottage this morning to find a pile of mail on the kitchen floor. Picking up a pristine white C4 envelope, she had turned it over to see whom it was from. He had tried to snatch it from her, but it was too late. She had already seen the stamped address of the sender, in bright blue lettering: Fertility Clinic in York. And as the letter was clearly addressed to Mr Oliver Clifford-Jones, there was no way he could get out of this, even if he wanted to.

She had stared at the envelope, then at her husband, and back at the envelope. 'Fertility Clinic York? But why—how—I don't understand! What does this mean?'

'Please, Daisy – listen. I can explain. It's just a brochure, okay? Just some information. I haven't booked an appointment or anything. Not yet. It might not be necessary. I – I am still waiting for some test results.'

'Test results? What do you mean, test results? What test?'

'I went to see Dr Palmer last week. Because I wanted to know what was wrong. I told him about – about our problem to conceive, and he advised me to have my sperm tested. You see, my sperm count may be too low, or—'

'Stop! Stop!' She had put her hands to her ears and shaken her head, refusing to listen. 'I don't want to know! Okay? I don't want to know!' Her eyes quickly filling with hot, angry tears, she had walked over to the window and stood there, her arms crossed in front of her chest, and her back turned to her husband. She did not want to look at him. How could he have hurt her so much? And ordering that brochure, too!

'Why didn't you *ask* me? Why didn't you talk to me? Aren't we a married couple? Didn't we say there should be no more secrets? And yet, you go off, make an appointment, have your … tests run … and even ask for *this*!'

She had flung the envelope onto the floor, startling the dog who had followed her to the living room. Drifter had made for his basket where he had curled up into a ball, watching Daisy with anxious eyes.

Oliver had not said anything. He had not even followed her, or if he had, she had not heard his steps. Eyes blazing, tears running down her cheeks, she had finally turned around – he was still standing in the same spot in the kitchen – and cried, 'How could you? How could you??'

Without waiting for an answer, she had stormed out of the house, and run over to the barn, where she had saddled Ruby, all the while crying and hoping he would come and take her in his arms. Calm her, soothe her. Tell her everything was going to be alright.

But he hadn't. Not one word, not one step. Nothing.

And what does that tell me about my husband, she thought, as she pushed Ruby into a canter, giving her free rein to run, and her tears free rein to fall. They had reached the broad, level track below the kilns, and as there was no one about, Daisy thought it safe to let the horse run. Her eyes blind with tears, she did not see the boys who were sitting in the mine entrances, smoking. But when one of them threw an empty beer can onto the track, Ruby shied and rose on her hind legs. Taken completely by surprise, Daisy could not hold on to the horse, and fell off. She hit the ground headfirst, then with her shoulder, before she came to lie on her back, numb with pain.

There were two things Daisy saw before everything turned black: the boys running off in one direction, and Ruby, mane and tail flying, in the other. The last thing she heard was the ringing of her phone.

***

'SHE'S NOT ANSWERING the phone – what if she has had an accident? If she is hurt?'

'Now don't panic, Oliver.' Abi, who had just come back from her shopping, slammed the door of her battered old Range Rover shut. 'She is an excellent rider, and she knows the area by now. And Ruby is a good horse. If anything happens to her, I'm sure Ruby will come running home. But I don't think anything *has* happened to her,' she hurried to add when she saw the stricken look on Oliver's face. 'I think she is probably just enjoying a good old canter and can't answer her phone. That would not be sensible, would it?'

'No,' he mumbled, absent-mindedly tapping redial, even if he knew Daisy wouldn't pick up. 'I suppose not.' He could not bring himself to tell Abi about their dispute earlier, and that Daisy, hurt and disappointed, had run off in a fury. Abi did not even know about their problems – and why would she? It was bad enough that he had gone behind Daisy's back, he would not go and tell others about their conception issues now, would he?

'So what are you going to do? You can't ride, can you? Otherwise I'd suggest you take Ronnie and go after her. Do you know which way she went?'

'Yes … up to the kilns. She loves riding along the old railway track. I guess I'll just take the car then. Come on, Drifter!' he called, and the little dog came running out of the cottage. 'Let's go find your mummy.'

Abi shook her head. 'But you won't get far in the car, will you? She will have gone up through the woods, and then—'

But Oliver did not hear her. He had already picked up the little dog and walked to the car with him, cursing himself for not stopping his wife when there had still been a chance. But he had been angry. Sulking, too, probably. And, worst of all, too proud to run after his wife. Who was she to tell him he could or could not make an appointment with their GP? It irked him to know (and admit) that she was right, too – he should have asked, or at least *told* her. Most of all, he should never have emailed that Fertility Clinic and requested a brochure to be sent to him. That was most definitely the stupidest thing he could have done. No wonder she was hurt. Had he been in her place, he would have been hurt, too.

'Please God,' he prayed as he started the engine,

'please let me find her. Please keep her safe.'

***

GRITTING HER TEETH, Daisy tried to sit up. She was in excruciating pain. Her shoulder hurt, and she could not lift her left arm, never mind put weight on her hand, or even close her fingers. Turning it up, she saw the palm was a mess of dirt and blood and tiny stones, and winced. That did not look good. When did she have her last tetanus shot? She couldn't remember. As a teenager, probably. She should be alright then, shouldn't she? It was bad enough that she had a feeling she might have broken her collarbone, or at least bruised her shoulder really badly. Trying to shift her bodyweight, she was now leaning against a rock with her knees pulled up. Her left arm hanging limply, she used her right hand to try and get her phone to work, but the battery was dead. Also, the screen was smashed to pieces.

Bother, she thought. Now what? Would Ruby have run back to the farm, or to Birchwood Park? Or would some farmer find her grazing in his field, as if nothing had happened? She had no idea, but the thought of anything happening to the precious horse was unbearable, especially since it was not even hers. How would she ever explain this to Ellen? It was unforgivable!

She bit her lip. What on earth had got into her, shouting at her husband and then storming off like that and racing a horse that was not even her own up the hillside? She did not normally lose her temper like that. In fact, she *never* lost her temper. And now look where that got me, she thought, wishing she had a tissue to blow her nose. I am hurt, I have lost Ellen's precious horse, and on top of all that, I am also making a spectacular fool of myself.

'Stupid me,' she whispered underneath her breath, 'stupid, stupid me!'

She was still angry, but right now, the pain numbed all feelings of resentment. All she wanted now was for Oliver to find her, and take her home.

CHAPTER 23

'Oh dear! How did that happen?'

Startling at the sound of an unfamiliar voice, Daisy lifted her eyes to see Mr and Mrs Colbeck standing on the path, in full walking gear, and looking down on her with a mixture of pity and curiosity. Pity, mostly. Mrs Colbeck sat down next to Daisy and was about to put an arm around her shoulder, but Daisy instinctively shrank away. 'Don't! Please. I'm sorry, but it really hurts.'

'Oh. In that case, I won't touch you. But you will allow my husband to help you up, won't you? We need to see if you can walk at all, or whether we will have to summon a helicopter.'

Daisy's eyes widened. 'A helicopter? Oh no! I don't think that will be necessary.' The thought of spending an entire Saturday in A&E was enough to dampen Daisy's mood. The last thing she needed was extra attention, and on the day of the Midsommer Fest, too. The party everyone had been talking about all week. Well, she thought, I will not be making an apple crumble now, that's for sure.

Mrs Colbeck rummaged in her rucksack for a water bottle while her husband squatted down next to Daisy, offering a sympathetic smile. 'Do you think you'll be able to get up and stand, if I support you? I promise I won't touch your left arm. Or any other part that is hurting.'

Despite her pain, Daisy found herself smiling at him. He was such a perfect gentleman! Somehow, he did not quite fit her picture of a police officer. But then, neither did Oliver fit the picture most people had of a vicar either, did he? Which just went to show that one should not believe in types, but in people. And not be prejudiced. 'That would be kind, thank you. I believe it's my left side altogether. My shoulder, arm, hand, and hip.' She gave a little laugh. 'I expect I will be covered in bruises and not fit to wear a skirt for weeks to come. Oh well. As long as nothing is broken.'

'Except the arm, which looks very much broken to me, if I may say so,' came Mr Colbeck's rather dry remark. 'Did you fall off a horse?'

Daisy nodded, then winced in pain, and bit down her tears. In moments like these she almost wished she could swear. Loudly and colourfully.

'Oh, don't worry about the skirts, love. You can wear those lovely, floating, long ones that suit you so well. You are such a pretty young lady, Miss, I am sure you will always look elegant whatever you wear. Have a drink of water. And I have a chocolate bar, too. I always take one or two for emergencies.'

Mrs Colbeck held out a slightly squashed KitKat to Daisy, which she took gratefully. 'Thank you. That is very kind.'

'Not at all. Philip will call your husband, if you have the number? I'm sure he must be worrying, especially if the horse came back with an empty saddle. Do you think it will have run back to Fern Hill Farm?'

'I don't know, to be honest. She might have made for Birchwood Park, since that is her home … Ruby is one of Ellen Maverick's horses, you know. I hope very much that she is safe!' Close to tears, Daisy looked at the chocolate bar in her hands, quietly wondering how she was supposed to open it with her hands scuffed and sore as they were. But Mrs Colbeck, sensing that Daisy was struggling, kindly took the chocolate and unwrapped it for her. 'Thank you,' Daisy sniffed, and took a small bite. The tears were almost choking her. Quickly, to stop herself from sobbing, she took another bite, and another, until the KitKat was gone.

'I have Oliver's number,' Mr Colbeck said, already pressing his phone to his ear. 'He called me only yesterday about those—oh, hello, Oliver? It's Philip Colbeck. We found your wife. She fell off her horse on the track that runs along Rosedale East Side—you're already on your way?—Five minutes? Oh, good.—Yes, of course. Will do. Bye.'

***

Abi was kneading bread dough when Lily came in from the yard, shaking her head and muttering something about 'that wretched pony!' under her breath.

'Why, what has he done?' Abi asked, thumping the dough ball onto the floured surface with flourish. 'He hasn't escaped again, has he?'

'Oh yes, he has. And he has cheerfully eaten his way through the entire village – Nate called me from the Bridge Café, saying Jolly Jumper had just walked in and stolen the scones from the plates of two astonished customers!'

Abi dropped the dough ball with a thump. 'No!'

'Yes. And I am not ashamed to admit that I wish I had seen it – it must have been hilarious! No doubt there will be photos on the village Facebook group. Anyway, I had just gone out to deliver a book to the Barry's place, so by the time I got back, Jolly Jumper had already made his exit – with a nod of thanks to the laughing crowd and nicking a gentleman's cream slice on his way.'

'Oh, Lily! That's embarrassing! We can't let that happen again! And of course we will have to make up for the damage.'

'But they *love* him, Abi! That's the thing. They think he is *funny*! Well, not the people who didn't get to eat their scones and cream slice perhaps, but … anyway. In the end, I found him on Brook Farm where Mr Marston had tied him up good and proper. Unfortunately, that was after he had caught him stealing a walnut and coffee cream cake his wife had unwisely left on the windowsill to cool off. Victoria and Edmund were still laughing hysterically when I came. They thought it was a tremendous joke, no matter how hard Mr Marston tried to explain that it wasn't funny because it was their Uncle Tom's birthday cake, and he was coming for tea. They don't understand, do they? Aw, but I think they are sweet. They just see the funny side of everything – maybe we all should.'

'Well,' Abi remarked wryly, 'that rather depends on which side of the fence you are. I'll make a cake for Eliza's brother-in-law, just as soon as the bread is in the oven. You can bring it over later – but make sure that pony can't get out and follow you!'

Lily grinned. 'Oh, I will, don't you worry. Mr Marston said, "And tell your Auntie Abigail she may be a saint for

putting up with the pony *and* that goat, but I am not!" –
Now, I take that as a warning, even if Jolly Jumper does
not!—Tea?'

A few minutes later, Lily poured the tea and passed
Abi a mug. 'I met Oliver and Daisy outside just now,
when I was putting Jolly Jumper back in his stable. Oliver
says they have just been to A&E – do you know what
happened?'

Abi pursed her lips. 'Not really, no. Only that Ruby
shied, and she fell off. The next thing I knew was he
was bundling her into the car and taking her to A&E in
Whitby. She looked a right picture of misery, if you ask
me. Thank God she was wearing a helmet.'

'Oh dear. I hope they'll be able to come to the party
tonight. It would be a shame if they missed their first
Midsommer Fest.' Draining her mug, Lily looked at Abi.
'Are you sure you'll be alright looking after three dogs
tonight? Don't you want to come to Maddie's party?'

'Oh, quite sure, thank you! I am past the party age,
and more than happy to settle in front of the telly with a
glass of sherry. Just as long as the goat and the pony are
under lock and key!'

***

'I AM SO glad Ruby came back to the farm. It's amazing,
isn't it, how she instinctively found her way back here,
instead of running home to Birchwood Park? I would
have died of shame, had Ellen seen her. I will tell her, of
course, but still – I'm glad she is not hurt.'

Daisy was sitting on the sofa, pale and tired, but
otherwise just glad to be home again. They had only just

come back from A&E, the staff at the small hospital in Whitby having been very capable as well as sufficient – they had left the premises in just under three hours, and that included x-ray and the fitting of a temporary cast. Also, they had used the time to talk about things they should have talked about weeks ago. Like why Oliver had decided to go and see the GP about their fertility problem, and chosen not to tell her.

'I wanted answers, Daisy. I'm a man. I needed to know why things were not … well, working as they should. Why we could not have a baby. Or not just yet. I can't just sit and watch you getting unhappier with every passing month, with every negative test, with … with your life. I promised I would always strive to keep you safe and happy, and look what a mess I've made of it! I have never seen you so wretched. Not getting pregnant, not having your horses anymore … you even dream about that. And don't tell me the one thing doesn't have to do with the other. I know you never think, or dream about anything else. Horses, babies, shattered dreams. My poor darling. And there was I thinking moving to the country would be the answer. The peace and quiet we'd find here … But it isn't that simple, is it?'

'Life never is,' she had said quietly, taking his hand. 'And you are wrong – you haven't made a mess of anything, Oliver. We should have talked about things, been more honest with each other. But we'll do better from now on, won't we? We'll take better care of each other.'

'We will.' He had gently put an arm around her right shoulder, pulling her close, and kissed the top of her head. 'Don't you worry now. I'll keep you safe, my darling. Always.'

Handing her a mug of tea now, he sat down next to her. 'Yes, I'm glad, too. But I am even more glad that the Colbecks found *you*, my love. Because no matter how precious or valuable that horse may be, I am sure Ellen would agree with me that you are worth more. You are irreplaceable, a horse isn't. It's as simple as that. And yes, I know you would argue that it was her late mother's horse, but … oh, Daisy, can't you see? You mean the world to me! Had you been seriously injured …' He shook his head. 'I don't even want to think about it. I'm so glad to have you back.'

She smiled. 'Yes, me too. Glad to be home – and back with you. I'm sorry I ran off. I shouldn't have done that. It was childish of me, and quite unnecessary.'

'Yes, but you were hurting, and I was too blind to see that. I was too proud to run after you. I should have done that. And you were right, too: It was wrong of me to make that appointment without telling you. I'm sorry, Daisy, for everything. Most of all for behaving like – like an idiot. And a very selfish one at that. Please forgive me.'

Daisy hesitated. Come on then, Daisy, say it. Just say it. But somehow, she couldn't. The words remained stubbornly stuck in her throat. Why do I find this so hard, she thought, shaking her head. He has been nothing but kind to me, and it was me who walked out on him, not the other way round. It was me who got him worried. Again. Because I always go and do these stupid things, don't I? Like missing a flight and panicking at the prospect of having to spend a night in a hotel in Amsterdam … or forgetting to take my phone when I was walking on my own when we had only just arrived here, and I got lost … or falling off a horse because I rode too fast and did not pay attention to my surroundings, like any responsible rider should.

She swallowed. Then she took a deep breath and turned to look at him, tears in her eyes. 'Of course I'll forgive you. And I'm sorry, Oliver. For being so difficult.'

He put a hand on her shoulder. 'You are in pain, darling, you have every right to be difficult. We'll talk some more tomorrow. Okay? Now rest, or I won't take you to the party. If you're sure you still want to go?'

She frowned. 'Of course I do! Why wouldn't I?'

'Well, because—oh, never mind. I'll make us an omelette now. Mushrooms, tomatoes, and bacon?'

'Yes, please. All of it. And cheese.'

As she sipped her tea and watched him break the eggs for an omelette into a jug while Drifter was watching his every move (no doubt hoping one of the eggs would land at his feet), she suddenly felt very small and very foolish. She was so lucky to have Oliver. She should not doubt him. The only way forward now, she thought, is openness, honesty, and talking things through. With each other, and with God. After all, it was Him who had the plan.

***

IN YORK, MISS Lavender was trying to enjoy the sunshine, but found that she couldn't. She was restless, and could have done with a nice, brisk walk, but of course they would not let her walk alone, so she had to content herself with sitting on a bench instead. The last thing she needed was yet another extension of her stay because she had broken the rules. It was bad enough she had to stay the weekend. Everyone knew nothing ever happened in hospitals at weekends. She only hoped Daisy would come to see her tomorrow, and bring some of Jessie's cake.

'I am going to collect you in fifteen minutes, Miss Lavender. And don't you go off and catch a bus home or walk into town for a sneaky cappuccino!' The nurse, a cheerful young girl named Annabel, had wagged her finger at Lavinia. 'You know there is a bus stop outside the gates, and I know that you know. So don't try to trick me. Fifteen minutes.'

'I don't *like* cappuccino! And I haven't even got my purse,' Miss Lavender protested, but Annabel had already walked away. No doubt to boss some other helpless old biddy around. She liked Annabel though. Not only was she cheerful, but honest and outspoken, and certainly not afraid of her.

Miss Lavender adjusted her glasses and looked at the small bundle of letters in her hands. Those from Hugh she had already read the night before her fall – he had not been much of a writer, so there were only five letters dating from the time of their secret courtship – and the others were mostly from her friend Joan, who had kept in touch until her death in 2009. She had always said she would come and see Lavinia in Yorkshire, but sadly, she had developed early dementia, and her letters had become sparse, until one day her daughter had telephoned Lavinia to inform her of her mother's death. She had not gone to the funeral. What would have been the point? Joan was dead, and she did not know anyone else there.

Her own father had long been dead by then, and left everything to his widowed sister's only son in Dorset. Back then, Lavinia could not have cared less. But now that she knew that the heir was no other than Daisy's father, George Miller, she suddenly cared very much. In fact, she was uncommonly excited. She had asked Daisy not to tell her father just yet, though. She needed more time to get used to the idea of having family again. For now, Daisy was enough.

Carefully tugging at the string, Miss Lavender untied the bundle of letters and took the last one Joan had ever written to her. It was dated June 2008.

My dear Lavinia!

I can't believe I am to have another birthday without you coming to celebrate it with me. Sixty-six! That is quite old, isn't it? Or what we considered old back then. Do you remember the time you made a cake for me, but used salt instead of sugar? It was absolutely inedible. And my father took the first bite. I don't know why, really – it should have been me, shouldn't it? Oh, but Dad loved his cake. He was such a sweet tooth! I remember my mum always putting a slice of fruit cake into his lunch packet though she knew your mum would provide cake, too, for everybody, down to the least of the stableboys. She did not serve the tea herself, of course. Your mum was such a grand lady! I was a bit afraid of her, you know, because she was so beautiful, so elegant, and so very, very ladylike, in a haughty sort of manner. She could have come straight out of a Dickens novel – or should I say Brontë now that you have become a proper Yorkshire Lass? Anyway, I was afraid of her. Your father, I could never quite make out. Was he serious, or teasing me, or flirting when he touched me and said I was pretty? Was he just being kind in a fatherly way, or was he really making a pass at me, like you said afterwards? You were outraged. But Lavinia, we were only children! I am sure it was quite harmless. Anyway, I'm rambling. My husband has bought a very nice Victoria Sponge, that will have to do. Let's hope it's not salty!

Yours truly, Joan x

Lavinia shook her head. It was so sad – Joan's husband had left her long before she had written that letter. After twenty-five years of marriage, he had run off with his secretary. Joan had never got over it. Especially since their only daughter lived in Spain, so she was left quite on her own. Poor Joan. Maybe that had even started the dementia – a state of constant denial and pretence? Joan was always *fine*. Norman had just nipped out for some milk. He would be back any moment. He had never come back though, not even for their daughter's wedding, or his wife's funeral.

'Well,' she sighed, folding the letter and putting it back in its envelope, 'at least I know that my cousins will hopefully have the decency to attend my funeral, now that we are acquainted with each other. At least, Daisy and I are. George… funny, I can hardly remember him at all now. But then, they seldom visited, did they? Always kept themselves to themselves down there. Never assuming they would inherit the estate, the title, and all that from my father because I ran away. Oh well.' She rose to her feet, stiff-legged. 'I suppose I'd better get back – and there is Nurse Annabel coming to get me.—No chance to nip off to Bettys now, is there?' she called, and the nurse laughed good-humouredly.

Thinking that a slice of Jessie's carrot cake would do just as nicely, Miss Lavender followed the nurse inside, her thoughts once again drifting back to Daisy, and Bishops Bridge. And to the little dog who had started it all.

She smiled to herself. *The dog in the churchyard.*

CHAPTER 24

THE GARDEN BEHIND the Hunters' farm house was lit up with hundreds of fairy lights, strung from tree to tree and along the wooden fence that ran behind the rustic picnic benches Jonathan and his dad had put up the day before. It was nearing midnight, and some of the guests were already a little worse for the drink, while others had gone home because they had to get up early the next day. But a lot of people were still here, celebrating the longest night of the year, and waiting for Madeleine to announce it was time to gather around the wish tree.

Daisy, who was sitting next to Lily and Lucy at one of the tables at the far end of the garden, was surprised to find herself enjoying the evening, despite being in pain because of the bruises she had suffered. It was a beautiful, balmy night, and she was wearing Oliver's favourite dress, a red and white gingham dress she had had for longer than she cared to think of. But she knew he loved her in it, and had put it on especially for him.

'Would you like another glass of wine?'

Daisy looked up. 'Sorry?'

'I offered to get you another glass of wine, but to be honest, you look so exhausted, I'm afraid you'd fall asleep. My poor darling! Perhaps I had better take you home?'

'Absolutely not. I want to see that wish tree thing – even if I'd rather not take any part in it. Too mystical. But look, the children are all getting excited now, whispering to each other, and comparing their ribbons ... Does it matter what colour the strips are, or how long they are?'

Lily laughed. 'Not a bit! But to the kids, it does. Look, there is little Hester Sue from Thorgill showing off her ribbon to her arch enemy, Patricia Morgan. Hester Sue Barry lives on Mill Farm. You know, where the water mill is. Her Nana reputedly sees fairies dancing by the pond in the garden on moonlit nights. Only last weekend, Mr Colbeck found her wandering around the village in her nightie and took her home. She also believes there is a ghost up on the hill, guarding his treasure – oh, but you know *that* story.'

Daisy sighed. Yes, I do know that story. And I have had quite enough of your fairies, thank you very much. Or any fairies for that matter.

Thankfully, Madeleine chose this moment to grab the microphone from the DJ, calling, 'Right, everybody, I know you're having a great time, and I hate to interrupt you, but I just wanted to say that the tree is now ready and waiting for you! You can all come, pick a rag or use the one you have brought, and hang it on the tree. Don't forget to make your wish! Oh, and Deirdre is going to play on her lute, so it's going to be ... *magical!*'

Everyone cheered and clapped as a tall, slender woman in a purple medieval gown stepped onto the makeshift stage, carrying her lute. Sitting down on an antique wine keg, she took her time arranging the folds of her skirt, then carefully tuning her lute, and finally, pushing back her long, black hair over her shoulder before she was ready to look up and smile at her audience.

'She is something, isn't she? What a stunner. We used to go out, the fair Deirdre and me, when we were kids. God, that's ages ago, isn't it? How old are you, Oliver?'

Ben had sat down next to Oliver, taking a sip from his beer now. He was reasonably sober, and Daisy had seen him talking to Nate and Jessie a while ago. They had seemed to be getting on quite well, and once in a while she had even heard them laughing. She hoped they could still be friends after all, and that Jessie could stay in her sweet little cottage for a bit longer. Sooner or later she would probably marry Nate, and then the cottage would be too small, anyway. Especially if they were planning to have more children ...

Stop it, Daisy! Just stop it. Not everyone is constantly thinking about having children.

'I'm thirty-five. Where is Cindy, by the way? I thought you might have brought her, since she wants to move to Bishops Bridge?'

Lily and Lucy promptly began to snigger, and even Daisy found it hard not to laugh. She loved Oliver's dry humour, and knew that people were often taken by surprise because they did not expect something like that from a vicar. *Well, thank God Oliver is different from what people would expect,* she thought, a smile twitching at her lips despite her best attempts to hide it.

'Oh, Cindy ... nah, she doesn't want to live in the country. She wants her shops and her beauty parlours and what have you. She will probably just stay where she is, or perhaps move to Thirsk ... oh, what do I know? Women, eh?'

'Well, she seems old enough to make her own

decisions, and if she doesn't want to move to the country, then there is no more to be said, is there? And if that means that Jessie can stay in her cottage, so much the better. You know she loves that cottage as if it was her own, Ben.'

'I know.' Ben gave a sheepish grin. 'I suppose I just wanted to show Cindy off … she is really quite nice behind all that glamorous exterior. And she likes Bishops Bridge. Says it's a sweet little place, and Jessie's cakes are absolutely delicious. I couldn't agree more. She's made one for tonight, hasn't she? Some showstopper of a sparkling lake meets dark green forest and all-glittering-trees sort of thing. When are they going to cut that then? After the wish tree humbug?'

Daisy smiled. So she wasn't the only one who thought it was all humbug. Well, well.

Just then the fair Deirdre took up her lute, bent her head, and began to play. It was beautiful. Really, really beautiful. Whether it was magical or not, Daisy could not tell, but she began to relax into Oliver's arms, and closed her eyes when he kissed her.

Ben groaned, muttering something about the vicar getting carried away, and got up. 'Come on, guys, let's go make a wish, and leave the two lovebirds here to it. But don't miss the cake!' he called back over his shoulder to Lily and Joseph.

But Daisy was not listening. She could always have cake tomorrow. Without the magic.

The others had only been gone for a minute when somebody called, 'Hello there? Don't you want to come and make a wish?'

Turning around somewhat reluctantly, Daisy saw

Madeleine striding towards them in her usual brisk, purposeful manner. Daisy had never seen a woman stride more briskly, or more purposefully, than Madeleine Hunter – and certainly not at thirty weeks pregnant. Or whatever week it was.

'You alright, sweetie?' Madeleine sat down next to Daisy. 'You look a bit pale. Bit too much excitement for one day, eh? First that nasty fall, then an afternoon in A&E, and now this crazy farmer's wife asking you to tie a piece of rag around the tree when all you want to do is go to bed and sleep.'

Daisy was just going to say, yes, absolutely, when Madeleine wagged her finger at them and said, 'Aw, but you can't go home before you have made a wish! It's an Irish tradition, but widely spread throughout Britain, too. It's quite harmless, really. You take a rag, make a wish, and tie it to the hawthorn by the old well behind the house. And then you leave it there to rot!' she laughed, but stopped when she saw the anxious expression on Daisy's face. 'It's just a bit of fun, Daisy. Most of the rags are actually put there by children who wish for a pony, or teenagers who wish they will magically pass their GCSEs without revising, or something. You can also say a prayer, if you like. That's fine.'

Daisy was not convinced, but Oliver took her by the hand, saying, 'Come on, darling, let's make a wish then. We can say a prayer together. I'm sure God will understand. And you know He always answers, tree, or no tree.'

Daisy nodded. She hoped very much that God would take her pain away first of all. Then they could see about the rest.

Lit up by dozens of warm white solar lights which had been stuck in the ground around the trunk, the hawthorn tree stood by the old well behind the house. Here, the garden sloped gently down towards the stream that divided the Hunter's land from the neighbouring farm. The grey and withered tree was at least forty feet high and looked like it had been there since medieval times. Although that was perhaps unlikely, Daisy could not help being in awe.

'This is beautiful,' she murmured, placing a hand against the trunk, and feeling the roughness of its bark. 'And it certainly looks ancient! – Does it still bear flowers, Madeleine?'

'It does, and they smell divine, if you don't mind me saying that. Do you want to pick a rag? They are in that wicker basket over there.' And with that, she left them to it.

'You pick one,' Daisy whispered to Oliver.

'Okay,' he whispered back, his lips brushing her ear. Giggling, she shook her head and gave him a playful shove. 'You are impossible, Oliver Clifford-Jones! Absolutely impossible!'

While Deirdre played a series of Tudor tunes on her lute, more and more people came and tied their rags around the tree, some of them muttering something, but most of them in silence. The children all giggled and nudged each other on their way back to their parents, and Daisy smiled. She noticed that many of them (especially the younger girls) had really pretty rags which looked far too nice to be "left to rot on a tree".

After they had tied their own piece of cotton around a branch of the hawthorn tree, Daisy and Oliver stood back and watched in silence, having decided to leave their prayer for later.

'Do you think I can risk wishing the Johnsons to move away? Or for their dog to go mute?'

On turning around, Daisy saw Jessie standing behind her, holding hands with Nate. They all laughed at her wish, Lily and Lucy almost bending over, and then Nate nudged Jessie and said, 'Go on, what harm can it do? You are not wishing the plague upon them, are you?'

But Daisy did not laugh. Something had caught in her throat, making it difficult for her to swallow. 'Oliver,' she whispered, grasping his hand, 'I want to go home.'

'Now?'

'Yes, please. I—I'm really tired and – I suppose I should have taken some painkillers, but I haven't, so …'

He looked at her, concern showing in his warm, grey eyes. 'Of course I'll take you home. It's been a long day, and we probably shouldn't have—anyway, I'll take you home. Come on.'

She nodded, and smiled at him as she looped her arm through his. Though she was in pain, this was not the real reason for her wanting to go home all of a sudden. She did not know why (and she certainly would not tell Oliver), but she could not shake off this growing sense of unease, dread even, that had been with her all evening. It was a bit like last night when they had walked back from the castle, only more intense. A feeling of foreboding. A sense of fear she could not explain …

***

IT WAS ONLY later, when she lay in bed next to her

husband, and with the little dog in her good arm, that she felt herself slowly relax. Maybe she was just exhausted. Maybe her tired mind had been playing tricks on her, or maybe it was all that talk of ghosts and fairies that had unsettled her. It shouldn't unsettle her, she knew. She was quite safe with Oliver. There was no need to be afraid. No need at all.

CHAPTER 25

JESSIE AND NATE were among the last guests to leave the party, and Louisa May was asleep by the time Nate had turned the bend by the old churchyard. They were both surprised she had enjoyed herself so much, even if most of her friends had not been there, except Celine Barry, who had come with her mum and little Hester Sue. Her dad had stayed at home to keep an eye on her grandmother. 'Just in case she walks into that pond again in her nightie, thinking she had heard the fairies call her,' Celine had said, rolling her eyes. 'You wouldn't believe how *exhausting* it is to have a Nana like that! I mean, she is really sweet, and I love her to bits, but – talking of being away with the fairies! Honestly, it can drive you mad.'

Jessie smiled. Celine was a lovely girl, and she was glad she had come tonight, or else Louisa May might have got bored, and tried to sneak away to the castle, or the kilns, or wherever they were meeting tonight. The kilns, more likely, as the castle was too close to the Hunters' Farm, and people would have seen them. Not that there was anything anyone could do, of course, except make them clean up the next day.

'What's that light down there?' Jessie leaned forward in her seat, straining her eyes. 'It can't be the sunrise, can it? It's too early. And the village is in the west, not in the … oh, my God! Nate! It's a fire!'

Nate braked hard and sat staring ahead to where the red flames where rising high into the black sky like splashes of paint, or blood. It was a gruesome, yet almost surreal sight. 'Oh, shit … I hope it isn't … no,' he muttered, shaking his head, 'it isn't your café. It's the neighbour's house!'

Remembering how she had joked earlier this evening about wishing for the Johnsons to move away, Jessie felt sick. Even if she had not actually made the wish, it still felt as if she had just been punched in the stomach with an iron fist.

'What's going on? Are we home yet? Why—oh no! No!' cried Louisa May, suddenly wide awake. 'It's not your café, is it, mum?'

Jessie's throat felt so dry, she had to swallow several times before she could answer. 'No, sweetheart, it's the neighbours … the ones with the mad dog – look, there he is!'

Ossie, beside himself with fear, was running up and down in front of the house, barking furiously at the flames that were emerging from the little cottage. One moment they would show up like wild, angry flashes behind a window, the next they would burst through the splintering glass to lick at the stonework.

'Oh, my God …' Jessie shook her head, a hand on her mouth. It did not look like the fire had started only five minutes ago. Where on earth was the fire brigade? Had somebody even called them yet?

Suddenly frantic, Jessie pulled out her phone and cursed when she dropped it. Reaching down into the footwell, she cried, 'Nate? Do you think we should—'

But she was interrupted by the blaring of sirens, and then there was a flash of dazzling blue lights as the North Yorkshire Fire and Rescue Service came racing up the High Street, followed by an ambulance, and a police van.

'Oh, thank God! I hope they are not too late … do you think the Johnsons are still in there, Nate?'

But Nate did not answer. Instead, he jumped out of the car and darted down to the stream, splashed through the water, and up the other side, making for the Johnsons' house.

'Dad!!!'

Before Jessie even realised what was happening, Louisa May had pushed open the door and was running after her father.

'Louisa, no! Come back! Louisa!!!'

She cried with relief when she saw Mrs Colbeck stopping her daughter just before the bridge, holding her firmly by the shoulders until Jessie caught up with her. 'You'd better take her home, Jessie. And the dog – look, your husband's got him now. He is safe, and he's got the dog.'

Jessie opened her mouth to explain that Nate wasn't her husband but thought better of it. It didn't matter. He was safe, that was all that mattered.

Louisa May wiggled out of Mrs Colbeck's embrace and flung herself into her father's arms, sobbing desperately. 'Dad! Oh, God, Dad! I thought you were going to get inside … I thought you were …'

'It's okay, sweetheart,' Nate said, kissing the top of her head. 'It's okay … I was only trying to get the dog … I wouldn't have gone nearer, I promise.'

Well, thank God she doesn't know you are a voluntary fire fighter then, Jessie thought, her heart still pounding madly inside her chest. If the fire brigade had not turned up, she was not sure he would not have tried to get into the house, even without protective clothing. Shuddering at the thought, she quickly knelt down beside the dog, pulling him towards her. He was still barking, and trembling with fear.

'Oh, Ossie! Oh, you poor thing …' Jessie did not dare look over to where the team of firefighters were getting the hoses ready while trying to figure out whether their engines would fit through the narrow path between the Johnsons' end of terrace and her café. They wouldn't, of course, the old miners' cottages having been built much too close and with too little space at the back. This meant they had to carry equipment round the back of the house, thus wasting precious time. To make matters worse, the wind was blowing the flames across to Miss Lavender's house on the other side of the narrow path. Thank God the old lady was still in hospital. If they didn't get control over the fire soon, her house might yet burn down, café, bookshop, and all.

'Mum? Can we go home?'

Jessie hesitated. Of course they should go home. The police would tell them to any minute. Why hadn't they done so yet? Maybe they were busy supporting the fire brigade. It had taken them long enough to come out here. Why hadn't anyone had the sense to call them sooner? She tried not to look when she heard the violent cracking of wood. Windows were bursting, roof tiles were sent flying as the flames ate away hungrily at the wooden roof beams, screaming and howling. If the Johnsons were still inside, it didn't look like they were going to survive.

'Mum? Where is Mr Colbeck?'

'What?' Jessie turned her head, like in slow motion. Suddenly everything seemed to happen in slow motion. She tried to get Nate to look at her, but he was talking to Mrs Colbeck, putting a reassuring hand on her arm now and nodding as she spoke to him, quietly but urgently.

'… could not stop him … he was in his fireproofs and out of the house before I had opened my eyes!'

Jessie felt her mouth go dry. Mr Colbeck had gone into the house?? But he was a policeman, not a fireman, was he? Or maybe he had had training in that department as well, she did not know. Was it part of a policeman's training? She did not think so. She shook her head. It did not make sense. She must have got it wrong. It couldn't be Mr Colbeck. They had to be talking about someone else.

But then Nate turned his head and gave a slight nod in her direction, confirming her fears. She shut her eyes for a moment, digging her nails into the palms of her hands. So he *had* gone into the house, presumably before the fire brigade had arrived on the scene! Was that very brave or very foolish of him? She could not tell. Both, possibly. Even with training and fire-retardant clothing.

'I don't think we should go just now, sweetheart,' Jessie whispered. 'Let's wait until we know that Mr Colbeck – I mean, everybody – is safe, shall we?'

'But everybody else is gone. The police don't want us here, do they? They said we should go. Didn't you hear them?'

Jessie couldn't remember. Had she heard them?

'I'm scared, mum, I want to go home! You are scared, too, aren't you?' she said to the dog, sitting down in the grass with him and putting an arm around his shivering body. Having finally stopped his frantic barking, Ossie lay with his head on his paws, his eyes fixed on the house.

'Mrs Colbeck?'

Jessie turned around at the same time as Mrs Colbeck did. Oliver had arrived and was putting a hand on Mrs Colbeck's shoulder. The poor woman was shaking, and Jessie thought she had never seen a face so white. They were whispering for a minute or two; then she saw Oliver taking Mrs Colbeck's arm and leading her away. She could hear her weeping softly, and her heart lurched – please, God, she prayed, make him come back. Please bring her husband back.

'Tea, my dear?'

Jessie turned at the soft woman's voice and was astonished to see old Mrs Flite standing there, holding out a mug of steaming tea. On the bench beside her was a tray full of tea things, and a plate of homemade plum cake. At ninety-eight, Elizabeth Flite was the oldest resident of Bishops Bridge and she still lived by herself in a tiny cottage on Blacksmith Lane. There was nothing she liked better than to sit in the Bridge Café with her friends and talk about the card she would receive from the Queen on her hundredth birthday. Or the King, in case Mrs Flite should outlive her royal namesake.

Where on earth had *she* come from now? And why hadn't she been sent home by the police? She was tiny, to be sure, but …

'Thank you, that's very kind of you, Mrs Flite. But—'

'We cannot do anything, my dear,' the old lady insisted gently. 'It is all in God's hands. Trust, hope, and pray. There is nothing else we can do. Drink your tea, dear. I shall go and offer some to Mrs Colbeck now, and see that she eats some cake, too.'

Jessie doubted Mrs Colbeck would eat cake now, and yet, she could not help but admire Mrs Flite. There were some very kind and lovely people here in Bishops Bridge, and she was one of the kindest, and loveliest. She could not bear to think about another woman, and her husband, who were well liked and respected for their friendliness, and their unfailing helpfulness. Was it only this morning – no, yesterday morning – that they had found Daisy injured after her fall, and brought her back to the village? Could all of this really have happened so fast – and was there nothing they could do to make this nightmare end?

***

OVER AT FERN Hill Farm, Daisy was pacing the little cottage, worrying herself sick about the fire. From here, she could not even see anything, except that the sky over the village was brighter than it should be at two in the morning. Oliver had received an urgent message from Nate, asking him to come at once. Daisy knew she would be of no use at the site of the fire, especially with her arm in plaster, but being trapped here was almost worse. If only Joseph and Lily would come home! Then she could drink tea with Lily, and wouldn't feel so alone. But they were still at the Hunters', and Abi was asleep, oblivious to what was happening in the village, so there was only Drifter and her.

Deciding she might as well have coffee while she waited, Daisy put the kettle on, and leaned against the door of the fridge. This could be a long night. A very long night indeed.

A message flashed up on her phone just as she was spooning coffee into a mug.

> Mr Colbeck is trapped. He went in before the fire brigade arrived, and has not come out yet. Neither have the Johnsons. Please pray.

'Oh no. Oh, please, God, no!' Daisy felt her knees wobble, and she had to sit down. Thinking how they had all laughed this evening when Jessie had wished for the Johnsons to move away, she felt ashamed. Mortified. Had she laughed, too? She could not remember. All she could remember were the fairies Nana Barry could see, and the wretched rags they were to tie around that wretched hawthorn tree. And the feeling of dread in the pit of her stomach … or had it been foreboding after all? Had she sensed that something terrible would happen?

She got up, took her coffee, and walked slowly back to the window. She could not see the fire from here. She could not see anything.

Why did they have to be in such a remote area where it took so long for the fire brigade to arrive? Had nobody even called them before it was too late, and Mr Colbeck had got in, trying to rescue the Johnsons? Had they all been at the party, dancing around that stupid old tree, too drunk to notice that down in the village, a house was on fire??

Realizing there was no point in asking these questions now, Daisy briefly closed her eyes and sighed. 'Sorry, God. Sorry,' she whispered, shaking her head. Then she took a cushion from the sofa and pressed it to her chest as she sat down. And there she sat, her eyes fixed on the yard, and prayed until the coffee was cold, and the cushion in her arms wet with her tears.

***

THEY HAD ALL been sent home and told to keep their doors and windows shut. The police had been very clear about who was allowed to stay, and who wasn't: Oliver and Mrs Flite had taken Mrs Colbeck back inside her house, where they sat and waited for news, and everyone else had gone home. Jessie and Nate had taken the dog with them, as there was nowhere else for poor Ossie to go. He was curled up on the sofa with Louisa May now, while Jessie was making hot chocolate.

This is my fault, she kept thinking, sniffing as she put the milk pan on the hob. This is all my fault. If only I hadn't wished for the Johnsons to move away, this would never have happened. Stupid tree. Stupid wish. And stupid, stupid me!

What if the Johnsons should perish in the fire? Or Mr Colbeck? She would never be able to forgive herself if anything happened to any of them.

'Jessie?'

She spun around, dropping the wooden spoon she had been holding, and bent down to pick it up. When Nate took her hands and pulled her back up, she promptly burst into tears.

'Darling! Don't cry. Please. Look, I have brought you your phone. There is a message from Oliver. Do you want me to read it first? In case it's—'

But Jessie had already snatched the phone from him and swiped the screen with a trembling finger. Her hand flew to her mouth, and she gasped. 'No! Oh no! No!!!'

***

THEY HAD FOUND Philip Colbeck's body buried underneath the smouldering remains of a timber beam that must have fallen on him when the roof collapsed, knocking him unconscious. One of the firefighters had carried him out of the house, where paramedics had taken over, immediately starting resuscitation. But it had been too late, Oliver said when Nate spoke to him later. They had not been able to bring him back.

The Johnsons, on the other hand, had been saved. They had been taken to the nearest hospital with minor burns and, in Mr Johnson's case, with smoke inhalation, but were expected to be released after a couple of days. They would not have a home to return to though as their house had burnt down to the ground. It was not until the early hours of the morning, when Mrs Colbeck was already weeping over her husband's lifeless body, that the fire brigade had at last been able to extinguish the last of the flames. To Mrs Colbeck, of course, that did not matter at all. The only thing that mattered was that she had lost a most beloved husband who had meant the world to her.

Tears were streaming down Jessie's face as she stood there in the kitchen of her little cottage, her head buried in the folds of Nate's shirt, while Louisa May was making the hot chocolate. How lucky I am, Jessie thought in between sobs and hiccups, to have these two. How lucky we are to be alive, and safe. Life, she thought, is such a fragile thing. It can be shattered in an instant, and suddenly all our certainties are stripped away. Everything we believed in, everything we lived for – all gone with the person we loved most in the world. And the cruel thing was – and she had experienced this herself when her sister had died – for everyone else life would go on. Tonight, people might go home thinking things would never be the same again in Bishops Bridge. They would though. They would. The house would be rebuilt, and sooner or later, life would go on as it had before. Perhaps it was cruel, perhaps it was for the best. Or perhaps it was just the way things were.

CHAPTER 26

THE ENTIRE VILLAGE was stunned into a shocked silence that lasted for several days. It hung above the rooftops like a dark and heavy cloud that could not be lifted, its gloomy atmosphere filling every nook and cranny in every wall of every room in every house. Even when people left their homes to go to work (some wishing they didn't have to, others being grateful for a chance to escape the eerie atmosphere for a few hours), they would walk in respectful silence past the blackened ruin that had once been the Johnsons' house, or past the Colbeck residence in its prominent plot on the corner of Church Lane and Brook Lane. Jessie and Lily had agreed on not opening their shops again until after the funeral. Jessie would provide cakes and sandwiches for the wake, and Abi had promised to help her.

'The whole of Rosedale will turn up, you'd better be prepared,' Abi said to Oliver when he came and brought Drifter on Tuesday morning. He was just heading out to meet Mrs Colbeck and her family, to talk about the funeral, and Daisy had an appointment at the hospital to have her proper cast fitted. 'Philip Colbeck was very well-liked and respected among the villagers. He will be sadly missed – unlike the Johnsons, I'm afraid. I know it's not kind to say it, but I think it would be altogether better if they did not return.'

Oliver nodded. 'Yes, perhaps – but if they do, they deserve a chance to be forgiven. After all, it isn't their fault that the fire broke out in the first place, and it isn't their fault Philip Colbeck died either. If his widow does not blame them, who are we to do so?'

'You are right, of course. I still think they would find it difficult … anyway. It is not for us to say what will or will not happen, is it? Time will tell. And hopefully heal.'

Oliver put a hand on her arm. 'I'm sorry, I didn't mean to sound patronizing. It would be difficult for them, no doubt, if they returned to Bishops Bridge.' Then he nodded towards the car, where his wife was already waiting for him. 'I'm afraid I have to go now – you sure you'll be alright looking after the little one?'

'Course I am. Take your time now, don't rush, and I'll see you later. – Come on, Drifter, let's go find Theo, the old lazybones,' she called to the dog who followed her, tail wagging, to the farmhouse.

When she had put Drifter down and watched him clamber into Theo's basket (an intrusion the older dog bore with an air of admirable stoicism), Abi stood in the kitchen for a few minutes, not quite sure what to do with herself. It was not like her to be judgemental, or downright unkind, and she hated to think that that was how Oliver saw her now. Of course the Johnsons were not to blame; she had never meant to say that they were. The fire had been caused by a defective power supply to the Johnson's ancient TV set, and not through carelessness on Mr Johnson's part. Abi felt sure she had not been the only one to suspect Mr Johnson of having fallen asleep on the sofa with a burning cigarette in his hand. Once the initial explosion had set the living room on fire, it had rapidly spread all over the ground floor and up the stairs before the Johnsons, sound asleep, had even heard or smelt anything. What a dreadful shock it must have been to wake up and see the smoke creeping in underneath their bedroom door! To feel the imminent heat of the fire that was raging outside the door, knowing it would not be long until the flames found their way inside. What an unimaginable horror! If anything, she should pity them.

'You alright, Abi? You look a little pale.'

'What?' She turned around with a start. 'Oh. Hello, Joseph. I never heard you come in.'

He frowned. 'No, you didn't. And I seem to have just missed Oliver. Shame, I wanted to ask him something … never mind, it can wait. Tea?'

'Yes, please. I'll put the kettle on. I have shortbread, too.'

'Lovely. Is Lily in, too?'

'No, she's gone to York to collect Miss Lavender from the hospital, since Daisy cannot drive. Also, she has an appointment in Whitby to have her permanent cast fitted. That is, after they have talked to Mrs Colbeck about the funeral arrangements … I'm afraid it will be down to Lily to tell Miss Lavender about the fire, and prepare her for the sight that awaits her when she comes home.'

Joseph scratched his head. 'Oh, yes, of course. Lily mentioned that this morning. I forgot. Sorry.'

'Nothing to be sorry about. I'm glad you have time for a cup of tea. This fire business is really getting to me … I can't stop thinking about it.'

He gave a sad smile and shrugged. 'None of us can.

Sit down, and I'll make the tea.'

***

THEY HAD JUST been sitting at the table for a few minutes when Jessie walked in, closely followed by Ossie. The collie dropped at her feet the moment she sat down, putting his muzzle on his paws. Drifter, who had come to say hello, found himself being resolutely ignored, and sat down at Abi's feet, hoping for attention. When she didn't bend down to stroke him, he curled up into a ball, pushed his nose under his front paws, and sighed as if he was carrying the weight of the world.

Joseph laughed at the picture. 'Now there is a dog who has found his mistress! Ossie, I mean. We all know that little Drifter here has found his home alright. Would they let you keep him, do you think?'

'Oh, I don't know. I can't imagine they would but …' Jessie shrugged and helped herself to a shortbread finger. 'You never know, do you? Louisa May would be more than happy to keep him, of course, even if I have to remind her that Ampleforth College is not some nineteen-fifties school from an Enid Blyton novel, where pupils can bring their dogs.' Turning to Abi, she said, 'Anyway, I was wondering … is Daisy in? Or Lily?'

'Sorry, but no. Lily has gone to York to pick up Miss Lavender, and Daisy has gone with Oliver. They are meeting Mrs Colbeck and her family. To talk about the funeral.'

Jessie nodded and bit her lip. Clearly, there was something on her mind – something to do with the fire probably, thought Abi. And the dog would always remind her of that terrible night. Maybe it would be better if the Johnsons took him back after all.

'Sorry, ladies, but I've got to go,' Joseph said and pushed back his chair. 'Thanks for the tea, Abi, and I'll see you later. Take care, Jessie!'

As soon as he was gone, Jessie looked at Abi, tears shimmering in her eyes. 'Abi? Can I ask you something?'

'Of course. Anything.'

'At the party … when we were all waiting to make a wish, I … I said something … um … I made a silly joke – about how I wished the Johnsons would move away.' She swallowed. 'And now … and now they have lost their *home*! Oh, Abi! Do you think—'

'Of course not!' Impulsively, Abi reached for her hands. 'Oh lass! You don't really believe this happened because you made a *joke*? Surely that would be taking things a little too far, don't you think?'

'I don't know – would it?'

'Yes! And I am sure Lily, Daisy, in fact *everybody else*, would agree with me. Don't blame yourself, lass! That won't bring him back … apart from the fact that it's nonsense, of course. You are *not* to blame. This is *not* your fault. Do you hear me?'

Jessie nodded, but did not look at all convinced. Ossie had sat up and put his head in her lap, gazing up at her with his clear blue eyes. He certainly did not blame her for anything.

'Jessie,' Abi said, 'I know what you saw was terrible, and I can imagine how helpless you must have felt watching the house burn, but you're not *to blame*!' She didn't know why but she felt the need to explain things to the poor girl who felt so guilty about something that was not her fault at all. 'It was unlucky that most people were still at the party at the time the fire broke out. There was hardly anyone at home in the village, you see. By the time Mrs Colbeck woke up because of the noise, her husband was probably already putting on his clothes, or maybe he'd already gone. She couldn't have stopped him, lass,' she said, gently rubbing Jessie's hands, 'no one could. It was what he did, what he lived for: to *rescue*. His wife knew she could not have stopped him from going into that house, unless the fire brigade got there first. Sadly, they didn't.'

'His father and grandfather had been firefighters, and all of his siblings are either that or in the police force,' she went on to explain. 'Philip Colbeck grew up in a family of men whose *mission in life* it was to protect and rescue others. He knew what he was doing because he had done this all his life. He was a fireman first, you see, before he was married. Then a friend of his, also a fireman, died in a fire, and he could not save him. He was devastated. So his fiancée persuaded him to go into the police force instead. She thought that if he had to have a dangerous job, she would rather have him patrolling the streets of York than risking his life getting inside burning buildings …' Abi pursed her lips. 'Only he never stopped being a fireman at heart. And now …' She shook her head. 'It's sad, but at the end of the day … that's what Philip Colbeck lived, and ultimately died for. That's who he was.'

Jessie buried her face in her hands and shook her head. 'But I still feel bad about that joke! I can't help it. It just … haunts me.'

Abi took her hand and gave it a little squeeze. 'I know. I'm sorry, lass.'

This fire, she thought, when Jessie had gone with the dog at her heels, will haunt us all for a long time yet.

***

OUTSIDE THE COLBECKS' house, Daisy stood at the car and said, 'I think I don't want to go straight to the hospital now, Oliver. I need a little break, to be honest … and the appointment is not until a quarter past three. Can we stop at Rievaulx Abbey perhaps? We always said we would go but haven't been so far … would that be okay?'

'Of course. It's not even twelve yet, so we have plenty of time. I was going to take you out for lunch, but we can have a little something at the Abbey café, that's fine, or stop in Helmsley. Yes, let's do that. You certainly deserve a treat – you were an absolute angel, Daisy! So kind, so patient, so full of compassion … I really couldn't have done this without you.'

While Daisy had sat with the grieving widow, Oliver had been able to talk to Philip Colbeck's son and daughter, learning much about the deceased one's life, and what he might have wanted for the funeral. As the Colbecks had not been churchgoers, they did not know many hymns, but his daughter insisted they include *Nearer My God to Thee*. Oliver had managed to keep his sigh in, and made a mental note of asking Ellen. He needn't have worried though, as Mrs Colbeck herself had brought up the subject of Ellen during her tearful talk with Daisy, asking her if she thought Ellen would sing for her husband. Daisy was certain she would, thinking that this might perhaps have a somewhat healing effect on Ellen, after what she had been through at her father's funeral. On the other hand, it would bring back painful memories that might still be too fresh … but they would find out when they asked her.

If she says no, Daisy thought, I will offer to play the *Ave Maria* on the violin. And *Nearer My God*, too, if they insist.

Daisy blushed. 'Thank you, but I didn't really do very much. I asked a few questions – a very few – but mostly, I just offered compassion, and listened. Maybe I should— oh. Is that your phone?'

Hoping it would not be anyone to prevent him from spending precious time with his wife, Oliver tapped at the dashboard to answer the call via Bluetooth. 'Yes, Oliver Clifford-Jones speaking, what can I do for you?'

'Is that the vicar?'

'Yes. Who is speaking, please?'

'It's Johnson. Cedric Johnson. I am calling from the hospital.'

'Oh. Yes, of course. How are you then, Mr Johnson? And how is your wife?'

'That's why I'm calling. I'm calling to say that it would have been nice if one of your lot might have paid us a visit by now, and help us with this mess. Insurance and what have you. Isn't that part of your job as a vicar?'

Oliver rolled his eyes at his wife. 'Well, no, not really. Of course we would try to help but you and your wife do not belong to my congregation, Mr Johnson. You are not members of the Anglican Church at all. Still, if you would like me to come and see you, I am sure I can—'

'Oh, don't worry, I won't bother you then. Bloody doctor already said I would have to get a lawyer, though how I am going to pay one is a different matter, but that's only by the by. But you can tell that wretched woman she can keep that daft dog if she wants to, or do with him as she pleases, because we can't have him anymore, not without a house or garden to call our own.'

'Right,' said Oliver, setting the indicator to get onto the A170. 'I'll speak to her. Is there anything else I can do for you? Really, I don't mind—'

'Yeah, yeah, you can mind your own business, that's what. We are not coming back to bloody Bishops Bridge, and I am not going anywhere with that whining old wife, either. We are done. Finished. She can find somebody else to tie her blooming shoelaces, and pick up the stuff she drops all over the place. I've had enough. Of her, and all of you.'

And before Oliver could say anything, he had rung off.

'Nice chap.'

'Mmm …' Daisy was already tapping into her phone. 'I'm texting Jessie. So she knows they have now officially adopted Ossie. It's funny, isn't it, the way we get dogs here in Bishops Bridge? I find mine in the churchyard, Jessie has hers dumped on her by her nasty neighbours … sorry, that was not kind. What did he say about Mrs Johnson's shoelaces and the things she dropped? I didn't understand that.'

'I didn't get that either. But we can ask Abi tonight. I'm sure she will be able to explain. Now then, next stop – Rievaulx Abbey!'

***

MEANWHILE, MISS LAVENDER closed the door behind her and sat down on a kitchen chair. There were flowers on the table and a card sat propped up against the vase, with her name written on the envelope. She would read the card later. It was probably from Daisy. Lily, who had collected her from the hospital earlier, had brought a large bag of shopping, together with a chicken casserole and a few slices of Abi's farmhouse loaf. She had been reluctant to go, saying she did not like to leave her on her own now, but Miss Lavender had left her with no choice. She needed to be alone. She needed to think. And what a lot there was to think about!

First, there was the trifling little matter of what to do about the shop, and the house. Maybe the doctor was right, maybe she should think about retiring. She was seventy-seven, she had worked all her life. But this shop was her lifeblood. How could she expect people, especially strangers like the doctors and nurses at the hospital, to understand? Thinking of working at her age! Crazy. Mad. Completely round the bend. Well, maybe she was. But even so, she could not imagine Bishops Bridge without the village shop. Where would people buy their milk and newspaper in the morning?

She sighed. They would do their shopping on their way home from work, and go to the big supermarkets on Saturdays, like most of them did, anyway, for their weekly shopping. And read the newspaper online, as many people seemed to do these days. Maybe Lily was right. Maybe it was time for a change. For all of them. Because one thing was clear: The fire had destroyed more than just the Johnsons' home, and Mrs Colbeck's life when she had lost her husband. It had destroyed the sense of peace in the village.

The silence Miss Lavender had perceived as they had driven up the deserted High Street had been palpable, almost oppressing. Bishops Bridge was mourning. Even the Little Egret that lived by the stream was gone. Lily had remarked she had not seen him since last week, and she had been here every day.

The ruin was a gruesome sight even in daylight, and Miss Lavender had shuddered when she had seen it. The site had been fenced off, and a sign had been put up: 'Danger! Keep out!' It was so sad. She had no idea what the owners of the cottage (Mr and Mrs Johnson had been renting) were going to do. Claim insurance and sell up, most likely. What was it to them, anyway? An investment, nothing more. They had never lived here.

Absentmindedly touching the silky petals of the flowers (pale pink roses and fragrant white carnations – only Daisy knew that she loved those the most), Miss Lavender got up and went over to the window. She threw up the sash, leaned out and closed her eyes, inhaling the sweet June air.

When she opened her eyes again, she saw Ellen standing by the stream, and a tall, feisty looking girl she had not seen before. They were looking up to her and waving.

'Hello, Miss Lavender! Good to see you back!' Ellen was wearing a long, floaty summer dress that looked very much like it had once belonged to her mother. 'We were going to walk to Rosedale Abbey for a coffee, but I can get the car if you would like to accompany us? It is rather warm, and I'm not sure how far you would want to walk. That is, if you want to come with us.'

Miss Lavender hesitated. She was supposed to rest. And she really wanted to be alone, and think. But she did not want to miss the opportunity to see Ellen and catch up with her before she went back to London. Now that both her parents were gone, Miss Lavender was not sure how often Ellen was going to come back to Rosedale. If she was coming back at all, that was. But would she have the heart to sell Birchwood Park unless she really had to?

She sighed. Only time would tell.

'That would be very kind of you, thank you,' she called down. 'If you don't mind getting the car?'

***

'BUT MRS JOHNSON *can't* be on her own!' Abi shook her head angrily. 'What *on earth* is that man thinking? The poor woman can't even tie her own shoelaces, for goodness' sake!'

Oliver and Daisy were sitting in Abi's kitchen, the dogs asleep under the table. Daisy had her brand new cast, which she still eyed suspiciously ('Four weeks!' she had exclaimed on the way home. 'What am I going to do for *four weeks?*' – To which Oliver had replied, 'Not ride, I'm afraid. Ruby and Starlight will have to content themselves with running around in the fields') and they had brought pies from Helmsley, which they were now enjoying with a bottle of red.

Oliver refilled their glasses. 'That's what Mr Johnson said. Why, what's the matter with her?'

'Mrs Johnson is a very sick woman. Rheumatoid arthritis,' Abi explained. 'I think she first had trouble with her hands when she was in her early thirties, or even before that. When they moved here about ten years ago, she was already completely dependent on her husband. That's why she never leaves the house.'

'Oh.' Daisy put a hand to her mouth. 'Poor Mrs Johnson! It's a very painful condition, isn't it? And him leaving her – why, that is cruel!'

'It is. But it's not unlike him, I'm afraid. Most people thought they were both bad, but really, it was only him. Like I said, she never left the house, and they hardly ever welcomed guests into their home. Well, she did venture into the garden sometimes, but never far, and never for long. Poor woman.'

'But – why did they get a dog then? If she could not even walk, or be left on her own?'

'Ah. That was Mr Johnson's idea. He thought if he had a dog, he would have an excuse to get out of the house for a few hours every day. While I cannot blame him for that, I suspect the real reason was that he could not stand the constant nagging of his poor, crippled wife, which is not very charitable, is it? Now *he* says – this may or may not be true – that she made him stay at home all day, in case she needed anything. So he spent his days sitting in the garden smoking and letting the dog do as he pleased while she was seated in an armchair by the window, in the summer, or by the fire, in the winter. I can't remember the last time I actually *saw* her …' Abi frowned. 'Anyway, now I think about it, I can guess what that poor dog would have wanted: either a proper job, like herding, or to be allowed to look after his mistress. But she was inside, and he was outside. No wonder he was always so wound up. Well,' she concluded, 'I suppose he will calm down now. He already has, from what I saw this morning.'

'Do they have any children?' asked Daisy, shocked to learn that they had been so mistaken about Mrs Johnson.

'Anyone Mrs Johnson could go to, if her husband is really going to leave her?'

'Oh yes, you bet he is. And they have children, yes – three, if I am not mistaken. But they don't live nearby, and even if they did, I doubt that they would care. Their youngest daughter might, she is the nicest of the lot, and the only one I remember having met once or twice. I think she lives on the Isle of Skye now – and I can't see Mrs Johnson living *there*, not at her age, and in her state of health. I never thought I'd say it, but I feel really sorry for her. She might end up in a care home – and not one of the nice ones where they serve afternoon tea on a silver trolley.'

CHAPTER 27

'But what if I fail? If I can't do this?'

'You won't fail,' Katharina assured her friend, 'you never do. You can always sing, in every situation, you said so yourself. And I have known you long enough to know this to be true.' She rubbed her hand gently up and down Ellen's arm. 'Please promise me you'll say yes.'

Ellen sighed. She got up, went to stand at the French doors that led out onto the raised patio, and crossed her arms in front of her chest. Looking out at the landscaped gardens, she felt her eyes smarting with unshed tears as she thought of her mum. The garden had been her domain. While they had always had a gardener to do the heavy work (Ellen made a mental note of emailing him to tell him she would no longer be able to afford his services, or not after this summer, anyway), Angela had tended to her flower beds and herbaceous borders until she was eventually forced to give up because she could not leave the house anymore. Her father had said that was when he knew she was not going to live. But until the day she died Angela had insisted she were taken to the window and sat in a chair, wrapped up in blankets, so she could look down into her beloved garden. She did not want to die in a hospice, nor in a hospital, but at home, and God had granted her that final wish: Angela Maverick had fallen asleep in that armchair, a smile on her lips, with her husband and daughter beside her.

A single tear rolled down Ellen's cheek. For all that her mother's death had been so peaceful in the end, her father had not been able to cope. Just three short weeks after the funeral, he had walked into the wood and shot himself.

Today, this was four months ago.

'Ellen?'

'Yes?' Ellen did not turn around. She did not wipe her tears away either – she had not even realised they had come, and found their way down her cheeks. She just stood there and looked out into the garden, thinking of her mum.

Mama.

Another tear, and another. But still, she did not move. She did not even put a hand to her cheek to wipe the tears away. She just let them fall.

'Do you want me to reschedule my flight? I could stay with you for another week. Until after the funeral. Or however long you think you might need me here.'

Ellen hesitated. She knew it was kindly meant, but she could not keep her friend here when she knew she really wanted to go home. Her parents were waiting for her in Vienna. Katharina was an only child, and she had not been home since Christmas. Her mum and dad would want to make the most of the summer they had with their precious daughter. It was not Katharina's fault that her own parents were dead. That she was all alone, with no one left in the world.

'Ellen?'

'It's fine. Go home, your parents are waiting for you. I will take you to York tomorrow, as promised.'

She felt Katharina's hand on her arm and swallowed. Too much sympathy would only open the flood gates, and she really did not want to cry so much for her own sake. This was not about her grief now, it was about Mrs Colbeck's. Oliver had said she had asked her to sing at the funeral next Tuesday, and she knew she had no right to deny her that wish. Just the *Ave Maria*, fittingly known as *Ellen's Gesang*. It almost made her smile. Dear old Schubert. But she did not feel like smiling. In fact, she seemed to have forgotten how to smile.

But you have not forgotten how to sing.

'Mama?' she whispered, putting a hand to the door frame and listening intently. But the only sounds she could hear were the joyful chirping of the birds in the trees, and the bleating of her neighbour's sheep in the distance.

'Are you sure?'

Katharina had not heard a voice, of course. And why would she? She had only heard it in her imagination. Her mother was gone. She would never hear her voice again. Not trusting herself to look at her friend, Ellen did not turn around as she nodded. 'I am sure. I will take you to York tomorrow, so you can catch that plane on Friday. To go home.'

'And you will sing at Mr Colbeck's funeral?'

'I will.'

She felt her arm being gently squeezed. 'That's good. Mrs Colbeck will be so pleased. If that is the right word. I don't know. I am sorry – I have never lost a father, or mother. Or any loved one, really. I even have two sets of grandparents. I am so lucky, I know. I'm sorry, Ellen. For you, and for Mrs Colbeck. But mostly for you.' She hesitated. 'If there is ever anything I can do for you – anything at all – you will let me know, won't you?'

Ellen swallowed. There was nothing Katharina could do for her. Or anyone. But she smiled through her tears and said, 'Of course.'

***

'So what did she say?'

Daisy was trying to wriggle into a sweater and found it ridiculously hard. But the more often she got stuck, the more determined she became. She knew Oliver was watching her, ready to come to the rescue, but she had insisted she could manage. It was bad enough that she could not look after the horses properly, let alone ride. But now that Ellen had said she would stay a bit longer, she felt a little less bad about it. And she could still do some of the jobs, like leading the more docile ponies like the two Lady Greys, to the field and back. One at a time, of course.

'She said yes. I must admit, I am relieved – after what the poor girl has been through herself lately, I admit I was surprised to hear her say she would not only stay all summer, but sing at the funeral, too. I'm sure she is doing it for Mrs Colbeck, but still, I'm relieved. And glad.'

Holding the sleeve of her sweater between her teeth, trying to pull it down her arm, all Daisy could do was nod. She was glad, too, especially as she had realised she would not have been able to play the violin with her left arm in plaster. Funny how this had not crossed her mind before. Ellen's singing would have them all crying, no doubt, but she knew it meant a lot to Mrs Colbeck. She and her husband had been so fond of Ellen, and had often invited her to stop by for a cup of tea when she had been practising her singing in the church. Mr Colbeck had also been the one who had found her father, and driven straight down to London to tell Ellen in person.

'No one should hear such things from a stranger, and certainly not over the phone. I know they would send some London officers to her flat, or tell her principal at the college, but I'd much rather she heard it from someone who actually knew her father, and cared about him,' he had explained. His wife had agreed to come with him, and together, they had brought her home.

And now, only four months later, she would sing at Philip Colbeck's funeral.

'She is so brave,' Daisy said. She had finally managed to pull the sleeve down and reached for her water glass on the table. It was amazing how exhausting such a simple task could be!

'She is, yes. Um … talking of being brave … I – I had a phone call this morning, Daisy. While you were out feeding the ponies.'

Putting the glass down, Daisy turned slowly around, her head pounding. 'Yes?'

'It was Doctor Palmer. He has got the test results.'

I knew it, she thought. I knew it was going to be bad news. Now what?

'Yes.' Oliver bit his lip. 'It's – it's what I feared. It's my fault. I'm sorry, Daisy.'

Daisy felt tears welling up in her eyes but fought hard to keep them from falling. She could not cry now. She had no right to cry. They had just talked about Mr Colbeck's funeral, and about poor Ellen being all alone in the world, without any family at all – how could she be so selfish as to think of her own little worries? This was nothing compared to what others had to go through. Nothing.

'Darling?'

Yes, she thought, but could not speak. I heard you. No children. No hope.

'Would you like me to make you a cup of tea?'

She nodded, then frowned. How could he be so calm? And so kind? Why wasn't he angry? He had every reason to be angry. With himself, with her, with God. He could rant about the unfairness of it all, couldn't he? Or he could be sad. He never cried. Why did he never cry? Why was he always so infuriatingly calm, as if nothing could ever shake him?

'Then I'm going to put the kettle on now.'

He turned and slowly walked through to the kitchen, his arms hanging limply to both sides of his body. As she watched him go, her water glass clutched in her hand, she realised she was wrong: He was not calm at all, even if his physique betrayed his emotions. He was devastated. Broken.

Suddenly she jumped up, knocking her water glass down. 'Oliver! Wait!'

She could not let him do this for her, when really it should be *her* comforting *him*. Had she got so used to him being the strong partner in their relationship? The one who would always comfort, always soothe, always encourage, even when he had nothing to give because he himself was feeling empty and low? She had to be strong now. Stronger than before – and not, as usual, looking for her husband to help her. Always fretting, always worrying. And always thinking of herself first. *Me, me, me.* Constantly complaining about her lot in life, she had been nothing but a spoilt, immature girl who didn't know *just how lucky* she was! How blessed, and privileged.

Coming into the kitchen, she put a hand on his shoulder – and flinched when she felt his body go tense. Was he resenting her now? But why? It was not her fault, was it? Of course it wasn't his, and she was going to tell him, but it wasn't hers either – it just was not meant to be, and they would both have to come to terms with that. The sooner the better.

'Oliver, please, don't do this now. Please. Sit down. I'll make the tea.'

'I'm fine.'

'No, you are *not* fine! I can see you aren't. You're upset, and you have every reason to be upset. This is … devastating. Especially for you. But we are married, Oliver, we must carry the weight of this together. There is no need for you to—'

'There is every need, yes! Because it's my fault, isn't it? I cannot give you what you want, what you need so badly. Any other man could perhaps, but not I, your husband. You said you were useless – now look who's the useless one!'

And he spun on his heel to face her, his face contorted with pain. 'I cannot make you happy, Daisy. I cannot give you what you want. What you need. Not now, not ever. The decent thing would be to let you go—'

'No!'

'Yes! Don't you see, Daisy? You were born with everything, and I have given you nothing. You left your home, gave up your career, left your horse behind – all for me! And look how I have repaid you! Look! This is what has become of you – a wretched, motherless, unhappy woman. You don't deserve this. You—'

'I don't deserve to hear such *talk*! I forbid you to talk like that! Stop it!' Her voice had turned shrill, and the dog began barking and jumping up at them in turn. Daisy ignored him. She only had eyes for her husband now, even though it did not seem to make a difference to him. 'Please, Oliver, you mustn't talk like that!' she pleaded. 'We can work it out! Look, I've got the horses now, I have a plan – I'll tell you about it later – *and* I have Cousin Lavinia! And we have Drifter. Just think of all the good things that have happened to us since we came here. We have so much, Oliver, so much! Friends, and a home, and—'

His eyes darkened. 'A home? What's a home without children? The sound of little feet? The Rectory is huge, you keep reminding me it is far too big. And it is! It's ridiculous! How many dogs do you want to fill all that space? A dog is not a child! It is not the same!'

'I never said it was, but …'

'I need to get out of here!'

Grabbing the car keys from the kitchen table, Oliver pushed past her, yanked open the door and slammed it shut behind him.

CHAPTER 28

NOT KNOWING WHERE else to go, Daisy took Drifter and walked into the village. It was hot and humid and by the time she reached the old stone bridge, she just wanted to sit down in the shade and rest. 'Come on, Little One, let's sit by the stream. I can put my feet in the water, and you can have a little paddle. Would you like that? Yes?'

She did not know how long she had been sitting there, watching the dog a little half-heartedly, when she felt a hand on her shoulder. It wasn't Oliver's hand – she would have known his touch from anyone else's – so she was reluctant to turn around, too weary to even look up. It was Lavinia's gentle voice that made her lift up her tear-streaked face.

'My dear girl. How long have you been sitting here?'

Daisy shrugged but did not say anything. Well, she didn't know, did she? It might have been half an hour, it might have been for ever. The sun had disappeared behind thick, dark clouds, and the air was laced with the smell of rain. The wind had picked up quite a bit, too, and Daisy was shivering in her thin dress.

Maybe I had better get back, she thought. Make the most of the last remaining days in our dear little cottage. They would move to the Rectory next weekend, and she had not even started packing yet. Their furniture had arrived last week, so it was mostly clothes and personal things. It would not take long. And yet, she was dreading the move more than ever. What was there to look forward to? A ridiculously large, empty house. A house that would remain empty, unless they filled it with books and dogs. She shook her head wearily as she recalled Oliver's bitter words.

How many dogs do you want to fill all that space?

She sighed. Yes, how many?

'Do you want me to walk you home? Or would you like to come over and have tea with me? You look like you could do with a decent cup of tea, if you don't mind me saying so.'

But Daisy shook her head. She didn't want to go anywhere. She just wanted to sit here and wait for the storm to pass. Literally. 'No,' she said at last, 'I'm alright. But you had better get back home, Lavinia, before it starts to rain. I believe there is a storm coming.'

'Well then, let's go and sit in the church. The rain can't hurt us in there, can it?'

Daisy sighed. There was no point in arguing with Cousin Lavinia. She would not get rid of her so easily. 'Okay,' she gave in, wearily getting to her feet, 'but we'll have to take Drifter. He may be frightened of thunderstorms.'

The old lady tutted. 'I doubt that. He will have encountered quite a few of those during his lost days. But of course he can come with us. I'm sure Oliver wouldn't mind.'

Daisy bit her lip. She had much rather they did not speak of Oliver right now. She did not want to cry in front of Lavinia, and she did not feel she had the right to tell her about the quarrel they had had. If it had been a quarrel – it hadn't, though, had it? He had just stormed off, leaving her to pick up the pieces.

Like I did last week, when I took Ruby and rode off. Looks like there are two who can play at the game, she thought wryly as she followed Lavinia into the church.

***

Having driven around Rosedale aimlessly for an hour or so, Oliver finally parked the car on the verge of the track that led to the farms. Then he sat there and tried to think of what to do. Should he go home? Would Daisy still be there? Would she be angry with him, or worse still, in tears? Probably. She always cried at the smallest of things. Sometimes he found himself losing patience with his wife. Why couldn't she be stronger? Why couldn't she fight for what she wanted in life? Why did she always give up so easily, or simply rely on him to sort things out? He couldn't be strong all the time. Not now, he couldn't. He had reached a dead end himself.

'What do I do now, Lord?' he asked, putting his head on the steering wheel. 'What do I do?'

Maybe I'll walk up to the kilns, he thought, before the storm hits the valley. Or I can walk up anyway, and watch the infamous ghost guard that treasure of his. After all, I am not afraid of thunderstorms, am I, or of ghosts? Fears are my wife's department. Especially irrational ones. Who would be afraid of fairies? They did not even exist! The fear of deep, impenetrable waters he could understand after she had so very nearly lost her baby sister in the pond, but fairies?

Stop it, that's not fair. She went to the Midsommer Fest with you, even though she had every reason not to go. And not because of her fears, but because she was hurt. And yet she went, and she tied a wish around that tree, too.

A wish that has just come to nothing. A wish not even God would grant them, never mind a stupid old tree.

With a weary sigh, Oliver started the motor and drove up to the farm. We can't run away, he thought. There is proof now of my inability to father children. Proof of my failure as a husband. We might as well get it over with, and go our separate ways.

It's for the best, a voice inside his head was saying. Clearly that had to be the voice of reason. – You know you can't live without her, a different voice reminded him. That was his heart speaking. By the time he reached the farm, Oliver felt dizzy, confused, and utterly wretched. And he still had no clue what he was going to do, or what he was going to say to her.

When he let himself into the cottage, his heart in his stomach, he was relieved to find it empty. But then he looked up at the darkening skies and frowned. Where was she? Drifter was gone, too. Where had she gone? She would not have gone over to Abi's for a tea and a chat. He knew her too well to know that when she was upset, she would either turn to him, or want to be alone. So what was he supposed to do now? Should he get back into the car and look for her? Did he even have the energy to do that? After all, it was only one week ago that he went to find her after she had walked out on him and got herself into that pickle with the horse.

And now you have done just the same. Looks like

two can play at that game, doesn't it?

Only he had not acted like a responsible, never mind loving, husband last week, ignoring her pain and letting her run off, hurt and confused. And today, he had pushed her away when she had just been trying to be kind. She had wanted to comfort him, and what had he done? He had walked away and left her to pick up the pieces.

'Alright then, I'll look for her,' he said, not sure whether he was talking to God, or to himself. Sometimes it did not seem to make such a big difference. The truth was, he felt very much alone with this mess. And what a mess it was! What a mess they had both made of it.

***

'How CAN I help him when he pushes me away?' Daisy turned to look at Lavinia, her face drawn and tired. 'It's not as if I am not wretched myself. We can't have children, and that's final. We can't. So what's next? And how do we find out if he won't even talk to me?'

Lavinia sighed. 'That's a lot of questions, lass. I'm afraid we won't find all the answers today. But one thing you really have to know: it is not you he is rejecting now. He just finds it hard to accept it, and that will take some time. He will come around, don't you worry. Courage, dear heart.'

Daisy sniffed. Courage. That was exactly what she didn't have these days. She used to be quite brave, didn't she? When she had taken Destiny from one event to the next, proudly presenting her to the judges, and challenging her to take even the most difficult hurdles and run faster than all the others, leaving them to take second and third place … because she had wanted to win. And she had loved every minute of it! Soaring the heights … she had been so confident then. Even when she was little, she had never been afraid of anything – well, apart from the pond, or any deep waters, for that matter. Her parents always said she had saved Kate's life that day because she had been so brave. She probably had – and yet, even today, all she could feel was guilt and shame. She had not looked after her like she should have. She had let her fall in, and nearly drown. Had she died, it would have been her fault.

But she didn't drown, did she? She is alive.

Yes. And she is a mother, too. I am the only one of us who isn't. Perhaps it's because I am the one who can't be trusted to look after a child?

'My little sister nearly drowned when I was eight,' she heard herself say, 'in our pond at home. I was supposed to look after her, but I was dreaming. I was not watching her like I should have. And then she fell in … I got her out, but the doctor said it had been very close. Had she died …'

'Oh, lass!' Lavinia put an arm around her shoulder. 'What a nightmare that must have been, and you only so little! – But she didn't die, did she? You saved her! I'm sure your parents were very proud of you. And grateful, too. – Does Oliver know about this trauma of yours?'

Daisy nodded. 'Yes. He does, and he has been really good about it. He could lose his patience with me, you know, and say, get over it, girl. It's in the past, and anyway, she did not die. But he would never speak to me like that. He has always been so good to me … always protected me … never challenged, never doubted me.' She scrunched the damp tissue she had been fiddling with into a ball and stuffed it into her pocket. 'When I told him I would give up event riding and not pursue an equine career after all, he accepted that, too. He knew I wanted children. He did, too, of course. That's why he never questioned my decision, I suppose. And since the competitions would have taken me away from home ever so often, it probably seemed sensible for me to stay at home. He knew I wanted to be a good mother. The *perfect* mother …' She shrugged and pulled out another tissue. Somehow the tears did not want to stop flowing.

Lavinia nodded. 'I see. And he knows that, of course, and now he feels guilty. Guilty because he never questioned you, never tried to persuade you to pursue your riding career – and guilty because now he knows that all the time it had been him. It's not his *fault*, of course, don't get me wrong! But he may think differently. He can't cope with the thought of having let you down. Failed you even.' She put a hand on Daisy's. 'You must be patient, Daisy. Give him time. And then, when he sees a little more clearly, you can talk and consider options. But not before that.'

'I don't want to talk. I don't want to consider options,' she wailed. 'I just want to show him how much I love him, how much I *care*!'

'I know, lass. I know. And he knows that, too, I am sure. Now, why don't you ring him and tell him where you are and that you would like him to come and pick you up? I believe it won't be long until that storm hits, and I don't have a car to take you home in. And you need to get home, Daisy. The sooner the better.'

She nodded and dug in her pocket for her phone. Tapping Oliver's number with trembling fingers, she held her breath as she waited for him to pick up. But he didn't.

***

OLIVER WAS WALKING down the track towards the village, his hands deep in his pockets. What with the thunderstorm hanging over the dale as it did, it did not seem likely that Daisy had walked up to the kilns, so he supposed she had gone to the stream, or perhaps the churchyard. He knew that was her favourite place to go when she needed to think. And by God, he had given her a lot to think about. And a lot to cry about, too. Because he had hurt her. Failed her.

But what about me, he thought as he stopped outside the gates to Wood End Farm. I have a lot to think about, and I am sad, too. Wretched. After all, it is my fault we cannot have children. And I have gone behind her back to do that test. It serves me right, doesn't it? Serves me bloody right.

'Oh no,' he muttered, kicking angrily at a stone, 'you are not going down that road now! No self-pity. Absolutely no—'

'Hello, Oliver! What are you doing here? I thought you had moved into the Rectory by now. Sorry, I'm not really good at keeping in touch. I've been busy with work. Lots of commissions – which is good, of course, but it does keep me a little out of touch with the real world. Susanna says I might as well put up a tent in the workshop. Fancy a cuppa?'

Relaxed and easy-going as ever, David Stanton was standing in the yard, leaning on an axe, and grinning back at him. Suddenly Oliver was reminded of his days as a carpenter, and he said, 'Not sure about that cuppa, but if you'd let me chop some wood, that would be great. I used to be a carpenter, you know, before I trained as a vicar.'

'Oh? Like Jesus, eh? Well, yes, chop away, by all means. But are you sure you want to do that in these clothes? You look rather smartly dressed, if you don't mind me saying so. Daisy might not be impressed when she sees you all covered in wood shavings and sawdust.'

Oh, sod Daisy, Oliver thought grimly and opened the gate.

***

WHILE DAISY WAS in the church crying her heart out to Lavinia, Oliver found himself opening up to David – whom he hardly knew at all, but maybe that was why – and felt much better for it. By the time he had told David everything, the wood was chopped, and he was covered in sawdust and sweat. His arms ached from the exertion, and the cup of tea David offered from his battered thermos flask was more than welcome now.

David drained his own cup, put it down on a pile of wood and said, 'Wow. That's a lot of information. I had no idea you were trying for a baby and – well. I have not known you for long, have I? And it's not the kind of thing you'd discuss with strangers. Or anyone really. Thank you for trusting me with that.'

'Thank *you* for listening. I know it's rich of me to complain when poor Mr Colbeck has just perished in that fire, Mrs Johnson has been deserted by her husband and has nowhere to go, and Ellen—'

'Yes, but we are not talking about Mr Colbeck or Mrs

Johnson or Ellen now, are we? We are talking about you, Oliver. You have a right to be sad, worried, angry … all of that, just like every other man. And you have an awful lot on your plate there, if you don't mind me saying so. Um – a question … why do you not talk to another clergyman, or anyone from the PCC perhaps? I thought, as a vicar, you'd have some sort of counsellor available. Isn't there anyone in charge of the clergymen's personal welfare in the Anglican Church? Or shouldn't there be someone?'

'Probably. But to be honest, I think talking to you has already helped me a lot. The next step, I suppose, will be to try and talk to my wife … only that seems rather difficult now. I did not exactly treat her well this morning, and then I just walked off, didn't I? I hurt her, David. I let her down.'

'You probably did, but I am sure she will forgive you the moment you take her in your arms and tell her you are sorry. She loves you so much – everyone can see that.'

Oliver nodded. 'I know … the point is, where do we go from here? With the Baby Issue, and everything? I thought we had already made such progress since … God, was it only last Saturday she found that letter? Anyway, we talked about that at length while we were sitting in A&E, and I thought were finally getting somewhere. We said we would look forward now, not back.'

'That sounds promising, doesn't it? Hopeful.'

Oliver looked at this hands. They felt red and hot, and would be covered in blisters after all that chopping. But boy, it had done him good! All the anger was gone, and what was left was a deep sense of regret.

'Yes, you would think so, wouldn't you? If only I hadn't—'

'Oliver! No ifs, no buts, no what-might-have-beens. No regrets. There is no point – it's all in the past. You cannot change what happened. But you can do something about the present, and the future. Do you know,' he said as he began to put his tools away, 'it took me all of twenty years to come to my senses and return to Rosedale. I could not believe my luck not only to bump into Susanna here – literally, because I hit her car – but find her single, too.' He grinned. 'Turned out she still loved me after all these years. Now if that does not prove that love survives everything, I don't know what does!'

He finished putting his things away and slid the door to his tool shed shut. 'You will sort something out, I am sure. Whether it's adoption, or IVF, or whatever. But first, you must get back together. Go home, Oliver, and tell her.'

Oliver sighed and rose to his feet. 'You're right. I can't run away from this, can I? For better, for worse. That's what we promised.'

'That's right. For better, for worse.'

'Okay.' Oliver drew a deep breath. 'We'll sort it out. One way or another. Anyway, thank you, David. You've been a big help.'

But David just shrugged as he picked up his thermos. 'Aw, but I haven't done anything, have I? Uh-oh, it's starting to rain. I say, we'd better run!'

So they did. And while David ran on ahead to Rose Cottage, Oliver turned into the drive leading to Fern Hill Farm, hoping to find Daisy there.

***

DAISY WAS WAITING for him by the door, Drifter at her feet. She had been offered a lift by Lily earlier, when she and Lavinia had emerged from the church to the crash of heavy thunder, and accepted it gladly. Finding that Oliver had not come home yet, she had just been about to put the kettle on when the electricity had gone off. Thank God that was when she had seen Oliver approaching the gate.

It was raining hard now, with thunder following lightning in rapid succession – and yet, Oliver slowed down when he saw his wife standing there, until he came to a halt a few yards before the cottage. He was not sure what to do. Should he just hug her? Say he was sorry first? Or both at the same time? Would she even let him touch her?

'Don't you want to come inside?' she called against the wind. 'You are getting soaked!'

His heart missed a beat when he saw the smile on her face. That famous Daisy smile he loved so much. 'Yes!' he cried, his voice thick with relief, 'I do!' And then he broke into a run, closing the remaining few yards with just a few long strides. Enveloping her in his arms, he held her tight, like he had hoped he would before this day was over.

'I'm sorry, Daisy,' he whispered, kissing her hair. 'I'm so sorry I walked out on you. I never meant to hurt you like that.'

But she just smiled, and shook her head, and silenced him with a tender kiss. 'We're going to be alright,' she whispered, even though there were tears hanging in her eyelashes.

And he thought he had never loved her more than in this moment.

CHAPTER 29

THE DAY OF the funeral arrived and the cloud of mournful silence that had been hanging over the village now seemed to have descended on the congregation that was gathered in the parish church of St Peter's. The bell tolled solemnly to let everyone know that Bishops Bridge had lost a much loved friend and neighbour, and everyone stood as the door opened and the pallbearers came in, slowly carrying the coffin down the aisle. When they had put the simple oak coffin down and the last echo of the last chime had faded, Ellen stood and sang the *Ave Maria*. Her strong, clear voice filled the church and the hearts of the mourners, and Daisy saw that even Mrs Higgins, sitting in the opposite pew, was dabbing at her eyes with a handkerchief. Somewhat satisfied that even that spiteful woman's heart had not been left untouched, Daisy put her hands in her lap and turned her eyes on her husband who was taking up his Bible now, ready to greet the congregation.

Following the greeting and opening prayer, they rose to sing the first hymn, *Abide with me*. Daisy could not bring herself to sing the final verse that went "Hold thou thy cross before my closing eyes", knowing she would never be able to stop crying once they got to the final line

— "In life, in death, O Lord, abide with me".

Next, one of Philip Colbeck's two brothers gave the eulogy. He was a tall, haggard-looking man in his early sixties, and looked so much like his deceased brother that Daisy thought it was almost uncanny. She closed her eyes and leaned against Lavinia's shoulder, her hands clutching a well-used tissue.

'He was not afraid, and even though he knew how dangerous it was to go in there … that he might not get out alive … he did not hesitate. Philip was a man of action, a man who would always put others before himself. His wife, his family. His friends and neighbours, and anyone in need …'

Daisy swallowed, remembering how only a couple of weeks ago, Mr Colbeck had come to her rescue, too, when she had stupidly fallen off her horse because she had not been careful enough. Both Mrs and Mr Colbeck had been so kind to her! No doubt he would have carried her all the way home, had Oliver not come. She still had the crumpled bit of paper in her pocket that had contained the KitKat Mrs Colbeck had given her. She knew it was silly, but she could not bring herself to throw it away. It would forever remind her of the last kindness Philip Colbeck had done her.

'… he was the best and kindest brother I could have wished for, and I am sure you will all agree with me when I say … when I say …' Here the tall, erect man's voice broke, and his daughter hurried to bring him a tissue. When he had collected himself, she remained quietly at his side with a hand on his arm, her head bent low, and he went on. 'He just never thought about himself. He always put others first. His family, his friends, his neighbours.

Perhaps that was the only fault he really had: that he never thought of himself. I remember one incident when we were children. It was a hot summer, and we were at home, trying to keep ourselves occupied and cool. We never went on holidays during the summer, and we didn't live near the sea. There was not so much as a stream in our neighbourhood, so the only thing we could do was to turn up the hose and splash each other, or pretending to put out ... to put out a fire, like Dad. Yeah ... that was a favourite game. And it lasted until Mother came and scolded us for wasting precious water. Anyway, I had got a new bike that summer, and we raced up and down the lane behind our house, sometimes taking our hands off the bars, sometimes stretching out our legs at ridiculous angles for the sheer fun of it. We had a lot of fun, until Philip's foot suddenly got stuck in the spokes. But even then, he insisted he was alright. He didn't even cry when we walked back to the house. So we put our bikes in the shed first, checked on the rabbit – I think I remember Philip giving him fresh water – washed our hands, and went in for dinner. Suddenly Philip began to sway and fainted in the hallway! And no wonder, there was a huge hole in his foot! There was not a lot of blood, which was curious. And which was why we probably thought it wasn't so bad. And do you know what he did while we were waiting with him in A&E? He was cracking jokes to stop our little sister from crying!'

Had he looked up, he would have seen a few melancholy smiles among the congregation as some of them remembered Philip Colbeck's dry sense of humour, and his humbleness. He then talked about his brother and sister-in-law's love for walking and the stunning photographs he had taken over the years, especially of the North York Moors. 'This village here, and Rosedale, was his home. He always said he had never been happier anywhere else, and he wanted to grow old here with you all … sadly, he didn't.' Overcome with grief, he shook his head and mumbled, 'Sorry, I don't think I can go on. I know what Philip would say, of course – he would say, yes, you can. Because you must. And so we will – because we must.'

He leaned on his daughter's arm as she led him back to the family pew where he sat staring ahead while the congregation sang *Nearer My God to Thee*. Everyone was sobbing their way through this hymn rather than singing it, and everyone seemed to be relieved when Oliver said a final prayer before they all joined in for the Lord's Prayer. After a moment of silence, Ellen sang one last hymn – fittingly, *I Vow to Thee My Country*. At last, the pallbearers stood up, bowed their heads, and proceeded to carry the coffin out of the church where the hearse was waiting to take it to the graveyard of the old church. Apart from Mr Colbeck's two brothers, his son, and his brother-in-law, two men from the village had volunteered to be pallbearers. One of them was Alexander Cartwright, the other Jonathan Hunter.

Outside, they stopped briefly under the lychgate, not to take a rest, but rather for tradition's sake, and so that Mrs Colbeck could lay her hand on the coffin one last time before it was lifted into the hearse. Everyone watched as it drove away, and then made their way to their own cars.

***

'Greater love has no man than this, that a man lay down his life for his friends,' Oliver said at the grave, and everyone bowed their heads, humbly acknowledging the truth of these words from the gospel of John, chapter 15. Then he threw a few handfuls of soil onto the coffin, and stepped aside to let Mrs Colbeck and her family do the same. When Mrs Colbeck threw the single white rose she had been holding in her hands throughout the service, the other mourners stood in silence, some of them reaching into their pockets or handbags for a tissue.

Ellen stood a little apart from everyone else, trying to breathe. And trying to stop herself from singing. If only she could cry like the others! Nobody would think that odd. But singing while the vicar was praying? She really could not do that. She would only draw attention to herself, and that was the last thing she wanted. But no matter how hard she tried, she could not keep the memories from coming, making her eyes sting with unshed tears. If only I could breathe, she thought, putting a hand to her chest. If only I could breathe …

'You alright?' Lily stepped forward and caught her by the elbow, motioning for Abi to take her other arm. 'You look ghastly pale! Is it the heat? Do you need to go and sit in the shade?'

'No, no,' Ellen hurried to say. 'I am – um … quite well.'

The way she raised her eyebrows at Abi, it was clear that Lily did not believe her, but Ellen did not care. It didn't matter. Today was not about her and her losses, no matter how much they were haunting her. Today was not about her at all, but about the man who had given his life for others. Greater love indeed …

Her lower lip wobbled, and she put a hand over her mouth to stifle a sob. And suddenly Daisy was there, taking her by the arm, and gently steering her away from the crowd. 'Come, come,' she said soothingly, 'you need to sit down awhile. I will do some breathing exercises with you if you feel ready, and otherwise, I will just hold you. It's okay. It will pass. It will pass …'

They had just about made it to the padlocked door to St Mary's Chapel when Ellen broke down, sobbing uncontrollably. 'I'm sorry!' she cried, nearly choking. 'I'm sorry! I should never have left you! I should – never – have – left you!'

Daisy did not have to ask to know that she was talking to her father. To her Papa, as she had called him. Or still did. For even though Daisy had not known Ellen for long, she could feel the deep bond between her and her adoptive parents. A bond that even death had not been able to destroy.

***

ELLEN HAD NOT come to the wake but walked back home, changed into cropped denim shorts and a T-shirt, and pulled on her walking boots that were still standing next to her father's in the boot room. His words of advice still echoed in her head whenever she set out to walk on the moors: 'If ever you feel like the worries and anxieties of life are getting too much for you to bear, I suggest you take a walk through nature with open eyes, that you may behold the beauty of God's wonderful creation, and feel his soothing presence and powerful might in every bush, every flower, every animal that you glimpse. May you feel comforted by the thought that all of this,' and he had pointed to the heather-clad moors, 'is part of the almighty God's wondrous creation. And so are you, my darling girl,' he had added, putting an arm around her shoulder.

Darling Papa. Oh, how she missed him now! How she missed their walks, often spent in companionable silence (apart from the intermittent humming on her part perhaps – but he had never minded her humming, or singing). And how she missed coming home to her mother's tea, as always prepared to perfection in the saloon, the conservatory, or outside on the patio. Thinking back now, she sometimes thought she must have dreamed all this. But why was the taste of her mother's strawberry jam she had used to fill the Victoria Sponge with still on her lips?

Ellen walked briskly all the way up to the kilns, along the footpath that led past the majestic remains of the mine entrances, with the rolling fields to her left and Bishops Bridge deep down at the bottom of the valley, looking as peaceful as ever. Only it wasn't. Death had come to the sleepy little village once too often in too short a time. First both of her parents, and now Mr Colbeck.

Standing in the churchyard earlier this afternoon, Ellen had thought it seemed like yesterday that they had buried her father. It seemed impossible to believe it was four months ago. Back then, she had been the one to let the single red rose fall onto the coffin, too stunned to cry. Today it had been Mrs Colbeck. She had not cried either, at least not openly. But no one could see the tears you cried inwardly, could they? Oh yes, Ellen knew a thing or two about unshed tears, and how much they hurt. How they burnt your heart from within, eating slowly at your innermost feelings like the flames that had eaten at the Johnsons' house … until you could bear it no longer, and finally broke down, and cried.

Daisy had been nothing short of brilliant. She had sat with her all the time, and even when the other mourners had begun to make their way towards the gate, she had stayed with her. Oliver had come over and put a hand on his wife's shoulder, and she had whispered something in his ear – probably explaining that she would follow. Only when everyone else had left and all was quiet, Ellen had actually been able to stop crying and do the breathing exercises with Daisy. Feeling a little calmer, she had slipped Daisy a note for Mrs Colbeck in which she had explained why she would not come to the Rectory, where the wake was to be held. Because she needed to be alone for a while. She had promised she would come to see her tomorrow morning instead. Mrs Colbeck would understand. She was just the kind of person who would – because that was just what she was like. What she and her husband had both been like …

By the lone chimney Ellen sat down in the grass with her knees pulled up to her chest, and her head resting on them as she gazed into the distance. Then she did what she always did when she did not know what else to do: She began to sing.

***

MISS LAVENDER SAT down on her sofa without bothering to take off her shoes. She was hot, tired, and thirsty, but she did not get up to drink. She just sat there, motionless, for an hour or more, and thought. Thought about Mr Colbeck and the many encounters they had had over the years, thought about how strange it would feel to open her shop again next month, knowing he would never come again for his milk and newspaper. He had been a man of habit. Every morning he would come, and buy exactly the same two things: two pints of semi-skimmed, and a copy of The Guardian. She could not remember him having ever bought anything else, except the odd bag of sweets for a visiting grandchild. When Jessie had told her how he had come here with his youngest granddaughter, Jubilee, only days before his death, she had wished she had been there and not in that stupid hospital. It would not make a difference now, of course. It would have happened anyway. Fate. Destiny. God's plan. Because at the end of the day, it all came down to just that, didn't it? That God knew best, even if we could not see it that way when we were hurting so much.

She was also thinking about Ellen and what she would do now that she was on her own again. And finally, her thoughts turned to Daisy, and Hammond Hall, as they usually did these days. Part of her wanted to get on the next train and go home, and part of her wanted to stay here and hide from her family for a while longer, until she was ready.

Will I ever be ready though? Or will I keep on hiding until it is too late?

If Philip Colbeck's death should have taught them anything, it was that time was a precious thing, and should not be wilfully wasted.

'So, no time like the present then,' she muttered and got up, having finally decided what she was going to do.

She went to the kitchen, poured herself a small glass of sweet white wine from the fridge, and took it to her desk in the corner of her living room.

The Victorian mahogany rolltop desk was one of the few items Lavinia had brought over from France when her grandmother had died, and she had instructed the French lawyer to sell the villa for her. The desk had originally stood in her mother's writing room at Hammond Hall, and she had had it sent to France when she had left her husband. Had she known she would not live for much longer, she might have left it where it was, and it would have been lost to Lavinia. As it was, it had become one of her most treasured possessions.

Taking her writing paper out of a drawer, and the Montblanc fountain pen she had been given by her father on her sixteenth birthday, she found that the ink inside had dried up because she had not used the pen in years. With a sigh, she took it apart and began to clean it very carefully. When she was satisfied with the result, she took a bottle of royal blue ink from one of the little shelves on the desk, and refilled the pen by slowly drawing the ink through the golden nib. Finally, she took a small sip of her wine, and began to write.

CHAPTER 30

'Do you know what Ellen will do? About Birchwood Park, I mean?'

Two weeks after the funeral, Lily, Jessie, and Daisy were sitting together in the café garden. Jessie had reluctantly opened her café a few days after the funeral, not at all sure what to expect. But the locals were glad to be able to meet at their usual place again, and talked about the tragic events over tea or coffee and Jessie's homemade cake. After a while, they talked about other things, of course. The ruin remained a ruin, but life in Bishops Bridge went on, just like Jessie had said it would. Even her own anxieties had ceased to be such a burden, and that was mostly thanks to Daisy, whom she had been able to talk to about feeling so guilty about the fire. Ossie, now officially the Bridge Café Dog, never left his place by the back door, watching over his new mistress's every move. He never barked these days, except when Louisa May came in after school. Then he would rush to greet her enthusiastically, and they would walk home together. Exiting through the back door, of course – unless one of them forgot the No-Dogs-Rule still applied even to Ossie.

'I don't know. I don't think I have seen her since the funeral – have you, Daisy?'

Daisy finished her cake and pushed her plate aside. 'Yes, I have. She sometimes comes to the farm to help me with the horses, and I think she likes to sit in the kitchen and talk to Abi. Abi says the Colbecks had always been very fond of Ellen, and Mr Colbeck had promised to help her sort through the papers and decide what to do. Now he is gone …' She shook her head. 'I don't know. She does not really know anyone else in the village, does she? Apart from us, and Lavinia. It's a very difficult situation. Poor Ellen.'

The others nodded and stirred their cappuccinos. Poor Ellen indeed.

'Talking of Lavinia – was it you who persuaded her to reduce her shop hours, Daisy? Or is it doctor's orders?'

Daisy pulled a face. 'Neither. She would not take orders from anyone, as you well know. It was her idea. She said she had worked long enough, it was – here comes! – *time to think about gradual retirement.*'

'Retirement??'

'That's what she said.' Daisy shrugged. 'She might change her mind again, of course, but to be honest, I don't expect her to. She even suggested she would—oh, is that my phone? Excuse me, please.—Yes, hello? Oh, Louisa May! Did I forget you?—Goodness, I am sorry.—Yes, I'm coming. That is, if Lily would be so kind—'

Lily had already got up and was dangling her car keys in front of her. 'I'm on my way. Five minutes. Bye!' Secretly, Daisy was glad of the distraction because she felt she had already said too much. It was not her place to talk about Lavinia's plans; she would tell people herself when the time was right for her, and not sooner. As for Oliver and her, there was more to discuss, and more to decide than she could get her head around to …

Suddenly everything happened so quickly that a nearly forgotten riding lesson was a walk in the park compared to that, even with an arm that was still in plaster! She could not wait to get rid of that thing, though the doctor had warned her that she would have to take things slowly even then. But as long as she would be fit to start her first course in September, she would neither complain nor despair.

***

'I'M SO SORRY to barge in like that … I didn't mean to disturb your Friday afternoon, as I'm sure you have lots to do … or maybe just want to enjoy a spot of gardening?'

Ellen indicated the gardening tools Oliver was holding in his hand. Standing next to a rather dubious looking old wheelbarrow, the vicar was dressed in a pair of old jeans and a faded T-shirt and looked more than a bit surprised to see Ellen. But his kind grey eyes showed genuine concern, and he hurried to offer her a seat and a glass of lemonade.

'You are very welcome to interrupt. Here, have a glass of lemonade. Homemade by Abi,' he explained as he poured them a glass each.

'Thank you.' Ellen sat down and drank thirstily. 'Oh, that was good. I'm so sorry, Oliver. I know how busy you are … I wouldn't have come if—'

'Please, Ellen,' he said, holding up his hands. 'Don't apologise. Never apologise for seeking help – if that is what you have come for? If you have come to tell me how beautiful our garden looks, even if it's full of weeds, or how skilled I am at handling that beastly old wheelbarrow, you are very welcome to do so, of course.'

She laughed a little, but he could see the tears shimmering in her eyes, and his heart went out to her. 'I'm sorry. I should not make light of such things. Of course you are unhappy. You have been,' he was going to say *to hell and back*, but decided that was probably not the appropriate expression here, 'going through a very difficult time. I cannot even begin to imagine what this must be like for you. I'm so sorry.'

Nodding, she took a tissue and turned away to blow her nose. 'I suppose most people can't,' she said when she had collected herself a little. 'It is hard enough, you know, to lose one's parents … and in so short a space of time … and then the suicide …' She shook her head and excused herself once more. 'But having grown up without even knowing my real parents, never mind being loved by them …' She shook her head. 'You know, when Charles and Angela first brought me back to Birchwood Park, and showed me everything, I thought I had to be dreaming. A room all to myself – so lovingly decorated, and full of toys! And the house! I had never seen anything like it. I could not believe I was to live there. And when they told me a few weeks later that they had decided to adopt me, and would I like to call them Mama and Papa … and they called me their darling little girl, right from Day One. It had to be a dream, I thought. Because only in dreams had I ever been so happy before … had I ever been *loved* like that before.' Here, she burst into tears, and Oliver passed her a packet of tissues, wishing there was something he could do for Ellen. But what could anyone do for her? How could anyone help? Charles and Angela

Maverick had been all she had ever had, and she had been everything to them. Everyone in Bishops Bridge knew that. They could not have loved her more had she been their own flesh and blood.

He would never admit it, but Ellen's story made him sometimes doubt the fairness of it all. In truth, it made him almost doubt his own faith at times … How could God let the poor girl suffer so much? And who were they, Daisy and him, that they thought their world had come to an end just because they could not have children? For pity's sake! Honestly. Yes, he had grown up without a mother, but he and his brother had still had a father, who had done a fabulous job of raising them. They had never been alone, and they had always felt loved. And Daisy, too. What did either of them know of pain and sorrow?

He stole a sideways glance at Ellen, noticing a scar that ran down the side of her left temple. From what Reverend Thompson had told him, her early childhood had been anything but rosy. There might well be more scars, hidden underneath that thick, long, dark blond hair of hers, or her clothes. Not to mention the invisible scars. The ones that were left on our hearts …

'You know why I did not come to the wake after Mr Colbeck's funeral,' Ellen said quietly. 'It's because I couldn't bear to be there, among so many people. The funeral was already a bit too much for me … as you will have noticed. Daisy was quite wonderful – but still, I had to get away, had to be on my own. I went walking. Papa used to say to me, if ever I felt like the worries and anxieties of life were getting too much for me to bear, I should take a walk through nature with open eyes, and behold the beauty of God's wonderful creation, and feel

His soothing presence and powerful might in every bush, every flower, every animal that I glimpsed.'

Oliver was just going to say what a beautiful piece of advice that had been, and how right her father had been to suggest she seek refuge on the moors, when suddenly Ellen's eyes darkened, and her voice turned angry and bitter. 'So why did he walk up to the wood and shoot himself then? Why didn't he take his own advice? Why did he take a gun instead? Who was he to tell me how to handle stressful situations, when clearly he couldn't cope himself?' Her eyes were ablaze with fury. She did not look at Oliver but straight ahead, to some point in the distance, or to nowhere in particular at all. 'How could he let me down like this? Didn't it cross his mind that I might need him, too??' Then she broke down and sobbed, and Oliver put an arm around her shoulder.

When she had calmed down a bit, she said, in a desperate whisper, 'I don't know what to do … I just don't know what to *do*! I have an appointment with Papa's solicitor in York next week, and Mr Colbeck said he was going to come with me … how was I to know that he would leave me, too? Everyone is leaving me!'

'No, Ellen. Not everyone. We are here, and we are your friends. I hope you know that.'

She nodded. But then her face clouded over once more, and she asked anxiously, 'Do you think they are right, Oliver? The people who say I am bad? Am I – am I a curse, do you think? Have I always been nothing but a curse to everyone whose life I have touched, no matter how hard I tried to be good? Or why do they all die??'

Though his heart was breaking to hear her talk like that, Oliver shook his head vehemently. 'No, Ellen. No.

You are *not* a curse. You are not bad at all – your mother called you an angel, didn't she? You are lovely and kind and so very, very gifted. Who would have sung at somebody else's funeral just a few short months after they had buried both of their parents and were still grieving them? Mrs Colbeck was so grateful, Ellen. Everyone was. There are always people who think they know best, and there are those who are … not kind. Even in Bishops Bridge. And I have never known a friendlier place than this! But Ellen, please don't listen to those who lie. Don't say you are bad. Your parents would be so sad to hear you talk like that. You meant the world to them!'

She scoffed. 'I did, didn't I? So much so that my father took his own life three weeks after my mother's funeral, instead of looking out for me, as he had promised on her deathbed! *That is* how much, or how little, I meant to him.'

'No, Ellen, no!' Oliver was aghast. 'No! It had nothing to do with you. It did not even have anything to do with your dear Mama, or the promise he made and could not keep. Ellen, your father was severely depressed. Reverend Thompson told me in confidence. He had been on medication all his adult life, though very few people knew about that. Without his wife … he just couldn't cope.' He shook his head. Then he briefly put a hand on Ellen's and said very quietly, 'I am sure he did not plan to take his life. He did not break his promise on purpose. He just … he just could not see another way.'

'No,' she admitted, hanging her head. 'I suppose he couldn't.'

For a long time, they sat there, watching Drifter dash about the garden chasing butterflies, until he finally caught one and swallowed it – whether on purpose or accidentally, they could not tell, but the look of surprise on the little dog's face made them both laugh.

'He is so cute! Why couldn't *I* have found him? I would love to have a dog … a companion … but I suppose it is not practical. I'm going back to London in September, and then …' She shook her head and sighed. 'I don't know. You see? I still don't know what to do. Crying does not help. Neither does singing. But I need to decide what to do about the houses and all that, and soon. Do you know anyone I could ask? Would you perhaps be able to help me?'

Oliver had been afraid she might ask him, but he did not have a clue about inheritance matters, death duties, and all that. But he knew just the person who did – only he was not here. He would call him tonight though. No one had more insight on these matters than his father-in-law. It was time he came to meet his long-lost cousin, anyway. That was, if he even knew he had one. Had Daisy told her father by now, or had the dramatic turn of events over the last couple of weeks kept her from doing so? He was ashamed to admit he had not even asked her lately.

'I'm afraid I can't, but there is somebody I could ask. I'll ring him tonight, okay? Why don't you stay for tea, Ellen? I am sure Daisy will be delighted to have you.'

***

THE FIGURE OF an elderly woman with a slightly hunched back retreated from the hedge. 'I knew it! I knew this ever smiling vicar was too good to be true! And with the saintly Ellen, of course. Just you wait, Madam! Just you wait …'

And she hurried home to phone her friend and tell her all about it.

***

At Fern Hill Farm, Daisy was watching Louisa May ride Willoughby in a steady trot around the outdoor school. The lesson was drawing to an end, but Daisy was in no hurry, and neither, she suspected, was Louisa May. They never really watched the time.

'Can I ride a little faster? Try a few jumps even?'

Daisy smiled. 'If you like? But you will have to put them up yourself, as I can't lift the poles. Only two though, to get him used to it. Remember he has not done any jumping before, and we do not want to frighten him.'

'Course not. Will you hold him for me?' Sliding down from the saddle, the girl handed Daisy the reins. Then she ran over to the far side of the school where Abi kept a few simple standards and poles, and quick as a flash, she put up a vertical like a pro. Mounting the horse again, she turned Willoughby around, and pushed him into an easy canter first, before gathering speed as they approached the obstacle.

Daisy watched the two of them taking the low fence with no trouble at all, and laughed when Louisa May asked her if she could add another pole. 'One more,' she nodded. 'Be careful not to tire him out, or ask too much of him. Willoughby is not the cleverest of horses, I'm afraid. I hate to admit it, but Jolly Jumper has more brain.'

When she had finished, Louisa May came to a halt in front of Daisy and bent to pat the horse's neck. 'You did very well, my boy, even if you don't have Jolly Jumper's brains. – When can I have my next lesson, Daisy?'

'Do you have time tomorrow? I think we have got a fan and a crossbar, too. They are easy obstacles for practising. I'll ask Abi where they are.'

'Yay!' Louisa threw her hands in the air, and Willoughby whinnied in response, performing what looked like a happy little dance on the spot.

Daisy smiled. As she watched the pair of them making their way towards the stable block, she saw Mr Marston coming up the drive with Victoria and Edmund. They waved excitedly when they saw her, and Daisy waved back. 'Hello, Mr Marston! Hello, Victoria, and Edmund! How are you today?'

'We are fine, thank you. How is that arm of yours? Healing nicely, I hope?'

'Oh yes. It's amazing what you can do single-handedly if you put your mind to it – and if you are lucky enough to be right-handed, which I am, thank God. I was just going to feed carrots to the ponies – would you like to do that, Victoria? Yes? And you, too, Edmund? Great,' she said when the young man nodded enthusiastically while his sister gave her the thumbs up. 'Come along then, let's see who is the hungriest today.'

'Jolly Jumper!' cried Edmund and gave a raucous laugh.

His sister joined in, and their father threw up his hands. 'What can I say? They love that naughty fellow!'

Daisy laughed. 'That's alright, we love him, too. Mr Marston, it's okay if you want to go and find Abi. Victoria and Edmund will be fine with me, won't you?'

Edmund, whose speech was less affected by his condition than his sister's, shouted an enthusiastic 'Yay,' spinning around in his wheelchair, as was his habit.

Victoria reached for Daisy's hand and gave her a shy smile.

A few minutes later, Daisy watched them as they fed a carrot to each of the ponies in the field behind the cottages. Ronnie, the gentle giant, blew his warm breath at the girl in the wheelchair without minding the strange contraption at all. Daisy's heart filled with gratitude and love, for both the horse, and the girl. Victoria was of a slight built and had lovely dark curls that came down just to her shoulders. Her green eyes sparkled behind her thick glasses, and Daisy smiled at her. 'Is that good? Yes? Oh, look, he has finished. He wants another one! But that wouldn't be good for him. We'll go and find William and Delilah now, shall we?'

Victoria did not speak, but the smile on her pretty face said everything. She was really a very special young woman, just like her brother was a very special young man. Daisy had no doubts whatsoever that spending time with the ponies would boost their self-confidence no end, and do them a world of good. It would also make their parents proud and happy to see them engage with the ponies on a regular basis, and do something that brought them joy.

If Daisy had been in any doubt regarding her decision to sign up for a course in equine therapy (she wasn't), it would have been swept away the moment she heard Edmund say to his sister, 'Look, Vicky, there is Dad. And Auntie Abi. – Hello, Auntie Abi! Look, we are feeding a pony!' Edmund did not pronounce the words quite as clearly, but Daisy could understand him well enough. The more often they came here, the easier she would find it to understand them both, despite their impediments. She was looking forward to it immensely.

As she absent-mindedly fed Jolly Jumper another carrot, she thought she had not felt so sure about anything since marrying Oliver. Without her being aware of it, a tiny little seed had been planted today – and that seed's name was hope.

CHAPTER 31

'BUT IF YOUR grandfather suffered from Parkinson's, how could he have run the estate? Did you know him at all? Didn't you say he died when you were quite little?'

Daisy was cooking dinner ('single-handedly,' she had said as she had picked up a spoon to stir olive oil through the pasta water, 'literally!'), and Oliver was watching her fondly, a glass of wine in his hand. When he had told her about Ellen coming for tea, Daisy had insisted she cook pasta primavera. 'That's simple enough. If you chop the vegetables and grate the cheese, I can do the rest.'

'Yes,' she said now, stirring sun-dried tomato paste into the sauce. 'He died in a care home near Newmarket when I was five. My dad had placed him there when it became too difficult to care for him at home. He was never going to run the estate, which is why my Dad went with him when he heard he had inherited. They even took Great Grandma Emmeline who was still alive at that time. I was always sorry I never met her. She must have been a wonderful person. And so brave! Married at eighteen, a mother at nineteen, widowed at twenty. She lost two brothers and a husband during the war, but she never gave up. No! Wait. Her husband died of the Spanish Flu in 1920. Anyway, Lavinia said her father adored his sister.

Although he never forgave her for marrying a man from Dorset, and remaining in the south all her life.'

Oliver handed her her wine glass. 'That is sad. Your poor grandfather! Having been uprooted at that age, and with his illness, too … only to end up in a care home far away from the home he had known all his life. Did you say he was widowed, or divorced?'

'Divorced. My grandmother ran off with an American singer and actor when my dad was six. She never came back. We never talk about her either. It's like she never existed. – Pass me the salt, please?'

Handing her the salt mill grinder, he nodded. 'Oh yes, I remember that story. That's why your Dad was so close to his grandmother, wasn't he? Because she literally doubled as grandmother and mother for him.'

'Yes. As I said, she was the most important person in my dad's life until he met my mum.'

'Understandable. So when your father inherited, he had to start the whole business more or less from scratch because old Sir Winston had pretty much ruined it in his lifetime, hadn't he? Were there even any horses left?'

'Oh yes, quite a few. It wasn't so bad, really. My dad always was a hard worker, and he knew a lot about horses. And then of course he was lucky to meet mum, who had grown up on a stud farm herself. They always were a wonderful team, those two.'

'Amazing, yes.' He drank his wine slowly, never taking his eyes off his wife. God, she was so beautiful! 'I'm glad it all worked out so well for your dad. For all of you,' he said. 'I know how much you love your home, and your family.'

'Including new additions of the unexpected sort, yes.'

Daisy smiled, quite unaware of him watching her every move. 'I cannot wait to tell Dad about Lavinia, but she asked me not to just yet. I don't think they would have met very often, with him having grown up in Dorset, but still – it will be wonderful to bring them back together after so many years."

Oliver nodded. Then he glanced at the clock above the kitchen door. Ellen would be here any minute. Suddenly he wished he had not invited her – he wanted to be alone with Daisy, talk to her about the things that really mattered. Their relationship for instance, and what they were going to do now they knew there would not be any children. At least none of their own. He also wanted to know more about her plan to get a degree in equine therapy. Was she strong enough to go ahead with this? Or would she need some time to come to terms with things first? But then he really did not want to stop her doing something she loved. He had done that before, hadn't he? He had stood by and watched her throwing her career away, claiming it was her choice, her decision, and who was he to stop her? Truth was, he should have. He should have stopped her.

While giving up event riding had seemed a sensible choice when they got married, he had never expected her to give up riding altogether. She had worked so hard for her degree in horsemanship, only to waste her talent in some small riding school in rural Derbyshire. He knew she had done that because she had thought she would get pregnant soon and be a mother – and being Daisy, she had wanted to be a *perfect* mother. And in Daisy's books, being the perfect mother would begin long before that child was even born.

Oliver shook his head dismally. What had all the sacrifices been for now? Just because Daisy had said she had made up her mind, he had accepted that as her decision and had left it at that. They had never talked about it again. He had focused on his career, thinking he would have to provide for a family soon. And that had made it okay in his mind. Only it hadn't. It shouldn't have. Even though she had insistcd that that was what she wanted, he should have known her heart was breaking. And yes, she had played her part well – so well, in fact, that he never saw her struggling. How could he have been so blind?

'Oliver?'

He turned around. 'Yes?'

'Are you all right? You look preoccupied. Are you thinking about … about the baby thing?'

Quick to shake his head, Oliver put his winc glass down and put the knife and chopping board in the sink. 'No, no. I mean – yes, but not like that. I mean, it's not about the test result.'

'Hm.' She scrutinised him for a minute, then turned the heat down and fiddled with the strap of her apron until Oliver came over and undid the knot for her. 'You know you can always ask for help, don't you?' he offered, planting a soft kiss in the nape of her neck.

'And you,' she said, turning around to face him, and putting her right hand to his cheek. 'You can ask for help, too. I am happy to listen, whatever it is. Remember, we said we would find a way together. Don't bottle things up, Oliver. Please.'

Cupping her face in his hands, he smiled. 'I won't. But we don't have much time left before Ellen comes, so there is no point of talking about it now. Shall I set the table?'

'I have already done that, flowers and all. It's amazing what you can do with only one hand! – Do you think I'm doing alright?'

'I think,' Oliver replied, kissing her, 'you are doing great. But we haven't kissed since the morning, and that, Mrs Clifford-Jones, won't do. That,' he kissed her again, 'will not do at all, I'm afraid.'

***

ELLEN WAS STANDING by the window of the spare room where Daisy and Oliver had put her for the night, insisting she stay and not go back to her empty house. She had been too tired to argue. They meant well, she knew that. And they were right, too: she probably would have cried all night, had she gone back. She looked about her, taking in all the loving little details of the room. With three of the walls painted white, and the fourth one blue, there was an almost nautical feeling to it, especially with the white floorboards, and the blue gingham curtains in the dormer window. On the bedside table was a jug filled with wildflowers which Daisy had probably picked in the field behind the Rectory. There were flowers everywhere in the house (she had been given a tour), reminding her of her mother, who had had flowers displayed in every room throughout the year. From March to October, they had all come from the garden, and during the winter months, her father had brought them in from the orangery. The orangery had been his domain. He had grown orange and lemon trees in there and of course, flowers for his lady.

On every Sunday in Advent, Angela would make up a fresh bouquet of a single amaryllis and a few roses, bound together with holly and twigs of fir. When Ellen was younger, she and her mother would sit at the kitchen table and stud oranges with cloves and put them on sideboards and shelves around the house. Such sweet, simple ideas.

Pushing open the window, Ellen leaned forward and rested her chin on her clasped hands. It was a warm, balmy night, and the air was laced with the scent of honeysuckle, star jasmine, and the almost intoxicating scent of the night lily. She closed her eyes and inhaled deeply. Yes, that was good. She would sleep with the window open and breathe in the scent of the flowers until she slept. She had hardly slept at all since Katharina had left. Instead, she had sat at her father's desk into the early hours, trying to get on with the dreaded paperwork. Thankfully, her parents had been well organised, and everything was filed away in clearly labelled folders: *Insurance. Tax. Birchwood Park. The Cairns, Argyll. London apartment. Angela, medical records. Ellen.*

There was no need to open this folder, as she had a copy of its contents in her London flat. But seeing her name written in her father's old-fashioned hand had made her put a hand to her throat. How would she ever get to the bottom of it all when her emotions tripped her up every time she sat at his desk, remembering him?

Oliver had not been able to get hold of his father-in-law yet, but had said he would try again tomorrow and let her know if he might be able to help her. It was kindly meant, but what she really needed was somebody she knew and could trust, and not some stranger from Suffolk who knew all about race horses and grand estates that had been in the same family for goodness knows how long. She would have to rely on the family solicitor. Mr Hamilton had known her parents for years; he had explained the will to her back in March, and he would help her make the right decisions. She had already decided to sell The Cairns, and keep the flat in Kensington. What she was supposed to do with Birchwood Park was a different matter. This was the only home she had ever known. The one place where she felt safe and happy. How could she ever give this up?

She sighed. Too many questions. And no answers. No answers at all.

***

THE NEXT MORNING, Ellen offered to look after Drifter, so Daisy could go to church with Oliver. 'I'll walk him up to the churchyard, say a prayer for my parents, and Mr Colbeck, and take him back to Birchwood Park. We can play in the garden, hey, Drifter? Do you want to take your ball?'

Drifter ran to fetch the red rubber ball Joseph had given him as a welcome gift, and dropped it at Ellen's feet. Then he sat and looked up at her expectantly, his bushy tail swishing the floor.

'I would say that was a resounding yes!' Oliver laughed and turned to his wife. 'Come on then, let's go. Thank you, Ellen. We will come and pick him up after the service.'

They all left the Rectory together a few minutes later, with Daisy and Oliver walking across to the church, and Ellen and Drifter turning right to walk up the hill.

***

'And do you know what he did next? He kissed her! Full on the mouth!'

'No!'

'Yes! And do you know what she did?'

'Slapped him, I hope?'

Marion Higgins shook her head. 'No. We are talking about Ellen High-and-mighty-Maverick, aren't we? She can't resist an opportunity to cause scandal, can she? Even if she thought nobody saw her. She kissed him back, that's what she did! And then,' she added, looking over her shoulder to where Oliver was standing, 'they went into the house and closed the door behind them …'

'You are not suggesting—you don't think they actually—you know what?! I can't believe she would do that, to be honest. Seducing,' Mrs Blythe lowered her voice, '*the vicar* of all people!'

'Well, yes, I find it hard to believe, too, but I saw what I saw, didn't I? And I don't think they went inside to make tea.'

Mrs Blythe frowned. 'But wasn't his wife at home? She has a broken arm, and a wee dog to look after, surely she must have been somewhere about?'

'Well, I saw her coming back from Fern Hill Farm an hour later, passing my house. So—' Marion Higgins looked at the small group of women, eagerly anticipating their reaction to the juicy piece of gossip she had just fed them.

Mrs Blythe shook her head. 'Well, I know she is a strange girl, what with her singing all the time, but – an affair with the vicar? Of all people? I don't think that is likely. You must have misinterpreted the situation, Marion. Maybe he was counselling her, and she cried, and he felt obliged to hug her. That would be more like him. He is such a kind-hearted man, is Oliver.'

'That's as maybe. But do you know,' said Mrs Lennox, the former deputy headmistress of the village school who only came to church for the gossip afterwards, 'I always thought that man too good to be true. Reverend Thompson was well-respected, too, and he did not have people calling him by his Christian name or anything, unless you knew him really well. And even just *hugging* a member of your congregation is highly unprofessional, if you ask me, whether there was any kissing involved or not.' Satisfied, Mrs Lennox finished her tea and smacked her lips.

'May I ask what you were even *doing* on the other side of that hedge, Marion Higgins?'

Everyone turned around to find Mrs Cartwright standing there, a cup of coffee in her hand, and a look of decided disapproval on her face. She and her husband had lived in the village for over thirty years and were well-respected among the people of Bishops Bridge. Having looked after many of the village children in her time (Louisa May had been one of them), Mrs Cartwright was a pillar of the community. Next to her stood old Mrs Flite, looking daggers at both Mrs Higgins and Mrs Lennox.

But before she could think of a witty reply, Marion Higgins was approached by Daisy herself. Smiling sweetly at her, the vicar's wife said (rather cheekily, Mrs Higgins thought), 'Yes, I did pass your house, Mrs Higgins, and I saw the curtains twitch, too. Really, you must improve on your spying skills. Have you never watched *Rear*

Window? A very good movie. They use a telescope. That would save you the trouble of trespassing, I dare say, and risk being reported to the police. And can I ask you to stay on the footpath in the future, as is the common rule when walking in the country. The footpath does not run alongside the hedge at all, you must have strayed a good bit to be able to 'see' through our yew hedge. Which is quite dense, by the way. And high. As to what you might or might not have seen, I will reserve the right to find out about that myself when I speak to my husband. Good day, Mrs Higgins. – Oh, and Mrs Lennox? You are free to call us Mr and Mrs Clifford-Jones, if you'd rather. In fact, I think my husband and I would prefer that.'

***

LATER, WHEN THEY were walking up the hill together to relieve Ellen of her canine charge, Daisy remarked quite casually, 'Mrs Higgins seems to have seen something quite interesting when she peered through our yew hedge yesterday afternoon.'

Oliver frowned. 'Through our—but why would she do that? And what business does she have there, anyway? It's not part of the public footpath.'

Daisy shrugged. 'Because she is a nosy, nasty, meddlesome old gossip, that's why. Now I do not believe a word she said but I think you need to be careful. This is a small village, Oliver. If you just as much as touch another woman, no matter how briefly, or how innocently, it could … well. Get you into trouble.'

When he did not respond, she stopped and asked, perhaps a bit more pointedly than she meant to, 'You did hug Ellen yesterday, didn't you?'

Oliver looked confused, and hurt. 'Yes, but – she was crying, Daisy! What else could I have done? What would *you* have done?'

'Oh, *I* would have hugged her. Of course I would. But that wouldn't be a problem, would it, because I'm a woman. You are a man. A married man, and a vicar. You can't do that, full stop.' There were tears in her eyes, but she quickly blinked them away. 'I'm sorry. I didn't mean to criticise you. Just – just be careful, okay? For your own sake, for Ellen's, and for mine.'

He nodded, somewhat dumbstruck. 'Of course. You are right … I wasn't thinking, I suppose. I'm sorry you had to hear that from Mrs Higgins, even if it is none of her business. What did you say to her then? Or did you just walk off?'

Suddenly an uncharacteristically impish grin spread over his wife's face. 'Well …'

And when she had told him, and they had finished laughing, he took her by the hands and said, his eyes gleaming with merriment, 'Well done, you! I would have loved to see her face! Oh, I am so proud of you!'

And he was. How had his helpless, frightened little wife, who could not be left on her own for one night, become such a strong, confident woman who was not afraid to speak her mind? Was it Rosedale, or the dog, or the horses – or finding Miss Lavender? All of it maybe? Whatever it was, something had clearly worked its magic in Daisy, and he could not wait to find out where it would lead them.

CHAPTER 32

'WELL, IF YOU don't have Darjeeling, or any loose tea at that, I will have a glass of water instead.' Miss Lavender looked about the conservatory where Ellen had set the table for a light lunch. There were fish finger sandwiches, a bowl of leafy green salad along with a bottle of Sainsburys salad cream, a plate of flapjack squares that looked like they were straight from an M&S box, and a big bowl of strawberries. 'You shouldn't have gone to so much trouble, lass! We did not expect the full Sunday lunch, did we, Daisy? But you know, I think I will take a stroll around your beautiful garden before we eat, if you don't mind?'

'But Miss Lavender,' Ellen began to protest, 'the fish finger sarnies will get—' But Miss Lavender had already gone and was walking down the cobbled garden path, stopping every now and then to admire the flower beds.

'Never mind. I don't think she cares much for fish finger sandwiches,' Daisy shrugged and helped herself to one. 'But I do. And I can tell you, I am starving!'

Ellen sighed. 'That woman is such a mystery! Do you know anything about her private life at all? Like, who she is, and how on earth a fine lady like her ended up in Rosedale, and running a grocery store?'

'Oh, erm … yes, as a matter of fact, I do. I am not sure

I should tell you, but ... oh, I suppose it doesn't matter if I do. She grew up on a very grand estate in Suffolk, but left home, and her family, to marry a Yorkshire farmer! Unfortunately, the young man died on the day before the proposed wedding ... but she did not want to go home, so she stayed in the area, worked in a shop in Thirsk for a few years, and then discovered Rosedale, and Bishops Bridge. She bought the house, took over the then rundown little grocery store, and called herself Miss Lavender. And that's the end of that story. Oh, and she is my great-aunt, or something like that. We have only just found out. Because the estate she grew up on is my own childhood home, Hammond Hall.'

Ellen stared at her, fish finger sarnie in hand. 'No way!'

'It's true. Of course it is not quite as simple as that, but as I said, it's not really my story to tell. I hope she does not mind me sharing that much – but since it's you, I'm sure she doesn't.'

'But you and Miss Lavender,' Ellen marvelled, 'that's just – wow! Now you mention it, you do look alike. The eyes! Yes, that's it. You have the same eyes. And the cheekbones, too. Wow. I think I might just need a glass of wine – will you join me?'

'Oh, go on then. Erm ... Ellen, there is something I have been wanting to ask you ... do you think I could ...' She drew a deep breath. 'You see, the thing is I am going to start a course in September. I don't know if you have ever heard of equine assisted therapy but – well, I would like to train as a coach and start my own business here in Rosedale. They say you do not need to have your own facilities, but I thought ...'

'Why don't you ask Abi? I'm sure she would be more than happy to help. What's more, I think she would be delighted to let you use her ponies. I am not sure about my mum's horses, as they are both a bit on the spirited, high-strung side, but her lovely little Welsh Ponies would be perfect therapy partners, I am sure. And the donkey of course.'

Daisy gave a small sigh of relief. She had hoped that Ellen would say that. Of course she could have asked Abi directly, or even Lily – but somehow she did not have the courage to do that. Ellen had become a really good friend over the past few weeks. Lily would probably call us "kindred spirits", she thought and smiled. 'Do you think so?'

'I absolutely think so. And if I were you, I would not hesitate to ask. – Here,' she said, handing Daisy a glass, 'to horses and new adventures!'

'To horses and new adventures.'

They were just chinking glasses when Lavinia returned, a wistful smile on her lips. 'I am glad to find you so cheerful together. I always thought you might be good friends. Would you like to pour me a glass, too, Ellen?'

While Ellen was busy in the kitchen, Lavinia said down, gingerly took a fish finger sandwich and placed it on her plate. Then she sighed. 'Well then, I suppose I'll have to be polite about this. And talking of being polite, there is something I would like to confess … it is something to do with your very kind offer, you know, of letting me live at the Rectory with you. I want you to know that I have made up my mind.'

Daisy put her wine glass down. 'Okay?'

'Yes. I will come and live with you – if that offer of the

studio flat above the garage is still on, that is. I wouldn't want to get under your feet in the big house. And talking of big house … there is something I would like you to do for me.'

'Anything, Lavinia, you know that.'

The old lady smiled. 'Yes, dear. I know. Now, as you know, I have been in regular touch with your father, whom I should dearly like to meet soon. So when I am ready – and I don't think I am just yet, so no need to get the car out! – but when I am ready … will you take me back to Hammond Hall?'

'Oh, Lavinia!' Daisy cried, flinging her arms around the old lady's neck. 'Yes! Of course! Anytime you want – tomorrow?'

***

That night, when once again sleep failed to come, Ellen stole herself away to the bit of woodland where her father had ended his life. Taking a lantern instead of a torch, she walked steadily towards the end of the second field, where she stopped at the gate and put her lantern down. Nothing in the world would make her actually walk through that gate, beyond the lining of trees that were set against the darkness of the sky.

The moon was partly hidden behind the clouds, and the stars seemed to have gone to sleep long before morning. Maybe they had not bothered to get up at all tonight, saving their light for brighter times. Maybe they, too, were tired of the heat, or of the deep melancholy that still lingered in the village, and in many people's hearts.

Ellen's heart was heavy, too, for all that it had been such a lovely, fun-filled afternoon. The days were not the problem at all – it was the long and lonely nights here at Birchwood Park. At night, she felt the loneliness so much more … was that what had driven her father to end his life? The loneliness? The empty house? The long, dark hours before dawn?

Leaning against the gate, she curled her fingers around the wooden post, and thought about why she still felt so wretchedly lonely when actually, she was making new friends. Lily, Jessie, and Daisy. Miss Lavender and Miss Abigail. But they were here, not in London. Suddenly she did not want to go back at all. But what else could she do? What else did she have but her music? Katharina was gone, and everyone else seemed to know what to do with their lives … even Daisy had found her true vocation. And she was pleased for her, she really was!

And yet. And yet …

'I don't know,' she whispered. 'I don't know what to do …'

For a long time, she stood there, staring ahead into the impenetrable darkness of the wood, remembering her father. Not the lonely, desperate man who had taken his own life, but the kind, patient, generous man she had called Papa. She remembered how he had taught her to read because she had not learned properly before, and because no one had taken the time to sit down and practise with her. How he had dried her tears when she had come home from school crying because the other children did not want to play with her. How he had always advised her later, when she was older, and did not know what to do with her life. All she had ever wanted to do was to sing.

'And why shouldn't you be a singer? The Lord God has gifted you, my darling girl, with this beautiful voice.

Why do you think He has done that? Because He wants you to use that talent. He wants you to sing! *We* want you to sing. Come on, let's find out which is the best college or university for you to go to.'

And then they had come across the Royal College of Music, and before Ellen knew it, her father had called the Director and arranged for all three of them to go down to London. She had applied, auditioned, and been accepted – all within a few months of her crying to her father that 'all she ever wanted to do was to sing'.

'Papa,' she whispered, almost choking on the word. 'Papa – can you hear me? It's me, Ellen. Can you – can you see me?'

But there was only silence around her, and a soft, velvety darkness, engulfing her like a cloak, though she did not feel warmed by it. Nor did she feel her father's presence. Of course not, she thought, quickly wiping her eyes. He is not here. He can't be here. He is in heaven, with Mama.

Or were they right when they said people who committed suicide did not go to heaven? How did they know? Had they been there? Were they wiser than God Himself? Were they the better judges? Of course they weren't. They did not know her father like she did; they certainly did not know him like God did. So why did they think they could judge him? And why, if she knew they were lying, did she feel so frightened?

'I know you are not here, Papa. That is what scares me so. You are gone. Mama is gone. I am alone in this world, all alone! They talk about community and friendship and family, and they say I am one of them, but I know I am not. It's not the same. It just isn't the same!'

She began walking up and down, hugging herself against the cold. When had it become so cold? Or was it because she was not sleeping, nor eating properly? If Miss Lavender and Daisy had not turned up, she would not have eaten at all today. And who would remind her that she had to eat once she was back in London? With Katharina gone, there was no one left. She wished more than ever she could stay here instead. Here, she felt safe, and close to her parents, even though they were gone. But she knew that sooner or later, she would go mad with grief and loneliness – and ultimately, with boredom. Also, she could not let her parents down. She had to keep her promise, and keep on singing.

She was about to turn and walk back to the house when she felt something soft and warm brush her cheek. Thinking she heard a whisper, too, she leaned across the top rail of the gate and strained her ears, but could not hear anything except for the wind rustling in the trees.

I must be imagining things, she thought. It wouldn't be the first time either, for she had often imagined her mother's warm hand touching her, or her soft voice speaking words of comfort. Putting a hand to her cheek, Ellen felt nothing but the cool softness of her own skin. Of course there had been no voice either; it had only been her imagination playing tricks on her. Grief did the strangest things to you. And yet, she did not feel afraid, but calm and at peace.

Picking up her lantern, she made her way back to the house, singing one of her mother's favourite songs, *Amazing Grace*. And as she set the lantern down by the back door and blew out the candle, she suddenly knew what she would do.

CHAPTER 33

ROSEDALE HAD NOT experienced a summer like this since the heatwave of 1995, with temperatures rising steadily until they reached the mid-thirties, and not a drop of rain except for the heavy thunderstorm last week. And even that had not brought more than an hour's worth of rain. With July drawing to a swift close and August a mere couple of days away, the heat still lingered stubbornly in the valley rather like a guest who had long outstayed their welcome. Everywhere the grass had turned yellow and dry, and people tried desperately to keep on top of things, watering their gardens at the most ridiculous hours. Even the stream did not sparkle and gurgle along as cheerfully as it usually did, but seemed to take its time, as if it had grown weary and tired.

Lavinia was sitting in the shade of her porch, waiting for Daisy to come and collect her. They had decided to celebrate her finally getting rid of her cast with an Afternoon Tea at Bettys in Northallerton. Also, she and Oliver would officially move into the Rectory next weekend, though they already spent more time there than they did in the cottage.

'I am so glad!' Daisy had said when she had called Lavinia this morning. 'I can't tell you how tiresome it is to always have to remember where one has put this cardigan or that vase … really, it's exhausting. Everyone has promised to help – Lily said it was because they could not wait to get rid of us and rent out the *Lapwing* to tourists at last! But you know what Lily is like.'

Lavinia had chuckled. 'Yes, I know what Lily is like. She has become a good friend though, hasn't she?'

'She has. She and Joseph and Jessie … and Ellen, of course … all of them. Sometimes I have to pinch myself, you know. I can't believe how everything has worked out so well for us here! Which is why I am taking you out. We could go to York,' she had said, 'but personally, I don't think it's worth the trouble of driving there. Bettys in Northallerton is just as nice, and we can do the shopping afterwards.'

Daisy, Lavinia thought, would be alright. She had well and truly blossomed during the course of one summer, and it was a joy to see her now as she became more and more involved with village life and her newly found friends. It was as if she had always lived here, always belonged here. In a way, Daisy had settled in just like she herself had all those years ago …

It was all about the right place and the right time, wasn't it?

Lavinia put up a hand in greeting when Mr Barnsley came slowly down the lane, his Golden Retriever, Honey, trotting by his side. He would only take her down to the stream for a paddle now, and sit on one of the metal benches in the shade for a while. Deciding she could just as well sit with him while she waited for Daisy, Miss Lavender crossed the street and called out, 'Good afternoon, Mr Barnsley. How are you bearing the heat then?'

'Oh,' he said, feeling for the bench before he slowly lowered himself into a seating position. 'Not too bad, Miss Lavender. Not too bad … We stay indoors most of the time, don't we, old girl?' Patting Honey's head, he turned the subject on Daisy – by now the entire village had heard of their relationship, and if Daisy had not put her foot down, she and Lavinia would have made it into the local newspaper.

'So how is that charming great-niece of yours? Have you met your cousin yet? The one you have not seen in sixty years, as they tell me?'

Miss Lavender smiled. Sitting down beside him, she answered, 'No, I haven't seen him yet. But we have been exchanging regular letters, George and me, so when we do meet – hopefully soon –, we will not feel as if we were strangers meeting for the very first time. And it's not sixty years, merely fifty-seven.'

'Oh!' Mr Barnsley chuckled. 'Only that long, eh? Well, well.'

But Lavinia was already lost in a long-forgotten memory, brought back so vividly to her through her cousin George's letters …

Do you remember that last Christmas we all spent together at Hammond Hall? We had come up especially for the occasion. I think I had a secret crush on you then … a case of puppy love, no doubt. I was thirteen! A bit embarrassing, but at my age, I don't mind admitting that I admired you greatly back then. You were beautiful, and so wonderfully spirited! And you could ride a horse like any man. Better, even.

Anyway, we had come with Grandma Emmeline, as we would, and I still remember her telling your father off for one thing or another. Possibly for flirting openly with the maid.

Lavinia smiled wistfully. No doubt for flirting, yes. Emmeline had been the only one who had dared criticise Sir Winston Featherstone, Baronet. She had been a great lady, her Auntie Emmeline. So kind. So gentle. And yet, from what Lavinia had heard while she still lived at home, she had clearly been the head of her little family down in Dorset. Despite working full-time as a midwife at a privately run maternity home in Bournemouth, Emmeline had still found time to run the house for her son (there had been no money for staff, and she would have been too proud to ask her wealthy brother), and raise her grandson.

Lavinia liked to think she would have welcomed her and her baby, too, had Timothy lived … but then she had hoped to go to France and live with her mother and grandmother. Only that had not worked out either, had it? Even today she wondered how she had been able to survive all that grief – and on her own, too. Maybe that was why she could understand Ellen better than most. She knew what it was like to lose all her dear ones in so short a time …

'Lost in thoughts?'

Lavinia looked up, slightly confused. 'Sorry?'

The old man put a hand on her arm. 'I may be blind, Miss Lavender, but I can sense when something is wrong. When somebody is sad. You have been through a lot in your life, my dear. Much more than most of us could ever imagine. Or I can't, anyway. I have been so blessed with my family, I am still blessed today. Three children, six grandchildren, two great-grandchildren. And I wish that you, too, will find your peace with your family. I hope you will meet them soon, and get the chance to return to that childhood home of yours … what is it called again?'

'Hammond Hall. It's in Suffolk. I am not sure I want to go back though … or at least, not yet.'

'Oh? Whyever not? Too many painful memories?'

'Something like that, yes. It doesn't matter now.' But it did, and she knew she could not fool Mr Barnsley, just like she could not fool George, or herself.

Mr Barnsley did not pry though, and so she sat with her eyes closed, and let the memories come back once more …

In her mind, she could see herself riding Duchess across the open fields and meadows that were part of the vast parkland at Hammond Hall. Only when on horseback, she had felt so wonderfully wild and free. As soon as she had handed Duchess over to the groom though (sometimes she tended to her horse herself, but she knew her mother did not like that; she said it made her smell "like a common stableboy") and stepped back into the house – and thus reluctantly slipping back into the role of dutiful daughter – that feeling of exhilaration had left her. It was only when she ran away, that the sense of freedom, the courage, and the confidence she had felt then had returned, and remained with her until the day Hugh died.

Her spirit, like her heart, had been broken beyond repair.

***

'WE ARE ALL requested to come to the *Dog & Partridge* on Friday night,' Daisy said as she got into the car and started the engine. They had thoroughly enjoyed their Afternoon Tea in Bettys air-conditioned rooms, and had been given dainty little boxes containing their leftover cakes. Lavinia had insisted Daisy take hers for Oliver. 'Including you, Lavinia.'

'Me?' The old lady looked at her over her horn-rimmed spectacles. 'I never go to the pub! Whatever would I want there?'

'Celebrate something, I suppose. Lily is very vague in her message. She says it will all be revealed on Friday evening, in the garden of the *Dog & Partridge*. And if you want to know what it is about, you had better come.'

Lavinia harrumphed. 'Well. We'll see about that.'

'I'm sure Abi will come, too, and *she* doesn't usually go to the pub.'

Out of the corner of her eye, Daisy could see the old lady's mouth twitch. If Abi was coming, then maybe she would come, too. Daisy knew how much Lavinia valued her. With Lavinia leading such a secluded, private life, Abi was probably the closest she had to a friend here.

'Well, you have three days to think about it. And you have not far to go either, so Oliver and I can just collect you on our way. Drifter is coming, too, of course.'

'Is he now? Hm. I thought he might like to spend a quiet evening with me.'

'Nope. He will not want to miss out on all the fun. All the dogs are coming. Even Ossie.'

'Did you just say *nope*??'

***

When Daisy got home, Oliver was waiting for her, a large, brown envelope in his hand. 'Hello! I have a letter for you – it's from Berkshire.'

'Ooh, that's exciting! Will you have time to look at the brochure with me? Or are you going somewhere?'

'I am, as a matter of fact. I'm meeting a group of teenagers who would like to join my youth group. And I'm late already—is that for me?' he asked with a hopeful glance at the pretty cardboard box in Daisy's hand.

'Yes. Leftover cake. Oh, but I'm pleased for you, Oliver, about Bishops Bridge teens showing an interest in your youth group. That is a great achievement! Especially after that car park and litter picking encounter they had with you …' She could sense that he was in a hurry to get away and asked, 'When will you be home then? Before eight, I hope?'

Oliver shrugged. 'Better not wait for me when you get hungry. But I will join you for a glass of wine on the patio later. Bye now, sweetheart.'

When he had gone, Daisy took the envelope containing all the paperwork and the brochure she had requested into the house with her. It was still too hot to sit outside, even in the shade. Briefly closing her eyes, Daisy took a deep breath. Then she slit the envelope open and took out the brochure about Equine Facilitated Learning. A minute later she was so absorbed in the fascinating world of equine therapy, she did not even notice the ringing of her telephone at first.

'Daisy, for goodness' sake! I have been trying to call you like *hundreds* of times!' Jessie sounded exasperated, but Daisy knew her usually so sweet-tempered friend was only in jest. 'Did you get the same cryptic message? From Lily?'

'There is nothing very cryptic about it, is there? It says we are to meet at the *Dog & Partridge* at seven on Friday. Dogs welcome.'

She could almost see Jessie rolling her eyes through the telephone. 'I know! That is what I call cryptic. I'm sure she is planning to tell us something. Maybe they are getting married?'

'Maybe. Or maybe Joseph is going to open a veterinary practice on Fern Hill Farm?'

'Oh! Yes, that could be it, couldn't it? Of course, why didn't I think of that——No.' She sounded deflated. 'Surely we would meet at the farm then, and not at the pub.'

Daisy laughed. Tossing her brochure aside, she said, 'You know what? I'm coming over, and then we can speculate to our hearts' content. We could even make a list of the most likely and the most ridiculous reasons for a party. What do you think? And can I bring Drifter?'

'You can. Louisa May is staying with Celine tonight, and Nate is in Durham. Yes, do come!'

When they had rung off, Daisy whistled to Drifter. 'Into the car, little rascal! Too hot to walk. And that way, Jessie can't make me drink. Goodness, what has become of me?'

***

On his way home from the meeting, Oliver decided to walk up to the castle and watch the sunset. He had brought his camera, too. Maybe he would get a few good shots he could send to Michael. His brother was a hobby photographer and was always excited about the beautiful pictures Oliver took on the North York Moors, a landscape so totally different from the one he was surrounded by in New Zealand. Having received a text from Daisy, he knew she would not be home before ten, and he needed a little time to himself.

The meeting had gone very well, and he was really pleased with the outcome. Of course, having a young team from the National Park there had helped a great deal. The boys had hung on Lorraine's lips, and the girls had nudged each other and giggled every time they glimpsed a bit of Tom's strong, tanned forearms. But if it served the purpose of getting them on board, why not? He had sent them home with a letter to their parents, informing them of the weekend he planned to spend camping on the Moors with them at the beginning of September. He was looking forward to it immensely.

There was quite a lot he was looking forward to. Beginning with the surprise he was planning for his wife, and the wedding anniversary trip to Venice in late September she knew nothing about as yet. It would only be a few days, and he might have to reschedule because he had booked the trip before he had even had an idea what equine assisted therapy was, but he was sure he could work that out. They could work it out, all of it. If only they loved each other, and stayed close to each other, then they would be alright.

***

Laughter filled the garden behind the *Dog & Partridge*, and Oliver caught Daisy's eye as they opened the little gate at the back to enter. They had taken the public footpath across the fields, in the hope of tiring Drifter out, but that seemed an impossible task with a young working cocker. To Daisy's horror, he had even devoured a dead mouse along the way. Spotting Inigo now, he began to bark and tug at the leash, eager to greet his best friend.

'He is getting quite strong,' Oliver remarked, turning to Daisy. 'We'd better get him signed up for one of those dog classes, or he will soon be dragging you through the undergrowth in pursuit of some scent or other. He's a gundog after all.'

'Oh, no, he would never do that, would you, Drifter? But talking of misbehaved dogs – look, there are the pugs … oh dear! There are three of them now! Please tell me I am dreaming.'

Oliver laughed. 'I'm afraid not.'

'Hey! You're here at last, great!' Ben, who had come with Cindy, waved to Daisy and Oliver. 'We thought you had got lost on the way – come on, grab a glass, Joseph was just going to tell us something. Weren't you, Joseph?'

Joseph gave Ben a confused look. 'Sorry?'

'The announcement?' Ben prompted. He was drinking coke and had his arm around Cindy, who did seem to be enjoying herself – Daisy noticed her chatting quite amiably with Jessie and Lucy, and thought that perhaps they had misjudged her by her appearance. She really looked a bit like a Barbie Doll with her long, straight, blonde hair, immaculate make-up and manicure, and a short, figure-hugging, pink dress. But her laugh was actually lovely, like the ringing of tiny bells. Perhaps they should give her a chance just for that laugh. After all, people had given *her* a chance, hadn't they, even if they all thought she was terribly aloof when she first came to Bishops Bridge. Was it only three months ago?

Lily, who was wearing a pretty floral dress and her trademark denim jacket, dragged Joseph to his feet and said, 'Yes, he does have something to tell you. That is, we have. Because last Sunday, when we were sitting by the lone chimney watching the sun rise over the valley ...'

'Aaaaaaaw!' went all the women (including Cindy), exchanging knowing looks and nods.

'When we were watching the sun rise over the valley and eating our sticky buns, as we do on a Sunday morning when my darling is not working ...'

'Or being trampled nearly to death by a herd of angry cows,' Lucy whispered, and Daisy put a hand to her mouth, remembering the story. 'Because that was a Sunday morning, too, and they were going to go walking.'

Daisy nodded, and sat up to hear what Lily was going to say when Joseph took over, cutting it down to the one sentence everybody had been waiting for: 'To cut a long story short, I asked this lovely lady here to marry me, and you are all to save the date for the ... what was the date again?' Lily stood on her toes and whispered something in his ear. 'Ah, yes. The twenty-third of May next year. If you please,' he added, looking at Lily for approval. Laughing, she shook her head, and said, her amber eyes bright with joy, 'Yes, if you please everyone, you are all invited!'

'Hear, hear!' some of the men shouted, and then everybody got to their feet, cheering and calling, 'Congratulations!'

Joseph kissed his happy fiancée, and they all cheered

again. Daisy, who had tears in her eyes, turned to Lavinia and said, 'I told you it would have to be something special. If they wanted all of us to be there. Though why all the dogs, I don't know.'

'Maybe they want them to be bridesmaids and flower girls. If that is allowed in church.' Ben was in great form, one had to give him that. Daisy thought he actually looked happy.

'I'll think about it,' Oliver deadpanned.

'They are all boys though, aren't they? Have you noticed? All of them. Theo, Inigo, Hamish, Drifter, and Ossie.'

'Honey is a girl. And there are a number of Labradors in the village who are also girls,' said Jessie. Then she promptly burst into a fit of giggles, with Daisy and Lucy following suit.

The champagne flowed, and soon everybody was in a buoyant mood, celebrating the happy couple. Abi and Lavinia went to sit in a quiet corner at some point, and ordered coffee. Daisy, who was holding Sarah Elaine, was thoroughly enraptured by the sweetness of the little girl. Laughing and gurgling all the time, Sarah did not seem in the least tired, although it was past nine o'clock.

'Do you know where Ellen has disappeared to? Has she gone straight to London from York? She never said, did she?' Jessie tapped her foot, which prompted Ossie to sit up and cock his head to one side as he tried to make out if she was upset. 'She's been away for a while … two weeks, I think. Or maybe she is not coming back at all?'

'Oh yes, she will be back. She is just busy sorting out her flat and all that … and maybe she needed to get away for a bit. It has not been easy for her to come back to the empty house, lose yet another friend in the village … even sing at his funeral.' Daisy sighed. 'That's quite a lot.'

'Quite a lot, yes …' After a while, she turned to ask, 'So what are *you* going to do then? You said you were starting a new career, but never really elaborated. Is it a secret, or will you tell us?'

'No, it isn't a secret. I am starting a course in Equine Assisted Therapy in September, and am hoping to be able to set up business here when I have my degree. In the meantime, Abi and I will turn Fern Hill Farm into an Equestrian Centre of sorts – mainly as a riding school to start with, but we were also thinking about letting holiday makers go on guided rides on the moors. Lily says her guests will love that.'

'Oh, but that's great news, Daisy!' Jessie exclaimed, and hugged her friend. 'What a brilliant idea! Those horses need something to do, anyway. Will you use that naughty pony, too? Or the donkey?'

Daisy smiled at little Sarah and gently lifted her up and sat her down again. Sarah loved that and gave a happy little baby laugh. 'I don't know,' she replied, mesmerised by the baby's smile, 'maybe.' And then, surprising herself a little, she added, 'We'll see.'

***

AT THEIR QUIET little corner table, Miss Lavender – or Lavinia, as most people called her by now, since word had spread rather quickly about her newly discovered relationship with Daisy Clifford-Jones – and Abi were sitting and talking of the days when Bishops Bridge had been nothing more than a handful of houses, with a pub, a church, and farmland all around.

When Lavinia had taken over the shop in 1971, it had been rather run down, and most people tried to avoid buying there because the former proprietor had been unfriendly and it was not very well stocked. Also, the premises had been grubby and greasy with dirt that seemed to have been glued to the floor for longer than you cared to think about.

'I think I spent the first week just cleaning and painting and putting up new shelves,' Lavinia remembered, 'I worked night and day, determined to open as soon as possible. Anything else would have been a loss, which I thought I could absolutely not afford. With hindsight …' She shook her head. 'Oh, never mind. It worked out well, didn't it? No regrets.'

Abi nodded. 'No. I don't believe there is any point in that. And you have made it work, and all on your own! You have been very brave, Lavinia. But … there is just one question that has been on my mind for a while … do you mind if I ask it?'

'You can ask me anything. Whether I choose to answer is a different matter.'

'Yes, now why doesn't that surprise me,' Abi muttered, 'you would not be Lavinia Lavender if you did not get to choose, or have the last word. Talking of choosing – what made you take the name of Lavender? I can see how you did not want to keep your maiden name, or felt it was not right to take your deceased fiancé's name, but – why Lavender?'

Lavinia smiled. 'That's an easy enough question. When Mr Harris and I were shaking hands on the shop deal, he said to me, "Now then, Miss …" I realised then that I had not even introduced myself because I was so excited! So I looked about me and saw the lavender pots on the steps, and said, "Lavender. Miss Lavender." And that was that.'

Abi laughed. 'I see! And so you have been Miss Lavender ever since? Just like that?'

'Yes.' Her friend smiled. 'And you know what? I would not change that name for anything. What's more, I would not change the life I have lived here for anything, nor the friends that I have made over the years. But more than anything, I am glad I have found my family again – or has my family found me? I don't know.'

'Does it matter?'

Lavinia gazed out across the fields beyond the fence. 'No. It does not matter at all. We have found each other,' she said, nodding over to where Daisy and Oliver were sitting, laughing with their new friends, 'and that is what matters.'

CHAPTER 34

SUMMER WAS DRAWING to a close as August slipped away almost unnoticed, bringing shorter days and darker nights, and, finally, cooler temperatures. Ellen had been away for nearly three weeks now, and Daisy was busy turning the Rectory into a home. Instead of taking Jessie and Louisa May on a boating holiday, Nate had rather spontaneously put down an offer for Mrs Colbeck's house, while Oliver had helped Mrs Johnson find a place in a small, family run retirement home in Rosedale Abbey. She was now the happy resident of a tiny bungalow which she shared with another lady, a Mrs Dorothy Briggs. Dorothy had lived in Rosedale Abbey all her life, and was quite happy for Mrs Johnson to tag along as she went to her Bridge Club, Book Club, Sewing Circle, and Bingo evenings at the Village Hall. Jessie and Louisa May promised to visit as often as they could, and bring Ossie, too.

On returning from their first visit, they both declared they had hardly recognised Mrs Johnson. She was not grumpy or miserable at all, as they had half expected her to be, but open, friendly, and showing a genuine interest in what was going on in Bishops Bridge. She also enjoyed Louisa May's lively descriptions of Ossie and how he tried to make himself at home at Jessie's café, and of the notorious Shetland Pony that had come to live on Fern Hill Farm.

'I'd never have thought it possible, but Mr Johnson leaving her has actually been the making of her! She is such a sweet old dear, really. And Ossie adores her,' Jessie had commented when Nate had asked her how it had gone. He was away on business all week, and she had teased him by saying that he was giving her the perfect opportunity to go out with her girlfriends on Friday night, claiming she would 'never get the chance to do that these days'.

'When will you be back then?' Louisa May was eating ice-cream straight from the tub while her mother was getting ready for their evening in York.

'Oh, I don't know. Late, I guess. When are you going over to Abi's? Or do you want a lift? You're taking Ossie, aren't you?'

Louisa May looked up as if her mother had just asked a really silly question. 'Course I'm taking Ossie. He can run alongside my bike. He's become quite good at that, even off the leash. You're a good boy, aren't you, Ossie?'

Ossie wagged his tail. He was dozing in the sun by the French doors, calm as ever. It was hard to believe he was the same dog that had driven Jessie round the bend with his incessant barking when he had lived with the Johnsons.

'That's good. But please make sure he doesn't run off to try and herd Mr Marston's sheep again, like he did last time I let him off the lead. He is a sheepdog after all. Right then, have fun getting everything ready for the big day tomorrow, and thanks ever so much for doing this.'

Louisa May shrugged. 'It's okay, I like Daisy. Remember how I said she had to be related to Miss

Lavender? And you said you were sure they weren't? Ha! Just goes to show I was right after all. Instinct, sixth sense, or what?'

Jessie smiled. 'Whatever. And don't forget to give Abi the chocolates. And of course you know nothing, should anyone ask!'

'Who should ask? Dancer? Delilah? Or the donkey?'

'Well, you never know in Rosedale. Sometimes the trees have ears.'

'The trees, right?' Louisa May grinned at her mother. 'Don't let Celine hear that. Or her Nana. She is coming, too, by the way – Celine, I mean, not her Nana. We are going to sleep in the hay with Ossie and Bingo.'

'Who is Bingo?'

'Celine's collie. Anyway, didn't you say you were running late?'

Jessie grabbed her keys from the table in the hall and shouldered her handbag. 'I am, yes. I'll see you tomorrow then, either here, or at the farm. Remember you also promised to help in the café.' She was halfway out of the door when she remembered something. 'Oh, and thank you, by the way. I hear you have been kind to the Matlocks this morning. Mrs Flite told me you took their shopping up the hill for them. She saw you pushing your bike.'

Louisa May rolled her eyes. 'Well, I couldn't let them walk all the way up there carrying their annual stock of loo rolls, could I? The shelves at Sainsburys must be empty now – I swear they bought at least ten packets. Honestly! How often do they take the bus to go to the shops? And do they really not buy any food? I did not see a single loaf of bread. What *do* they live on??'

'I can't tell you, to be honest. I think they only eat fruit and nuts and vegetables, preferably homegrown. They go foraging in the woods ... you know, picking mushrooms, berries, and wild herbs.' Jessie shook her head. 'I think it's rather sad, really. It can't be healthy for them, and they must be permanently cold. They don't use gas or oil, I think. Anyway,' she shrugged, 'Have fun at the farm! See you tomorrow!'

***

DAISY ENJOYED THE evening with her friends immensely. Having grown up in such a close-knit family as hers, she had never had a lot of friends, and never thought she was missing anything either. During her time at boarding school, she had mostly kept herself to herself. Having spent most of her free time either with horses, or with family – usually both – she had been happy and content with her life. Before she had met Oliver, she had hardly spent time away from her parents' estate, other than travelling to horse events, of course. And even then she had usually been accompanied by either her father or one of her siblings, and not mixed much with the other equestrians. It was only during her time with the Royal Horse Society, where she had trained as a coach in horsemanship, that she had found herself reluctantly joining the other participants for a drink in the evenings, if they were persistent enough to persuade her. But that was years ago now, and she had lost touch with all of them soon after the third and final course was finished.

This time, she thought, as she studied the menu at the small riverside restaurant they were sitting in, I'll be more open. I'll make friends. I have managed to make friends here after all, so I know I can do it.

'What are you having?'

'Sorry?'

Lily rolled her eyes. 'What are you having? You have been staring at that menu for five minutes and the waitress has just been a second time. I'm having garlic mushrooms, followed by the lemon salmon.'

'Oh! Yes, that sounds good. I'll have the same.'

'If you're sure. Will you join me for a bottle of wine?'

'Erm …'

'Chardonnay or Pinot Grigio? Oh, they have a white Merlot. Now that sounds interesting … not that I know anything about wine, of course. Which do you prefer?'

Daisy shook her head. 'I don't mind, really. We can try the Merlot. And I have just changed my mind about that starter. I'm having the mozzarella sticks instead. Which reminds me, I should really be at home preparing that housewarming party tomorrow … why I ever agreed to have one, I will never know. I am not the party type at all, never mind my culinary skills. Or lack of them. Do you think I can get away with ready-made burgers for the barbecue?'

Jessie put a hand on her arm. 'Hey! Relax! It's just a housewarming party.' At this, Lily sniggered, and Jessie shot her a warning look. 'Don't worry, everyone will bring something. And of course ready-made burgers are fine, and sausages. It's not so much about the food, it's about the community.'

'Yes, I know. I just want to do my best – you have been so kind to me – to both of us, by welcoming us like you did. I must admit I was not at all sure how we would settle in here. If you had not been so friendly and helpful

…'

But Lily waved her comment aside. 'Oh, give over. That's just what folks are like around here. They are kind, and they like to help if you let them. And you are giving something back, you know – not only because Oliver is the vicar, and doing a great job, but you and your horse business … that's really cool. Abi is so happy that her horses are finally being put to good use. You are actually doing her a favour.'

'Am I?'

'Yes! And now let's eat. I didn't have lunch, and I am absolutely starving.'

Daisy smiled. Lily was a real tonic. She had told her how she had come to Bishops Bridge heartbroken and grieving last year, yet Daisy found it hard to imagine how this happy, bubbling, and constantly chatting person should have been so different then. On the other hand, she found herself quite different from what she had been when they first came here in May. She had not had a bad dream in weeks, but slept soundly all night, and woke up feeling truly refreshed. What was more, she felt that her relationship with Oliver was being given a second chance. The bond between them seemed stronger than before, and she was grateful and relieved. She was a lot more relaxed these days, which probably helped. Happier. And that was good – essential, even – because how was she supposed to help others if she was struggling herself? Her own mental health was paramount if she wanted her business to be a success, and help others to find health and happiness.

'You know what,' she confessed over dessert (she had chosen tiramisu), 'I have never felt so at home anywhere before. And I have never felt so happy either. I'm sure this was all meant to be – starting with the dog in the churchyard, and finding Lavinia.'

'Well, yes, that is two extraordinary things, isn't it? I'm not sure I want to believe in coincidence after this. By the way, you never told us – how come you never suspected the relationship? Are there no Lavenders in your family?'

Daisy smiled. 'No. It is not her real name. Or it wasn't then. She would have been My Lady Featherstone, because her father was Sir Winston Featherstone, Baronet.'

Lily dropped her spoon. 'Seriously?'

'Well,' Daisy replied with a rather nonchalant shrug (while discreetly brushing off the drops of cream that had landed on her blouse), 'they do exist, you know, these honourable noblemen. Even in the twenty-first century. And I think you will find they are often quite normal people.'

***

Later, Daisy stood at their bedroom window in the Rectory, looking out into the moonlit garden. Tomorrow, they would stick a lot of solar lamps into the ground, to create a romantic atmosphere for the party. The garden really was quite lovely. Oliver had put a lot of work into it over the past few weeks, clearing the neglected borders from dead plants and leaves, and planting new flowers and shrubs.

'I really enjoyed this evening, you know. I never thought it could be so nice to have girlfriends. I never missed it!' Daisy shook her head, laughing softly. 'Little did I know. It's amazing, isn't it, how far we have come in just one summer? Maybe it's true what they say – that sometimes, when we let go of the wishes dearest to our hearts, we find that something even more beautiful is waiting for us. Something we would not have found, or even seen, before. Because all we could think of was the One Thing that we wanted so much. And now we have found something else. That is, I have.' She turned around to her husband. 'But I have a feeling that you are just what the parish here needs, Oliver. You, too, have come to the right place. I am absolutely sure of it. Do you think that we have found our home at last?'

Oliver put his arms around her. 'Yes, my darling. We have. After all, this is where we found Drifter, and Miss La—I mean, Lavinia. Goodness, why is it so hard to call her that?'

'Because she is such a very fine lady, I suppose. Lady Lavinia Featherstone.' She chuckled as she remembered the look of surprise on her friends' faces tonight. 'I asked her about that grave, by the way. You know, when we were talking about where little Timothy might be buried. And you are right, he has a small grave and headstone in the churchyard in Thornton-le-Dale. Timothy Crawford, the inscription says. That nice vicar and his wife did that for her. Lavinia says she used to go once a month or so, but since she gave up driving and sold her car, she has only been a few times, far and between. She would love for us to take her. The vicar and his family have long since moved on, and most people will not remember the Crawfords, either. But that doesn't mean we can't go to the churchyard, and have a look around the village while we are there. Although the question I would really like to know the answer to is – when are we going to take her back to Hammond Hall?'

CHAPTER 35

DESTINY

The three friends were sitting on the steps of the porch outside the Bridge Café, enjoying a chat and a cup of coffee before Lily and Jessie would open their shops, and Daisy would go to Fern Hill Farm for Louisa May's riding session at eleven.

'Dad called me this morning to tell me he has finally persuaded Lavinia to come to Hammond Hall in September. She hasn't even told *me* yet – well, I suppose she must have made up her mind overnight. Which does not surprise me, seeing as she has been thinking about nothing much else these past few weeks. Oliver says he can't come with us, as he has about twenty weddings in September, but that's okay. We are taking Drifter, of course. Oh, I can't wait!'

'That's lovely, isn't it?' Lily smiled. 'So all's well that ends well. Even if I'm sure it will be very strange for her to see the house again after so many years. And her cousin, too – does she even remember him? Didn't you say your dad grew up in the South?'

'Yes, in Dorset. And they did not meet very often, no. But still, it's wonderful to think they will get to see each other again after so many years. And at Hammond Hall, too. What will she say, I wonder, when she finds that the oil painting of her horse still takes pride of place over the fireplace in the library?'

Lily and Jessie exchanged knowing looks, but Daisy was oblivious. 'What is going to happen to the Johnsons' place, by the way? Are they going to rebuild it?'

Now Jessie's face lit up. 'No, they aren't. In fact, that's some good news I haven't shared yet – the parish council have decided they would leave the corner plot free, so that in future a fire engine would have direct access to the back of the Brook Cottages. They are going to fix the Coopers' place, of course, but they will definitely not rebuild the end cottage. At least that's what Mr Cartwright told me. And I'm really happy about that because it means I can expand my garden a little. More outdoor seating, more customers, you know?'

'Ah, yes! That's great,' Lily enthused. 'And you will never have to put up with another Os—sorry, Mr Johnson, I mean. Ossie is alright, really, isn't he?'

Jessie ruffled Ossie's ears. 'Course he is! You are my lovely doggo, aren't you? Yes, you are …' She looked up and smiled. 'And I'm so glad things turned out well for Mrs Johnson. She did not deserve that husband! By the way, we are going to meet Mrs Colbeck on Monday, to finalise the sale. I am so sorry for her … having to give up that beautiful house. But she says she is glad Bridge House is going to belong to someone from the village rather than to a stranger who never knew them, or appreciated Bishops Bridge the way she and her husband did – even if they only lived here for the last five years.'

The other two nodded, and for a while no one said anything, each of them lost in their own thoughts.

'Have you heard from Ellen?' Lily asked, shaking out her coffee cup.

Daisy shook her head. 'Not a word since I explained about the equine therapy course to her. Well, she reacted with a thumbs up emoji, and sending a series of animated horses, but that's it. I am not even sure when she will be back. Didn't she say she only wanted to stay for a week or two? It's been almost—Oh, who's that?'

'Who?'

'That man over there! I have never seen him before.'

'Says the woman who has lived in this village for one whole summer,' Lily remarked drily. Curious, she followed Daisy's gaze across the street and noticed a tall man in a navy suit who was looking up at the church clock. She put him in his early to mid-thirties. 'But you are right, he is quite a looker. That jacket alone must have cost a fortune. He is very handsome!'

'I didn't say *anything* about his looks!' Daisy protested, but Lily laughed. 'Just teasing, Daisy. Just teasing you a bit. Do you want me to walk over and ask if I can help him? He does look a little bit lost. He can't be a walker, or he wouldn't be wearing a suit, and as far as I know there is no wedding scheduled for today. Otherwise I'd say he was suitably dressed for the occasion. – Why is there no wedding today, Daisy? It's summer, it's brilliant weather, what's not to love?'

Daisy shrugged. 'I don't know. Because they are all getting married in September, it seems.' Then she got up and stretched her back. 'I need to go, your daughter is probably already waiting for me. And she said she would bring her friend Celine, too. Looks like I am going to be busy today. I'll see you tonight then, at the Rectory?'

Lily and Jessie winked at each other behind Daisy's back. They would see her before that, but Daisy of course had no idea that there was a big surprise waiting for her at Fern Hill Farm. And Lily at least had said she would not want to miss the moment, so she was going to follow Daisy just as soon as Abi had called her, as per instruction.

'So you don't want me to chat up that gorgeous—oh. He is gone. Oh well,' Lily said, dusting off her jeans as she rose from the steps. 'Either we will see him again, and find out more, or … it's his loss for not getting to meet the Charming Three of Bishops Bridge.'

Jessie cast her a curious look. 'What was in *your* cappuccino then? Come on, girl, to work! – Bye, Daisy, see you later! Don't forget to chill the champagne!'

Jessie and Lily were still giggling and nudging each other when Daisy had disappeared around the bend. And just as soon as each of them had gone back into their respective shops, the man in the suit came out of the church and turned right, walking briskly up the hill in the direction of Old Broughton.

***

ELLEN SHUT THE door behind her and wiped her brow. It was not nearly as hot now as it had been back in July, and the air-conditioning in her mother's Mercedes was in perfect working order, but the drive up from London was still long and tiresome, especially on a Saturday when everyone seemed to be wanting to get away to the country. She had left at dawn, hoping to get here by mid-morning, so she could have a little lie down before the party tonight. Walking into the kitchen, Ellen took a glass from the cupboard, filled it with cold tap water and drained it in one. Then she refilled it and took it upstairs with her, leaving her suitcase in the hall. She had enough clothes in her wardrobe, and for now all she needed was a shower, and a bed.

Half an hour later she was fast asleep.

***

THE MOMENT THE glossy black horse truck with the golden lettering *Hammond Hall Stud, Suffolk*, turned into the drive, Daisy knew that her dad had tricked her with his phone call this morning. For all she knew, he might already have been on his way to Yorkshire then. But why had he come with the truck?

Suddenly she felt slightly dizzy as realisation dawned on her: This was not a surprise visit. This was not even just about Lavinia, who was coming out of the house with Abi and Oliver now. This was …

Daisy's hand flew to her mouth. 'Destiny,' she whispered. 'They have brought Destiny!'

Tears were pricking at the back of her throat until they were almost choking her. She could not move. She could only stand there and stare as her father jumped out of the cabin, and, giving her a cheerful wave, went to open the door at the back of the truck. A minute later he was leading Destiny down the ramp, and Daisy let out a gasp at the sight of her beautiful horse. Destiny's lovely dark chestnut coat had been brushed to a shine, her hooves had been polished, and her black mane fell loosely over one side of her gracefully arched neck. The mare stopped when she caught sight of Daisy and whinnied softly, tossing her head as if to say, What are you waiting for?

And then Daisy ran towards her, flung her arms around her neck, crying, 'Destiny! Oh, my lovely. My lovely, lovely horse …'

Everyone was cheering and taking pictures or filming with their phones, but Daisy was oblivious to all that. She had her horse, and nothing else mattered. All she wanted was to stand quite still and savour the moment. Breathe in her horse's sweet smell, feel her warm breath blowing on her face. Touch the warm, smooth skin she had not touched for such a long time. Lose herself in those liquid brown eyes and see the unconditional love reflected in them.

**

'OH,' LAVINIA SAID again, for the third time. But she could not really think of anything else to say. What *did* you say to a cousin you had not seen in almost sixty years?

George walked towards her, laughing. '*Oh*, Lavinia! Your *oh* sounds just as prim and proper as I remember it from long ago. Only the Queen herself could utter this sound with even more emphasis and meaning.'

'Yes, well, but – what can I possibly say? I am lost for words, even if you are not.'

He smiled fondly at her and took her hands. 'Oh, Lavinia—now, listen to me! I am no better than you are. But then I suppose that despite the letters we exchanged and the one phone call last week, it still seems we were both of us rather ill-prepared for this meeting. Come, let us sit on that bench over there. Everyone is busy making a fuss of Daisy and Destiny, and I rather think they are doing it on purpose, so that we can have a little privacy.

You can meet Helen and Albert and Georgiana later. Did I tell you that my daughter-in-law was called Georgiana?'

Lavinia shook her head, still mesmerised. 'No, you didn't …'

And as their voices trailed away, Daisy and her mother stood and watched the cousins walk arm in arm towards Abi's orchard.

'I only hope they will not come across Jolly Jumper, or Myrtle,' Daisy sighed. 'The orchard is their favourite haunt, except for the kitchen garden where Abi grows the sweetest carrots you have ever tasted.'

'Who are they? Jolly Jumper and – Myrtle?'

'Oh! We call them the Terrible Two. They are the naughtiest Shetland Pony and the naughtiest goat you have ever come across. I'm sure you will meet them later.'

Her mother laughed. 'I see. Well, in that case I'm glad we got your precious horse here with no trouble at all. She is a lovely mare, and so laid back these days. Doesn't mind travelling at all. Well, you have trained her well, you and your father. How old is she now? Eighteen?'

'Yes. I have a feeling she has also mellowed quite a bit by now. She is completely calm, isn't she? As if nothing could faze her.' She rubbed Destiny's nose. 'You're a good girl, Destiny. The best, actually.' She smiled as she looked over to where Abi and Oliver were standing, chatting amiably to her brother and his wife.

'Hello, Albert!' she called, waving to him. 'Hello, Georgiana! Where are the children? Didn't you bring them after all?'

Albert – who, at thirty-seven, was almost bald – shook his head laughing. 'No. I mean, yes, we did bring them – but you never said there was a *donkey*! As soon as

Belinda and June heard that, they followed your friend Lily to the field where she keeps him. She is nice though, Lily. Everybody is so nice. No wonder you are happy here, sis.'

Daisy frowned. 'Lily? I didn't even know she was here. I thought she was in her shop … oh well.' She shrugged. Knowing Lily, she probably had not been able to resist coming here and witnessing the reunion of the long-lost cousins. She was such a hopeless romantic! Louisa May and her friend Celine were here, too, of course, as they had had to pretend they wanted a riding lesson when, really, Louisa May had been dying to meet the famous Destiny. No doubt she would have her pictures posted on the village Facebook page before lunch was on the table.

'I am happy here, yes. Very happy, and very much at home.' She caught Oliver's eye and smiled at him, hoping he would see just how overjoyed she was, and how much she loved him. He had brought her Destiny! Had he known how much that would mean to her? Probably. She was not sure whether it had been his idea, or her dad's, or even Lavinia's. She would ask them later. Or maybe it didn't matter.

***

'So you have never been back? And never seen him again?'

Later that afternoon, Lavinia and George were sitting on a stone bench at the far end of the orchard, far away from the happy hustle and bustle in the yard. Lavinia shook her head. 'No. Not once.'

'That's sad. I'm sorry for you, Lavinia. And for him,

actually. He was a foolish old man. Quite unhappy with his life. I think he was very lonely, too, towards the end, when the ladies lost interest because he had gambled most of his fortune away … oh well, never mind. Let's not talk about that now. – Why didn't you go to France, by the way? You could have lived with your grandma? Didn't you say you had a good relationship?'

'Oh, I don't know …' Lavinia lifted her shoulders and dropped them again. 'I might have done that, you know, had little Timothy lived — had Mother lived … had my life taken a different turn. I did go to see her two years later, when I needed a bit of an escape. I … did not exactly have the easiest of starts in Thirsk,' she hinted but did not dwell on it. 'Anyway, I went to France, and we spent a blissful summer together, drinking champagne, eating escargots, and driving her open-topped car along the famous clifftop roads, the Mediterranean to our left, the vast lavender fields to our right. All the while singing at the top of our voices, of course …' A smile crossed her face. 'It was a lovely, lovely time. Granny died three years later, and left me the villa. Which I sold, as you know. By then I had declared Yorkshire my home, and had no desire to live in France, or anywhere else in the world.'

He nodded thoughtfully. 'Yes, I can see how you would be happy here,' he said quietly, taking in the scenery around him, with the heather-strewn hills in the background, drenched in the late afternoon sunshine. 'It's a beautiful place. Very peaceful.'

'Yes. It is.' For a long time, neither of them said anything. Then suddenly she grasped his hand, and said, 'Thank you, George, for coming here today, and for bringing Destiny. That was very kind of you. Very kind indeed.'

He squeezed her hand, and said nothing.

Destiny, Lavinia thought as she gazed out across the moors, a smile tugging at her lips. What a fitting name for the horse that, ultimately, has brought two long-lost cousins back together.

CHAPTER 36

IT HAD BEEN Oliver's idea to have the family reunion party ('we had to pretend it was a housewarming party, didn't we, or you would have guessed!') at the Rectory and Daisy, who was terribly nervous about it, kept flitting from house to garden and back to make sure everything was perfect. Abi and Lily had insisted they would be in charge of the kitchen so she could devote her time to her family, but they could not seem to calm her down.

'It's just your family and friends, the weather is perfect, and we are only going to throw a few sausages on the barbecue, so for heavens' sake, stop fussing!' Lily cried, trying to grab Daisy's sleeve. But her friend had already dashed off to double-check the table decoration.

'Sorry, I hope I wasn't too rough on her just now. – So, who else is coming? I thought I saw Ellen this afternoon, but I'm not sure – is she back yet, Lavinia?'

Lavinia had come into the kitchen for a little break – having been subject to her newly-found family's undivided attention all day, she was a bit worn out by now – and sat down on a chair. 'She is, and she promised to come, too. I expect her any moment.'

'What was she in London for so long?' Lily wondered. 'Do you know, Miss—I mean, Lavinia?'

Evasive as ever, Lavinia tilted her head to one side and pretended to watch a ladybird who had settled on the window sill. 'Maybe I do, maybe I don't. Why don't you wait until she is here? Then you can ask her yourself.'

***

WHEN THE LAST of the guests had arrived, they were all seated comfortably in cushioned vintage rattan chairs around the large, square brick table which the Thompsons had had custom made with a built in planting area in the centre. At first, Daisy had thought it was hideous, but now, filled with Michaelmas daisies and hardy geraniums from Ellen's mum's garden (Ellen had given her unrestricted access to the garden 'even when I'm not there'), she thought it looked rather lovely. Ellen looked lovely, too, she noticed. Radiant, even. She had told them with bright eyes that she had been to London 'to settle some things' – meaning she would not return to the Royal College of Music and her Kensington flat but stay here in Yorkshire for a while, to recuperate, and, as she had put it, 'to find herself'.

'I had a very good and very long chat with the director who also offered to help me find a tenant for my flat. It's only for a year, or two at the most, because I still think I am going to continue my studies. But for now, I just need a break. I intend to make the most of my time here, and spend it with the lovely people who have turned out to be such wonderful friends this summer. I also have an offer to work part-time at the *Red Grouse*. On the condition that I will not sing *all the time*,' she added with a twinkle in her eyes, making her friends laugh.

'I'm sure you will have plenty of opportunity to sing. Maybe later tonight?'

Ellen smiled at Daisy. 'Yes, maybe. If you get your violin?'

Meanwhile Lavinia, seated between her cousin and his charming wife, and opposite Albert and Georgiana, watched Daisy and her friends chatting away happily. It was amazing how much this girl had changed over the last few weeks. Gone was that dreamy, faraway look, and that constant sadness in her eyes. She still spoke with the same polished accent, but she did not use it to hide behind anymore. Lavinia was certain she had heard her say *now then* at least once in the course of this evening. Albert, who probably thought some mischievous spirit had taken his prim and proper little sister away and replaced her with somebody else, had sat there shaking his head in bemused disbelief. She had also seen him lean over to his wife and heard him say, 'She has changed so much, you wouldn't believe it is really her!' To which the feisty Georgiana had replied, 'I have never seen her so relaxed. Rural Yorkshire seems to suit her. I am glad for her – and to be honest, I like her a lot better now!'

That is probably because Daisy likes herself better, too, Lavinia thought. Because she has found her home, and her purpose. And an extra auntie into the bargain, as George had said with a wink. He winked a great deal, that man. But she liked him. She liked all of them, and wondered how much her life would change now she had found her family again. Time would tell.

'Will you sing for us?'

Everybody fell silent as they looked from Jessie to Ellen and back to Jessie. And back to Ellen. Daisy held her breath, hoping Ellen had forgotten about the violin. She wasn't even sure she had unpacked it yet. But it seemed she was in luck, as Ellen got up and walked over to the yew hedge. 'Okay,' she called, pushing her long, dark hair back over her shoulder as she turned around. 'What would you like me to sing?'

Mostly, the guests wanted to hear famous musical pieces, like 'I could have danced all night' from *My Fair Lady*, 'I dreamed a dream' from *Les Misérables*, or the epic 'Memory' from *Cats*. But when Jessie asked if she knew which opera Richard Gere took Julia Roberts to in *Pretty Woman*, and if she could sing *that* song, a strange expression came over Ellen's face. Whether it was concentration, thoughtfulness, sadness, or plain old dreaminess, they could not tell.

'It's from Verdi's *La Traviata*, I think,' Daisy whispered to Jessie. Her eyes, like everyone's, were fixed on Ellen.

'It's *La Traviata*,' Ellen called over to them. 'And the aria you mean is called *Amami Alfredo*. I'm not a Maria Callas of course, and I haven't got a partner to sing Alfredo's part, but I will do my best.' She brushed her hands on her jeans a few times, then sank slowly to the ground, and closed her eyes briefly before she began to sing.

When the aria came to an end, everyone was spellbound. They did not even clap at first, and Ellen, thinking they had perhaps not enjoyed it, looked at them anxiously.

But then they all rose to their feet and the cheering and clapping started, with loud shouts of 'Bravo! Bravissimo!' Ellen, overcome with tears of gratitude, bobbed a little curtsey, and was just about to walk back to her friends when a voice called from behind.

'Hello? Excuse me?'

They all looked up to see a stranger standing by the little gate in the yew hedge. Lily's eyes widened when she recognised the man in the suit – what on earth was *he* doing here?

'I missed the last bus back to Hutton-le-Hole where I am staying at a hotel, and my phone needs charging. I was wondering if you would let me use your phone to call a taxi?'

Ellen stared at him, confusion written all over her face. 'I am sure you can, but—who are you?'

He turned to look at her, and from the moment their eyes met, everything seemed to happen in slow motion. Coming through the gate, he walked towards Ellen, all the while gazing at her as if she were a dream he could not believe to be true. Taking her hands in his, he said, in a low, husky voice, 'I'm sorry. Please don't think I am making fun of you, miss. I swear I am not. I am quite in earnest, as anyone would be with this name … I didn't choose it after all.'

Ellen smiled softly, then blushed and dropped her gaze, feeling that if she kept looking into his dark grey eyes just a second longer, she would do something silly. Like kissing him. A perfect stranger she didn't even know by name! She would die of shame – and so would he, most likely, if she did. Especially in front of a large group of people he did not know. 'Of course not. Your parents did, I assume,' she heard herself say. 'So you are—'

'Alfred. Alfred Matlock.'

Had he added, at your service, ma'am, the surprise could not have been greater. Even Lavinia could not help staring when she heard that name.

Ellen stared, too, and was glad he was still holding her hands, or she might have fainted. 'But—how is that possible? I have never seen you here before! Do you not visit your parents often? I had no idea they even had children … stupid of me, really, to assume they hadn't but—do you have brothers or sisters?'

'A sister, three years younger than me. Ophelia. She lives in London. And … and where did you say you came from?'

'I am Angela and Charles Maverick's adopted daughter. From Birchwood Park?'

'Oh yes! I think mum said something about your parents—did they … I mean …' He struggled for words, and when he did not find any, he held her hands a little tighter and shook his head. 'I'm sorry,' he said, 'I forgot what they said. Will you tell me what happened?' His voice was gentle, and his hands felt warm and strong. Safe.

She nodded slowly, not quite sure how to start. His eyes were the colour of the sea after a storm, and she wondered why he was so embarrassed about not knowing what had happened to her dad. How was he to know?

'There is not much to tell … I am an orphan – twice over, actually. My parents died earlier this year … both of them. I mean, Angela and Charles Maverick. I don't know about my real parents. I don't even know my biological father's name, and my mother took an overdose of heroin when I was two, so I don't remember her at all. To me, Angela and Charles were the only parents I ever had. I called them Mama and Papa.' I'm babbling, she thought. He probably thinks me very silly. And rightly so. I'm sure he must have heard his parents' version of Papa's death, and how I was so unworthy, I—

'I'm so sorry for you. What a nightmare! Poor, poor you …' And he instinctively pulled her in his arms, and she put her head against his broad shoulder, burying her face in the folds of his jacket as if it was the most natural thing in the world. As if she *belonged* here. It was the most extraordinary sensation. How could she feel so safe in his arms when she barely even knew him?

After a while, she pulled back though, embarrassed. 'It's fine,' she mumbled, her gaze dropping to her feet. She did not want to talk about herself. Rather, she wanted to know why she had never seen him before, and for how long he was staying. Only she wouldn't ask him that, of course. Instead, she looked up and said, 'I can't believe we have never met before – but then I have been in London these past six years, so maybe we just missed each other every time you came … where do you live?'

'At sea,' he replied, and she nodded. 'At sea. Yes, that makes sense …'

'I am an officer on a cruise ship,' he explained. 'Which means, I get four months of leave after having worked four months on the ship. I am just in the middle of my vacation now. Which is why I am taking the opportunity to check on my parents. They have not been very well – and before you ask, yes, of course it's because they do not eat properly, and are constantly cold in that ramshackle old shed they call a house, because they refuse to get connected to the gas pipe. Also, they are getting older … too old for this kind of life, really. My dad will be seventy-two in October, and mum needs a new hip. Urgently. But will she listen to me? No. They never listen to me. They never listen to anybody.'

He raked his hands through his short brown hair a few times, then shook his head and sighed. 'Sorry. I'm sorry. I shouldn't bother you with that. So, tell me a little more about yourself.—Oh for shame, I never even asked for *your* name! It's Ellen, isn't it?'

She smiled, feeling ridiculously pleased that he knew. And even more pleased with the way he had pronounced her name just now. *Ellen.* 'Yes. And there isn't much more to tell, really. I am a student at the Royal College of Music in London, training to be an opera singer. I was going to stay on for my Artist Diploma in Opera, but—' She hesitated only for a brief moment. 'I have just decided to take a break … I'm not coping very well with … with all that grief.'

He nodded. 'Of course. I understand. So this aria from *La Traviata* … you can just sing this stuff without even having the lyrics at hand, or an orchestra to support you? That is absolutely amazing! I've never heard anything so exquisitely beautiful. Ellen Maverick, you are an angel! An angel of music!' Taking her by the hand, and by surprise, he twirled her around on the spot until she was out of breath, dizzy, and laughing.

'I only hope,' he said, as he caught her in his arms and looked deep into her eyes, 'there is no Phantom of the Opera lurking in the background though, making you sing *only for him*.' His eyes were twinkling, but she sensed a more serious question behind that *Phantom* remark, and it made her stomach flutter. He wanted to know if she was free.

'That was one of the pieces I chose for my final exams this summer, which were at the same time part of the audition for the course I was going to start on this autumn. Only I won't for now. And there is no phantom involved in my singing tuition, or elsewhere in my life,' she added, turning her mouth up to his. 'I take it that is what you were asking?'

***

'HONESTLY,' JESSIE SAID, topping up their wine glasses. 'They do not even know each other! What on earth are they *talking* about? Did you know the Fruitcake Couple – oops, sorry! I mean Mr and Mrs Matlock, of course – had children?' She turned to Lavinia who seemed to be the only one whose eyes were not constantly wandering towards the yew hedge.

'I did, yes. But they never lived here. The Matlocks came here about five or six years ago, I think, and retreated into the woods. It was as if the woods had swallowed them up. And as you know I never listen to any sort of gossip, I'm afraid I can't tell you anymore.'

Jessie sighed. 'Oh well. I suppose Ellen will tell us all about him later. If she ever comes back, that is.'

Daisy shook her head solemnly, a dreamy look on her face. 'It doesn't look like it. I wouldn't be at all surprised if they just disappeared through that gate hand in hand, walk up the hill, and ....' She had almost been tempted to say, *into a faraway land.*

'But they *can't*! He is a complete stranger!' Lily stared over to where Ellen and Alfred were standing, chatting and laughing as if they had known each other forever. Only to Lily's knowledge, they hadn't. 'What if he is a fruitcake, too??'

'Lily!'

Just then Ellen and Alfred stepped out of the shadows and made their way towards the group of curious but friendly looking people. 'Sorry we have been so long!' Ellen laughed, her face still flushed from the kiss. 'Any chance of a glass of wine and a bite to eat for a poor, hungry stranger who has missed the last bus?'

The poor, hungry stranger threw up his hands. 'Sorry for inviting myself like that! I'm Alfred Matlock, and my brimstone parents have no electricity in their shed, never mind a charger. Which I also forgot, as it turns out.'

'Dickens!' Lily whispered, grasping Jessie's wrist. 'That's Dickens! He's just quoted from *Bleak House*! The brimstone bit, I mean. Isn't that amazing? I'm sure it's a sign!'

'I have *no idea* what you are talking about,' Jessie returned, 'but he seems very nice, yes. Pass me the brownies?'

***

LATER, WHEN EVERYONE had gone (Alfred would have insisted on calling a taxi, but Daisy and Oliver had been adamant and said he was to stay at the Rectory for the night), and Daisy's family had gone to bed, Daisy and Oliver were sitting alone in the garden, the remains of the last bottle of wine between them.

'What an evening!' Daisy said with a sigh. 'What a day!'

'What a summer!' Oliver suggested, throwing a stick for Drifter. He was not tired at all, even though it was so late – or rather, it was early, since it was gone two in the morning. They had sat together for over two hours after Alfred had turned up, and by the time the party was officially over, everyone said they felt like they had known each other for much longer.

'Oh yes! I suppose we can all agree on *that*!'

Drifter barked and wagged his tail. 'See?' Daisy turned to her husband, laughing. 'He agrees! And why wouldn't he when it all started with him? If I had not found him in the churchyard that day …'

'Oi!' Oliver put a hand on her arm. 'What's that?'

'What?'

'Over there!' He pointed to the laurel bushes that grew along the border to the church. 'The lights! Do you see them? Fireflies. Hundreds of them! Aren't they pretty?'

Giving a small sigh of relief – she had half expected to see Mrs Higgins on the other side of the hedge! –, Daisy nodded. 'Very pretty.' And turning to her husband, she said, somewhat dreamily, 'And they dance just as prettily as fairies. Even if not everyone can see *those*,' she added.

His face broke into a slow smile, making the edges around his eyes crinkle. 'Can you?'

She looked wistful for a moment. Then she shook her head and smiled. 'In nights like these, I almost wish I can – but I can't, no. And I don't have to either. Because everything I need, and everything I want, is right here. I am happy here, Oliver, and at peace. This is where we belong. Everything will be alright – *we* will be alright.' And this time, there was no anxious *won't we?*

Oliver drew her close and kissed her hair. She did not have to know how relieved he was to hear her say that. 'Yes, my darling. We will be.'

They sat there for a little while longer, sipping their wine and enjoying each other's company, before they walked back to the house arm in arm at last, closing the door to the darkness of the night.

Epilogue

'If you please, Auntie Lavinia, Mummy says tea is being served in a few minutes, and will you come down to the library?'

Lavinia turned around and smiled at Albert's youngest who was hovering in the door, a wriggling black spaniel in her arms. 'We were going to have tea by the pond, but it is raining so hard, Mummy says it's better to have it in the library. Then you can look at your horse again. Do you want me to wait for you, or do you need a few minutes?'

Sensing that the dog wanted to be free, the little girl squatted down and let him go. He dashed towards Lavinia and then jumped up onto the window seat where he sat and pressed his nose against the cool glass. If Lavinia did not know better, she would have thought he had been here all the time, waiting for her.

'You go ahead, Belinda, and tell them I will be down in a moment. I just need to wash my hands.' And take a few more moments to stand at the window, looking out into the garden my eyes have not seen for so many years. It looked different now of course, but the memories it held were still there – the happy ones, and the sad ones, too. They were lingering in every flower and every tree, the rain washing away the bitterness she might have felt, leaving the air clean and fresh and full of hope.

Stepping back, Lavinia took a deep breath. Then she picked up her woollen shawl, draped it around her shoulders, and walked towards the door of her old bedroom. It was fifty-seven years since she had last walked through this door, thinking she would never come back. But never is a long time, and time, as everyone knew, had a habit of changing things, and people, and hearts.

Today Lavinia Featherstone had come home.

Seeing the portrait of her beloved horse above the fireplace in the library had made her heart flutter for a moment. Then she had closed her eyes, said a little prayer for her parents, and walked on to the table by the window where Daisy and her father had been sitting over the stud book, trying to find out whether Destiny might be related to Duchess. She wasn't.

'It's better this way,' Lavinia had said, laying her hand upon Daisy's shoulder, 'Duchess is part of my past. But Destiny is part of your life, Daisy, past, present, and future. Sometimes it's best to let go of what used to be, and lift your eyes, and see what lies ahead. And I believe only the best does for you, Daisy girl.'

There had been no need for Daisy to ask her if she could do the same. In coming here today, she already had.

'Now then,' Lavinia said, putting a hand to the door, 'let's see if they know how to make good scones at Hammond Hall. I'm sure they cannot compare to Jessie's, but I am willing to give it a try. Come on, Drifter.'

Thank you!

As ever, to my darling Wolfgang – thank you for your standing by me through each and every storm that has come our way over the last thirty years, and for always being able to calm me when the waves hit high. You mean the world to me, and every moment spent with you is precious.

To Lukas and Rahel, my pride and joy. Because family matters, and so do you!

To my own Mama, who sadly is not here to read my books anymore, and Papa. I miss you.

To Ali, Deborah, Ruth, and Geoff, for your friendship, your encouragement, and your prayers. Not to mention providing the tea and the cake whenever we pass through Oxfordshire. And the picnics. We will continue to do our best and always bring the sunshine.

To Dieter and little Whisky for putting a smile on my face each morning when we meet, and for reading my books before anyone else does (Dieter, not Whisky – that's the dog!!!).

To John, the vicar who married us, and who has known me nearly all my life. Faith is a gift – thank you (and your lovely Dorothea) for helping me find it.

To all the friendly people of "Bishops Bridge" – thank

you for making me feel so welcome, and letting me be a part of your lovely community.

Thank you to my amazing editor, Shirley, for embarking on this adventure with me. I am already looking forward to the next one!

Also, to Ken for designing such a beautiful cover, and for doing the typesetting just so. You have been a great help, and very patient with me, thank you!

Last not least to our Benny dog for keeping me company, whether walking, dreaming, or writing. You're the best dog ever.

About the author

ANNE LIVES BETWEEN the North of Germany and the North York Moors, where her stories are set in the fictional village of Bishops Bridge. Married to the love of her life and mother of two amazing grown-up children, she also calls a very beautiful (though not very bright) lassie dog her own.

When she is not writing, you will find Anne roaming the Moors, sometimes singing, often dreaming, or completely lost in thoughts (approach with care, lest she fall off that ridge!).

For updates, you can follow Anne on Instagram @ bishops_bridge_books and Facebook @AnneWhorlton.

Printed in Great Britain
by Amazon